SO-ABR-882

WITHDRAWN
...DRAWN

MANY LIGHTS IN
MANY WINDOWS

MANY LIGHTS IN MANY WINDOWS

TWENTY YEARS OF GREAT FICTION AND POETRY FROM THE WRITERS COMMUNITY

EDITED BY LAUREL BLOSSOM

A Writers Community Book
Jennifer O'Grady, Series Editor
YMCA National Writer's Voice

The Writers Community, celebrated around the country as a premier training ground for American writers, is a workshop and residency program. The oldest and one of the best community-based writing programs in the nation, The Writers Community celebrates its twentieth anniversary in October 1997.

The Writers Community became a nationwide program of the National Writer's Voice of the YMCA of the USA in 1986.

LAUREL BLOSSOM, *cofounder of The Writers Community*
JENNIFER O'GRADY, *Program Director of the YMCA National Writer's Voice*
JASON SHINDER, *Executive Director and founder of the YMCA National Writer's Voice*

The characters and events in some of these contributions are fictitious. Any similarity to real persons, living or dead, is coincidental and not intended by the authors.

©1997, Selection and arrangement by Laurel Blossom.
Each author holds copyright to his or her contribution.
All rights reserved. Except for brief quotations in critical articles or reviews, no part of this book may be reproduced in any manner without prior written permission from the publisher: Milkweed Editions, 430 First Avenue North, Suite 400, Minneapolis, MN 55401
Distributed by Publishers Group West

Published 1997 by Milkweed Editions
Printed in the United States of America
Cover design by Adrian Morgan, Red Letter Design
Cover art by Fran Gregory
Interior design by Will Powers
The text of this book is set in American Garamond.
97 98 99 00 01 5 4 3 2 1
First Edition

Milkweed Editions is a not-for-profit publisher. We gratefully acknowledge support from the Bush Foundation; Target Stores, Dayton's, and Mervyn's by the Dayton Hudson Foundation; Ecolab Foundation; General Mills Foundation; Honeywell Foundation; Jerome Foundation; The McKnight Foundation; Andrew W. Mellon Foundation; Kathy Stevens Dougherty and Michael E. Dougherty Fund of the Minneapolis Foundation; Minnesota State Arts Board through an appropriation by the Minnesota State Legislature; Challenge and Literature Programs of the National Endowment for the Arts; Lawrence and Elizabeth Ann O'Shaughnessy Charitable Income Trust in honor of Lawrence M. O'Shaughnessy; Piper Jaffray Companies, Inc.; Ritz Foundation on behalf of Mr. and Mrs. E. J. Phelps, Jr.; John and Beverly Rollwagen Fund of the Minneapolis Foundation; The St. Paul Companies, Inc.; Star Tribune/Cowles Media Foundation; Surdna Foundation; James R. Thorpe Foundation; U.S. West Foundation; Lila Wallace-Reader's Digest Literary Publishers Marketing Development Program, funded through a grant to the Council of Literary Magazines and Presses; and generous individuals.

Library of Congress Cataloging-in-Publication Data

Many lights in many windows : twenty years of great fiction and poetry
    from the Writers Community / edited by Laurel Blossom. — 1st ed.
        p. cm. — (A Writers Community book)
    ISBN 1-57131-218-8 (acid-free paper)
    1. American literature—20th century. I. Blossom, Laurel.
    II. Series.
    PS536.2.M36 1997
    810.8'0054—DC21   97-11722
                                                                          CIP

This book is printed on acid-free paper.

Many Lights in Many Windows

 *Foreword*

Writers, who seem to require more response and gratification than almost any other group I can think of, often lack access to channels that might make them feel as though they aren't writing into a void. This is especially true for new writers, who might not have already done the requisite colony-hopping and conference-going that provide a loose community of familiar faces. I was fortunate enough to find myself engaged with other writers almost immediately after I graduated from college. That autumn I spent six weeks at the MacDowell Colony, where I made close friends and traded work back and forth. After the six weeks were up, I returned to New York, to a loosely knit community of friends who were writing novels and poems while teaching the occasional class or waiting tables. I took a job teaching writing at The Writer's Voice of the West Side YMCA, and there I was introduced to another group of writers: students.

Teaching helped me feel validated as a writer and made me realize that I actually had some advice to pass on to others. The more I taught, the stronger my voice became, and I realized that the energy that went into teaching was naturally recycled back into my own writing. Teaching didn't sap me of energy; it just made me more excited about my own work. Later, when I taught at The Writers Community, my students were truly gifted and I learned a good deal from their work. I felt comfortable with them and knew that their concerns were largely my own.

I've taught writing in a variety of settings. Once, while teaching in a southwestern university, I had a class made up of students who hadn't really been exposed to much fiction in their lives. As part of the curriculum, I taught Tillie Olsen's great short story "I Stand Here Ironing." This heated up the class, creating arguments among the students about what kind of a mother the narrator was. To these students the narrator was real and could be held up to moral scrutiny just like anyone in life. I understood, watching the debate going on in the classroom, that fiction can have tremendous sway, that a writing teacher can help new writers explore their excitement about fiction and put that excitement to tremendous use.

Writing is inevitably solitary, of course, but the idea of a community of writers is invigorating to think about when you're all alone with your thoughts and it's three in the morning and you just can't find a way to end the paragraph. Sometimes, when I'm up very late working, I'll look out my window and see other lights in other windows, and I'll imagine that there are writers in those rooms, doing essentially what I'm doing. In a strange way, this is always a comfort.

MEG WOLITZER

MANY LIGHTS IN
MANY WINDOWS

Introduction

I

The Writers Community is an organization. Put most simply, The Writers Community provides community-based creative writing workshops and residencies to poets and fiction writers at several points along the curve of their professional careers.

But the writer's community is also an idea, and it is primarily that idea—of a community of writers among themselves, and of writers in creative community with audience, readers, and humanity in general—that this anthology seeks to explore.

As an organization The Writers Community began, as has many another good idea, with a walk on the beach. It was the summer of 1975, I was spending a couple of weeks on Martha's Vineyard with my friend and colleague Helen Chasin, and she was describing to me her idea of the perfect writing workshop. At that time, according to statistics from Associated Writing Programs, there were perhaps twenty creative writing programs at universities in the United States; today AWP lists about 230. Even then, however, Helen saw that something else was needed: a writing workshop that would uphold the standards of the academy without requiring academic courses, an academic approach, or academic prices; a workshop that would concentrate on the craft of writing, that would be taught by working mid-career writers of achievement and promise, and that would incorporate writing into the ordinary lives of its members by meeting in their own community.

That was the bare bones of the idea.

Nine months later, in January, 1976, with the help of a $35,000 grant from the William Bingham Foundation, The Writers Community offered its first workshops in poetry and fiction under the auspices of the Academy of American Poets.

A year later it went out on its own, renting a former chiropractor's office next to the Dalton School on East 89th Street in New York City. Independent workshops were offered in the spring of 1977, and from this date is measured the twentieth anniversary that the present anthology celebrates.

I've often thought there was something symbolic in the fact that our space had formerly been used by a practitioner of a marginal form of medicine, unrecognized by the mainstream medical profession; a form of medicine that nevertheless helped thousands of people every year to better health; a form of medicine that, by cracking bones or by a subtler kinesthetic approach, relieved their pain and aligned the very structure of their skeletons.

How like the situation of poetry, how like the effect of a successful short story or novel! It makes me think of The Writers Community as a kind of chiropractic of the imagination, promoting emotional and spiritual health among its residents, its members, and the people that eventually read their work.

Over the ten years of its independent existence, The Writers Community gained a reputation not only as among the first, but also as among the best community-based writing workshops in the country. Many of the writers hired as residents, and not a few workshop members, unknown or little known at the time, have gone on to become MacArthur Fellows, university department heads, or otherwise recognized literary figures. A number of them are included in this anthology.

The Writers Community was adopted by The Writer's Voice of New York in 1986, becoming the professional training apex of its multilevel writing workshop program. In 1990 a grant from the Lila Wallace-Reader's Digest Fund established the National Writer's Voice Project (now the YMCA National Writer's Voice), through which have developed more than twenty literary arts centers at select YMCAs across the country. The YMCA is the perfect partner for the National Writer's Voice's mission "to give voice to people through a democratic vision of the literary arts and humanities . . . to narrow the distinctions between artist and audience, and between cultural institution and community, making the arts more accessible and life-enriching to the widest possible audience." As part of this potentially vast national—and even international—network, The Writers Community currently offers its workshops and prestigious residencies at five to eight YMCAs each year on a competitive basis. According to the Academy of American Poets, The Writers Community is currently the only countrywide community-based writing residency program; and of all residency programs, it is the largest.

I recently learned that the YMCA began as a Bible study group in London in 1844 and came to Boston in 1851 via a retired sea captain who was also a lay missionary. It seems appropriate that an organization founded for the study of the spiritual meaning and significance of words in an age of spiritual upheaval should return, in another such age, to that same study in a broader cultural context, through the practice and appreciation of the literary arts.

So I'm thrilled that our most recent brochure calls The Writers Community "a core program of the YMCA National Writer's Voice."

I still have to pinch myself to believe it!

II

In a speech to the 1996 Associated Writing Programs annual conference in Atlanta, Doris Betts called workshops "the American how-to version of Paris in the 20s." This witty insight captures both aspects of the writing workshop experience: first, the training by a mentor in literary craft and literary business; and second, the enormous excitement of talking shop with one's peers. Saul Bellow has often spoken, and marked the disappearance, of the New York literary salon of the 1950s, in which writers like himself made contacts, met other artists and writers, and were inspired by the intellectual ferment of their times.

The Writers Community has tried to recreate that milieu in its readings and workshops, though our logo shows a monk sitting at his desk, quill in hand, alone. We chose that image, Helen and I, to emphasize what seemed to us at the time to be the oxymoron of the program's name. Over the years, however, I have come to believe in the name without irony. My own sense of isolation as a writer has practically disappeared, and I understand more and more that writing is, in fact, a community act, a collaboration. Contrary to the dictates of the outmoded Romantic mythology of the brooding poet starving heroically in his loft alone, The Writers Community and other programs like it provide the nourishment writers need, make a space for them to share their work with other writers, exchange points of view, evaluate and revise, revise, and revise in response to ideas, until (and if) a poem, a story, an essay, or a novel can be finished. Auden said a poem is never finished, it is only abandoned. The work passes from the author's hands into the hands of its readers, who are the ones to complete it.

This collaboration with an audience has long been acknowledged and exploited on stage and screen: in the double ending of Harold Pinter's screenplay for *The French Lieutenant's Woman*, in the Broadway script for *Nicholas Nickleby*, and in the interactive productions of *Tamara* and *Tony and Tina's Wedding*, to name a few. More recently, cyberspace publishing has given writers the opportunity to explore, and readers the ability to choose among, a number of possible developments in a poem or story, leading to alternate conclusions or mysteries.

Writers, therefore, are like pebbles thrown in a pond: our community ripples out from us in little, overlapping waves. In the shared experience of a story or poem, we become, without regard to time or distance, an entity in communion—reader, audience, and writer together. Writers in this volume, asked to contribute a statement about what community means to them, have looked at this experience from a variety of viewpoints and have helped define its meanings.

Sophie Cabot Black and Michael Cunningham talk about the loose-knit community of contemporaries whom writers meet in workshops and conferences, at readings and publishing parties, through correspondence or over the internet, to whom they show their work, who publish them in magazines, write reviews of their books, encourage them and comfort them, as Meg Wolitzer says, at night when, working late, they see other lights burning in other imagined writers' windows across the street.

There is also, of course, the community of ancestors, those predecessors whose literary work writers cherish and with whom they are in constant dialogue in their own writing.

Allan Gurganus evokes the workshop community, in which teacher and students bond in the mutual endeavor of getting the story right.

Sterling Plumpp explores the cultural community of race, gender, and class from which writers come and to which they each owe their inspiration.

Sharon Thomson includes the intentional community, entered voluntarily for the service of consensual goals her writing supports.

There is the regional community, an accident of geography that may, nevertheless, command writers' loyalties and for which they may serve as voice.

There is the political and economic community called America, of which we all, in the community of this anthology, are part—*e pluribus unum.*

You will think of others.

Last, there is the human community to whom it is the writer's calling to give expression in the most profound and humble spirit.

The Writers Community has made every effort to live up to its name, so that all those who come in contact with it, as residents, members, or audience, will feel that they have entered a special place. Fees were nonexistent at first and have been kept consistently low so that no one need be excluded from the workshops for financial reasons; the program has remained small and focused so as to keep its commitment to serious purpose, intensive individual attention, and support for under-recognized mid-career writers; we have tried vigilantly to create a safe place for writers to be most fully themselves, to push the boundaries of what is possible in their work, and to make enduring friends of their colleagues.

In short, The Writers Community has tried to provide a community for writers among themselves, what Terese Svoboda calls "the last cloistered community," and, in conjunction with the YMCA of the USA, to encourage the writer's awareness of, and service to, the larger community of cloistered people, beyond the pale, that in one way or another includes us all.

III

The Writers Community has had the privilege of supporting residencies for some eighty-five mid-career writers over its twenty-year history and has offered workshops to more than one thousand of their working colleagues. With such numbers, to my regret, not every writer associated with The Writers Community could be represented in this single volume. One volume or more could have been devoted to the work of the writers-in-residence alone. An important goal in my final choices was to provide as near an equal balance as possible between the work of those residents and the work of the lesser-known writers who worked with them under our auspices.

Beyond that, the criterion was simple and singular. I tried to find, with the help of several readers, the best work I could in the submissions we solicited from writers who have been part of The Writers Community over its first twenty years. I want to thank those readers—Cornelius Eady, Barbara Elovic, Alice Fulton, Diane Lefer, Charlotte Nekola, Nahid Rachlin, and Terese Svoboda—for the careful and thorough attention they gave to their assignments.

There are others, too, I want to thank, without whose leg-, brain-, and spirit-work this anthology would never have happened: Jason Shinder, founder and executive director of the YMCA National Writer's Voice; Jennifer O'Grady, program director of the National Writer's Voice and series editor of Writers Community Books, the first of which this volume represents; Fionn Meade and Beth Blaney, National Writer's Voice interns; Emilie Buchwald, our enthusiastic editor at Milkweed Editions; and Fred Courtright, permissions editor and major headache reliever.

Finally, there are many, many people to thank for the existence and survival of The Writers Community over twenty years; I am bound to have omitted some, but my gratitude and appreciation extend to you all, whether or not your names appear here. Among those people are: Betty Kray, former executive director of the Academy of American Poets; June Fortess, Gregory Kolovakos, Jewelle Gomez, and Michael Albano, directors of the Literature Program at the New York State Council on the Arts (NYSCA); Literature Program directors at the National Endowment for the Arts (NEA), including Frank Conroy, Mary MacArthur, and Gigi Bradford; Sheila Murphy at the Lila Wallace-Reader's Digest Fund; Jeanie Kim at the Lannan Foundation; Cynthia Gehrig at the Jerome Foundation; trustees of the William Bingham Foundation; Helen Chasin, John Frederick Nims, Michael Washburn, Jane Gregory Rubin, Thomas Guinzburg, Patricia Spear Jones, and Scot Haller for their service on The Writers Community Board of Directors; executive directors Linda Corrente, Susan Charlotte, Sharon O'Connell and their staffs; Jason Shinder, Cynthia Sosland, Jennifer O'Grady, and Micki McGee of the YMCA National Writer's Voice for their faith in, and faithfulness to, the mission of The Writers Community as they integrated it, first into The Writer's Voice at the West Side Y in New York, and then into the YMCA of the USA; Lynne Vaughn, director of program development, YMCA of the USA, whose leadership on behalf of the Y's arts initiative smoothed the way; members of the National Writer's Voice Program Committee, including Cornelius Eady, Stuart Ewen, Daniel Halpern, Lawrence Joseph, and David Unger; members of The Writers Community National Advisory Committee, including Carol Anshaw, Alison Hawthorne Deming, Cornelius Eady, Diane Lefer, Nicholas Samaras, and Terese Svoboda; George Plimpton, Frank DeFord, Tammy Grimes, and all those who put their hearts and souls into the three Writers Community Bowling Tournaments; and, finally, all the members and writers-in-residence whose devotion to writing and The Writers Community has given it its particular spirit.

In the end, of course, the decisions concerning the selections presented here are entirely my own responsibility. I'm proud of the result, like a mother presenting her children to the world for the first time. Each piece is individual, with its own personality, strengths, and weaknesses, admirable on the whole and often unreservedly fine. Together, I think they speak well for the family! At the very least, they make a combined statement that will tell you more about The Writers Community than a thousand introductions by a prejudiced parent.

So I invite you to come in, sit down, and once again, for the umpteenth time, join the fellowship of reader and writer, one person to another to another and another, around our common human fire.

LAUREL BLOSSOM

BETH BAUMAN

The Middle of the Night

Allie's father is asleep beneath the azalea bush. Allie stands on the lawn, barefoot, in her nightgown, watching him breathe. His open mouth vibrates. She plucks a flower off the bush, drops it over him, and watches it bounce off his chin and land on his chest. She kicks him. He doesn't stir.

A breeze lifts Allie's nightgown, making her shiver. This is the middle of the night, she thinks. She has never seen the middle of the night. She darts across the moist lawn, quickly, in a rush of glee. She leaps with her arms outstretched. Then she runs in figure eights until she tumbles to the ground and lies on her back, panting. It is so quiet. Every house is dark except for theirs, which is lit from basement to attic. The stars look icy and faraway. Lifting her arm, Allie covers a handful of the sky. The phone rings and she runs inside.

"Hello," she says.

"You sound little," the voice says.

"I'm not."

"How old are you?"

"Nine."

"Are you your father's child?"

"Yes," Allie says.

"I'm the woman your father *shtups.* Do you know what that means?"

"No," Allie says, leaning against the counter.

"Where is your father, sweets?"

"He's busy and can't come to the phone right now."

"Well, I really didn't want to talk to him anyhow. I think I like you better."

Allie climbs up on the counter, shivering. The breeze blows

through the front screen and out the back. Papers on the desk flutter. Shriveled roses in an empty vase tip over.

"What's your father doing?" the woman asks.

"Sleeping."

"With your mother?"

"No . . ." Allie jumps off the counter.

"I didn't think so."

Last week Allie's father staggered up the driveway with the weed whacker, singing the New Year's Eve song. Allie's mother fell to her knees, announced it was the last straw, and said, "How could you sever the heads of my petunias?" Her mother then drew the shades and climbed into bed with a cool washcloth on her forehead. When Allie made her a Harvey Wallbanger, her mother groaned, "I'm on the wagon for good, darling," and she made Allie flush the Harvey Wallbanger in the upstairs bathroom.

"I knew that union was doomed from the beginning," the stranger now says. "I bet you live in a real nut house."

"Are you my father's friend?"

"Well, yes and no."

"I'm going to hang up. Good-bye." Allie hangs up. She runs outside, taking a leaping jump off the porch. She runs in circles past her sleeping father and gallops one end of the lawn to the other.

Allie sleeps late. Outside it is already hot. She walks into the hallway sleepily, feeling crabby and wanting to crawl back into bed.

Yesterday Allie watched as her mother moved into the attic. Her mother, pale, with hair springing out of her bun, pulled down the hatch in the upstairs hallway, and the tiny set of stairs tumbled to the floor. She raced up and down those stairs, carrying a thermos, a sleeping bag, pillows, bananas. Like a squirrel, Allie thought, storing nuts for the winter. "I'm going to live up here for a very short while," her mother said, rushing down the little stairs, blowing her nose.

Allie watched quietly.

"I need to gather my wits," her mother said with wet eyes. She lit the flame in the lantern and hurried to the top of the tiny stairs and climbed into the hole. She blew a kiss. The yellow light illuminated the blackness behind her. "Do you have anything to say to me?" she asked.

Allie sensed something final and desperate in her mother's ghostly face and with a shaky voice said, "I've been to Mount Rushmore and when I looked at the presidents' stone heads I could see their greatness."

Her mother seemed to twitch and pulled up the hatch, and the tiny set of stairs folded back in.

This is Allie's interesting sentence and before that moment she hadn't had an occasion to use it. Her teacher once wanted an interesting sentence, and at the time Allie couldn't think of one. Her teacher had said children without imagination were guilty of sloth and headed for a life of despair.

Now Allie stares up at the hatch. She pictures her mother eating a banana in that spooky light. There are bugs up there and spiderwebs. Her mother is frightening her. How long is a very short while, Allie wonders.

Her father is crumpled in the recliner, looking shrunken, as if his skin is too big for him. He is in the clothes he wore yesterday, and his bare feet are soft and white and thick with blue veins. He smells bad. As Allie sits on the couch, he winks at her. His eyes are wide and alert. "Hey, sleeping beauty," he whispers. There is a twig in his hair. "Your mother wrote you a letter." He hands it to her, but she doesn't take it. Instead, she rests her head on the arm of the couch.

Her father opens the piece of paper with a trembling hand. He winks at her again. The room is bright with sunlight. Allie knows he doesn't feel well. When she closes her eyes she feels an ache behind them.

"Well," he says after a moment. "Maybe we'll read it later." Allie reaches out her hand for the letter, but her father does not offer it. "What do you say we go to the grocery store and buy a watermelon?"

Allie does not want to go to the grocery store. She walks over to the window and stands behind the drape. It is hot and quiet in the neighborhood, the kind of day when the cement sidewalk will burn the feet, but later on it will cool off. The sun will set and most people will go to bed, but not Allie.

Her father says, "We'll go buy a watermelon a little later, a nice watermelon for the three of us." He sighs and sinks down into his chair. "Honey, don't marry someone with a flair for melodrama. Get yourself a straight arrow, a beer drinker." Allie pokes her head out from behind the drape.

Her father sighs again, running his hand through his hair. He plucks out the twig, looks at it in a funny way, and tosses it onto the coffee table. He and Allie glance away from one another.

Allie came into the world too early. At three pounds, she fit into the palm of a hand and was hairy like a monkey. There are many things her parents have told her that she does not believe and this is one of them.

Her parents are older than other parents. They never cook and like to take long drives. They think Allie should do what she likes, whenever she likes. As a result Allie is quiet and shy and self-disciplined.

Until recently the three of them would drive to hotel restaurants or taverns for drinks and finger food. Often her parents' friends joined them; Allie didn't like these friends, who always wanted to know why she was so quiet. "Talk," they would say to her, and silently she would drink her cherry cola or swirl the ice in the glass. What did they want to hear, she wondered. Or they would address her with, "Well, hello!" as if she was small and in diapers, or one of them might swing an arm over her shoulders and say, "As we know, men are the root of all evil in this hideous life."

Allie would then explore the bathrooms, where she would tap-dance on the tile, line up the little soaps, and sit on a lounge chair with her legs crossed, pretending to smoke a cigarette. There were things for her to do in these hotel bathrooms, it was true, even if she did get lonely. But she knew that later she and her parents would snuggle on the couch in front of the TV, her parents peaceful and cheery with liquor, and Allie herself would be happy to be sitting between, her lids half closed, on the verge of sleep.

The last time they did anything together was their day trip to Atlantic City to ride in the diving bell. Her father said beneath the

Atlantic was a magical place where sea serpents glided in the waves and where the tentacle of an octopus might wrap around you as a school of stingrays and porpoises casually crossed your path. Allie nodded her head, believing all of it but knowing the part about the stingrays and porpoises to be true as she sat between her parents on the couch with her lids half closed. "Yes," her mother had said. "The diving bell from the days of the Steel Pier. Remember the diving horse, Jack? Mr. Salty Peanuts? Oh, those were the days!"

So on a limp, grey day in the spring the three of them climbed into the car and headed for Atlantic City. A fine mist covered them on their walk to the pier, where the diving bell sat bloated and crusted with barnacles. They were the only ones in line. An old man with a hacking cough opened the oval door and said, "Hop in."

Inside smelled unpleasant, like a worn, sweaty shoe. The three of them knelt on the plastic seats with their faces pressed close to the window. Slowly the diving bell was lowered off the pier. They hovered over the water's edge and with a jolt plunged into the water. Surrounded by a cascade of bubbles, they descended to the bottom of the ocean.

When the bubbles cleared, there was nothing but green murk as far as Allie could see. She waited expectantly for a squid or a shark with many rows of teeth to come gliding by. Kneeling on the bench, Allie waited until her sweaty knees grew stiff, making her crouch on the seat with her forehead against the glass. Allie imagined that at any moment they would be pulled back to the pier, but they remained in the pulsating, murky water, where the low hum of the diving bell lulled Allie into a daze. "This isn't really the sea," Allie said finally. Her parents continued to stare out the windows, their jaws slack and their skin pasty white.

"Why won't they lift us?" her father asked, unsteadily, licking his lips.

"I don't know," her mother said quietly, opening and snapping shut her purse. Her mother's makeup seemed to have melted on her face, and her lipstick extended past the border of her lip. Her eyeglasses sat crookedly on her face.

"I feel sick. You think there's enough air here?" her father asked.

"Stop frightening us," her mother snapped. "Can't we do something?"

"Stop talking." Her father sat very still and only moved his eyes.

"How do you think we get it to go up?" her mother asked in a small, hollow voice.

Allie directed her steady gaze out the window, willing something to happen out there, willing her body to make something happen until her hot breath steamed up her window.

"Maybe there's a lever or a buzzer or an intercom," her mother nearly shrieked as she circled the inside of the diving bell. "Maybe we can find it here, somewhere!"

Her father slumped against the bench, clutching his heart. "Don't use up all the oxygen. Goddamnit," he said.

Allie's mother fixed a savage look on Allie's father.

Allie took shallow breaths of hot air. Looking out the window at the murk, she felt like she'd been had, and the disappointment surrounded her in a squeeze, bringing tears to her eyes.

"You're a terrible person in a crisis. Why I married you I'll never know," her mother hissed into his ear. She adjusted her glasses on her red, hot head.

"You should have had a martini with lunch," her father said in a booming voice. "You're an awful traveling companion when you haven't had a martini with lunch." He stood up, clutched his heart and then sat back down.

"I don't need a martini," her mother said sadly. "Not now, not ever."

"You do! You do! We all do!"

Shaking her head, Allie's mother took off a shoe, stood on the bench, and tapped the top of the diving bell with it.

They later learned one of the cables had broken. Huddled together, they were pulled lopsided to the pier. The local news was there with a camera when they climbed out of the bell, but her parents yanked Allie to the car, where silently they drove home.

The next night Allie bounds down the stairs. The front and back doors are open, and the house is like a wind tunnel. Her hair blows crazy across her face. She climbs up onto the kitchen counter, but she doesn't see her father in the yard. Then she spots him in the Allens' yard, sleeping in a chaise lounge. The phone rings.

"Hello."

"Hello, you," the woman says. "Do you feel like blabbing? How would you like to hear about one of the greatest love stories in history? Should I tell you? Let me ask the eight ball." Allie hears a rattle. "Should I tell the kid my stories? 'It is decidedly so.' All right."

"Who are you?"

"I'm your father's flame. Your father's a very attractive man, but you'd never know it by looking at him. We have the kind of love affair where we can't keep our mitts off each other."

"You don't know my father," Allie says.

"Look kid—"

"What's your name?" Allie asks.

"Why?" the woman asks. "What's yours?"

Allie looks at her reflection in the oven window. She looks afraid and this frightens her.

"Tell me something. Who do you look like, your mother or father?"

Allie looks at her colorless reflection. "I have brown hair, long hair." She looks at her crooked teeth. "I'm in my nightgown. What do you look like?"

"Tell me what you think I look like."

"Ugly."

"Don't get saucy with me, béarnaise." The woman hangs up on her.

Allie wanders outside. Her nightgown fills with air, making her balloon. The ground is moist beneath her feet. Barefoot, she walks into the Beckers' backyard and touches the roses, which are all in rows by color. The petals are velvety and moist. She picks up a pair of hedge clippers and wonders about its uses, for cutting roses certainly, but maybe for giving a friend a haircut. She clips flowers off several of the stems and they fall to her feet. She wonders if this act will send Mrs. Becker to her attic.

On a table by the Beckers' pool are a stack of books. One is called *Correct Behavior for All Occasions*. She likes the cover; it pictures a large house filled with silhouettes of delighted-looking people, all with good hairdos, all of them leaning close to one another in cozy, gold-lit rooms.

She wants the book. Vaguely she wonders if Mrs. Becker will fall to her knees and scream when she sees her beheaded roses. Will she miss her book?

Tonight the sky is filled with bright stars. The wind is crisp. It swishes under her hair onto her bare scalp, filling her with a vibrancy that makes her feel disconnected to the earth, disconnected to the life around her. On her way home she thumbs through the book.

The next afternoon her father searches for his tooth beneath the recliner—his head is bright red with the strain of bending. Allie reaches her own small hand into the carpet beneath the chair as she feels for the tooth. Did he have it when he went to sleep last night, she wants to know. He sits back on his heels, cocks his head to the side, and smiles sadly at her. "I believe I had a full set then," he says. The dark gap in his smile makes him look like a stranger to her.

Allie is annoyed and scared that a tooth could disappear just like that. It is one thing when you send two socks down the laundry chute and only one comes back, but something very different when you go to bed with a set of teeth and wake up one short. "Dad!" she shouts.

Her father sticks his finger into the gap, as if the tooth might be there after all, as if it is hiding. "It was a cheap plastic cap," he says. "I should have had it replaced. I've had it since the age of the dinosaurs." He carelessly sweeps his hand over the carpet. "Well, maybe I swallowed it."

"Really?" Allie says.

"Who knows." He shrugs.

Allie feels like bawling. A panic starts thumping through her, making her want to run very fast. What is going on here, she thinks. Today a tooth, tomorrow a foot or a head.

"Where is it?" she yells.

Her father is looking at her now, but he doesn't seem to see her. She looks behind herself where his gaze falls—it is a warm summer evening, an ordinary evening. The curtain billows in the breeze. There is the smell of a barbecue not far away.

"Allie, come sit with me," he says. "Your mother will come back to us. It's like she's on a vacation, honey."

Her father is pale with pink cheeks. "Come sit with me." Allie sways from leg to leg. She does not want to sit; she will trace his tracks and find that tooth. "Tell me everywhere you went last night."

On the back porch the world seems much bigger and harder to weed through than it had from the living room. Allie will not search for the tooth. How do you find something fingernail-sized out there, where do you start?

Besides, she is lazy during the day. She sits a lot, spacing out, feeling weary. Her bones seem to have curved and shifted.

She slumps on the steps, eating potato chips and quietly reciting curses. She waits for the night, when her vision will sharpen, when her energy is up and her spirit yawns and stretches, standing up straight and taking her creaky bones with it.

Tonight is calm and starry. There is no wind as Allie sits on the front steps blowing bubbles through the wand. The yard is filled with translucent blue bubbles and the low hum of crickets. The phone rings.

"I know it's you," Allie says, picking it up.

"You're a mind reader. How are you, sweets?"

"Good."

"How come I always do all the talking? Lemme ask the eight ball something." There is a rattling noise. "Should the kid talk for a change? 'Signs point to yes.' Okay. Act alive; say something."

Allie crunches the phone cord in her hand, thinking fast. "If you had to have a pet snake, a pet rat, or a pet tarantula, which would you have?"

"None! My god! Why would I want one of those things?" The woman is silent for a second. Then she says, "Your problem, kid, is that you take too much crap. You gotta learn to say 'fuck off' once in a while. Don't let anyone push you around. Say it. Say, 'fuck off.' For practice."

"Fuck off," Allie says.

"Like you're mad, say it like you're mad."

Allie says it again louder.

"Try 'go piss up a rope.' Say it with an attitude."

"I like the middle of the night. Do you?"

"What are you interrupting me for? You show a lack of concentration, kid. Your problem—"

Allie hangs up the phone and thinks this is the last straw. She doesn't know what she means, but when she looks at her reflection in the oven window she looks like a person whose feelings have been hurt.

Outside a few fireflies glimmer near the azalea bush. The moon is a toenail clipping, and a breeze blows back her hair.

Allie wanders into the next development, where all the houses are dark and quiet. She roams through the backyards like a spirit in a nightgown. On the back stoop of one house a long-necked watering can catches her eye and she waters her feet, leaving wet footprints on the concrete. The back door of the house is open, and Allie peers through the screen down the dark hallway to where a light shines. She steps inside, imagining a sleeping family there, a mother and father and a few children tucked in their beds. She walks down the hall as though she is invisible.

In the darkened living room a man sits on a couch with a long-haired woman curled up next to him. Soft voices come from a small TV, which gives the room a yellowish glow. Both the man and the woman look up at her standing in the doorway.

"Who are you?" the man says.

"Is that a kid, Marshall?" The woman sneezes three times in a row. "God, I feel like shit," she whispers in a raspy voice. "Am I hallucinating or is that a kid?"

"It's a kid."

The man gently pushes the woman off his lap. Standing, he runs his fingers through his hair as he looks from the woman on the couch to Allie. "This is kind of fucked up," he says.

The woman sneezes again and lets her head fall to the couch. "I must have a fever. Am I a hypochondriac, Marshall?"

"You're allowed," he says. "Where are your parents?" he asks Allie.

Allie leans against the wall silently. Something smells good in the kitchen. She looks toward the smell.

"Come here," the man says. He is very tall and slouchy in his body. He wears faded jeans and flip-flops.

Allie follows him into the kitchen, where soup boils on the stove. The can says "Chicken with Stars." He stirs it.

"I'm going to walk you home after she eats."

"Oh, I know the way."

"It wasn't a question, it's a statement."

Allie nervously pulls her hair. "Well, good-bye," she says, losing her nerve. As she turns he grabs her by the back of the nightgown.

"It's two o'clock in the morning. Just hold your horses." He directs her to the stove, where he pours the soup into a bowl. It is boiling hot with steam. He leans over and blows in it. This man smells like grass. "Can you pour that ginger ale into a glass?" he asks.

Allie does. "You want some?" he says. She does not. But as if in a dream she remembers the book with the silhouette people, *Correct Behavior for All Occasions.* In the chapter on food it says to always accept a small offering of food or drink, it's the polite thing to do. Allie takes a glass off the drainboard and pours herself some.

The man takes a box of Saltines down from the cupboard. "Carry the drinks," he says. Together they join the sick woman on the couch.

"Oh, Marshall," the woman says, in a high, pained voice. "I'm all clogged up."

The man sets the food on the coffee table and puts his arm around the woman. Her hair is matted to her head and her face is shiny with sweat. In her feverish daze she takes tiny, delicate sips of soup.

Allie sips her ginger ale with similar grace.

"Give me something to wrap around my neck. My throat's so sore," she says to Marshall. He puts a sweatshirt over her and wraps the sleeves around her neck.

"That's much better, Marshall. Much better." She eats steadily, delicately. Looking up at Marshall she says, "You're all right, you know that." Marshall kisses her lightly on the forehead.

"What's the kid doing here?" the woman says.

Marshall studies Allie with kind, searching eyes.

"What's the deal with you?" he says.

Allie does not know what to say, or what she might say if she could say something. Nothing feels certain to her.

"Do you love each other very much?" she says in a sleepy voice. She asks because she knows what the answer is and wants it confirmed, to know that she is right.

Marshall nods.

Suddenly Allie needs to get home, to check and see that everything is all right. She is out the back door and into the next development before she realizes no one is following her. She is alone, it is the middle of the night, and her house is not far away.

Her house is dark, even the attic. In the silence she senses her father is asleep here in the house, maybe in the den. Allie stands in the hallway, waiting for her eyes to adjust to the lack of light. The house is very still, there is no movement, no wind, no creaking floors, no life it seems except for her pounding heart, which is too loud to be hers alone and must really be three pounding hearts, the one in the den and the one in the attic and hers here in the hallway.

BETH BAUMAN ON COMMUNITY

Thank God for The Writers Community; the workshops attract great writers and they're affordable. The workshop I took in the spring of 1994 with Michael Cunningham had the right ingredients: gifted writers with unique voices; a talented, thoughtful, funny instructor; and ample amounts of kindness and encouragement. It's been my experience that a good workshop creates energy, an abundant supply, which gets passed back and forth among the writers so that creativity can flourish.

BETH BAUMAN *holds an M.F.A. in creative writing from the University of Arizona. Her work has appeared in* Pleiades. *She is currently living in New York City and working on a novel.*

SOPHIE CABOT BLACK

Higher Ground

Into your hands they hammered the idea
You would lose something if you turned back. No longer
Safe to want salvation, so close to dawn

And its impatience for everything
All of a sudden. It's not the loneliness
But the disappointed path back

Explaining. And if we ask too many questions
One of us will wander off, the careful language
Of hope, of revision, dissolving

Until it becomes the simple sound
Of feet moving over ground. I go over this part
Again. The place we learned

To slip in with the damp faith
Of bartenders, hoarding white lilies
And powders; the place my trembling mouth

Leaned into a mirror and prayed for fame;
The place where out of spent pastures comes
A muddy and expensive city: these places

Do not go away quietly or easily, perhaps
Will not even kill. How we come to hate
Our story and end up walking one

Behind the other, toward the hillside
And the ordinary eyes of horses where there are signs
They have been staring too long into the face

Of winter.

The Misunderstanding of Nature

I cannot stop watching her and thinking
Of ways to follow. Against the window
Her urgent spring buds strangle,

Summer aches with what longs to loosen,
A wet fall leaf hits clapboards. By winter
She pulls back into ice, but even then gives herself away;

To push myself right up to her, looking hard into
What it is she leaves behind. I believed I'd learn
How to change my life, like getting in a car and slamming the pedal

Until it goes into beauty then beyond
Beauty, then staying there until my blood also starts
To give itself away. Only I am still

In my own room, talking myself into a new gratitude.
Each evening a transaction breaks the landscape:
A child at the door, the cow crossing to the barn.

Only then does the light finally change. The child
Wants to know about trees not growing to the sky,
About rivers running north, about the length of night;

The cow makes deep sounds, the old complaint,
And the light falls suddenly like that,
Down into patient arms

Yet has been falling all afternoon, giving itself away: the great
Wheel turns, gently passes over mountains,
Over their dark green breath, over my blood

That curls and uncurls waiting, over all that time
I was sure something was wrong,
Over those democracies she will always bring

Of cow, ice, light, and child.
Each with a gift for the other: it is perhaps
Without waiting or corresponding to anything at all.

SOPHIE CABOT BLACK ON COMMUNITY

Community. I cannot think of a more important element to writing, save its very opposite, isolation. Always the balancing act between the two.

In all the different classes I teach I find myself stressing the same news: you will not do well "networking" with the older and mostly inaccessible writers who "teach" you. Instead, look around. Those sitting in the workshop across from you, by you, are your peers. If you don't like them, change them. But connect with them. They are the ones who you will be showing poems to, running into at readings, and, sometimes, they will become the ones who will review you, edit you, teach your books. This is where you will find your community — right under your nose.

This became clear to me during the few years just after attending a writing program in New York City. I was the perfect candidate for such a program — I desperately needed to immerse myself in poetry and poets — having not had any such experience in my undergraduate work, or anywhere else in my life. But I knew no writers and was terribly lonely in the Big City. So those connections became terrifically important as a source of energy to lean on, to glean from, to make me braver.

There also comes (back?) the time you cannot wait to be away from community. I believe we need to honor those times; that is when the real work is germinated.

SOPHIE CABOT BLACK's *first book,* The Misunderstanding of Nature, *received the 1994 Norma Farber Book Award from the Poetry Society of America. Her poetry has appeared in a variety of journals and anthologies, including* Best American Poetry 1993. *She was recently a Fellow at the Bunting Institute at Radcliffe College.*

PHILIP CIOFFARI

Love Is for Vanishing into the Sky

The Maestro arrived the first sunny day in July, 1950. His truck, red as a clown's nose, rolled down the main street of our project like a float in a parade. A brassy marching song burst from the loudspeaker on top, echoed off the facades of the ten-story buildings, and encouraged some of us to walk the street in a ragged line. We weren't exactly *marching,* but this was no idle walk either. We kept our eyes on the back of the truck straight ahead, hands stiff at our sides, though sometimes our grins would twist out of control, self-conscious. Following the Maestro's truck was a privilege, like stepping onto a stage, and all the project watched—or so we imagined—from thousands of windows that climbed skyward on walls of brick.

The truck leaned sideways on a small rise, against a line of trees at the end of the street, where the shadows of the buildings didn't quite reach. Behind the trees the swamp's grassy lowlands shimmered in the sunlight for a mile, maybe more, toward New Rochelle and the Long Island Sound. We formed a circle around the truck. Inside, a tapping sound, something heavy sliding across the floor. The back doors opened: the Maestro, a man with a broad face, a moustache, and eyes that were always smiling even when his lips were drawn, appeared from behind the curtain. From the back of the truck he waved to us with the flat of his hand, then stood over his grinding wheel and wiped a rag across the wheel and its metal stand.

Within moments, it seemed, the women of the project formed a line behind the truck. The street filled with the sound of the Maestro's wheel moving against the steel of a blade, a high-pitched scraping whine so thin, so piercing, it seemed to belong to another world: the cry an angel might have uttered, falling from paradise, banished forever from the face of God. The Maestro leaned over his machine. His dark eyes stared into the celebration of sparks the wheel sent forth, as if he understood the mystery of light, the invisible fire only he could touch into life.

His real name was Ennio Castelli. On the side of the truck that faced the street the letters E. CASTELLI PROP. were painted in gold, and above that the words KNIVES AND TOOLS SHARPENED SATISFACTION ASSURED. He came from Avellino, Italy. George, my stepfather, named him "the Maestro" because of the way he flourished his arms like a conductor before setting a blade to the wheel, and because of the symphony of shrieks and squeals he created as he honed the blade's steel edge.

"You're a case, you know that?" my mother said the night George came up with the nickname. She laughed, and George winked at her. She often told him in that same laughing way that he was a case, and I wondered if that was why she married him. I wondered if she had liked my real father for being "a case" too, if it was an attraction she transferred from one husband to another.

This was my tenth summer. I was four when my father left for the war. We stayed in the same two-bedroom apartment, fifth floor, facing east toward the corner of another building and the swamp, with a distant view of the Hutchinson River as it curved through tall grass toward the Sound. When my mother married George last year, she removed the wedding picture of her and my father from her dresser and stored it in a box on the top shelf of the hall closet. When nobody was home, I took it down sometimes and dusted it off.

My real father was a tall man, thin, angular, with a thick moustache that curled in an arc around his upper lip, like the Maestro's, and a startling look in his eyes, as if he was overjoyed at what fate had given him—his new bride, her beauty, the promise of a good life ahead.

Fifteen thousand families lived in the project, and though not all of them used the Maestro's services, many did. They brought their knives in paper bags or boxes or sometimes unwrapped, just holding them in their bare hands. We children sat on the grass, fascinated by the sparks and the unearthly squeals. That first night I stayed longer than the others, later into the evening, and he let me stand on the back of the truck while he skimmed a blade across the revolving wheel.

"A knife," he told me, "must be sharp, so sharp to shave the hair from your arm." He stopped the wheel, held the knife flat just below his elbow, and drew it downward. "Look." He extended his arm. The skin was bare where the knife had been: a narrow strip cleared between the black, curly hairs of his forearm.

The first two years of the Maestro's visits, it had just been my mother and me; after that, George always attended the Maestro's farewell carnival with us, shouting his *bravos* in a voice rough as a bear's growl and clapping louder than anyone else.

George was an archer. When he moved in he brought bows, arrows, quivers, tools. He carved a bow from osage wood, whittled his own arrows, stitched a quiver together with rawhide and leather. He called me "little buddy" and wanted me to go into the swamp with him for target practice. He would nail a bullseye to a tree and walk me back fifty paces. He would show me how to string an arrow while he talked to me about trajectory. My arrows didn't land anywhere near the target. The bow stood taller than I did; and the string pulled so taut I couldn't draw it back more than an inch or two. Besides, what I really wanted was to climb the ledge above the alley and take practice jumps to the cement below, my arms raised in a V above my head.

Someday I intended to join the army, the Ranger division, become a parachutist, a hero. Falling through the alley's gray air—a twelve- or fifteen-foot drop—I thought of my father floating through the skies above Italy, airlifted on a mission of danger. I landed on my feet, but the impact knocked me forward on hands and knees, and sometimes I fell all the way forward, lying face down on hard ground, closing my eyes, pretending I was dead.

The second day of the Maestro's visit, I watched him sharpen knives from early morning until night. I saw sparks everywhere: if I looked at a tree, or swamp grass, or the brick slab of a building. George came out to tell me I'd better come home for dinner quick, if I knew what was good for me. The next night George came out in his undershirt, yanked me up from the grass, and smacked me hard

on the side of the face. The night after that I hid in the trees when I
saw him coming. He scowled as he poked around the truck, then finally walked off.

After dark the Maestro hummed a song inside the truck. Light
gathered in a yellow crease at the edges of the curtain; smoke floated
above the small chimney on top, near the loudspeaker. When he
stepped through the curtain to light his pipe, he saw me standing
nearby in the shadows.

"You still didn't go?" he said in a friendly voice. He breathed in on
the pipe, but no smoke came out. I thought it was another magic
trick. "You like to see my house?" he said.

Inside the truck the air smelled of him, a grown-man smell of
sweat and metal. There was a stove, a narrow bed, a tiny dresser, a
table, and a single chair. Photographs—in bright color—of hilly fields
and farms blossomed like flowers on the walls. He stood in the center
of the room and extended his arm in a wide circle. "Everything I
own," he said, "it is for me to reach out with my hands to touch."

Sitting on the back of the truck he lit his pipe, told me about
Avellino, high in the hills near Naples, yet within a day's drive of the
sea. Insects hummed in the trees along the swamp; beneath the
streetlamps tree shadows shimmied in the sour breeze. One day he
would return to Italy, he said. And when he found his true love, he
would marry her on the isle of Capri, on a cliff above the bluest sea
in the world.

At home my mother sat alone at the kitchen table. A cigarette
burned low between her fingers. "George is losing all patience with
you," she said, jabbing the stub into a coffee cup. Her eyes had a hol-
lowed, gaping look, the way they became when she cried a lot; her
lips gathered in a thin, tight line. "He's out right now, God knows
where, because *you* made him so upset."

I stood at the edge of the table, red stains—wine and tomato
sauce—marked a trail from one end of the tablecloth to the other.
"I want to go to Italy."

"Oh, honey," she said. "We've been through this before. The
army's searched and searched. You know that."

"I don't care."

She came around and stood behind me, leaning down, folding her arms around my shoulders, rocking me; but I remained rigid. "He's buried inside us now," she said. "His grave is in our hearts."

Julie Waters showed up mid-afternoon of the Maestro's fifth day. She wore shorts and a thin jersey top; she leaned barefoot against the back of the truck, in full view of the Maestro at his wheel. The women waiting with their knives cast sour looks in her direction. Julie was older than the children who followed the Maestro; she was seventeen, maybe eighteen. A tall girl with sunken eyes and cheeks, she always stood with slouched shoulders as though fearful of hitting her head on something. The high school boys gave her money to do things to them. She lived two floors above us, in 7C. Her mother had run off. Her father drank too much beer and threw things against the walls. Julie often walked with her face down, to hide the bruises.

The Maestro glanced at her when he wasn't holding a knife to the wheel and sometimes even when he was. The women on line complained that he was taking too much time, that the knives didn't come back as sharp as they should. At night Julie sat beside the Maestro on the back of his truck. His hands moved as he spoke, his words coming out fast, some of them in Italian. He didn't notice me standing in the shadow of the trees.

The following night I watched again from the trees. They sat on the grass, the Maestro talking fast again, drawing pictures in the air with his hands, Julie leaning toward him, listening hard, as if for directions to a place difficult to find. The high school boys complained that Julie no longer hung around the playground. They called the Maestro a dirty old man, but he wasn't old. He was thirty-eight. The same age my father would have been.

The night before the carnival his truck was dark. The other children sneaked close to peek through a crack in the curtain. But I crossed the street, climbed ten flights in a dark stairwell. From the roof I looked across the shadowy pools of the swamp, past the tracks of the New York-New Haven-Hartford line, to the Sound, where ship lights floated on an invisible line that divided sky from water. The air smelled of salt and of cool, wet grass.

I thought about tomorrow's carnival. Every year it was the same. The loudspeaker on top of the truck played Mario Lanza's "The Loveliest Night of the Year." The red curtain parted and the Maestro—wearing a top hat, a black tuxedo, and white gloves— stepped into view on the truck's platform. "Welcome to the Circus Minimus!" he said, removing his top hat and bowing.

He juggled four tennis balls at the same time, he balanced eight cups and saucers on the handle of a broomstick, he swallowed fire. The magic tricks came last. Coins disappeared from the palms of his hands, he pulled a purple scarf the length of a city block from his shirt pocket, a rabbit appeared in his empty top hat, and then another, and still another.

"Arrivederci," the Maestro said, cradling the three rabbits against his chest and bowing. His face was flushed, his eyes aglow. People leaned from the windows of buildings across the street. They whistled and shouted. The Maestro blew kisses to them, and to those of us on the grass. "Until next year," he said.

Then we stood in a loose circle around the tire scars on the grass. The truck glided between buildings dulled the color of rust in the direction of Gun Hill Road, where elevated subway tracks lifted in a long arc toward Manhattan. I imagined him driving from station to station, neighborhood to neighborhood, and then somewhere south for the winter.

Shouts interrupted those pictures in my mind. Directly below, on the grassy rise behind the truck, two men were fighting, the Maestro and Mr. Waters, holding each other close like boxers sometimes do, then swinging wide punches back and forth. It looked like Mr. Waters was winning. He hit the Maestro hard in the face, and twice in the stomach. I felt the air go out of me. Mr. Waters stumbled backwards. The Maestro held a knife; the blade shivered with the light of a streetlamp. Mr. Waters shouted something as he backed away, rubbing his wrist.

At the carnival the next day Julie's left eye was bruised. Between tricks, the Maestro smiled down at her. He smoothed his moustache slowly with his thumb and forefinger. When he pulled a rabbit from his empty hat, his eyes seemed to have sparks flying in them as he

beckoned her to come forward. He leaned down to hand her the rabbit, brown and furry, wriggling to free itself from her hands. She slid
her thumb back and forth between its ears and rocked it in her arms
like a baby.

The Maestro appeared one day that January, his only trip to the
neighborhood in winter. Snow fell on the streets and walkways of the
project, gathered in thin lines on windowsills and fire escape railings,
along the ledges of alleys. It sketched the trees in white. It fluffed
like pillows on the marsh grass and bunched against the cattails.
Knuckles of ice swelled from the banks of blue tidal pools.

In the falling snow the Maestro stood on the back of the truck
and, in a new white top hat and tux, presented a shortened version of
the carnival. Julie sat on a chair beside him. She wore a white dress,
and her straw-colored hair, the exact color of the swamp grass in winter, fell in soft waves to her shoulders.

For his final trick the Maestro plucked a white dove from his
empty top hat. The bird fluttered its wings as if to fly, but remained
perched on his fingers. The Maestro held out his hand to Julie.
Snowflakes gathered in her hair like a veil. She was not a pretty girl
but her face seemed, at that moment, brighter and softer. She stood,
slightly stooped but still taller than the Maestro, and held his hand.

"I come for my bride," he said to the small crowd that stood on
the whitened grass. "In Capri, very soon, we will marry."

His face flushed; his dark eyes burned through the veil of falling
snow. *"Amore,"* he said, squeezing Julie's hand, "it is for vanishing into
the sky."

He lifted his arm. The dove fluttered above the truck, its wings
spread wide against the falling snow's blinding whiteness. In one
magical moment, it became indistinguishable from the snow, and the
sky around it, and was gone.

That winter the heavy snows turned the swamp grass completely
white; lids of blue ice sealed the tidal pools. One Sunday afternoon
Julie's father jumped or fell from the roof of our building. And most
nights I came home with my arms and knees bloodied from jumping

the ledges. My mother cried a lot because I wouldn't talk to George. "Just try," she would say. "All I'm asking is for you to try." But all I thought about was riding across the world in the truck with the Maestro and Julie.

In the summer the Maestro returned alone. His face had a shut-down look, and when his eyes took you in, you knew right away he was seeing something else. No music came from the loudspeaker. He didn't talk to anyone; he wouldn't answer any questions about Julie. He hunched over the wheel, and his eyes stared down at the sparks rocketing this way and that, as if they were nothing special.

There was, of course, no carnival.

One morning I awoke, and his truck was gone.

After that I stopped jumping from the ledges. Once in a while I went with George into the swamp. My arms were stronger so I could draw the bowstring back, almost as far as he could. On a slope at the edge of the swamp I would raise the bow and watch the arrow leap sky-ward, higher and higher into the blue of empty space, until it became nearly invisible, about to be lost forever in a sky of its own, before its final arc and return. All things fall from orbit.

Once, watching the arrow rise, I imagined the Maestro's wedding day at Capri. High on a cliff above the blue Tyrrhenian sea, the bluest sea in the world, he reaches toward Julie and parts her veil. His eyes have a startling look, as if he is overjoyed at what fate has given him: this woman, this place, this promise of new life. He leans forward to kiss her and, just as his lips touch hers, she disappears.

PHILIP CIOFFARI ON COMMUNITY

For me, as a writer, a sense of community means two things. First, it means an association, formal or informal, with writers, artists, and other intellectually and emotionally curious people who share an ap-proach to the world that includes not only *living through* experience but also the desire to *record* that experience in some way and make it available to others. Organizations like The Writers Community and the YMCA National Writer's Voice are successful examples of such a community. Secondly, a sense of community means to me a sensitivity to a particular place or region or neighborhood that serves as a literary background for the writer's work, offering people, issues, situations, mood, and atmosphere from which the writer draws, then returns in the form of a mirror, a recognition, an affirmation of both that community's dreams and its failures.

PHILIP CIOFFARI IS *a professor of English at William Paterson College. His short stories and poems have appeared in* Playboy, Michigan Quarterly, Northwest Review, Midwest Quarterly, Southern Poetry Review, Gulfstream, Turnstile, *and other publications. "Love is for Vanishing into the Sky"—written in a 1992 Writers Community workshop conducted by Ed Vega and first published by* Southern Humanities Review—*received the New Voice Fiction Prize of the New York Writer's Voice and was nominated for a Pushcart Prize. He is presently working on a novel.*

MICHAEL CUNNINGHAM

Ignorant Armies

Tim and I would have been incest. We've been together longer than we've been alone; when he bites his tongue I feel it in my mouth. I used to ask: Did we grow up gay because we were friends, or did we veer together in an Illinois schoolyard out of creaturely recognition? At the age of ten did we already carry homing devices, little silver beads of difference? It doesn't matter. We found one another. Our blood just spoke.

Plenty of others have fallen. Tim is the beauty of us, the one with the vast, reluctant smile. He has the shoulders, the heavy blond forearms: he has some serious business between his legs for anyone who gets that far. People always knew, even when he was ten. By the time our voices started changing, he'd turned dangerous.

He wasn't stupid. He just came from silence. He was a farm boy—he'd grown up with a father who knew the Bible through rumors and a mother who couldn't read flour off the sack. The hogs and chickens did more speaking. Tim listened. He watched. Anyone who called him stupid had never looked inside his head, where the mute wonders lived. There were grottoes inside him. There were underground caverns and schools of luminous fish.

Nancy was the first one. I fell in love with her too, or thought I had. This was high school—you lived by telling stories. Tim and Nancy used to kiss, they showed their flesh to one another, but that was as far as it went. She called it respect; she joked about marriage. Nancy was a figure skater, with all that implies about strength and flashing, razor-edged ambition. She had dark-blond hair, thighs like the branches of an ash tree. Tim and I would pick her up after practice. We got there early to watch her turn and jump, the blades making their immaculate sounds on the cloudy ice. Tim said, "Beautiful."

"She's a vision, " I said. "She's an ice goddess. Don't you wonder what it's like to be inside her skin?"

"Mm-hm," he said.

At fifteen, it was still possible to confuse desire with the ordinary love of beauty. It was possible to dream of knives on the ice and tell yourself it was all you wanted.

When she was finished, Nancy would cut over to us, stop in a little shiver of crystals. She'd kiss Tim on the lips, and sometimes she had a quick dry kiss for me too. "Hi, boys," she'd say breathlessly. Because she was going places, because she acted generous, I could imagine she loved us both. You live by telling stories.

As we left the rink, I said to Nancy, "You look complete out there on the ice. You look like a whole world, all by yourself."

She laughed. She considered me comical, but she didn't mind hearing what I had to say. She slipped her slender hand under Tim's big elbow.

"I just want to qualify for the Springfield finals," she said. She had a jock's habit of modesty. "I don't need to be a poem or anything. I want to skate in Chicago."

"So do you think being a vision of perfection could keep you from skating in Chicago?" I asked. "Would the judges hold it against you? Speak into the microphone, please."

"Oh, be quiet, you," she said, but I knew she was glad enough to be reminded of her beauty. Tim smiled, either at Nancy herself or at the living ghost of her, spinning on the ice, touching her own dim reflection at the two electrified points of the blades. We walked together across the parking lot of the mall. Scraps of bright paper from McDonald's scudded past us in the wind.

This is Nancy, Tim, and me on a summer night in Illinois, out by the reservoir. There are starfields and the racket of bugs; there's a moon sliding over black water. Nancy sits on a rock, slightly apart, with her chin on her knees. Tim and I pass a wine bottle.

I say, " 'And we are here as on a darkling plain, swept with confused alarms of struggle and flight, where ignorant armies clash by night.'" Back then, I had a few lines of poetry memorized, and I used to mumble them as if I were consoling myself for a loss so huge it could only be expressed by someone already dead. I offered scraps of poetry in place of height or handsomeness.

"You're such a weirdo," Nancy says.

"I know." I'm happy to be called anything by her.

Tim swigs at the bottle. A cold circle of moonlight slips along the dark-green shaft. He says, "It's a pretty night." He offers the bottle to Nancy, who doesn't want it. She wants something, but she won't say what.

"You want to go swimming?" I ask.

"In that water?" she says. "No, thanks."

"It'd be like swimming right out into the stars," I say. "It'd be blacker and more silent than anywhere you've ever been."

"Sure," Tim says. "I'll go."

"Go ahead," Nancy tells him. "I'll watch."

"Okay," Tim says.

"Okay," she answers.

Tim and I stand up tipsily on the rocks, get out of our clothes. I work myself around so that Tim's size, his arms and haunches, are closer to Nancy. I say, " 'The sea is calm tonight, the moon lies fair upon the straits,' " and am just drunk enough to imagine that in the dark, for a moment, she'll put together the sight of Tim's body and the sound of my voice.

She says, "I can't stay out too late, you know. I've got early practice tomorrow."

Tim and I step into the black water, the cool ooze and suck of the bottom. Sinking in this water is like disappearing—that much less of you, then that much, then that. We're just heads and flashing white arms, swimming out. We make soft splashes, no other sound. The sky is crazy with stars, and for a moment it seems we'll have everything, all our delirious dreams. We swim a distance, float. I say to him, "This is heaven. It could be heaven. I mean, if we turn out to spend eternity floating around in dark water watching the stars, that would be okay with me."

"Yeah," he says. "Me too."

We stay there until the ecstasy starts to pale, until it's edged away by thoughts of snapping turtles and pet alligators from Florida that were dumped here years ago and have somehow survived the winters. We swim back with a certain speed, pull ourselves out onto the rocks. Nancy says, "Have a nice swim?"

"Uh-huh." We stand there, naked and glistening. I reach for my shirt. Nancy sits on her rock, a thin girl in jeans and a Mexican peasant blouse. Tim, wet in the starlight, is big and quiet and glossy as a horse. He lifts his arm, pushes a lock of wet hair off his forehead, and looks around as if he's surprised and delighted to find himself here, on earth, where specks of light flick over water and dark smells of grass and manure blow up from the fields. For a moment—for the first time in memory—beauty reverses itself, and it is Nancy and I who are the witnesses. She shrinks, a practical and reluctant little figure sitting on a gray slab of rock. Tim expands. I watch it happen. I watch beauty become what Tim is, innocent and powerful, heavy with muscle, looking out at the world and finding there aren't words for what he wants to say. I check Nancy's face to see if she's seen it too, but Nancy is a practical person. She wants satisfaction. She wants to skate in Chicago.

Tim says, "That was great. Wow, Nance, you don't know what you missed."

"You'd better take me home," she says. "I've got to be on the ice at seven."

Tim and I didn't fight, though the ordinary clock of friendship suggested it was time. We were getting our final size, sprouting our hair and finding our voices. We loved the same girl. But we just never fought; it wasn't something that could happen between us. When Nancy left him, I was there to share the bottle of gin. I was beside him when he drove his father's truck off the road, and I was there, howling with him, as he tumbled out of the cab and screamed his curses up at the white sky. That was the day we left his father's truck, nose down in the ditch, its radio still playing, and walked out across the fields as if we both lived somewhere out there, in the huge shimmering heat that buzzed and crackled beyond the orderly streets of town.

"Goddamn her," he said. His voice was thick with the gin. Grasshoppers whirred around us. Cornstalks flashed their leaves, put out a hot green smell.

"She's just stupid," I told him. "Forget her. She doesn't know what she wants."

I was lying. She knew exactly what she wanted. She wanted more than kisses, more than ordinary admiration. She wanted a boyfriend as devoted to her body as she was to the ice.

"Stupid," Tim said. "Right, stupid. Shit, man."

He stopped to take a long draw from the bottle. The gin was clear and bright in the sun. After he'd swallowed he sat down hard. He disappeared among the corn. I went and found him.

"Forget her," I said. The corn leaves crisscrossed over his pale hair. He wore cut-offs and a Rolling Stones T-shirt among the dusty shadows.

"She's got my favorite shirt," he said. He spoke into the bottle. "She's got all my Springsteen records."

"You can get a new shirt."

I sat down beside him. His face was square, clouded, lost in his study of the bottle.

"You can get more records," I said.

"I can. Yeah, sure I can."

"We can go shopping tomorrow."

"Yeah. Okay."

He looked up from the bottle and we kissed, just once, down in the shadows of the corn. We'd been waiting to do it since we were ten. For a moment we left our lives, and kissing became something we could do, drunk, dazzled by the heat. His mouth tasted of gin and of something else, his blood and being, a taste particular to him. We kissed without touching at any other point. Then he was up and running. "Shit, Charlie," he said. I got up, unsteadily. I saw him run off into the fields, frantic, weaving and swaying, as if a flock of invisible crows were chasing him, trying to peck off his clothes and his flesh, everything he owned.

We fell away for a while, but I always knew him. I was a radio that picked up his station. He went west, tried acting, not because he had talent but because he hoped it might help explain his precise and langorous beauty, his exact way of carrying himself. It might help explain his trouble with the flesh—he was otherworldly, an artist.

Men changed everything. Suddenly there was no bottom to what Tim could inspire. Suddenly he was valuable, and he didn't need to perform. It was enough to lie naked beside a pool. It was enough to sit in the passenger seat, to drink whatever was poured. He made a brief career out of being who he was, a farm boy with cheerful compliancy and shoulders broad and graceful as the wings of a plow. He went to Paris. He made two movies, in which he appeared as a fireman and a mechanic. In both of them, he obeys the commands of dark-haired, insistent men. In both he has a shy, beatific smile and visible trouble staying hard.

I'd guessed all that, more or less. When Tim moved back to Illinois, almost ten years later, I could tell him the story of his life nearly as fluently as he could tell it to himself.

We kissed hello, a quick dry peck on the lips. We stood together in adult bodies in my Chicago apartment. By then, Tim's beauty had darkened. It hadn't faded, but his face had taken on a new gravity. His skin was stitched directly to the bone now. He had pale feathery hair and a tan. As he sat on my sofa, drinking Scotch, he told me he'd come back to the Midwest because it was real.

"Isn't every place real?" I asked.

"Man," he said, "I guess you haven't gone on a casting call and gotten in an elevator with six other guys who look exactly like you."

"No," I said. "I go to committee meetings instead."

He smiled. It hadn't changed, his smile. He had a talent for making you believe you were the answer. You were what he'd been waiting for, and whatever you wanted was what he wanted too.

"You like being a teacher?" he asked.

"No one likes being a teacher. But hey. There are moments, not many, but there *are* moments when I feel like I'm doing something useful."

"That's good," he said. "I always knew you'd end up doing something like this. You know. Something good in the world."

"Well, at least I'm not doing any harm," I said.

"Come on, Charlie," he said. "You always been too modest. I'm proud of you, man, I am."

Though he was like my brother, it was impossible not to think of how many men, ten times richer and more powerful than I'd ever be, had paid real money for this: Tim sitting on their sofas, drinking their Scotch. I thought, for a moment or two, that we might become lovers. That our stories were carrying us there. But it would have been incest. When Tim fell asleep on my sofa that night, he looked the way he had at ten. He muttered fretfully over a dream and curled up with his hands tucked between his thighs.

He found an apartment on the North Side, got a job tending bar. We saw one another often, and I admit that, for a while, I let people believe we were together. It's something to walk into a restaurant with a man like Tim. He didn't understand about that. He'd always lived inside his beauty, the tick and moment of it. He didn't know how little happens to most of us, how time can lie in a room.

He cut a path across Chicago. If his beauty hadn't been quite enough to make him famous in Hollywood, it was more than sufficient along the curve of Lake Michigan. I heard all the stories. I heard about the farm boy, Tim's own ghost, who stole the sheets they made love on and the teacup Tim had drunk from. I heard about the chef so devoured by jealousy he slapped his hands down flat on the grill and grinned at Tim as the flesh began to sizzle and smoke, saying it hurt less than the ordinary moments.

I had affairs myself. I didn't live in solitude. But no one filled me with panic or crazy light. There was sex shot through with kindness, coffee in the morning. There were new movies, the movements of nations, everything to talk about. I dated an Edward, a Stanley, a Dan.

Sometimes, not often, I spent money I couldn't spare on big blond hustlers who, for an hour or two, would do everything I told them to. Yes, they tended to look like Tim. No, I didn't bring cornstalks to the hotel rooms. I didn't dress them in cut-offs and T-shirts, or ask them to gargle with gin.

I'm not stupid. I know about desire's shallow bottom; I know the dances envy can make us do. A tin cup and a little hat, a serrated smile. What did I want? Not Tim, exactly, though I loved him. I seemed to want something I couldn't quite name. I wanted other skin. I worried that I would always just be more of this: a small man, light in the chin, already losing hair on top. No one ever stole a cup because I'd drunk from it.

Tim had been in Chicago almost two years before he met Mark. Every man like Tim may have a Mark waiting for him, someone older, prosperous, handsome as a good leather suitcase. A man with a country house and crystal glasses, a man who's been so many places he's had all the little fears scoured off. Tim was thirty that year. He was ready. He'd grown tired of smiling at drunks from behind the bar. A pair of brackets had started etching themselves on either side of his mouth. He and Mark found one another at a party, and all Tim had to do was not say no.

This is Mark, Tim, and me on the dock at Mark's house in Michigan. July sun flicks over the water, sailboats belly and sigh. Mark lays his hand on Tim's blond kneecap and says, "You know, sometimes I think there might be order in the universe. There might be something out there that wants us to be happy."

At twenty, Mark had had a lethal beauty, and now, at fifty, he lives inside what's left of it. Big jaw, straight solid jut of nose; an aura of proud, bulky sorrow. He is precise and certain as a carpenter. He loves Tim the way a carpenter loves wood.

I say, "Order in the universe is probably easiest to imagine when you're sitting by a lake and the maid is making lunch." I can't quite pick up the habit of being kind to Mark, though I accept his invitations. I'm an in-law, with attendant privileges.

"Oh, okay," he says. "Let me put it another way. I'd like to formally thank whatever agency might be responsible for this moment. And Carla's not a maid, she's a friend with a catering business. This is a gift she's giving us today."

Maybe Mark's most insulting gesture is his unwillingness to be insulted by me. He runs his big square hand along Tim's calf, cups the arch of Tim's foot in his palm. There is something about that, the sight of a masculine hand tenderly holding a graceful, powerful foot. For a moment, I can imagine what their sex is like.

Tim says, "You want to go for a swim?"

"Sure," Mark answers.

"Come on, Charlie," Tim says, and I say all right. Tim dives in, Mark follows. They send drops sparking up into the air. I'm about to follow, but I change my mind. Something closes in front of me—the moment doesn't have enough room. I sit on the warm boards of the dock and watch them as they swim out. They speak to one another, laugh, speak again. I can't hear what they're saying.

I admit that I was jealous, at first. I admit I could be bitter about simple fairness. Didn't I work hard, listen compassionately, treat my students with respect and my friends with honor? I was a good man—where were my surprises, my gaudy nights? Where was the love that pierced? But time passed, and I got used to Tim's new happiness. I did well in my job. I joined more committees, started in on a reputation. I finished my first book, a study of the inverse relationship between beauty and power in medieval society. I graded my weight in papers.

On their second anniversary, Tim and Mark bought rings. They were simple gold bands, marriage rings, with that pure businesslike shine. Mark didn't want a ceremony—he said he'd feel like a fool—but he did want the rings. He and Tim lived together in his apartment on the fifteenth floor. As far as I know, they were faithful. I saw less and less of them, I was so busy with my work, but when I did see them they looked complete. They had that telepathy; they laughed over invisible jokes. For the first time, Tim didn't tell me stories. It was Mark who made the conspicuous efforts in my direction. It was

Mark who invited me to dinners and weekends, Mark who asked me to come along and help them pick out the rings.

"Hey, Charlie," he said once after dinner, when Tim was out of the room. "Do you know how much Tim cares about you?"

We sat together in the gray and black silence of his apartment, with candles shivering. City lights blazed behind the gauzy curtains.

I shrugged. I said, "We've been friends a long time, Mark."

"You're almost more than friends. You're Tim's family, don't you think? Much more so than his blood relations."

I nodded. Tim's mother was dead, his father had remarried and moved to Canada, where he could keep a disapproving eye on the earth's icy curve. His sister lived in a trailer park, screaming her religion at the passing cars.

"You're like his brother and his father at the same time," Mark said. "It's an interesting combination." Mark had a solemnity, a steady kindness, alert gray eyes. At moments, I may have been in love with him myself.

"I suppose so," I said.

"No question about it," Mark said.

There was something in his eyes, a cloud of meaning. I had some unkind things ready to say about a friendship so old it outranked money and sex, the temporary comforts of the flesh. I was deciding how to phrase them when Tim came back, and Mark looked away from me. We talked about whether we'd go to the movies or just stay in for the night.

There was only a moment, half a moment, that I felt simple vindication when Mark received the news. I never told anyone. I left it behind and took up my truer, more complicated feelings. When Tim found out about himself I held him so hard he choked. We wept together, we three. I'm still not certain whether, mixed with my sorrow, I felt a certain thread of relief. I hate to think that I did.

Mark's family couldn't keep us from the funeral, but they refused to let him wear his ring. They buried him in a blue suit, with foundation caught in the corners of his nose. A week after the funeral, Tim and I rented a car and drove back to the cemetery in Wisconsin, a vast field of crosses and tablets and angels bent under the weight of their stone wings. We found Mark's grave, still without its headstone, and sat down on it. We ran our hands over the grass. We could have been touching the place where Mark's chest was, or his head, or his crotch. Tim dug out a plug of grass and put the ring in the dirt. He said, "I hope I'm not putting this over his feet."

We sat for a while. Birds carried on in the trees. Dragonflies blued the air. "When I go," Tim said, "make sure I've got my ring on my finger, okay? Make sure I'm buried with it."

I nodded. I didn't speak.

"Promise?" he said.

"Sure."

He sat with the sun on his milky skin, looking at the place where he'd planted the ring. I saw a vine creeping out of Mark's grave, pale as new asparagus, quiet as an eel. I watched Tim's face and saw—it couldn't have been for the first time—how much he'd lost. His face was empty, and worse than empty. He might have had all the blood sucked out of him. Trees shimmered over the field of stones. Our rented Honda Civic gleamed nearby. When we couldn't sit there anymore we got back in the rented car and had breakfast at a diner. We ate in silence, like old people who've been married so long they've outlived everything they had to say to one another.

When we got back to my apartment Tim lay down on my bed and I lay beside him, as we'd done a hundred times before. But this time, after twenty years of chaste friendship, I leaned over and kissed his lips. This time he responded, maybe out of love, maybe out of loneliness. Now I was all he had. We kissed, and I ran my hands along his rib cage. We worked our clothes off. I touched the new smallness of him, the hard little knots of muscle. I put my lips on his lesions. I lathered his cock with spit, took a breath, and put it inside me.

"Hey," he said. "What are you doing?"

"Nothing."

"Oh, no. Stop."

I didn't stop. I said, "I'll take it out before you come." I wanted to

have this awful beauty in me, this pale sure knowledge. I pictured
him gone. I pictured a wave crashing over the land and soaking
everything, the stores and the carpets and the bread. I could see windows breaking, green water rushing in. I moved up and down on his
cock. I saw the hairline network of his blood, the crazy pattern of it. I
saw the whole of his being, the bloom of his end. I wanted to enter it.

"No," he said, after a minute.

"Come on," I said. "I've been waiting twenty years for this."

"No, oh no," he said, and he shrank inside me. I kept after him.
When he fell out I turned around and put it, limp, in my mouth. I
could taste both our smells. He took handfuls of my hair and pulled,
hard.

"Charlie, stop," he said. "Stop."

"No."

He pushed away from me, got out of bed. It wasn't easy for him.
He stood breathing, terrified, on the rug. He looked at me as if I'd
betrayed him, told his most precious secret, and I realized we'd
finally reached a moment all the others had passed through before
me. This moment had been waiting for all of us, when we went too
far. When we showed him how much we wanted to walk through
the world in his skin, to inhabit the hush and shimmer. To take
possession.

"Okay," I said. "Sorry. Come back, I won't do anything."

"Charlie. Aw, Charlie. Please."

"I know. I got a little nuts. Come here, I just want to hold you for
a little while."

"Please don't, man. I can't stand it."

"It's all right. Come on."

He got back into bed, uncertainly. He had nowhere else to go.
His flesh was sparse now, his hair dull and brittle-looking. I held him,
thinking he'd fall asleep. He didn't sleep. He kept turning the ring
around on his finger. After a while he got up and found a Kool I'd
had in my drawer for over a year and we lay smoking it together,
watching the ceiling as if we had, in fact, made love. I ran my palm
over his chest, breathed the changing smell of him, though I knew
he didn't like my touching him that way. Smoke curled up from his

fingers, and he passed the cigarette to me. He coughed, the same sound Mark had made. A squeaky cough, bone dry, wire brushes scrubbing a balloon. "You shouldn't smoke," I said.

"This is my last one."

We lay there, not speaking. It seemed we should have had so much to say. It seemed we should have examined the history of our devotions, explained ourselves, told the final truths. But once the silence established itself, it was impossible to break. I stroked his hair. We lay smoking that stale Kool, while cars bleated in the street below.

Today, he has a different beauty. He's a figure drawn with a hot wire in white cement. He has a greyhound's economy of flesh; beside him, the nurses look bloated as manatees. They squeak on the linoleum, they bump one another with their soft heavy flanks. It's not hard to imagine them lolling in brown water, moaning, slapping their flukes. Tim is pale and exact as a fire, prickly with what he knows. You can't touch him. His fingers are thin enough to pick a lock.

He says, "Girls, give it a rest, you're just going to set the alarms off, and then where'll we be?"

Over a month ago, he stopped making sense. He doesn't need to anymore; he's got a gaunt dignity that's better than logic. Now, finally, he's found his voice. He has a large crazy presence, a self-assurance that borders on the regal. When you see him these days, big-eyed and ivory-colored, surrounded by machinery, you think of kings who ordered castles and monuments that broke their country's banks, that crushed slaves and starved peasants for generations and then lived forever as evidence of human accomplishment. Only the insane and the almost-dead can see the ferocious splendor that lies beyond regular pain and loss.

"Everything's fine here," the older nurse says, "Don't worry, you're just going to feel a little pressure."

"Don't *you* worry," Tim says suavely to the young nurse who can't find the vein. "We can just phone this one in, really, there's no point in alarming the public." I can't think where this style came from, this pilot's voice he's developed. Think of Van Heflin at the wheel of a 747, that gruff sense of command.

"Here," the young nurse says, and the older one nods. The older nurse wears a badge that says her name is Florida.

"Got it," the young nurse says, and the needle slides into the vein like it had always belonged there, like there was some magic attraction between steel and flesh. Tim doesn't wince. He has a new set of priorities—the needles don't bother him, but a potted chrysanthemum or a wrapped present can drive him crazy. He seems to fear anything inefficient, anything that sheds.

"Oh, you've got it," Tim says. "Tell me, do you like the rumba? Does it speak to you?"

He sounds like me. His voice has my cadences, my way of biting off the consonants.

The younger nurse giggles, and a panicky look skates across her eyes. She hasn't had enough practice with the flirtations of the dying. The younger ones are sometimes better prepared for high drama than they are for odd little jokes and non sequiturs. They hadn't expected the gravely ill to be so strange.

"I don't know," she says.

"The rumba," Tim says, "is the dance for you. It'll set your body free and bring your soul right up into your mouth. Trust me on this."

"I think we're all set here," says the older nurse, Florida. She helps the younger one tape the needle to Tim's arm, gives his intravenous bag a little shake. "Mm-hm," she says, and her mouth makes a firm line. Florida has been to Tim's room at least a hundred times, but she always treats him with the same distracted semi-attention, as if he's an illusion that won't coalesce or disappear. Back when he made sense, when some of his old beauty still held, he did a better job of charming nurses.

"Thanks," I say cheerfully. "We appreciate it."

The younger one gives the intravenous bag a shake of her own, and they move off down the hall. I'm alone here, with Tim, in the pale yellow of the room. The hospital has a hum and a steady aquarium light. Wheels turn along the halls.

"The truth of this bed," Tim says, "is the way it adjusts itself. Is it facing north to south?"

"Yes," I tell him.

"Good. Don't let a lot of people come."

"Okay," I say.

There's never a crowd, never much of a crowd. Friends stop by when they can, but I'm the one who's here from hour to hour. I'm the one who watches time pass: This much less, then this much, then this.

I pull the curtain all the way around Tim's bed, stroke his damp hair. He is looking straight ahead, staring at the air in front of him as if blazing letters were forming there, beginning to spell something important but illegible. I inhale, searching for the smell of him threaded in with the smells of medicine and hot machinery and instant mashed potatoes. No one wants him now but me. I run my fingers along his cheekbone, slip my hand down to his shoulder and then under the hospital gown to the hard plates of his chest. He growls, a low sawing sound that lives deep in his throat. I glance toward the door, to make sure no one's coming, and put my lips on his. His breath is sharp and dank. It tastes vaguely like him and it tastes like the bitter medicine that pumps by the quart through his veins. I whisper to him. I say, close to his ear, "Tim? Can you hear me?"

Nothing happens in his face. He looks ahead, murmuring. I hold his hand, feel the sharp smooth surface of the ring that's grown too big for him.

"'And we are here as on a darkling plain,'" I say, "'swept with confused alarms of struggle and flight, where ignorant armies clash by night.'"

He laughs. He looks at me, and for a moment he's present.

"Tim?" I say.

"Hey, Mark," he answers. "Hey, baby."

Then he's gone again. His eyes turn inward, and he murmurs, "The truth of this bed is that it doesn't work. It's got nowhere to go."

I hold his hands. We're here, right here, as the future closes up around us. Something will happen next. Something always does. We live with unspeakable losses, and most of us carry on. We find new lovers, change jobs, move to another state. We continue to know animal pleasures; we eat and have sex, buy new clothes. Hardly anyone is destroyed, I mean truly annihilated, by loss. We're designed for endurance.

Still, I'd trade every chance of future happiness if he'd come back one last time. I needed him to look at me, see me, and give me this ring I'm wearing. I didn't want to have to take it off his finger like that.

MICHAEL CUNNINGHAM ON COMMUNITY

Along with all the other difficulties inherent in writing fiction, one hardly benefits from feeling like a fool for wanting to do so in the first place. I spent my early adult years in precisely that condition, trying to write in various apartments that tended to have views of freeways or Cineplexes, and when I'd explain to friends that I couldn't go to the beach or movie or bar or whatever because I needed to stay home and write, they seemed to believe I was fiercely protecting some arcane hobby, like painting on China plates or building replicas of famous buildings out of toothpicks.

Although I knew better, it was difficult to avoid lapsing at least occasionally into those suspicions myself. Few endeavors hold less promise of reward than fiction writing in the late twentieth century, and a ferocious dedication is almost as important, early on, as talent itself. I don't regret much in my life, but I do regret the hours I spent fretting over the futility of writing at all when I could have been worrying about how to wring the most music out of my prose or how to bring a character more convincingly to life.

A community-based program like The Writers Community would not have made me into a writer—I did that on my own—but it would have saved me considerable time and anguish. When I taught a class for The Writer's Voice, I was constantly aware that one of its most valuable aspects was the twelve young writers' exposure to one another. Here in a room, every week, were thirteen of us who believed that trying to write the most beautiful sentences possible was more than enough to do with your life. Here were other people who would understand why you couldn't go to the beach or movie or bar, and further would probably forgive you if you called after midnight to read the paragraph you'd struggled with all day.

After teaching the class, I've had the good luck to continue living with the awareness that those twelve young people are out there, all in different circumstances, all negotiating the need to write and write well. It would have made an enormous difference to me at twenty. It makes an enormous difference to me now.

MICHAEL CUNNINGHAM *is the author of the novels* Flesh and Blood *and* A Home at the End of the World. *His fiction has appeared in the* New Yorker, Atlantic Monthly, Paris Review, The Penguin Book of Gay Short Stories, The Best American Short Stories 1989, *and other publications. The recipient of fellowships from the National Endowment for the Arts, the Guggenheim Foundation, and the Mrs. Giles Whiting Foundation, as well as a Writers Community residency, he lives in New York City.*

ALAN DUGAN

Closing Time at the Second Avenue Deli

This is the time of night of the delicatessen
when the manager is balancing
a nearly empty ketchup bottle
upside down on a nearly full ketchup bottle
and spreading his hands slowly away
from the perfect balance like shall I say
a priest blessing the balance, the achievement
of perfect emptiness, of perfect fullness? No,
this is a kosher delicatessen. The manager
is not like. He is not like a priest,
he is not even like a rabbi, he
is not like anyone else except the manager
as he turns to watch the waitress
discussing the lamb stew with my wife,
how most people eat the whole thing,
they don't take it home in a container,
as she mops up the tables, as the
cashier shall I say balances out?
No. The computer does all that. This
is not the time for metaphors. This is the time
to turn out the lights, and yes,
imagine it, those two ketchup bottles
will stand there all night long
as acrobatic metaphors of balance,
of emptiness, of fullness perfectly contained,
of any metaphor you wish unless
the manager snaps his fingers at the door,
goes back, and separates them for the night
from that unnatural balance, and the store goes dark

as my wife says should we take a cab
or walk, the stew is starting to drip already.
Shall I say that the container can not
contain the thing contained anymore? No.
Just that the lamb stew is leaking all across town
in one place: it is leaking on the floor of the taxicab,
and that somebody is going to pay for this ride.

Love Song: I and Thou

Nothing is plumb, level, or square:
        the studs are bowed, the joists
are shaky by nature, no piece fits
        any other piece without a gap
or pinch, and bent nails
        dance all over the surfacing
like maggots. By Christ
        I am no carpenter. I built
the roof for myself, the walls
        for myself, the floors
for myself, and got
        hung up in it myself. I
danced with a purple thumb
        at this house-warming, drunk
with my prime whiskey: rage.
        Oh I spat rage's nails
into the frame-up of my work:
        it held. It settled plumb,
level, solid, square and true
        for that great moment. Then
it screamed and went on through,

skewing as wrong the other way.
God damned it. This is hell,
   but I planned it, I sawed it,
I nailed it, and I
   will live in it until it kills me.
I can nail my left palm
   to the left-hand crosspiece but
I can't do everything myself,
   I need a hand to nail the right,
a help, a love, a you, a wife.

ALAN DUGAN *has received numerous awards for his poetry, among them
the National Book Award, the Prix de Rome, and the Pulitzer Prize.
His most recent books are* Poems Six *and* New & Collected Poems:
1961–1983. *He has taught at* The Writers Community *and resides in Truro,
Massachusetts.*

CORNELIUS EADY

Gratitude

I'm here
    to tell you
        an old story.
        This
Appears to be
        my work.
           I live
           in the world,
Walk
    the streets
        of New York,
        this
Dear city.
      I want
        to tell you
        I'm 36
Years old,
      I have lived
          in and against
          my blood.
I want to tell you
        I am grateful,
              because,
              (after all),
I am a black,
      American poet!
           I'm 36,
           and no one

Has to tell me
        about luck.
                I mean:
                after a reading
Someone asked me
                once:
                        If
                you weren't
Doing this,
        what
                (if anything)
                would you be doing?
And I didn't say
        what we both
                understood.
                I'm
A black, American male
                I own
                        this particular story
                        on this particular street
At this particular moment.
                        This appears
                                to be
                                my work.
I'm 36 years old,
                and all I have to do
                                is repeat
                                what I notice
Over
        and over,
                all I have to do
                is remember.
And to the famous poet
                who thinks
                        literature holds
                        no small musics:

Love.
    And to the publishers
        who believe
        in their marrow
There's no profit
    on the fringes:
        Love.
        And to those
Who need
    the promise of wind,
        the sound of branches
        stirring
Beneath the line:
    here's
        another environment
        poised
To open.
    Everyone reminds me
        what an amazing
        Odyssey
I'm undertaking,
    as well they should.
        After all,
        I'm a black,
American poet,
    and my greatest weakness
        is an inability
        to sustain rage.
Who knows
    what'll happen next?
        This appears to be one
        for the books,
If you
    train your ears
        for what's
        unstated

Beneath the congratulations(!)
That silence
is my story,
the pure celebration
(And shock)
of my face
defying
its gravity,
So to speak.
I claim
this tiny glee
not just
For myself,
but for my parents,
who shook their heads.
I'm older now
Than my father was
when he had me,
which is no big deal,
except
I have personal knowledge
of the wind
that tilts the head back.
And I claim
This loose-seed-in-the-air glee
on behalf of the
social studies teacher
I had in the tenth grade,
a real bastard
who took me aside
after class
The afternoon
he heard I was leaving
for a private school,
just to let me know

He expected me
        to drown out there,
                that I held the knowledge
                of the drowned man,
The regret
      of ruined flesh
           in my eyes;
           which was fair enough,
Except
    I believe I've been teaching
              far longer now
              than he had that day,
And I know
      the blessing
         of a
         narrow escape.
And I claim
      this rooster-pull-down-morning glee
                    on behalf of anyone
                    who saw me coming.
And said yes,
        even
           when I was loud, cocky.
           insecure,
Even
    when all they could have seen
                was the promise of a germ,
                even
When it meant
      yielding ground.
              I am a bit older
              than they were
When I walked
      into that room,
           or class
           or party,

And I understand the value
                    of the unstated push.
                                        A lucky man
                                        gets to sing
his name.
            I have survived
                        long enough
                        to tell a bit
Of an old story.
                And to those
                        who defend poetry
                        against all foreign tongues:
Love.
            And to those who believe
                            a dropped clause
                            signifies encroachment:
Love.
            And to the bullies who need
                            the musty air of
                            the clubhouse
All to themselves:
                    I am a brick in a house
                                    that is being built
                                    around your house.
I'm 36 years old,
                a black, American poet.
                                    Nearly all the things
                                    that weren't supposed to occur
Have happened, (anyway),
                    and I have
                            a natural inability
                            to sustain rage,
Despite
        the evidence.
                I have proof,
                            and a job that comes
As simple to me
                as breathing.

CORNELIUS EADY *is the author of five books of poetry, most recently*
You Don't Miss Your Water *and* The Autobiography of a Jukebox.
He has received fellowships from the National Endowment for the Arts, the
Guggenheim Foundation, and the Lila Wallace-Reader's Digest Fund, among
other awards. He has taught at The Writers Community and elsewhere and
is currently associate professor of English and director of creative writing and
the Poetry Center at State University of New York, Stony Brook.

BARBARA ELOVIC

Angels

In the celestial hierarchy there are nine rungs:
angels, archangels, principalities, powers, virtues,
dominions, thrones, cherubim, and seraphim.

The Pope says they're often misunderstood,
always invisible, still surely hovering
outside each precinct of the world.

I like to think of them sitting
in some abandoned union hall,
their wings tucked under carefully

as choir robes, as they patiently await
their assignments—whose life
they'll be obliged to bail out

over and over until its end.
Languishing in the sky between emergencies,
the angels blanket themselves in clouds,

cup their ears, and make way
for passing airplanes.
The need to believe in them keeps us conjuring

likenesses out of cotton and crepe paper,
glitter, glass, and cookie dough. For they are
the guardians of the second chance,

the one that gives you the heart to start over
in the middle of a life that has come to nothing.
They recall what we love when we're about to give up:

words that resemble musical tones—alabaster,
cloisonné, periwinkle. The bells of the clock tower
chiming the quarter hour, as if to say

small steps will get you there,
the muffled sound of footfall on snow.
The white of ivory and pearls with which we endow them

springs from the spectrum: its promise that possibilities
persist, as each road seems to lead to a wall we can't scale
without the help of wings.

BARBARA ELOVIC ON COMMUNITY

I ran a poetry reading series in Brooklyn for a number of years and
was lucky enough to have it funded in part by both the National
Endowment and the New York State Council on the Arts, but our
staying power stemmed from the success we had enmeshing our programs in the ordinary life of the community. For two years we staged
the readings in a local art and frame shop on the corner of a busy intersection. The readings were held on Sunday afternoons, and our
audience was drawn partly from our mailing list, readers of the
New York City Poetry Calendar, but also neighbors out for a stroll.
Intrigued by the sight of a group of people sitting quietly in a sun-
drenched room (all right, on good days) and listening so attentively,
the passersby would wander in to see exactly what was going on.

One of my greatest points of pride was the number of people who
admitted attending their first-ever poetry reading under our auspices. We relocated to a local library system when the frame shop
closed, and with the aid of a public address system, we encouraged
people to hear poetry read aloud, again often for the first time.

We also sponsored an annual high school poetry competition that resulted in a reading and publication for the contest winners. In addition to small honoraria, we awarded the high school poets books donated by major publishers. The year we launched the event, we were operating out of a private club whose headquarters was modeled on a Venetian palazzo. The prize winners showed up really "decked out" along with teachers, parents, and fellow students, some of them sporting corsages. By coincidence, three of the eight winners came from the same small vocational high school.

After the reading people mingled and posed for the many cameras proud audience members had brought. The high school kids took themselves seriously, and so did the parents, teachers, and classmates there to support them. Elitism was nowhere in evidence that May afternoon.

Clearly we had fallen as far from the academic ivory tower as Timothy Leary from his Harvard tenure.

BARBARA ELOVIC *has published a chapbook of poems,* Time Out. *Her work has appeared in* Poetry, Threepenny Review, *and* Sonora Review, *as well as the anthologies* Waltzing on Water, Anthology of Magazine Verse, *and* Walk on the Wild Side: Urban American Poetry Since 1975. *She is president emeritus of Poetlink, a literary service organization based in Brooklyn, New York.*

LESLIE EPSTEIN

FROM *King of the Jews*

Late that same afternoon Trumpelman arrived back at Tsarskoye Selo. The Obergruppenführer dropped him off in his new Double Six. The Elder could hardly walk. His clothes were ripped, his cloak gone. There was only one lens left in his frame. He did not go into the mansion, but around it, to the gardens in back. Though early in springtime, the fresh green stems of garlic were pushing out of the ground. Trumpelman sank down among them; wearily, he shut his eyes.

No telling how long he might have stayed there if Bettsack, the schoolmaster, had not walked by carrying what looked like a gigantic squash. *Smuggling!* said the Elder to himself, and keeping low, keeping hidden, he followed the young teacher to the edge of the plowed-up field. There the orphans—both the old-timers and the ones who had joined the Asylum in the last years before the move to the Balut—were waiting. They all had caps on, and coats, and were holding such things as nuts, the head of a cabbage, and a pink India-rubber ball. The sun had dropped well down in the sky, and the air was chilly now. Bettsack was a thin fellow, poorly whiskered, with threads that stuck up from his collar. He made his way to the center of the field, set down the gourd—it was as big as a washbasin, really—and began to call through his hands.

"Stations, children! Positions, if you please! You! Shifter! Leibel Shifter! Further back. Further back! Tushnet! You go back, too!"

The children began to scatter over the field. Shifter, the mad boy, the dog, kept going backward. Every minute or so he would stop, but Bettsack waved him farther on, until he was practically out of sight. "Stop!" the schoolmaster shouted. But Shifter still backpedaled, and the message to him had to be passed from orphan to orphan, from Krystal to Atlas to Tushnet, across the length of the field.

Finally they all held still. Bettsack bent down and picked up the dried squash; he just had the strength to lift it over his head. The next thing you knew the schoolmaster, a grown-up, responsible person, was rapidly spinning around. "Flicker!" he gasped to the boy who was nearest. "Citron!" he called, to the lad next farthest out. "Begin rotation!"

Trumpelman could hardly believe what he saw: both boys, and then Gutta Blit, and then all the others began to spin on the spot. It was like madness. Round and round they went, stepping all over their shadows. "West to east, Miss Atlas! Not like a clock!" Rose Atlas stopped; she reversed direction. The rest kept going, holding their little spheres. Bettsack had begun to stagger a little. The breath came visibly from his mouth.

"Now! Revolutions!"

Little Usher Flicker—between his fingers he had a pea from a pod—began to trip around the teacher, in a circle more or less. A bit farther out Citron was doing the same. The amazing thing was that as both boys went in this circular orbit, they did not stop whirling about. Gutta Blit, with the pink rubber ball, was spinning like a dervish too, and also Krystal, and so was everyone soon. Even Leibel Shifter, way out on the edge of the field, a half kilometer off, had started to run. However, because of the distance between him and Bettsack, he hardly seemed to be moving. Flicker, for instance, had run three times about the center, before Shifter, his legs thrashing, covered any noticeable ground. It would take him forever to complete a revolution.

"Attention! Moons!" Bettsack, with red patches that showed through his beard, with his necktie coming undone, practically shrieked this.

From behind the hill that led to the cemetery grounds fifteen, twenty, more than twenty children came pouring. What they did, with a whoop, with a shout, was to pick out some of the whirling orphans—Gutta, Rose Atlas, the puffing Mann Lifshits—and then begin to race as fast as they could around them. For a time the whole field was covered with these whizzing children, making circles inside of circles, curves within curves.

Then Trumpelman stood up in the dimming light; he walked into their midst. Through his split, puffy lips, he demanded of the reeling Bettsack, "What is the meaning of this? Speak!"

The schoolmaster dropped his squash. He started screaming. "It's the whole solar system! Including the new planet of Pluto! In correct proportions! According to the system of Sir J. Frederick Herschel!" Then he threw his arms around the Asylum Director, clinging to him the way a drunkard does to a post. Just then Nathan Hobnover, an eight-year-old boy, came roaring over the hilltop, making a sizzling sound: *zzzzzzz!*

"Comet," said Bettsack, and sank down about Trumpelman's ankles.

The exhausted children saw the old man in tatters; they wobbled to a halt. Mann Lifshits, whose heavy cabbage represented Jupiter, simply dropped, as did his eleven moons. One by one the others collapsed. They lay on their backs, with their coats spread, their breath coming up in a mist. Only the man from Vilna, for all his scratches and bruises, remained on his feet. Then he sat down, too. Tushnet caught his breath before anyone else and addressed the schoolmaster.

"Sir, what will happen when the sun goes out?" He was some way off, but it was so still you could easily hear him.

Bettsack said, "What do you mean, Tushnet? It goes *down*. It does not go *out*."

"I mean, when it burns up. Will we burn up, too?"

A high voice broke in. "It can't just go on forever. Sometime it has to run out of fuel."

"That is only a theory, Flicker. It has not been proved."

"But what if it's true? What then? Everything will be dark. It makes me nervous." That was Rose Atlas.

"I don't think it will burn up," said Mann Lifshits, from his spot on the ground. "It'll just get colder and colder. Everything on earth will get colder, too. It will be like the ice age. Nothing but ice."

"But it scares me," Rose replied.

"Listen," said Bettsack. "This is speculation. In any case, it won't happen for thousands of years."

"See? You said it was going to happen! It's going to happen!"

"We'll all be frozen to death!"

"Please!" their instructor said. "Why do you worry? In a thousand years none of us will be alive."

"I don't care! I don't want it to go out! I hate the idea of the cold!"

"I do, too!"

"No one alive! No one! There won't even be animals on earth. It's terrible!"

"Don't talk about it! Don't think about it!"

The children begin to whimper and moan. So Bettsack spoke in a loud, firm voice. "Pay attention, if you please. The sun is not going to stop burning. It is made in a certain way. And even if it should go out after all, by then men will have invented spaceships, and they will fly off to live somewhere else. To other planets, to other worlds. There is nothing that science cannot achieve. Perhaps in the universe we shall meet other forms of life. Perhaps even people just like ourselves. Think of that! What a wonderful day that will be! How much we shall learn!"

The moaning had completely stopped. Everything was quiet. Then, so that everyone's heart leaped and pounded, there was an awful wail from Leibel Shifter. "Help! I'm so far away! Help! I'm afraid!"

Trumpelman, sitting upright, answered. "Come. All of you. Come closer."

Silently, on all fours, the boys and girls began to crawl toward the center. They drew near to Trumpelman, who, through his swollen eyes, his single lens, was staring off to the west. They looked, too.

There, on the horizon, the real sun was leaking something. Red stuff, like jam, came out of it and spread over the nearby sky. "Like a raspberry drop," said Usher Flicker. He took the Elder's hand. Citron, a new boy, had curly blond hair coming from under his cap. He laid his head across the Elder's knees. Dark Gutta Blit leaned on his shoulder.

"It's beautiful," she whispered, gazing off to where the sun, cut by the earth's edge, still pumped the sweet-looking syrup from its center. All the children—the planets, the satellites, Hobnover the comet, and at last even Shifter—pressed close to Trumpelman, and to each other. They were like his missing cape.

LESLIE EPSTEIN ON COMMUNITY

The connection between the writer and the community is, in my opinion, vital for the writer—at least for this writer, since there are a few (Proust springs to mind) who thrive best in isolation. But I would lose my bearings without some degree of contact, if only once a week, with a community of either my peers or my students, with whom a voice can be established that is not merely an echo. That voice, quibbling or striving or criticizing, in prayer or praise, in outrage or gratification, is what tells the writer, in what would otherwise be a sea of silence, that he is yet alive.

LESLIE EPSTEIN *has published seven books of fiction, including* King of the Jews, Goldkorn Tales, Pinto and Sons, *and* Pandaemonium. *His articles and stories have appeared in* Esquire, Atlantic Monthly, Playboy, *and* Harper's. *His awards include Fulbright, Guggenheim, and National Endowment for the Arts Fellowships, an award for Distinction in Literature from the American Academy and Institute of Arts and Letters, and a residency at the Rockefeller Institute at Bellagio. He has taught at The Writers Community and for many years has directed the creative writing program at Boston University.*

DAVID EVANIER

Shoes

I

When he was ninety-five, my father and I began to get to know each other better. It was a year after he entered the nursing home. Arriving there after living alone in Manhattan for thirty years, he had immediately called all his favorite waitresses in the restaurants he had frequented to bid them farewell.

I sat with him in his room in the nursing home in Roxbury, Massachusetts. "Coming into town with a corpse waiting to be shipped," he said. "A corpse in your mind, that's no good, Daniel. Please write the funeral home in New York that I am here and they should expect my body when I die. And I hope that will be soon. Tell them I'm to be buried in the Mannheim Gardens and give them the exact location of the burial spot. You've got it in the deed. I'm always trying to make things easier for you."

I'd taken the Amtrak from New York. Along the route I recognized the debris that haunted me on our car rides here ever since I was a kid, stuff that somehow reminded me of my father's life: mud, weeds, abandoned factories, rock piles, pieces of rusted machinery, nails and hammers, bathtubs, gutted cars, gas tanks, coiled wire, gnarled tree branches, stumps, logs, quarries, and a sea of old tires. I passed the New Life Strip and Finish Shop, and the Patent Scaffolding Company.

In the cab on the way from the station to the home, the Jamaican cabdriver had swerved to avoid hitting a pregnant young woman and intoned, "They don't want to work and we have to pay the taxes. I will help you with one child. But the second, you must work three days. And the streets are to be cleaned. The streets are dirty. I will furnish the bus to transport you. I will furnish the tools. I will give you the broom. I will even give you the gas. But I want every street as clean as a penny . . ."

When I left New York for Los Angeles, in his panic and dependency my father had thrown himself on the mercy of my cousin, who worked as a secretary to the director of a nursing home in Roxbury, my father's hometown. He'd made her executor of his estate, and then removed her two months later.

Now my father lay on the bed, his legs like sticks. He had pneumonia, had lost his hearing, and needed a cataract operation. He could no longer read his beloved *New York Times*. When I had called to tell him, through a staff interpreter, I was flying to see him, he said he didn't want me to come. Then he called me back and shouted, "Do not come! Do not come! Do not come! You must not come!" On the following day he left a message on my answering machine: "Come."

"I didn't want you to see me like this," he said when I arrived. "You know I'm on drugs now. I'm not eating. I want to die. They won't let me. I see no reason for living. You shouldn't be here. I don't want to antagonize the big shots. I want to remain on good terms with them. They got very angry when I called the police and the fire department. They could send me up to the pit with all the queers. I should be dead. I want to be dead, but I can't. They won't let me." He looked at me. "Don't be angry for my wanting to die, Daniel. It would give me the peace I don't have."

My father could not hear me at all, so I wrote notes in response to his questions, or questions for him to answer. He told me to tear up every note in little pieces and to flush it down the toilet.

A nurse came in to give him his pills. "Thank you, dear," he said. As she went out, he said in his very loud voice, "She's no good."

II

On the next morning my father said, "Getting up in the morning, shaving, nothing to look forward to. Every minute is an hour. I just want to close my eyes. You used to think you could take care of me, Daniel. I never wanted to live this long. I want to die. But can't."

When the lunch tray came, my father began eating solid food again for the first time in ten days.

I wrote him dozens of notes: that I would come back to be with him for the cataract operation, why he must eat, must live, that he was too suspicious of people—

"You're right," he said to this, and made me tear up the note.

We walked down the hallway, my father with his cane. The men and women stared into space, some with mouths misshapen, holding on to their pocketbooks. My father was animated and purposeful, a dynamo beside them.

His voice bounced off the walls. "They sent a big colored man to look you over when you were in my room. See that big black Negro over there?" I saw the guard's shoulders stiffen as he walked in front of us. A blank-faced, stooped young man paced from one end of the hallway to the other. For the fourth time my father said, "See that poor idiot? He's a rabbi's son." This time the young man turned and said, "Grandson." My father did not notice or hear him. I told him.

"No kidding? I'm too loud."

We sat down in the hallway. "Remember my roommate, Bob? He moved out. He was a spy. He was. Not a spy. A friend of management. A nice man. I liked him. He took me out, wheeled me around when I couldn't walk. But now he's left and he mailed me thirty Bic pens. So you see? He was a nice man. But he was a spy." He looked at me. "You must think I'm crazy. But there are things about your cousin I can't tell you yet. Daniel, she tried to rob me blind."

When we said good-bye, I held my father in my arms and wept. I promised again to come back for the cataract operation.

In the cab, a familiar deep voice said, "I will furnish the tools . . . I will give you the broom."

III

My father had begged my cousin Tova to help get him into the home. He felt abandoned and had entered into one of his cyclical rages against me. Tova and her husband drove to New York, helped him pack, and transported him to the home.

As a boy visiting Roxbury with my father, I had slept in Tova's bedroom, listened to Jack Benny with her, played games, told stories, and dived beneath the blankets, hoping the night would go on and on. Her father, a Jewish Republican, was in a rage against FDR long after Roosevelt's death. He did not speak to his wife from 1946 to 1949 and again, from 1951 to 1953.

Now, forty years later, the voice on the phone was Tova, speaking with deep sighs, world weary, coping with the burden of my father and his money. "Dad is doing well, he's getting his pills, we all get old . . ." More sighs, no mention of cash. But after all, she was there and I wasn't. She deserved the five thousand dollars my father gave her. His suspicion turned on her now, as it had turned on me.

Then the phone call from my father's social worker. "Your father's mail was found opened in your cousin's office. We have severed all contact between them."

IV

On my next trip to Roxbury, I waited for my father in his room after the operation. I had written him constantly, since his physician told me his hearing would probably not return.

When my father came into the room with dark glasses, he laughed with pleasure that I was there. His hearing had returned. He had gained 13 pounds, was eating regularly, and was working out in the gym again.

He showed me a little bundle: shoes, gloves, pictures of me and my father together. "Tova left them in a heap at my door last week. She had kept them for a year, since she moved me from New York. I kept asking her about the shoes and the pictures, and she denied she had them. She said I must have dreamt it. So I only had one pair of shoes left.

"A shoe salesman came by once a month to take orders for shoes. Tova always hung around with him. I ordered shoes twice from him, and they never arrived. When I asked him about the shoes, he whispered, 'No can do' and walked off. So I knew she forbade him to sell me the shoes. I went to the head nurse and told her about it. In five minutes the salesman was at my door and I had the shoes in a week."

We walked into the cafeteria. To my astonishment I saw a patient, Harold Becker, who was the father of a woman I had worked with in New York City for five years; Jennie had introduced him to me when he had visited her at the office. Harold was staring straight ahead and muttering to himself. I reminded him who I was. He did not seem to recognize me.

Back in the room, my father said, "Leave the door open, and I'll watch and see if anybody's watching." He paused. "Daniel, your coming to see me again so soon must seem strange to them. They wonder why. They're being so nice to me now. They heat up my chicken and my soup. They come in to say hello. My case is so important to them, I don't know why."

It was quiet on the ward now. The TVs had quieted down. Suddenly a figure came charging into the room, his fists up, his bathrobe trailing. It was Harold Becker. Standing some distance from my father's bed, he spoke fiercely over my father's head: "If ever a guy had symptoms of psychic disease, it's him. Stupid bastard."

"You stay away from me," my father said.

"I'll keep away from you," Harold said. "You just watch it, that's all. Listen," he concluded, "I'll see you later." He strutted out, feinting with his fists.

We rang for the nurse and told her what happened. But my father was strangely peaceful. This was not what troubled him. He let it pass like a dream.

In the morning, my father told me he could read the entire eye chart. He had dreamed of Hebrew on all the walls. He laughed and shook his head.

We walked down the hallway, where other patients sat. We passed Tova's mother, Lillian, who was ninety-eight and had lived in the home ten years. She did not see us. "Lillian wants to die," my father said. "Well, she always did."

V

In the garden my father said, "I generally don't tip, but I gave this girl money because she had to bathe me, a naked man after all. After a while she wouldn't take my fifteen dollars. It was now too little, so she would leave it on the table. The next time, she put me in the shower, turned on only the cold water, and left me there. Then she came back with a second girl and they just stared at me.

"Then one day she came into my room and instead of speaking, handed me a note that said, 'You think I want to rob you.' Then she tore it up and walked out. Finally, one night late, I was in my bed in the dark. The door opened and she came in silently. She sat on the adjoining bed without speaking for a half hour.

"I had to decide what to do. If I ratted her out, I'd be in trouble with the whole staff. So I didn't go to the head nurse, but the one below her, and begged her not to tell. But she said she had to. It turned out okay. Now the girl is all smiles with me."

We walked into the cafeteria and sat down with Harold and his wife. After a moment Harold suddenly muttered, his head down, about me: "Of all the people I met at Jennie's office, he had the most presence by far. By far."

I reached over and touched him. "Thank you, Harold," I said.

In the evening I sat by my father's bed. A nurse peered in and took his blood pressure. "Another stall," he whispered to me. As she began to close the door, he said to her with a smile, "You can leave it open. I have nothing to hide."

This was our last night together. I would be returning to Los Angeles the next day. "Tova took all my money, not only the five thousand I gave her," he suddenly said. "She took all my savings when I came in here. I was so angry at you, Daniel, that I made her my executor. She said she would deposit the money in a joint account in my name and hers. But when I asked her where the money was deposited, she said she didn't know, that only her husband knew. This went on for weeks. I couldn't sleep. Finally I located the bank and went there. She had deposited the money in a joint account, but with

MANY LIGHTS IN MANY WINDOWS

her husband, not me. And I got it back! I got it back! I went down to the bank and told them what happened.

"On the day she and her husband picked me up in New York and drove me to Roxbury, first we went out to dinner, then to Tova's house. They got down to business about financial arrangements. I sat down at the table with her husband.

"But Tova, where was she? She didn't sit down. I looked around. She stood behind me, fiddling and pacing. She wouldn't face me. I asked Hal her husband what's doing with Tova? Why doesn't she sit down?

"'Oh,' Hal said, 'she's very sensitive about discussing financial matters.'" My father laughed and kicked his legs.

VI

It was almost midnight. He was very tired, and I heard him saying, "For years I gave Daniel an allowance."

"What?"

He looked startled. "Who did I think I was talking to?"

He took out the razor I gave him and told me he had trouble opening it. "But I've found a way. Look!" My father started wiggling all the fingers of both hands and smiled victoriously at me. Then he tried to open the razor. It didn't open.

"You try it, Daniel. We'll do it together." I was reluctant to wiggle my fingers.

"Come on, Daniel! Get with it!"

I began wiggling my fingers and my father wiggled his. We wiggled together. He was grinning. The nurse looked in, and popped her head out again quickly.

"Now!" my father said. "Let's try." I opened the razor. "You see!"

It was time to go. Visiting hours had been over for a long time. I walked with my father down the long corridor. He walked firmly, a spring in his step.

The cab was waiting at the front door. It was the same cabdriver.

I held my father and kissed him. "You're a good boy, Daniel." I got into the cab, closed the door, and looked through the window.

Planted solidly on the ground, his cane digging into the earth, my father surveyed the cab and held up his left hand in farewell.

I turned to the cabdriver. "He's still watching out for you," he said.

DAVID EVANIER *is the author of* Red Love *and* The One-Star Jew. *His work has appeared in* The Best American Short Stories 1980, Paris Review, Witness, New York Magazine, *and elsewhere. He has taught at The Writers Community and at Douglas College in Vancouver, and he currently teaches in the writing program at UCLA extension. He recently received a screenwriting fellowship from Universal/Amblin Entertainment and is currently completing a screenplay and a novel.*

CAROLYN FORCHÉ

Elegy

The page opens to snow on a field: boot-holed month, black hour
the bottle in your coat half vodka half winter light.
To what and to whom does one say *yes?*
If God were the uncertain, would you cling to him?

Beneath a tattoo of stars the gate opens, so silent so like a tomb.
This is the city you most loved, an empty stairwell
where the next rain lifts invisibly from the Seine.

With solitude, your coat open, you walk
steadily as if the railings were there and your hands weren't
     passing through them.

"When things were ready, they poured on fuel and touched
     off the fire.
They waited for a high wind. It was very fine, that powdered bone.
It was put into sacks, and when there were enough we went to a
     bridge on the Narew River."

And even less explicit phrases survived:
"To make charcoal.
For laundry irons."
And so we revolt against silence with a bit of speaking.
The page is a charred field where the dead would have written
We went on. And it was like living through something again one could
     not live through again.

The soul behind you no longer inhabits your life: the unlit house
with its breathless windows and a chimney of ruined wings
where wind becomes an aria, your name, voices from a field,
And you, smoke, dissonance, a psalm, a stairwell.

The Garden Shukkei-en

By way of a vanished bridge we cross this river
as a cloud of lifted snow would ascend a mountain.

She has always been afraid to come here.

It is the river she most
remembers, the living
and the dead both crying for help.

A world that allowed neither tears nor lamentation.

The *matsu* trees brush her hair as she passes
beneath them, as do the shining strands of barbed wire.

Where this lake is, there was a lake,
where these black pine grow, there grew black pine.

Where there is no teahouse I see a wooden teahouse
and the corpses of those who slept in it.

On the opposite bank of the Ota, a weeping willow
etches its memory of their faces into the water.

Where light touches the face, the character for heart is written.

She strokes a burnt trunk wrapped in straw:
I was weak and my skin hung from my fingertips like cloth

Do you think for a moment we were human beings to them?

She comes to the stone angel holding paper cranes.
Not an angel, but a woman where she once had been,
who walks through the garden Shukkei-en
calling the carp to the surface by clapping her hands.

Do Americans think of us?

So she began as we squatted over the toilets:
If you want, I'll tell you, but nothing I say will be enough.

We tried to dress our burns with vegetable oil.

Her hair is the white froth of rice rising up kettlesides, her mind also.
In the postwar years she thought deeply about how to live.

The common greeting *dozo-yiroshku* is please take care of me.
All *hibakusha* still alive were children then.

A cemetery seen from the air is a child's city.

I don't like this particular red flower because
it reminds me of a woman's brain crushed under a roof.

Perhaps my language is too precise, and therefore difficult to understand?

We have not, all these years, felt what you call happiness.
But at times, with good fortune, we experience something close.
As our life resembles life, and this garden the garden.
And in the silence surrounding what happened to us

it is the bell to awaken God that we've heard ringing.

CAROLYN FORCHÉ *is the author of three collections of poetry,* The Angel
of History, Gathering the Tribes, *and* The Country Between Us. *She
also edited the anthology* Against Forgetting: Twentieth-Century Poetry
of Witness. *She has taught at The Writers Community and elsewhere and
currently lives in Maryland with her husband and son.*

Dutch Elm

I left Wisconsin as the disease moved in, toppling all the heavy-crowned elms that for so long had made green tunnels of all our streets. But I didn't leave because the trees were dying, and I didn't go west because the disease hadn't yet crept that far. I'd simply reached the moving age, our house grown too small for my father and me both, and I went to Great Falls because it was as far away as I could reach. I had no plans of ever turning around. By the time I landed my first decent job I also had a wife and, though our first home was again shaded by rows of the giant trees, the slow death march of the elms couldn't have been further from my mind.

Jeremy was born that January, and all winter long we broke records for cold. On business trips I would hear what the temperatures were in Great Falls and have nightmares of boiler failures—returning home to find their two bodies curled by ice. That March the cold gave one last gasp and we read in the papers how the early calves froze to the ground in their placental sacks.

After the ice finally gave up, a pair of Great Falls park employees came down our street, stapling orange tags onto the first elms that would come down. I remembered back home in Madison that they had painted black, tarry bands around the trunks of our elms in hopes of slowing the encroaching disease. Feeling vaguely guilty, as if somehow I were the disease's carrier, I walked out front, asking the men about the tar, if they'd ever heard of it, if it wasn't something worth trying here. They only shook their heads. "There's no stopping it," one of them told me. "Only hope is that some of them just somehow survive."

The next year they came back, felling the elms, grinding their stumps, replacing them with spindly little maples and locusts.

We never had another winter that hard, and Monica was pregnant again by the next spring. Within six years Jeremy had two brothers and two sisters. After the other kids came along, we sometimes called Jeremy the Ice Man, remembering those early years. He was always vaguely proud of the name, thinking the cold had been something he was tough enough to get through, whereas maybe his brothers and sisters wouldn't have been.

Though I still traveled a lot, business was good and we moved to a bigger house in town. At night Monica and I stayed awake late, and I'd talk about trying something new, something without the travel. Monica wondered about finishing her schooling because the kids wouldn't always be there, and maybe after they were gone she would be too old. We were still young enough to laugh at the idea of being too old for anything.

It was all just daydreaming out loud. We had our house and our children, and our work went into them. This wasn't something we regretted or were bitter about. Not in the least. All our quiet talk in bed, after the kids were asleep, was our way of reaffirming this. We'd always fall asleep a little amazed at how lucky we were.

Driving home one spring, taking a new route that dropped down the river bluffs to the Missouri, out of sight of the mountains and the endless stretches of wheat, I was surprised to find the narrow band of riverbank covered by a lone cornfield. That fast I was back home in Wisconsin, surrounded by brilliant green corn, the light hazier and heavier than it was out here in all the open, turning nearly gold some evenings.

After talking it over with Monica we bought an old farmhouse on that riverbank and began what we hoped would be a tradition of shutting down the Great Falls house after school and moving out to the country for the summers. Only then did we learn that the corn was just a lark; something the farmer wanted to try. "Too cold for it up here really. Too short a season."

But that summer was hot and wet, perfect for the corn, and the kids went wild; building dams in the tiny creek cutting to the big river; playing hide and seek in the cottonwoods. They caught frogs and turtles and grasshoppers, and ran laughing down the rows of corn when it was still only waist high. But once the corn outgrew them they avoided its smothering walls.

Our last day there that first summer, Monica and I made a game out of packing the station wagon, trying to make it fun because no one wanted to go home. When the kids got distracted or mopey I chased them, scaring them with sudden charges. They scattered and I'd scoop up one or the other, tickling them until they howled. Then I'd go back into the house for the next box. Once I let the kids knock me down, and they all dove in to tickle the monster man. We were red with laughing, and had bits of dead grass and leaves stuck to our hair and clothes.

Toward evening the car was loaded, and Tim, our youngest, was already asleep on the pile of bedding in back. As I started rounding up the rest of the tribe Jeremy gave one last run, wanting to be chased, and I started after him.

He had quite a start on me, and I was surprised to see him head for the corn, which was ready for harvest and much taller than my head. But in he went, and so did I, having to slow and move sideways between the tight, towering stalks. I laughed demonically, rattling the stalks and shouting, "I'm going to get you, Jeremy!" I heard him giggle and run, and I stepped through a row but the leaves cut my view short. I moved on, laughing and threatening, crossing rows now and then, unable to see a thing.

Pretty soon I couldn't hear his giggles anymore. I stood still, my ears straining against the quiet rustle of the plants, but Jeremy had lost me. Finally I shouted that he had won, that it was time to go. "Come on, Jeremy," I called, and headed back to where I thought the house was.

I didn't like the constant brushing of the corn against me; the slick whish of it in my ears. It stole my bearings. By the time I reached the edge where Monica and the rest of the kids were waiting, I half expected to see Jeremy there taunting me, but the first thing Monica said was "Where's Jeremy?"

"He's hiding in there. He'll be out in a second," I said, but Monica's voice had a trace of the urgency I'd begun to feel thrashing through the last of the corn. She immediately started herding the rest of the kids to the car. I turned to the blank green wall of corn, and shouted for Jeremy.

Back from the car, Monica said, "We'd better start looking."

"I can see why they didn't like playing in there," I said.

"It's just corn," Monica said. "There's no place for him to go."

The car's horn blared and I turned quickly but Monica touched my arm and said, "I told them to. Every minute. It'll give them something to do and it'll let Jeremy know which way to go."

"He's just hiding is all," I said, but I looked back up at the golden tassels fringing the upper points of the wall of corn. "Jeremy," I shouted. "Enough is enough!"

"He's probably lost," Monica said. "Don't get mad."

"Well, I'll go back in," I said, hesitating. "You stay here in case he comes out."

"I'll go in too, over here."

I shrugged and ducked back into the green rows, knowing as soon as the flat waxy leaves touched my face that we would have done better just waiting. This wasn't the wilderness after all, and he had to turn up soon.

I counted the rows I crossed so I could retrace my steps, and I shouted his name now and then. The car horn honked every minute. I smiled, thinking what good kids they were and how smart an idea that had been of Monica's. Occasionally the horn gave quick, oddly-timed bursts, and I pictured the bickering over who got to punch it next.

As I pushed more and more leaves away from my face it occurred to me that I had no idea how far this cornfield went on, how soon it dropped into the river. It had only been a field before, covered with corn instead of wheat, but otherwise just like every other field between here and town.

Crossing through yet another row I bumped into Monica and she gave a yelp of surprise that nearly brought tears to her eyes. I was startled too, my breath quicker than it had been an instant before. "We'll never find him in here," Monica said.

"Let's head back. That's probably him blowing the horn now.

They're probably calling him the Corn Man already." I tried to sound reassuring, but I was hugging Monica in the middle of a jungle blackening with dusk, and our oldest child was missing.

We turned around, holding hands as we fought the corn. The sun set before we reached the house's clearing, but it was much lighter out of the smothering cover of the plants. For a moment things seemed more hopeful out in the open, but Monica's face was pale, her lips drawn tight and bloodless against her teeth. Her eyes flicked around the sides of the clearing, and she started for the car.

We stopped for a conference when we could see that Jeremy wasn't back at the car. Monica said she'd drive the dirt road that circled the corn. I'd run up the tractor track just this side of the little creek the kids had played in all summer. If Monica didn't see him on her first pass, she'd run to the farmer for help.

I gave Monica a hug before we split up and said, "Come on, Monica, it's only a cornfield."

She smiled back thinly, giving a shake of her head and a nervous giggle. "I know," she said. "We're being ridiculous."

But she turned for the car, and I ran to where the ruts of the tractor track cleaved the corn like a scar. We never said that he was anything but hiding in the corn, but we'd set up a search and started on it, even leaving the farmer to fall back on—to put our hope into if our initial sweep was a failure.

As I ran down the slash through the serried black-green ranks of the corn I began to mumble, "It's just a cornfield," over and over. There were horrible pictures lurking at the edge of my mind which the chant seemed to hold at bay. It was only a cornfield. It wasn't a city, where anything bad could happen at any time. There was the river, though, and we were in the country and I wondered if there were snakes out here, or wild dogs or bears. But I had never seen or even thought of anything like that before, and I could still hear the occasional bleat of Monica's horn, not too far away on the other side of the field. It was only a cornfield, and nothing bad could really happen in something like that.

Then, before the search had even really started, I turned the slightest of bends in the path, one I didn't think could have hidden anything, and there was Jeremy, running in the wrong direction—away from me—and when I called his name he ran even faster, as if it were me he was afraid of. He looked over his shoulder when I called again, then turned and stopped. I ran in and scooped him off the ground. He was crying harder than I'd ever seen him cry, the tears tracking down the sweaty dirt on his face. I rocked him back and forth, calling him the Ice Man, because I knew he felt brave with that name and I told him how scared I was so his fear would not embarrass him after it was gone.

He settled down a little before Monica drove into sight, bouncing wildly over the track that was never meant for any car. The lights caught us and I waved at her, to let her know everything was all right, and I brushed at Jeremy's tears so the other kids wouldn't tease him.

Monica skidded to a stop, erupting from behind the wheel and pulling Jeremy away from me, crying already herself. She kissed Jeremy over and over, until he was crying again too. Even some of the kids in the car were crying seeing their mom so shaken, and I was trembling myself, all the bizarre flashes I had while running down this road without my son pouring back in on me. I wondered if the night would be cold enough to kill him. I wondered if there might be old wells or sinkholes or something like that, that he could fall into and disappear. I even pictured him making it to some road I didn't know about, being picked up by somebody who would decide to keep him. That fast, I had imagined long nights holding Monica, going over every detail of watching Jeremy disappear forever into a row of corn that had no business growing in that country and would never be planted there again.

Putting my arms around both of them on the grassy road, I gently lifted them to their feet. I hugged Monica hard and took Jeremy from her arms, settling him onto my lap as I slipped behind the wheel, though he was far too big for that anymore. I held his hands on the steering wheel under my own hands, and said, "Why don't you drive us all on home, Ice Man?" Pretty soon the crying in the car fell behind us and Monica smiled at me and the kids started getting loud, fighting over their turns to drive, and, though that was the most wonderful sound, I started to shake again.

I suddenly saw all my children in those haunted milk carton black-and-whites, scattered vainly through the country. When Monica put her hand on my shoulder I looked down to see if I might crumble into a broken pile, as I would have in the cartoons the kids watched every Saturday.

We were on the highway then, flying past the short, safe wheat, the mountains bordering the sky in the west, and I felt Jeremy's hands hot under mine. There was a scrape on his narrow, naked wrist, and I thought of him tripping in the desperate, ebbing light of the corn jungle, scraping himself on the brittle shards of last year's harvest. His sharp hipbones dug into me and I felt him try to turn the wheel, anticipating the next turn. I squeezed his hands a little tighter and gentled out the curve for him.

As I calmed I stopped seeing the frightening pictures of missing children. Oddly enough, I thought of those men back home, when I was just a kid, painting the grim black rings around the still solid-looking trunks of our elms; trees that were really already as good as dead. Those rings hadn't meant a thing.

And, though I could see that clearly, I already knew that next year there would be rules about playing in the fields. Steering Jeremy's small, dirty hands through the next looping curve, I pictured Monica and myself as old people, holding each other in bed. In our big, quiet house we'll whisper to each other, asking if we remember the evening the Ice Man was lost in the corn.

Of course we'll both know we remember it. It will have become one of the family stories that gets told when the kids come home. They'll all laugh so hard when I admit I was scared enough to picture bears eating my son in the cornfield. They'll laugh about the honking of the horn too, which most of them wouldn't have been old enough to really remember.

But holding Monica in the darkness, years and years from now, with our like thoughts of the towering corn and our separate thoughts of our children spread out, facing all those dangers without us, I can feel her breath quiet on my neck, and I still imagine I can paint broad black bands around all of them.

PETE FROMM ON COMMUNITY

In many of the isolated Montana communities I visited during The Writers Community program, I was the first writer people had ever seen. Far from living in an ivory tower, they discovered I was almost too much like them. If a clown like me could succeed, anybody could. This gave the writers in the crowd confidence, despite the seven hundred rejection slips I displayed. The rest of the audience found that a writer can be anyone, not someone dressed in black, sipping espresso, thinking deep, dangerous thoughts. Most of the communities had never held a reading and only a few members of the audience had ever attended one. They found being read to fun, as they had as children, but more than that, they enjoyed discussing the stories afterward. One person said she'd hated literature classes because of the conjecturing over what the author meant, and how nice it was to finally get the answers straight from the horse's mouth. Also, discovering that there are writers writing about their area and their concerns made the entire process more believable to them, less something cloistered in unimaginable New York. And people wanted to know. In Glasgow, Montana, in January, in a blizzard, a red-cheeked woman arrived a minute late, apologizing and explaining that with the roads the trip over from Dickenson, North Dakota, (150 miles) had taken longer than planned. It was an honor to read to her.

"Dutch Elm" is part of PETE FROMM*'s newest story collection,* Dry Rain *(Lyons and Burford, 1997). His other books include the collections* The Tall Uncut *and* King of the Mountain, *the novel* Monkey Tag, *and the autobiographical* Indian Creek Chronicles, *which won the Pacific Northwest Booksellers Book 1994 Award. He lives in Great Falls, Montana, and taught at The Writers Community of the Billings, Montana, Writer's Voice in 1995.*

ALICE FULTON

Sketch

(for Hank De Leo)

Before the blank—full of fresh
    grain scent and flecked
        like oatmeal woven flat—
canvas, before the blank canvas
    is stretched or strained
        tight as an egg, before then—
                sketch. It doesn't catch
    commencement: it won't hook
    the scene like a rug,
or strategize too far ahead.
    It isn't chess. It doesn't expect
    the homestretch or the check.
            Each line braves rejection
of the every, edits restless
    all into a space that's still
the space of least commitment, distilling
            latitudes in draft.
    It would domesticate the feral
        dusk and stockpile dawn.
    It would be commensurate, but settles
        for less, settles
prairies in its channels. Great plains
            roar and waterfall, yawn and frost
    between the lines.
        From hunger, from blank
    and black, it models erotic
            stopped tornadoes, the high relief

of trees. In advance or retreat, in terraced
      dynamics—its bets are hedged—with no dead-
bolt perspective. Its point of view? One
         with the twister in vista glide,
    and the cricket in the ditch,
       with riverrain and turbine's trace.
                Inside the flux of
flesh and cunt and cloudy come,
      within the latent
marrow of the egg, the amber
      traveling waves—is where
            its vantage lies.
    Entering the tornado's core,
  entering the cricket waltzed by storm—
to confiscate the shifting give
    and represent the with-
      out which.

Slate

Neither pigeon, taupe, nor coal
black. Not a braille
pen embossing points on bond, the entrants
in a race, record of events, or gray
scales meshed in roofs.
Not "to foreordain." But
all of the above, the future
scrubbed with fleshburn brush,
threshold unscented by event as
yet, the premise, the blackboard's
dense blank screen, un-
reckoned rock complexion, the tablet un-
chalked with take and scene, opposite of

has-been, antonym to fixed, the
breadth of before, before
-lessness links with hope or mind or
flesh, when all is
-ful -able, and -or, as
color, as galore, as before

words. The above,
yes, and beyond
measure—unstinting
sky, green fire of cornfields, the how
many husks clasping how
many cells, the brain to say
rich, new, if, and
swim in possibility, as it is and
ever more shall be, to fold, to
origami thought,
look, no shears or hands, the

blizzard, unabridged, within the black dilated iris
core and hold
it—little pupil can—in mind, in utero,
sculpt the is, the am.

ALICE FULTON ON COMMUNITY

I believe it was in the fall of 1977 that I applied and was accepted for
a workshop taught by Thomas Lux at The Writers Community. At
the time, I was an undergraduate at Empire State College in Albany,
New York. The Writers Community, however, accepted students
solely on the basis of their writing. Factors such as age, academic
achievement, or letters of recommendation were not a consideration.
This policy, in its fair simplicity, encouraged a wonderful diversity
within the group.

Tom Lux's workshop was perhaps the most valuable learning experience I had as a young writer. Every week, I took the bus to New York City in order to attend the class, which met in a ground-floor apartment in the east eighties. My work developed as it never would have without Tom's encouragement and criticism. I also was introduced to other aspiring poets who lived in New York and to the many published poets whom Tom invited to class.

During my second term at The Writers Community, I moved to New York. A few months later, I accepted a position as an advertising copywriter. For almost a year, I devoted most of my time and energy to a business that viewed poetry with suspicion. The friends I'd made in Tom's workshop helped me remember that poetry was not universally despised. Although I had arrived in New York without literary connections, The Writers Community introduced me to a world in which books, and poetry in particular, were prized. Arriving from the nonliterary community, I was freely welcomed into The Writers Community, a generosity that affected the trajectory of my life, and for which I will always be grateful.

ALICE FULTON's *books of poetry are* Sensual Math, Powers of Congress, Palladium, *and* Dance Script with Electric Ballerina. *A recipient of fellowships from the MacArthur Foundation, the Guggenheim Foundation, and the Ingram-Merrill Foundation, she teaches at the University of Michigan, Ann Arbor.*

On Exploration

A hawk drops to the treetop
Like a falling cross.
The haybarn is ticking.
The Universe has everything.
That's what I like about it.
A single chubby cloud
Bee-lines downwind
Trying to catch up with the others.

Yellow leaves plane across the water,
Drifting the inlet.
The pond is a droozy eye.
Details tend to equal each other,
Making decisions harder.
Is polio an endangered species?
The Universe is mostly empty,
That's important;
A fractal palindrome of concentric

Emptinesses.
Is there life out there?
Are there lawns?
Columbus is famous for discovering a place
Where there were already people
Killing each other.
Nothing missing. Nothing new.

Let's pick wildflowers.
Let's take a meteor shower.
Let's live forever and let's die, too.

94

Two Horses and a Dog

Without external reference,
The world presents itself
In perfect clarity.

Wherewithal, arrested moments,
The throes of demystification,
Morality as nothing more
Than humility and honesty, a salty measure.

Then it was a cold snap,
Weather turned lethal so it was easier
To feel affinity
With lodgepole stands, rifted aspens,
And grim, tenacious sage.

History accelerates till it misses the turns.
Wars are shorter now
Just to fit into it.

One day you know you are no longer young
Because you've stopped loving your own desperation.
You change *life* to *loneliness* in your mind
And, you know, you need to change it back.

Statistics show that
One in every five
Women
Is essential to my survival.

My daughter asks how wide is lightning.
That depends, but I don't know on what.
Probably the dimension of inner hugeness,

As in a speck of dirt.
It was an honor to suffer humiliation and refusal.
Shame was an honor.
It was an honor to freeze your ass horseback
In the year's first blizzard,
Looking for strays that never materialized.

It was an honor to break apart against this,
An honor to fail at well-being
As the high peaks accepted the first snow—
A sigh of relief.

Time stands still
And we and things go whizzing past it,
Queasy and lonely,
Wearing dogtags with scripture on them.

JAMES GALVIN's *volumes of poetry include* Lethal Frequencies, Imaginary Timber, God's Mistress *(which won the National Poetry Series), and* Elements. *He is also the author of the prose classic,* The Meadow. *He has received fellowships from the National Endowment for the Arts, the Ingram-Merrill Foundation, and the Guggenheim Foundation. He has taught at the University of Montana, the Iowa Writers' Workshop, and The Writers Community and lives in Tie Siding, Wyoming.*

LOUISE GLÜCK

The Silver Lily

The nights have grown cool again, like the nights
of early spring, and quiet again. Will
speech disturb you? We're
alone now; we have no reason for silence.

Can you see, over the garden—the full moon rises.
I won't see the next full moon.

In spring, when the moon rose, it meant
time was endless. Snowdrops
opened and closed, the clustered
seeds of the maples fell in pale drifts.
White over white, the moon rose over the birch tree.
And in the crook, where the tree divides,
leaves of the first daffodils, in moonlight
soft greenish-silver.

We have come too far together toward the end now
to fear the end. These nights, I am no longer even certain
I know what the end means. And you, who've been
    with a man—

after the first cries,
doesn't joy, like fear, make no sound?

Daisies

Go ahead: say what you're thinking. The garden
is not the real world. Machines
are the real world. Say frankly what any fool
could read in your face: it makes sense
to avoid us, to resist
nostalgia. It is
not modern enough, the sound the wind makes
stirring a meadow of daisies: the mind
cannot shine following it. And the mind
wants to shine, plainly, as
machines shine, and not
grow deep, as, for example, roots. It is very touching,
all the same, to see you cautiously
approaching the meadow's border in early morning,
when no one could possibly
be watching you. The longer you stand at the edge,
the more nervous you seem. No one wants to hear
impressions of the natural world: you will be
laughed at again; scorn will be piled on you.
As for what you're actually
hearing this morning: think twice
before you tell anyone what was said in this field
and by whom.

LOUISE GLÜCK's *most recent collection of poems is* Meadowlands. *Her 1993 Pulitzer Prize for* The Wild Iris *was preceded by numerous awards, including the National Book Critics Circle Award and the Poetry Society of America's Melville Kane and William Carlos Williams Awards. Her collection of essays,* Proofs and Theories, *won the PEN/Martha Albrand Award. She has taught at The Writers Community and is currently professor of English at Williams College.*

JORIE GRAHAM

Notes on the Reality of the Self

In my bushes facing the bandpractice field,
in the last light, surrounded by drumbeats, drumrolls,
there is a wind that tips the reddish leaves
exactly all one way, seizing them up from underneath, making them
barbarous in unison. Meanwhile the light insists they glow
where the wind churns, or, no, there is a wide gold corridor
of thick insistent light, layered with golds, as if runged,
as if laid low from the edge of the sky,
in and out of which the coupling and uncoupling
limbs—the racks of limbs—the luminosities of branchings—
offspring and more offspring—roil—(except when a sudden
                    stillness reveals
an appal of pure form, pure light—
every rim clear, every leaf serrated, tongued—stripped
of the gauzy quickness which seemed its flesh)—but then
                    the instabilities
regroup, and the upper limbs of the tall oaks
begin to whine again with wide slappings
which seep ever-downward to my bushes—into them, through them—
to where the very grass makes congress with the busyness—
mutating, ridging, threshing this light from that, to no
avail—and in it all
the drumroll, rising as the ranks join in,
the wild branches letting the even drumbeats through,
ripples let through as the red branches spiral, tease,
as the crescendos of the single master-drummer
rise, and birds scatter over the field, and the wind makes each
                    thing
kneel and rise, kneel and rise, never-ending stringy

almost maternal lurching of wind
pushing into and out of the russets, magentas, incarnadines . . .
Tell me, where are the drumbeats which fully load and expand
each second,
bloating it up, cell-like, making it real, where are they
to go, what will *they* fill up
pouring forth, pouring round the subaqueous magenta bushes
which dagger the wind back down on itself,
tenderly, prudently, almost loaded down
with regret? For there is not a sound the bushes will take
from the multitude beyond them, in the field, uniformed—
(all left now on one heel) (right) (all fifty trumpets up
to the sun)—not a molecule of sound
from the tactics of this glistening beast,
forelimbs of silver (trombones, french horns)
(anointed by the day itself) expanding, retracting,
bits of red from the surrounding foliage deep
in all the fulgid
instruments—orient—ablaze where the sound is released—
trumpeting, unfolding—
screeching, rolling, patterning, measuring—
scintillant beast the bushes do not know exists
as the wind beats them, beats in them, beats round them,
them in a wind that does not really even now
exist,
in which these knobby reddish limbs that do not sway
by so much as an inch
its arctic course
themselves now sway—

JORIE GRAHAM *is the author of five volumes of poetry,* Hybrids of Plants and of Ghosts, Erosion, The End of Beauty, Region of Unlikeness, *and* Materialism. *Her latest book,* The Dream of the Unified Field: Selected Poems 1974–1994, *won the 1996 Pulitzer Prize for poetry. The recipient of a MacArthur Fellowship, she has taught at The Writers Community and is a permanent faculty member at the University of Iowa Writers' Workshop.*

ALLAN GURGANUS

It Had Wings

For Bruce Saylor and Constance Beavon

Find a little yellow side street house. Put an older woman in it. Dress her in that tatty favorite robe, pull her slippers up before the sink, have her doing dishes, gazing nowhere—at her own backyard. Gazing everywhere. Something falls outside, loud. One damp thwunk into new grass. A meteor? She herself (retired from selling formal clothes at Wanamaker's, she herself—widow and the mother of three scattered sons, she herself alone at home a lot these days) goes onto tiptoe, leans across a sinkful of suds, sees—out near her picnic table, something nude, white, overly long. It keeps shivering. Both wings seem damaged.

"No way," she says. It appears human. Yes, it is a male one. It's face up and, you can tell, it is extremely male (uncircumcised). This old woman, pushing eighty, a history of aches, uses, fun—now presses one damp hand across her eyes. Blaming strain, the luster of new cataracts, she looks again. Still, it rests there on a bright air mattress of its own wings. Outer feathers are tough quills, broad at bottom as rowboat oars. The whole left wing bends far under. It looks hurt.

The widow, sighing, takes up her blue willow mug of heated milk. Shaking her head, muttering, she carries it out back. She moves so slow because: arthritis. It criticizes every step. It asks about the mug she holds, Do you really need this?

She stoops, creaky, beside what can only be a young angel, unconscious. Quick, she checks overhead, ready for what?—some TV news crew in a helicopter? She sees only a sky of the usual size, a Tuesday sky stretched between weekends. She allows herself to touch this thing's white forehead. She gets a mild electric shock. Then, odd, her tickled finger joints stop aching. They've hurt so long. A practical person, she quickly cures her other hand. The angel grunts but sounds pleased. His temperature's a hundred and fifty, easy—but for him, this seems somehow normal. "Poor thing," she says, and—careful—pulls his heavy curly head into her lap. The head hums like a phone knocked off its cradle. She scans for neighbors, hoping they'll come out, wishing they wouldn't, both.

"Look, will warm milk help?" She pours some down him. Her wrist brushes angel skin. Which pulls the way an ice tray begs whatever touches it. A thirty-year pain leaves her, enters him. Even her liver spots are lightening. He grunts with pleasure, soaking up all of it. Bold, she presses her worst hip deep into crackling feathers. The hip has been half numb since a silly fall last February. All stiffness leaves her. He goes, "Unhh." Her griefs seem to fatten him like vitamins. Bolder, she whispers private woes: the Medicare cuts, the sons too casual by half, the daughters-in-law not bad but not so great. These woes seem ended. "Nobody'll believe. Still, tell me some of it." She tilts nearer. Both his eyes stay shut but his voice, like clicks from a million crickets pooled, goes, "We're just another army. We all look alike—we didn't, before. It's not what you expect. We miss this other. Don't count on the next. Notice things here. We are just another army."

"Oh," she says.

Nodding, she feels limber now, sure as any girl of twenty. Admiring her unspeckled hands, she helps him rise. Wings serve as handles. Kneeling on damp ground, she watches him go staggering toward her barbecue pit. Awkward for an athlete, really awkward for an angel, the poor thing climbs up there, wobbly. Standing, he is handsome, but as a vase is handsome. When he turns this way, she sees his eyes. They're silver, each reflects her: a speck, pink, on green green grass.

She now fears he plans to take her up, as thanks. She presses both palms flat to dirt, says, "The house is finally paid off.—Not just yet," and smiles.

Suddenly he's infinitely infinitely more so. Silvery. Raw. Gleaming like a sunny monument, a clock. Each wing puffs, independent. Feathers sort and shuffle like three hundred packs of playing cards. Out flings either arm; knees dip low. Then up and off he shoves, one solemn grunt. Machete swipes cross her backyard, breezes cool her upturned face. Six feet overhead, he falters, whips in makeshift circles, manages to hold aloft, then go shrub-high, gutter-high. He avoids a messy tangle of phone lines now rocking from the wind of him. "Go, go," the widow, grinning, points the way. "Do. Yeah, good." He signals back at her, open-mouthed and left down here. First a glinting man-shaped kite, next an oblong of aluminum in sun. Now a new moon shrunk to decent star, one fleck, fleck's memory: usual Tuesday sky.

She kneels, panting, happier and frisky. She is hungry but must first rush over and tell Lydia next door. Then she pictures Lydia's worry lines bunching. Lydia will maybe phone the missing sons: "Come right home. Your mom's inventing . . . company."

Maybe other angels have dropped into other Elm Street backyards? Behind fences, did neighbors help earlier hurt ones? Folks keep so much of the best stuff quiet, don't they.

Palms on knees, she stands, wirier. This retired saleswoman was the formal-gowns adviser to ten mayors' wives. She spent sixty years of nine-to-five on her feet. Scuffling indoors, now staring down at terry slippers, she decides, "Got to wash these next week." Can a person who's just sighted her first angel already be mulling about laundry? Yes. The world is like that.

From her sink, she sees her own blue willow mug out there in the grass. It rests in muddy ruts where the falling body struck so hard. A neighbor's collie keeps barking. (It saw!) Okay. This happened. "So," she says.

And plunges hands into dishwater, still warm. Heat usually helps her achy joints feel agile. But fingers don't even hurt now. Her bad hip doesn't pinch one bit. And yet, sad, they all will. By suppertime, they will again remind her what usual suffering means. To her nimble underwater hands, the widow, staring straight ahead, announces. "I helped. He flew off stronger. I really egged him on. Like *any*body would've, really. Still, it was me. I'm not just somebody in a house.

I'm not just somebody alone in a house. I'm not just somebody else alone in a house."

Feeling more herself, she finishes the breakfast dishes. In time for lunch. This old woman should be famous for all she has been through—today's angel, her years in sales, the sons and friends—she should be famous for her life. She knows things, she has seen so much. She's not famous.

Still, the lady keeps gazing past her kitchen café curtains, she keeps studying her own small tidy yard. An anchor fence, the picnic table, a barbecue pit, new Bermuda grass. Hands braced on her sink's cool edge, she tips nearer a bright window.

She seems to be expecting something, expecting something decent. Her kitchen clock is ticking. That dog still barks to calm itself. And she keeps staring out: nowhere, everywhere. Spots on her hands are darkening again. And yet, she whispers, "I'm right here, ready. Ready for more."

Can you guess why this old woman's chin is lifted? Why does she breathe as if to show exactly how it's done? Why should both her shoulders, usually quite bent, brace so square just now?

She is guarding the world.
Only, nobody knows.

ALLAN GURGANUS ON COMMUNITY

Tell Us It: Fieldnotes on Teaching Grown-ups Fiction Writing

If the creation of fiction requires cleanly solitude, its truest uses remain quite messily communal. Even now, telling—across every gripe of mortality, of race, class, sex, and simple orneriness—so ties us to each another!

My experience teaching writing to adults taught me how to write for adults. Humbling, a young man's weekly facing people far older, so many cataclysmic stories waiting in them, all on hold. Everything I had conscientiously invented in my own early fiction—deaths of children, hurricanes, genocide—already lived long lives within these folks. How dare I suggest a better way to shape each impatient tale?

One funny, acerbic lady of seventy-five arrived for class wearing a trench coat and carrying home-baked cookies for us all. She soon wrote how, as an actual pigtailed girl of eight in Mannheim, she'd skipped home from piano lessons. She found the door to her folks' apartment kicked in. Furniture was overturned, the wall safe hung opened, a potted palm now rested into the open grand piano. Her familiars were all missing, with the clothes on their backs, disappeared into the void of Nazi custody.

A janitor heard her, hidden in a closet, crying; he, an old man unknown to her by name, he, a Catholic, a Pole, smuggled her downstairs and—it being summer—hid her in the building's furnace. When winter came, he bought a horse cart, filled it with rutabagas. Then he asked the little girl to please strip naked. Trusting, helpless not to trust at least one person, she undressed. He then painted her the rutabagas' very white and purple; her body and her face were soon colorful and sticky, all bull's-eyes.

The child was packed, nude, beneath tubers, this in January. The janitor led a borrowed nag, the cart, out far out, toward a minor (easy?) checkpoint. When one Nazi border guard halted the vehicle and—with his bayonet—shoved vegetables aside, he figured he was looking down on just more rutabagas. He was actually studying the painted left buttock of a very brave girl.

I tell this story now as if the tale were mine. (I swear I could stretch it into a novel truly mine, because it's my own emotionally). It became so partway mine in the months I helped my so-called student to recast it, refine it. To reheat it to the white-hot heat it needed, to feel fully true again.

Living through a thing does little to save it. Living through it confuses you with allegiance to mere fact. The girl, after waiting sixty-seven years, was finally old enough, was carted far enough over the frontier for Fable to elevate a cart, a girl, a stranger's unexplainable goodness in a world unimaginably cruel.

She had lived it; and long afterwards, I—a goy, a boy, from her new country—helped her put it down; a bit more right with every try. "How did it smell, the cart, the road beneath the cart?" I asked, and she remembered. "Does that matter?" Then she wrote that in.

"Did you talk to him, from under rutabagas?" I asked.

"No, because I was trying so to be them, rutabagas." Then, please, tell us that.

Finally, she could believe it, the tale she'd made, the tale that'd made her. She could at last accept that it had happened. To some child—her, not her—but not so much unlike her that it was now impossible to feel. She could finally see it half clearly—through the film of decades and the hindsight we call History—she could observe it as if coming into the odd facts of this unlucky other life for the first time. Odd, it *was* the first time. Art allows us that.

She had put the "It" between the "Tell" and "Us."

The "you," as always, stays implied.

Till this adult class, I had taught only at colleges, taught privileged and very young folks. I soon learned that, however gifted undergraduates are, they're still just eighteen or twenty years old. Prodigies exist in mathematics, in musical composition; but there are no prodigies at living a hard sad worthwhile life. You just have to do it. Before you know you can. At that, alas, no one gets to offer you clever teacherly shortcuts.

I found that "my" grown-ups, with their lives and jobs, with little kids and big disappointments, were better equipped to know their own oh-so-tested strengths. They came oversupplied for the joy and task of living/telling memorable stories.

To sit at a table with a bike messenger, the girl Holocaust survivor who now designed hats, an editorial assistant, a writer-illustrator of children's books, an agent, a bond broker, a waitress-actress, an emergency room doctor. The resulting incongruous if generous conversation was one that any informed novelist would pay ready cash to overhear.

I just listed the occupations of class members I taught some years back at New York's Writers Community. Each of these people, from their legitimate fears and even wilder imaginations, had persisted in writing fiction. Communally, they responded to each other's solitary efforts. We made a circle.

Though their nominal teacher, I often felt as extruded, as beside the point as some nameless notary required to vouchsafe the wedding contract of two loving, sexy strangers. I was simply there, enjoying, refereeing, a cheerleading witness.

When one member of our class was murdered by her husband (another story) on the very day she planned to offer us her first story, the plot sickened. We knew that, in a world like this, we didn't need to make up improbable stories; we only needed make them seem half-credible.

She, the aforementioned editorial assistant, had been lively, beautiful, and gentle. The class's bond broker was a classic, genial woman-hating man, who simply did not know he was. We would later recall how this woman, now murdered by a man (who also sold bonds), had been so skilled and kind—in goading, teasing her young classmate toward seeing his own unconscious animosity toward the very woman he was trying trying trying to write toward life.

Mourning her, our choir of soloists drew in closer. As a group, we sat raggedly together at her funeral. From the pulpit, someone read excerpts from the very story our dead friend intended trying out on us the night she died. That story proved to be a love song to the beauties and dangers of loving difficult, violent, seductive men in Manhattan. Her prose proved shapely, visual, comic, deeply felt— an IOU of promise.

Nobody who ever tried writing fiction can long doubt both the impossibility and the necessity of our great enterprise. I mean: storytelling. How hard to trap (in black and white) the funny, baffling, horrifying, complicated, nose-thumbing truth. To manage that, nothing less than the slippery and imaginative techniques of a born liar will suffice.

And only a group of weather-beaten fellow survivors, ones still interested in remaining mostly good, can weekly remind you why you even bother. Why you persist in believing your experience is not just your burden and experience alone.

The others help make art's heartbreaking heart-mending goal seem—in your next draft, at least—nearly possible, eternally worthwhile.

Once upon a time, while listening to each other, while recalling the unaccountable kindness of a janitor, while burying a favorite, each one of us—finally told . . .

ALLAN GURGANUS *is the author of the novel* Oldest Living Confederate Widow Tells All *and* White People, *a collection of stories. His latest work, a novel, is* Plays Well with Others. *He has taught fiction writing at The Writers Community, Stanford and Duke Universities, The Iowa Writers' Workshop, and Sarah Lawrence College.*

JESSICA HAGEDORN

The King of Coconuts

Because, they would say. Simply because.

Because he tells the President what to do. Because he dances well. Because he tells the First Lady off. Because he dances well and collects art. Because he calls the General *Nicky*. Because he owns a 10,000-acre hacienda named *Las Palmas*. Because he employs a private army of mercenaries. Because he collects primitive art, renaissance art, and modern art. Because he owns silver madonnas, rotting statues of unknown saints, and jeweled altars lifted intact from the bowels of bombed-out churches. Because his house is not a home but a museum. Because he smokes cigars. Because he flies his own yellow helicopter. Because he plays golf with a five handicap. Because he plays polo and breeds horses. Because he breeds horses for fun and profit. Because he is a greedy man, a generous man. Because his wealth is self-made, not inherited. Because he owns everything we need, including a munitions factory. Because he dances well: the boogie, the fox-trot, the waltz, the cha-cha, the mambo, the hustle, the bump. Because he dances a competent tango. Because he owns *The Metro Manila Daily, Celebrity Pinoy Weekly,* Radiomanila, TruCola Soft Drinks, plus controlling interests in Mabuhay Movie Studios, Apollo Records, and the Monte Vista Golf and Country Club. Because he conceived and constructed SPORTEX, a futuristic department store in the suburb of Makati. Because he was once nominated for president and declined to run. Because he plays poker and wins. Because he is short, and smells like expensive citrus. Because he has elegant, silver hair, big ears, slanted Japanese eyes, and the aquiline nose of a Spanish mestizo. Because his skin is dark and leathery from too much sun. Because he is married to a stunning, selfish beauty with a caustic tongue. Because most people envy his wife. Because most people are jealous. Because his downfall is eagerly awaited, his downfall is assumed. Because his wife has had her tubes tied. Because he's always wanted sons. Because his only legitimate child is female. Because she is not exceptional or beautiful; because she hardly speaks. Because her name is Rosario but she is burdened by the nickname *Baby*. Because her mother dislikes her and almost admits it. Because her father flaunts his mistresses. Because her mother is discreet. Because her father has exquisite manners, and her mother is famous for being rude. Because her father threatens to acknowledge his bastard sons. Because he employs them in menial jobs. Because his bastard sons worship him, love him, plot against him.

Because he dances well, and collects art. Because he never finished school. Because men, women, and children are drawn to him, like moths to a flame. Because he is unable to maintain a full erection. Because it doesn't matter. Because he no longer drinks. Because he maintains a high-protein diet, and has trouble moving his bowels. Because he suffers from hemorrhoids, and has been operated on twice. Because he has premonitions about his death and believes in God. Because he dreams of cancer eating away his brain, his liver, his stomach, his balls. Because he dreams of morphine, how it won't be enough.

They call him king, Severo, "Chuchi," Luis. His employees and bastard sons call him *Don* Luis. His servants lower their eyes, call him *Sir*. His wife Isabel and his widowed mother Serafina call him by his first name, Severo. His daughter avoids calling him anything, even "Papa," except on public occasions. When his wife loses her temper, she calls him *hijo de puta,* whore's son, *cabron. Motherfucker* she learns to call him, after several trips to America. When she is really angry, she calls his mother a phony and a whore. She dares him to hit her; he never does, calling her a *real phony* instead. He is aware it is the worst possible thing he could say to her. They call each other every name in the book, they do not care if their daughter or the servants hear them fighting long into the night. He usually ends by calling his wife a hypocrite with the soul and manners of a common *achay,* a servant, a peasant, but with none of their warmth and appeal. He brags about fucking the servants, how they are more responsive than she could ever be. *You're dead down there,* he accuses her coldly. She tosses her head in contempt. *I'm dead to you,* she tells him.

It no longer affects her. It is nothing, an old story. Before the war. During the war. During the Japanese occupation. After liberation. Her mother is dead. Her father a weak man, a handsome man, a petty hustler. Her father coughs blood. She is a hostess at a night-club. Her father dies, in a barroom brawl. She wins a beauty contest. *Miss Postwar Manila. Miss Congeniality.* She is a starlet on contract at Mabuhay Studios. She cannot sing or dance. She cannot act. She is stiff and wooden on the screen. Because of her exceptional beauty, she is given small parts. The other woman, the best friend, the best friend's friend.

He's a wheeler-dealer, ruthless and ambitious. He does business with everyone. Japs, GI's, guerrillas in the jungle. He meets her, at a party. She is drunk. They are both in love with other people, but he is compelled by her beauty and amused by her bluntness. He meets her again, at another party. She is sober and knows exactly who he is. They marry. He later buys Mabuhay Studios, on a whim. She stops making movies, spends her time shopping for clothes. She takes a lot of airplanes, perfects her English. She is terrified by New York, intimidated by Paris, at home in Rome and Madrid. She develops a Spanish accent, learns to roll her r's. She concentrates on being thin, sophisticated, icy. Her role models include Dietrich, Vicomtesse Jacqueline de Ribes, Nefertiti, and Grace Kelly. She is an asset to her husband at any social function. She is manicured and oiled, massaged and exercised, pampered like some high-strung, inbred animal. She has reconstructed her life and past, to suit her taste. She is over forty, taut and angular, with marvelous cheekbones. She does not need a plastic surgeon.

It is a marriage made in heaven and hell. They love to fight when they are alone together, boast about their stormy union to bewil-dered friends. Small arguments over the most trivial things—this is how it usually begins. A witty exchange explodes into a shouting match, objects are thrown around the room. Breaking glass and shat-tering plates exhilarate her; no one really gets physically hurt. Their mutual contempt is a bond; they would never consider leaving each other. Their daughter is the burden they share, secretly she is the price for all their sins. They do not admit this to each other. They are exemplary Catholics, and donate large sums of money to the Church.

To a renowned American correspondent sent by a prominent American news magazine, Severo Alacran is gracious and self-effacing. "Please don't call me a visionary," he insists, "I'm really just a businessman."

Amiably, he poses for pictures. Eyes twinkling, his face friendly one moment and stern the next, he is photographed seated behind his massive desk, surrounded by mementos and awards, framed photographs of his wife and daughter, the President shaking his hand, the President and First Lady at some palace function laughing with him, a smiling group shot with the golf team he sponsors, "Manila Junior Champions." A creased snapshot of General Douglas MacArthur, Severo Alacran, and an anonymous Filipino man is displayed in a pewter frame on the wall above his desk.

He is thoughtful and relaxed in a solitary portrait which shows him standing next to one of his treasured paintings, "Farmers Harvesting Rice" by Amorsolo. "My enemies claim it's a forgery, that I can no longer tell what's authentic from what's fake," he admits casually. The correspondent frowns; he genuinely *likes* Severo Alacran. He hopes the rich man will elaborate. But the rich man breezily changes the subject, inviting the journalist to a private showing of his recent acquisitions later that afternoon.

Asked about his last name, he laughs heartily. He addresses the famous correspondent by his first name. *Steve.* A young man's name. Alacran, he explains, means "scorpion" in Spanish. "How about that, Steve? What's in a name?"

That same week, he is interviewed by Cora Camacho, the Barbara Walters of the Philippines, on her popular TV show, *Girl Talk.* He flirts and disarms her. "My dear Cora, of course I'm happily married! Aren't you?" He knows, as do most people in Manila, that Cora Camacho is single. She stifles a giggle, her overly made-up face feigning shock and dismay. "Mr. Alacran! I'm here to interview *you*—not the other way around." She smiles brightly at him.

He has decided she is hard as nails. "Of course," he agrees, smoothly. "How could I forget? Ask me anything. You know," he says, leaning closer to her, "I'm flattered to be on your show. You're our most celebrated media personality—a positive role model for all Filipinas."

Fuck you too, Cora Camacho thinks, her smile widening. "Why, thank you, Mr. Alacran!"

"Cora dear, you make me feel so *old*. You must stop calling me Mister!" He is aware that the age difference between them is slight.

Cora squirms in her TV chair, leaning forward for a camera close-up. "What shall I call you then—Sir?" She winks at her invisible TV audience, devoted millions who identify with her totally. Like them, she is a fan. Like them, she is demanding and devouring.

"You must call me by my first name. Severo."

"Se-ve-ro," Cora Camacho repeats huskily.

"There, you see? You make me feel young again," Severo Alacran lies on national television.

She hopes he will linger after the taping ends, maybe offer her a ride home in his limousine. She hopes her "Tigress" perfume isn't too overpowering. Maybe he drove himself to the studio today, in one of those fancy sports cars. A Maserati or Ferrari, something Italian and phallic. A young man's car. They could be alone, speeding on the highway, like in those American commercials where the road is endless and smooth, empty of other cars, trucks, buses, jeepneys, pedicabs, barefoot boys riding slow, plodding *carabao*. Cora Camacho loves the obvious, thinks she deserves to ride in an open sports car just once in her life, with the wind undoing her lacquered hair and one of the world's richest men driving beside her.

Cora Camacho moves closer to Severo Alacran. The camera closes in on her determined face. She is glad she always carries an extra toothbrush in her briefcase. The interview is about to end, and she only has time for one more question.

JESSICA HAGEDORN *is a poet, novelist, multimedia theater artist, and screenwriter. She is the author of* The Gangster of Love *and* Dogeaters, *as well as* Danger and Beauty, *a collection of poetry. Her recent awards include a Lila Wallace-Reader's Digest Fund Writer's Award, a National Endowment for the Arts Fellowship, and a 1993 Writers Community residency. Hagedorn was born and raised in the Philippines and moved to the United States as a teenager.*

LINDA HELLER

Brown Town

Last year a neighbor went headfirst through a windshield. She woke seeing auras around her nurses, flickering scenes from their lives that looked, she says, like early movies. This caused a career move. Now for fifty dollars she'll tell you your scenes. She also sells contraptions whose design she saw during her coma, squat door frames hung with copper pyramids, magnets, and crystals. Her flier urges spending an hour a day inside one. It states peace will come. I don't mention this as her shill; I've no investment in her company. I just want to be rid of the things that once surrounded me.

We were living on the outskirts of greater Roselle, but I called it Brown Town. That's what you saw, brown trees, brown houses, brown sky. Even our river had as its source some septic malfunction. Streets stopped abruptly, began again blocks later. These were roads without sidewalks, lined with lots gone to weed, and with handyman specials. Our place was tin and held together like a doll's house, by tin tabs bent through slots. It was a small house, but our family was small. We were a father, a mother, one child.

The walls had been papered by previous renters, people who believed what they wanted to, judging from the patterns they chose, 3-D brick in the kitchen, sand and shells above the tub, in the bedroom trellised roses. My parents never bought this fantasy, never thought their bathtub was the ocean. They always knew where they were, and each blamed the other. Such feelings scalded the other's skin and lifted the colors off the walls.

My father hadn't gone to high school, but he was studying aviation. He'd found the books on the street, a tall stack of them tied with cord, old books printed for a past war, with dry crumbling pages. At night, in the kitchen, he memorized their charts. I'd loll against his arm and imagine him a pilot, see him slip into an open cockpit. "I'll be loving you, always," he'd shout. He'd take off, fly scribbly loops before his plane fell. During the day my father worked in a factory making cleaning fluids.

He had and still has my heart. His name is printed across it the way a country's name spans a map. My love began while I was too young to know about risk. No one warned me, said, "Don't." Or, "Not that much." Not like years later, when friends tipped me off about certain men. No one said anything and so I dove into the notion of him the way you do into a pool. I can't remember his voice but I remember his smell and the hairs on his chest. In his presence, women tried to seem as attractive as he was.

Brown Town had a steep street of stores, stores that leaned against each other into the hill. Saturdays my father and I strolled to Roz's Stationery. Roz was a doughy, wheezing woman whose short hair was as sparse as the hair on my arms. I prayed she'd stay behind the counter. Her store was as stuffed as she was, and I wanted everything she had, especially the doll clothes in plastic boxes, the balls in the bin, though most were dead. My father waited in the doorway. He liked little balsa planes that had to be assembled. If he had money that's what I bought. Sometimes now I think, "Who would you rather have visit, God, a man to marry, or your father?" "My father," I answer.

My mother and her friends were always changing what they looked like. They dyed their hair, plucked out all their eyebrows, traded used makeup. Houses smelled from ammonia, and women usually had a splattered towel around their neck. The first dream I remember is one in which my mother's face continually slid off, revealing a new one. These were women who always laughed. They thought this showed they could take it. Men had muscles, they had laughs.

"He sneezed. Once. Next thing he's in a panic. 'What if it's cholera?' he asked. Tears came to his eyes. 'What if it's Saint Vitus' dance?'"

"Mine's so cranky I want to say, 'Sweetie, are you teething? Want Momma to rub rum on your gums?'"

I knew all these husbands, called most of them Uncle. Still, when

I heard this talk, I too saw babies, red faced and squalling, their whole bodies engaged in expressing their anger. I saw babies as big as houses, with fists the size of bedrooms, babies one had to tiptoe past, and not upset more.

"I didn't tell him."

"I hid the bill."

As a father, mine acted differently, quieter, more hidden. I'd stand against him, he'd move away. He seemed on a tilt, straining toward something secret.

At school we made a map on a large piece of plywood. Brown Town in silhouette looks like a birthmark, the kind that covers half a face. Our teacher passed out old newspapers and cans of watery paste. Roselle is rimmed by rocky hills. We added wet lumps. The teacher spoke while we worked. She held up an atlas.

"There are many kinds of maps." One, of our continent, seemed flooded by cooking oil and soap suds. "Population," she said. She showed us another that had arrows sweeping across it, and red and black spots. "Natural Hazards," she said. "Who would like to come up and point to those in our immediate area?"

I was a child who couldn't stand dread. Better to surrender, to have the worst over with. I raised my hand. Coated by paste, it looked ghostly. Perfect, I thought, for the task. I liked this ghost hand. For a moment it calmed me. I came closer and learned the symbols. Arrows were tropical storm tracks, red spots equaled earthquakes, black spots a high risk of tornadoes. Our area was free of these and colored a flat rust.

"I don't see any around here."

"Correct," our teacher said. "Greater Roselle is perfectly safe."

That night, in bed, I thought of the hills that surrounded us. What if wild animals hid in caves there? I pictured them gray and razor-backed, with many rows of teeth. What if, in the dark, they ran toward us? I myself had run down hills and knew how you picked up speed.

The owner of my father's factory bought a new machine. My father was chosen to run it. He stayed late to be trained and brought the manual home.

"It mixes fluids by pressure," my father said. "The place shakes like there's a sonic boom." This was during a time when sonic booms were frequent. Out of the blue, our house would expand and contract. We'd run outside, search the sky.

"I wouldn't want to work it," my mother said.

"You?" my father answered. "Who'd let you near it? No one in their right mind."

My friends and I traded love comics, *Ardent Romance, Hearts Entwined.* My favorite was about a stewardess. "When will my heart find its resting place?" she asked. She was anxious and at the plane's window. Below her, the earth looked very small and dark. Most stories were similar. A woman was loved by two men, one who was kind but too familiar, the way kitchen linoleum is. He'd be called Bob or Bill, have tan hair, wear tan suits. The other, Derek or Kyle, would be darkly handsome, romantic, wealthy, but unreliable. Forced to decide, the woman would fling herself across her ruffled bedspread. She'd cry, try to marshal her thoughts. Visions of Derek would swirl around her. He'd offer orchids, sips of champagne. She'd develop a fever, have to take sick days. Bob would quietly nurse her. During her turmoil her hairstyle would change in every panel. Her fever would break. She'd choose the good man. "My dearest . . ." "My darling . . ."

My mother learned to give manicures and gave them in the kitchen. Women chose purple polish, or amber flecked with gold or an oily-looking silver. They held their hands up under the light, admired their nails while they dried. I know their wish was to polish their whole lives, to coat them with smoothness and mean glamour. Instead they did this, and pretended they'd done more. Our teacher had a different look. She was Belgian, and I think she came here after the war. She looked scrubbed, but harshly, the way you'd scrub a vegetable. Her hair, a dry white yellow, was bluntly cut and brushed back. Her cheeks and brows also seemed aimed in that direction. Her gaze, though, was forward, her stare intense, open eyed, almost like a fish's. All this made her appear pulled in two directions, as if her eyes were riveted to a thing the rest of her wanted to leave.

At school our next project was a diorama, Greater Roselle during its first year. "Students," our teacher said. "Here's an interesting fact." We were making pipe-cleaner settlers, and few of us listened. "Children in this town have softer bones than do children in Belgium."

My neighbor, who went through the windshield, can also see the soul leave its body during death. She saw this first at the hospital, while she was in a large ward. Because of the room's size, an effort was made to make it tranquil. Blankets and walls were the gray you get when you mix milk with a drop of chocolate. For further harmony, each morning a nurse placed patients' hands outside their covers, all in the same position, as if they were dolls and would stay arranged. People were asked to whisper. No problem here. Most patients listen to their pain.

In this stillness my neighbor suddenly saw movement, a throwing back of covers. Then a soul took off its body the way a body takes off clothes. She says the soul is thin and looks a lot like a skinned rabbit. Later, in another bed, the same thing happened again.

Women always circled around my father, always found an excuse to talk to him. His attention stayed elsewhere though, on the brown sky or on a rough leafless tree. When I thought of my father I thought of trees. A lot of children do that. Their fathers seem so tall and they see the shared straightness, the permanence, the strength. In my case, some of this was wishful, meant to block my vision of his tumbling in a plane.

My parents slept in separate beds and with their backs to the other. When I think of them now, I see this facing away. Even out of bed they did it, took the position of people at the start of a duel. At work my father learned the new machine and was given more money. In our house we were making do with cardboard windows; even so he began flying lessons in an actual plane. This in November, when the sky's always dim.

In school our teacher had to shout above the heating system. Her thoughts were still on bones. "Children," she said, "if you fell out a window, you'd bounce like soft rubber balls. This is not true with children in Belgium. Quite properly, their bones would break. I mulled upon why this is so. And I think it's because here you are too coddled, life is hidden in lovely gift wrap. This I must fix. We will start by learning the correct human body." With help from a janitor, a skeleton was installed in a corner. Only partially intact, "Georgie Porgie" was scribbled across its forehead. A cheek was smashed. Its teeth were brown. More than anything, I didn't want its pointy fingers to touch me or to have it smile on my behalf. Our teacher passed out wire hangers, more old newspapers, and paste. I was told to make ribs. I'd never seen real ones before. Were they always yellowed and chipped like Georgie's? Was that what was inside me, that cruel-looking thing? I put my hand on top of my own ribs. Although hidden they seemed benign, their hardness comforting and familiar, like a night table's you might touch in the dark.

Now for the first time my father was happy, a child's happiness that should have been used long before, but wasn't. My father wore it awkwardly, the way children do new shoes.

Outdoors, in November, a gray covers the browns. That year, in our house, colors also changed. My father's happiness had a sweet pigment. It brightened his skin and lightened his eyes. While my mother, still facing away from him, seemed redder, the red of a coil too hot to touch.

At school we finished our skeleton and named it Hansel. It hung in a curve, one of its arms being longer and thicker than the other. "Deformities happen," our teacher said. Next she gave out thin green strips of foam rubber, the kind that pad wire hangers. "Children," she said. "I shall now speak about muscle."

My father was hardly home now. He missed dinner. My mother left it on the stove, cold and exposed for him to see. I looked and saw the sauce as blood, the cheese as raw flesh. "Daddy," I cried. In my mind I saw his plane broken and on the ground, him inside it, even more damaged. I thought, it's mother's wish. But now I think she saw herself in that pan.

My neighbor who went through the windshield no longer fears death. She says the soul is most happy unencumbered. On earth, to help it feel light, she recommends swimming.

Our teacher said, "What is it you say here? 'Make a muscle?' Well, do it." I made a fist and squeezed as hard as I could. A bump that looked like a little hill hardened in my arm. My arm quivered and I felt fear inside it. I was pleased. It was as if I'd met a new friend, one who felt like I did.

I asked my neighbor, "What about angels? Do we ever become them?" I saw myself as winged and pure white.

"No," my neighbor said.

In my father's case, I think he looks in death the way he did in the doorway of Roz's Stationery. I'm afraid to think otherwise. The smallest change frightens me, even the hump a salmon develops before it swims upstream.

It took days to weave the green foam around Hansel. When we finished, our teacher brought out red and blue yarn. "Blood vessels," she told us. I knew about those. My father had taught me. With my finger I'd press his skin and push blood out of his vein. The vein, a blue line, would vanish. Then, and this was my favorite part, the reason I'd started, I'd lift my finger, and the blue would rush back.

I came home from school. My mother's hair was turquoise. Something had gone wrong, a clash of chemicals or a process done too often. My mother was crying and whipping reeking liquids in a bowl. A sheet of instructions lay on the table. "Dazzle him. . . . Dazzle yourself." I read them and prayed for such a thing to be possible.

That night my father told me about a flight, a loop he'd made around Brown Town.

"I was up in the sky, and far below was my shadow. On the ground the shadow is always attached. Don't believe me? Then try freeing yourself."

I did, and saw he was right.

"But me, I can be far away, up in the sky, and my shadow, it can still slide along our street."

My neighbor says the soul's true nature is like the nature of a dog at the moment it sees you and flings itself on your legs. My neighbor's point is that the soul is as friendly.

"All of them?" I asked, unable to picture either of my parents bounding against anyone's legs. My neighbor qualified her statement. She said, "I'm only talking about souls I've seen."

Our teacher came into class carrying a large roll of batting. "Today," she said, "I shall explain flesh."

The owner of my father's factory developed a new cleaning agent. It was quite condensed and therefore cheaper to store. In its earliest stages it was mixed by my father's machine. During this process, my father wore protective gloves.

A seam burst, liquids that shouldn't have, mixed. I was in school when it happened, stuffing Hansel's fat arm into a nylon while my teacher lectured on skin. "It's our greatest protector," she said. No one came to tell me. Later, during vocabulary, he died.

Our second shock was that the factory had provided insurance, and the way my father died, my mother collected double the usual amount. After the burial, it was as if trucks filled with money dumped their loads on top of our house. Even so, for a while my mother shared my bed and we'd cry, our arms at our sides.

My mother bought a huge house in the good part of Brown Town and, using more of her new money, bought things to cover the brown, things such as grass, which arrived in large squares. She also bought clothes and had her hair bleached professionally. Our new lives were covered by colors, but above us I saw the brown sky, and the men my mother married, they didn't treat her particularly well.

I haven't told her, but I disagree with my neighbor. I don't think the soul likes to be freed. I think the soul can't feel wrapped enough. For example, in my case, I'll see the sky and think it's my skin.

LINDA HELLER ON COMMUNITY

I came to fiction late. I was an illustrator. A children's book editor asked me to write a story. At the time I thought there must be a set way to go about this, a list of procedures. I don't know why I thought this—it's certainly not how I approached visual art—but anxious to learn the correct method, I enrolled in a writing class. There my teacher did not let us in on a secret which made the act of writing easy. My big revelation was that writers patently reveal themselves in ways painters do not. Accordingly, I titled my first piece, "Another Woman in the Class Has Lost Her Man." But a part of the craft can be taught, and I took many classes at New York's West Side Y, a happy decision.

Except for my little dog, I'm alone when I write. My choice, but such a choice makes you crave a community. Life without one becomes thin and dim. We're social animals; most animals are. Even plants grow in clusters. And we humans are born wanting to broadcast what's happening to us and to interview others. We seek help and offer it.

For years The Writers Community was my community. I received encouragement there and learned practical facts: where to send my work, for instance. Most important, I gained close friends. A writer's life can be hard. You mail your story, it boomerangs back. A tiny printed note is attached. "We're too busy, too bombarded, de da, de da." Friends soften these blows and infuse you with hope.

Often a community needs a center to keep it strong, a place that remains fixed and draws people to it. A school can be that. For years I volunteered at a tutoring center. I gave little workshops. Children made books with actual moving mouths or lines of text that could be pulled along the page. The children's delight lightened me. I've read that our true nature is love. I experience it by participating in a community.

LINDA HELLER *received a 1996 fellowship from the New York Foundation for the Arts and recently completed a story collection,* In the Presence of Men. *Her work has appeared in* Ascent, Alaska Quarterly Journal, Northwest Review, Quarter After Eight, *and* New Letters. *She has also written and illustrated ten children's books and made an award-winning animated film. "Brown Town," written for Dinitia Smith's Writers Community workshop in 1989, was chosen as an honor story in* Best American Short Stories 1991 *and nominated for a Pushcart Prize.*

AMY HEMPEL

The Harvest

The year I began to say *vahz* instead of *vase,* a man I barely knew
nearly accidentally killed me.

The man was not hurt when the other car hit ours. The man I
had known for one week held me in the street in a way that meant
I couldn't see my legs. I remember knowing that I shouldn't look,
and knowing that I *would* look if it wasn't that I couldn't.

My blood was on the front of this man's clothes.

He said, "You'll be okay, but this sweater is ruined."

I screamed from the fear of pain. But I did not feel any pain. In
the hospital, after injections, I knew there was pain in the room—
I just didn't know whose pain it was.

What happened to one of my legs required four hundred stitches,
which, when I told it, became five hundred stitches, because nothing
is ever quite as bad as it *could* be.

The five days they didn't know if they could save my leg or not
I stretched to ten.

The lawyer was the one who used the word. But I won't get around
to that until a couple of paragraphs.

We were having the looks discussion—how important *are* they.
Crucial is what I had said.

I think looks are crucial.

But this guy was a lawyer. He sat in an aqua vinyl chair drawn up
to my bed. What he meant by looks was how much my loss of them
was worth in a court of law.

I could tell that the lawyer liked to say *court of law.* He told me he
had taken the bar three times before he had passed. He said that his
friends had given him handsomely embossed business cards, but

where these lovely cards were supposed to say *Attorney-at-Law,* his cards said *Attorney-at-Last.*

He had already covered loss of earnings, that I could not now become an airline stewardess. That I had never considered being one was immaterial, he said, legally.

"There's another thing," he said. "We have to talk here about marriageability."

The tendency was to say marriage-a-*what?* although I knew what he meant the first time I heard it.

I was eighteen years old. I said, "First, don't we talk about *date*ability?"

The man of a week was already gone, the accident driving him back to his wife.

"Do you think looks are important?" I asked the man before he left.

"Not at first," he said.

In my neighborhood there is a fellow who was a chemistry teacher until an explosion took his face and left what was left behind. The rest of him is neatly dressed in dark suits and shined shoes. He carries a briefcase to the college campus. What a comfort—his family, people said—until his wife took the kids and moved out.

In the solarium, a woman showed me a snapshot. She said, "This is what my son used to look like."

I spent my evenings in Dialysis. They didn't mind when a lounger was free. They had wide-screen color TV, better than they had in Rehab. Wednesday nights we watched a show where women in expensive clothes appeared on lavish sets and promised to ruin one another.

On one side of me was a man who spoke only in phone numbers. You would ask him how he felt, he would say, "924-3130." Or he would say, "757-1366." We guessed what these numbers might be, but nobody spent the dime.

There was sometimes, on the other side of me, a twelve-year-old boy. His lashes were thick and dark from blood-pressure medication. He was next on the transplant list, as soon as—the word they used was *harvest*—as soon as a kidney was harvested.

The boy's mother prayed for drunk drivers.

I prayed for men who were not discriminating.

Aren't we all, I thought, somebody's harvest?

The hour would end, and a floor nurse would wheel me back to my room. She would say, "Why watch that trash? Why not just ask me how my day went?"

I spent fifteen minutes before going to bed squeezing rubber grips. One of the medications was making my fingers stiffen. The doctor said he'd give it to me till I couldn't button my blouse—a figure of speech to someone in a cotton gown.

The lawyer said, "Charitable works."

He opened his shirt and showed me where an acupuncture person had dabbed at his chest with cola syrup, sunk four needles, and told him that the real cure was charitable works.

I said, "Cure for what?"

The lawyer said, "Immaterial."

As soon as I knew that I would be all right, I was sure that I was dead and didn't know it. I moved through the days like a severed head that finishes a sentence. I waited for the moment that would snap me out of my seeming life.

The accident happened at sunset, so that is when I felt this way the most. The man I had met the week before was driving me to dinner when it happened. The place was at the beach, a beach on a bay that you can look across and see the city lights, a place where you can see everything without having to listen to any of it.

A long time later I went to that beach myself. *I* drove the car. It was the first good beach day; I wore shorts.

At the edge of the sand I unwound the elastic bandage and waded into the surf. A boy in a wet suit looked at my leg. He asked me if a shark had done it; there were sightings of great whites along that part of the coast.

I said that, yes, a shark had done it.

"And you're going back in?" the boy asked.

I said, "And I'm going back in."

I leave a lot out when I tell the truth. The same when I write a story. I'm going to start now to tell you what I left out of "The Harvest," and maybe begin to wonder why I had to leave it out.

There was no other car. There was only the one car, the one that hit me when I was on the back of the man's motorcycle. But think of the awkward syllables when you have to say *motorcycle*.

The driver of the car was a newspaper reporter. He worked for a local paper. He was young, a recent graduate, and he was on his way to a labor meeting to cover a threatened strike. When I say I was then a journalism student, it is something you might not have accepted in "The Harvest."

In the years that followed, I watched for the reporter's byline. He broke the People's Temple story that resulted in Jim Jones's flight to Guyana. Then he covered Jonestown. In the city room of the San Francisco *Chronicle*, as the death toll climbed to nine hundred, the numbers were posted like donations on pledge night. Somewhere in the hundreds, a sign was fixed to the wall that said JUAN CORONA, EAT YOUR HEART OUT.

In the emergency room, what happened to one of my legs required not four hundred stitches but just over three hundred stitches. I exaggerated even before I began to exaggerate, because it's true—nothing *is* ever quite as bad as it could be.

My lawyer was no attorney-at-last. He was a partner in one of the city's oldest law firms. He would never have opened his shirt to reveal the site of acupuncture, which is something that he never would have had.

"Marriageability" was the original title of "The Harvest."

The damage to my leg was considered cosmetic although I am still, fifteen years later, unable to kneel. In an out-of-court settlement the night before the trial, I was awarded nearly $100,000. The reporter's car insurance went up $12.43 per month.

It had been suggested that I rub my leg with ice, to bring up the scars, before I hiked my skirt three years later for the court. But there was no ice in the judge's chambers, so I did not get a chance to pass or fail the moral test.

The man of a week, whose motorcycle it was, was not a married man. But when you thought he had a wife, wasn't I liable to do anything? And didn't I have it coming?

After the accident, the man got married. The girl he married was a fashion model. ("Do you think looks are important?" I asked the man before he left. "Not at first," he said.)

In addition to being a beauty, the girl was worth millions of dollars. Would you have accepted this in "The Harvest"—that the model was also an heiress?

It is true we were headed for dinner when it happened. But the place where you can see everything without having to listen to any of it was not a beach on a bay; it was the top of Mount Tamalpais. We had the dinner with us as we headed up the twisting mountain road. This is the version that has room for perfect irony, so you won't mind when I say that for the next several months, from my hospital bed, I had a dead-on spectacular view of that very mountain.

I would have written this next part into the story if anybody would have believed it. But who would have? I was there and I didn't believe it.

On the day of my third operation, there was an attempted breakout in the Maximum Security Adjustment Center, adjacent to Death Row, at San Quentin prison. "Soledad Brother" George Jackson, a twenty-nine-year-old black man, pulled out a smuggled-in .38-caliber pistol, yelled, "This is it!" and opened fire. Jackson was killed; so were three guards and two "tier-tenders," inmates who bring other prisoners their meals.

Three other guards were stabbed in the neck. The prison is a five-minute drive from Marin General, so that is where the injured guards were taken. The people who brought them were three kinds of police, including California Highway Patrol and Marin County sheriff's deputies, heavily armed.

Police were stationed on the roof of the hospital with rifles; they were posted in the hallways, waving patients and visitors back into their rooms.

When I was wheeled out of Recovery later that day, bandaged waist to ankle, three officers and an armed sheriff frisked me.

On the news that night, there was footage of the riot. They showed my surgeon talking to reporters, indicating, with a finger to his throat, how he had saved one of the guards by sewing up a slice from ear to ear.

I watched this on television, and because it was my doctor, and because hospital patients are self-absorbed, and because I was drugged, I thought the surgeon was talking about me. I thought that he was saying, "Well, she's dead. I'm announcing it to her in her bed."

The psychiatrist I saw at the surgeon's referral said that the feeling was a common one. She said that victims of trauma who have not yet assimilated the trauma often believe they are dead and do not know it.

The great white sharks in the waters near my home attack one to seven people a year. Their primary target is the abalone diver. With abalone steaks at thirty-five dollars a pound and going up, the Department of Fish and Game expects the shark attacks to show no slackening.

AMY HEMPEL *is author of three collections of stories,* Reasons to Live, At the Gates of The Animal Kingdom, *and* Tumble Home. *Her fiction and nonfiction have been published in* Harper's, Vanity Fair, New York Times Magazine, Esquire, Elle, *and* Vogue. *She currently teaches in the Graduate Writing Seminars at Bennington College. Hempel felt that "The Harvest" was appropriate for this anthology because it deals with the act of making stories, which is what she taught at The Writers Community.*

JOYCE HINNEFELD

Jump Start

Patty gets her jump start early—coffee in the morning, instant—and she gets in her car and drives. This is all she ever wanted, maybe all she ever wanted in her life. She's like a tune you can't stop singing in the corner of your whirling mind. She's traveling down the road like an animal that's sleek to a job you might not like to do.

Patty's driving like there's no tomorrow, or lots of tomorrows, she feels that good. It's the kind of day when she can think she's alive for some kind of wild and lovely reason; her mother and father are dead from the accident but she's alive and kicking and today she can think that sure, lots of things are sad, but today she's alive and she's driving her car.

It may be that the air is crisp and cool. Feel how crisp it is. Patty likes those kinds of changes, hot to suddenly cool and fresh, and she hopes that you do, too. The accident happened when it was hot— blazing hot sun on the asphalt—and ever since then Patty hasn't cared much for the heat. Plus she can smell pine behind the trailer court and the earth looks rich and dark, not pale and dusty like some goddamn migrant camp, which is what her father would have called the trailer court. In fact he probably did call it that—how else would Patty have thought of it now?

Patty knows the other girls at the packing plant laugh at her behind her back, knows they think she doesn't know, call her "the baby" and "the kid," even Essie, who barely speaks English and must not even know what those words mean. But on days when it's crisp and cool and she can smell the pine she doesn't care, she likes the drive and she's glad to see the girls again, doesn't care if they talk and they click their tongues about her dead parents and what happened to her brain when she's not there because she'll be there soon enough and then they'll all just laugh on their break anyway, sit out in the cool breeze at the picnic tables and laugh and carry on.

Each day on the way to work Patty drives by the clinic at the edge of town—drives by humming today, she's still got her jump start, still can smell the pine and see the shadow leaves outside the trailer where the sun shines through the branches above her car. She can drive and drive and never lose her jump start. Patty's a fine driver— just watch her, look at how alert she is—everyone knows the accident was not her fault.

At the clinic she sees Father McElvey again with his sign that says, "They're killing babies," and he waves at her and smiles and she smiles back but she's told him she won't come and hold a sign on her lunch break. And all he says is let me know if you change your mind.

But the girls at the plant call him fathead and *el loco padre* and worse, and they curse him in Spanish and laugh at him and all the people with him holding up their signs, the younger ones that the girls call "retards" and the old women with scarves tied around their heads even in the summer, even in ninety-degrees-in-the-shade summertime. Their wrinkled old fingers move fast along their rosary beads, and some of them hold dusty pictures of the Virgin of Guadalupe—who has dark skin and stands on top of what looks like a snake holding a moon, Patty's noticed—up against their chests like shields.

Since the accident Father McElvey likes to come by and talk to her and he wants her to come to his church. But Patty can't slow down long enough for that—not even long enough to go and hold a sign on her lunch hour, because she knows the surest way to lose her jump start would be to slow down that long, long enough to stop and think, like all that time in the hospital after the accident. And if she went and held a sign the girls would have that to laugh at about her, too. Some mornings she's seen one or two of their cars there at the clinic, Linda's maybe or Sandra's, and Patty can't make the connection between these slim girls in their tight jeans and their husky cigarette voices and the pictures of bloody babies that Father McElvey and the retards and the old women hold up in their faces when they walk out of the clinic. Because where, inside those skintight blue jeans, would a baby that size fit?

But Father McElvey seems like such a nice man and he smiles and nods at her and she doesn't think he would lie about the babies, and those old women with their rosary beads seem like they want to cry all the time, so somebody or something must die inside there, but Patty doesn't really know what to make of it all and the girls at the packing plant aren't too much help.

"Hey Patty, don't let him sink his claws in you," Sandra said to her once. It was the day Father McElvey pulled his car up alongside the picnic tables while they ate their lunch outside and handed Patty a flyer about a church potluck the following Sunday. "You start going to that man's potlucks and you'll never grow up, little girl." But I'm not a little girl! Patty wanted to say, she wanted to yell that at Sandra but she didn't say a thing. And she wondered why they all hated Father McElvey so much, what he did besides hold up the signs and the pictures of the bloody babies.

Patty wasn't Catholic though and she didn't think she ever would be. Her parents never went to church and she didn't know about her brother. He was in the army when the accident happened and now he was in Texas—he'd never come back—and after she'd stared at the dead bodies of her parents sprawled there on the highway for a while some woman she didn't know came up to her and said "I'll pray for their souls" and Patty stared at her because she didn't know what that meant, just stared at her until the hot sun made it seem like the woman was melting there in front of her, turning into something soft and rubbery right in front of Patty's eyes, and then the next thing she knew she blacked out and she never saw that woman again until one morning when she drove past the clinic on her way to the factory she saw her there next to Father McElvey with her rosary beads in one hand and a sign that said "Stop the killing" in the other one. It startled Patty to see the woman's face—it was solid now—and she heard the woman's voice all over again, heard it like it was just yesterday, heard her say "I'll pray for their souls" and still didn't know what that meant and didn't really care.

Because she'd lost her jump start for a while then. And she thought she might not want to be a Catholic after that, even though

Father McElvey was nice to her ever since the accident and it seemed like he always wanted to have her around.

Feel Patty's foot in her sneaker on the accelerator. Feel how she gets the pressure just right. Keeps it right there at fifty, then lifts her foot off just at the crest of the hill at the edge of town, right where the speed zone starts, lifts it off and watches the needle course back down, as smooth and gradual as the smooth hill Patty glides down, to thirty. That day last summer she'd looked down to check, to make sure she wasn't going over fifty-five so her father wouldn't yell (she'd just gotten her license, she was showing her father how careful she was, how she could drive the car just fine) and when she looked back up she saw the truck barreling right toward her face and so she swerved and he drove his giant truck right into the side of the car, right into her parents and they were covered in blood then and dead and her head was bleeding, too, but she lived.

At the bottom of the hill is the clinic and Patty is starting to lose her jump start just as she gets there so she looks for Father McElvey over in the parking lot, thinking maybe a smile from him will help her get it back, though she kind of doubts it. She doesn't see Father McElvey at first—he's not in his usual place. But then she spots him and when she sees what he's doing it takes her by surprise (but she keeps her eyes on the road—she's a careful driver, it might have slowed her down in other ways but everyone agrees she's a careful driver and they all decided she should be able to keep on doing that). He's walking alongside Dorrie Lambert, a young woman Patty has always admired. Dorrie's parked her car in the clinic lot and Father McElvey is walking right beside her toward the door and a couple of the old women are with them, too, walking along with their rosaries and sticking pictures of bloody babies in Dorrie Lambert's face and saying things to her that must be awful, the way their faces look (though Patty can't hear their words) and Dorrie is covering her face and looking down at the ground and trying to ignore them but it's clear that Dorrie is crying.

Leave her alone!

Patty screams it inside her car but the window is up. And as she screams she swerves to the right and for a split second she can't breathe, she feels like something has hit her in the stomach but she makes herself pull the wheel back the other way, straightens out the car and slows way down but keeps on driving. And she is terrified, her heart is pounding in her ears, and she glues her eyes to the road and concentrates as hard as she can all the way to the parking lot at the plant, and when she turns off the engine and steps out of her car her legs are shaky and she has to steady herself for a moment, has to hold on to the handle of the car door and catch her breath and get her heart to stop racing and her legs and hands to stop shaking, before she walks into the plant to punch the clock and go to work.

Patty's jump start is gone now, long gone, and she has too much on her mind. Usually Patty is one of the best girls on the line—she's fast and neat—but today the legs of the chickens seem to look too much like her own, their bumpy skin like the gooseflesh on her own arms that day after the accident (she remembers staring down at her right arm for the longest time, thinking how strange it was to have goose bumps, to feel so cold her teeth were chattering, there in the middle of that steaming hot highway), and even though she knows it's really just her own beating pulse that she's feeling when she rubs her gloved fingers over their bodies, inside and out, Patty can't shake the idea that she feels these chickens' hearts beating there at the tips of her fingers. She's slowing things down and at lunchtime the supervisor asks is she all right—and he looks nervous when he asks it, like he might have been expecting this to happen, Patty thinks—and she says she's fine, she just isn't feeling quite right and he says why don't you take half a sick day, go on now, I'll clock out for you, so Patty has to get in her car and drive again and now it's noon and not so cool and crisp but at least the women with their signs are gone when she drives by the clinic and so is Dorrie Lambert's car and Father McElvey is nowhere in sight.

Patty thinks that's good because she's decided that the tobacco stains on his teeth when he smiles make her feel sick and she never wants to go to his potlucks or be a Catholic, which from what she can tell means being a retard or an old woman with a scarf on your head

in the middle of the summer, making younger women who are pret-
tier than you are cry.

Dorrie Lambert was a high school cheerleader when Patty was
twelve and she had the best rhythm of all the high school girls by far.
At halftime at basketball games, when the band played songs with
drums pounding out the beat and the pom-pom girls in the bleachers
doing their routines, the cheerleaders stood at the sidelines doing their
motions in rhythm with the drums—slap the thighs twice, clap hands,
snap fingers, shake hips—and Patty and the other kids sat in the
bleachers and did the motions too, wiggled their butts on the seats
and clapped and shook their shoulders. Dorrie Lambert had it down
better than anyone, she always had the rhythm just right; just thinking about it Patty feels the beat inside her and moves to it there on the
car seat. She was always sorry when the halftime show was over.

Sometimes Patty and her friends would make up their own routines to songs on the radio in the backyard, but once she stopped
outside the kitchen door in time to hear her father say something
about "shaking her ass like some colored girl" and when her mother
clicked her tongue at him he slapped her and after that Patty only
did the dances by herself in her room with the door closed and the
music turned down low. As she got older she knew better than to
think she could ever be a cheerleader—it's the kind of thing you just
know—and she stopped dancing by herself in front of her bedroom
mirror because any time she tried she felt embarrassed.

The trailer is hot in the afternoon sun and Patty tries to sleep but
she keeps waking up sweating with a picture in her mind of the old
woman from the accident holding a picture of a bloody baby in
Dorrie Lambert's face. Patty thinks someone who got it all so right,
who moved just like that with the beat from the drums in high
school, shouldn't have to cry, shouldn't have to have Father McElvey
and all those women mumbling awful things in her ear, even if she
does have a baby inside her that she doesn't want to keep.

Patty lies sweating in her bed and she feels just like she felt after
the accident, and it frightens her to feel that way again. She knows
that something had better happen soon or her jump start could be

gone for good. When the sun goes down at last she walks outside to the woods behind the trailer court and she can smell the pine then, smell the pine and forget about the hot, hot highway and she wishes, then, in those cool woods with a breeze on her face, that she could take Dorrie Lambert in her arms and tell her not to cry. Back in the trailer she sleeps with the window wide open and the night air blowing in and she thinks she can smell the pine trees even there in her bed and she doesn't wake up once until her alarm goes off at seven A.M. in the morning.

Patty tries to get her jump start again—has her instant coffee in the same cracked cup her mother used—but it's not working now, she can't get the feeling right, and driving along the highway she knows it's because she's mad. She's mad at Father McElvey and all those women with their scarves and fat, dry fingers. "I'll pray for their souls" she said, and Patty thinks *el loco padre,* yes *el loco padre,* hears herself scream "Leave her alone!" and feels that terror in her chest again as the car nearly swerves to the right one more time.

This time when she reaches the crest of the hill Patty keeps her foot on the accelerator. She can see the tips of the women's signs ("They're killing babies!") and she pictures Dorrie Lambert crying on an operating table—what if she couldn't sleep? what if she felt them cutting into her skin?—and she catches a glimpse of Father McElvey's black-coated back.

Still Patty doesn't lift her foot. She watches as the needle stays at fifty, and then it's like a dream as her foot pushes down and the needle moves up to sixty, seventy, eighty (where you feel it first is the ball of your foot but it moves up fast to your chest and then your throat, it's almost like you're spitting something out that you've had inside forever), and she's heading right for them, right for that goddamn Virgin of Guadalupe (Sandra's voice: "Hey padre—what would you know about Nuestra Señora de Guadalupe!" Someone has left a pile of Catholic pamphlets in the plant lounge one day and Patty knows the girls all think it was her but it wasn't).

Now Patty points her car toward the Virgin and drives like there's no tomorrow, or maybe all kinds of tomorrows. She feels that good.

JOYCE HINNEFELD ON COMMUNITY

When I moved to New York City in 1987, I was twenty-six years old and full of a kind of premature maturity, a gloomy resignation that's plagued me, really, all my life—and the form it took then was a decision (I thought) to simply give up once and for all on being a writer and settle into life as a publishing professional. Fortunately, there's always been another side to that gloomy, mature part of me, and it was that side that prompted me, a few months after my arrival in New York, to sign up for a fiction workshop at The Writer's Voice of the West Side YMCA.

The rest is an unfinished history, a personal one that may not interest many people—but what needs to be said here is that while New York City can be a tough place to find a home, I found one in a group of women writers that emerged from that first workshop at The Writer's Voice. We've been together, in slightly different configurations, for nearly eight years; there are seven of us now, and four of us have been there since the beginning. We've survived various strains—deepening friendships and their accompanying disappointments; moves out of Manhattan and the accompanying difficulty of finding a workable meeting place; a divorce and some marriages; many, many jobs. Sometimes it seems like we're losing focus, losing the desire to continue. But then someone, in a burst of inspiration, will propose a weekend retreat outside the city, or a public reading for invited guests, and suddenly we'll be energized, and writing, again.

Sometimes it just feels too hard, still. All the rejection slips. The exhaustion of trying to make a living and still have something left when you sit down at the desk or the computer. Grim reports about the state of literary publishing. I get gloomy and still, though more rarely, decide sometimes that maybe I'd be better off giving up on this idea. The urge to write comes back, though, and while that may be something internal, something individual, the only way out of all the doubt, for me, is a conversation with other writers. This may be as good a time and place as any to say something I've always wanted to say—thank you to Ellen Kahaner, who was in Katherine Hiller's fiction workshop with me, Eileen Elliott, and Nancy Ludmerer in the winter of 1988, and who got our group together in the first place.

Publication is an increasingly hardscrabble business, and while online possibilities might alleviate some of the strain of a crowded world of print, I think those of us who've found our solace in words printed on pages we can hold in our hands are less comforted by the wonders of the World Wide Web than we sometimes let on. What places like The Writers Community program (its workshops, readings, publications, and various outgrowths) guarantee is a safe place for our words, a place where those pages can be held and read, where our voices can be heard—the kind of safety that allows risk, and discovery. For a writer, a crucial kind of home.

JOYCE HINNEFELD *is a writer, editor, and teacher whose work has appeared in* Farmer's Market, 13th Moon, Greensboro Review, *and the anthology* Prairie Hearts: Women's Writings on the Midwest. *She has worked in publishing and recently completed her first novel,* Rumer Rutledge Tells the Truth. *She teaches at Moravian College in Bethlehem, Pennsylvania.*

FROM *A Different Drummer*

Now the first time New Marsails (it was still New *Marseilles* then,
after the French city) ever saw the African was in the morning, just
after the slave ship he was riding pulled into the harbor. In them
days, a boat coming was always a big occasion and folks used to walk
down to the dock to greet it; it wasn't a far piece since the town
wasn't no bigger than Sutton is today.

The slaver came up, her sails all plump, and tied up, and let fall
her gangplank. And the ship's owner, who was also the leading slave
auctioneer in New Marsails—he talked so good and so fast he could
sell a one-armed, one-legged, half-witted Negro for a premium
price—he ambled up the gangplank. I'm told he was a spindly fellow,
with no muscles whatever. He had hard-bargain-driving eyes and a
nose all round and puffy and pocked like a rotten orange, and he always wore a blue old-time suit with lace at the collar, and a sort of a
derby of green felt. And following him, exactly three paces behind,
was a Negro. Some folks said this was the auctioneer's son by a colored woman. I don't know that for certain, but I DO know this here
Negro looked, walked, and talked just like his master. He had that
same build, and the same crafty eyes, and dressed just like him too—
green derby and all—so that the two of them looked like a print and
a negative of the same photograph, since the Negro was brown and
had kinky hair. This Negro was the auctioneer's bookkeeper and
overseer and anything else you can think of. So then these two went
up on deck, and while the Negro stood by, the auctioneer shook
hands with the captain, who was standing on deck watching his men
do their chores. You understand, they spoke different in them days,
so I can't be certain exactly what they said, but I reckon it was something like: "How do. How was the trip?"

Already some folks standing on the dock could see the captain looked kind of sick. "Fine, excepting we had one real ornery son of a bitch. Had to chain him up, alone, away by himself."

"Let's have a look at him," said the auctioneer. The Negro behind him nodded, which he did every time the auctioneer spoke, so that he looked like he was a ventriloquist, and the auctioneer was his dummy, either that way or the other way around.

"Not yet. God damn! I'll bring him up after the rest of them niggers is OFF the boat. Then we can ALL hold him down. Damn!" He put his hand up to his brow, and that's when folks with good eyes could see the oily blue mark on his head like somebody spat axle grease on him and he hadn't had time yet to wipe it off. "God damn!" he said again.

Well, of course folks was getting real anxious, not just out of common interest like usual, but to see this son of a bitch that was causing all the trouble.

Dewitt Willson was there too. He hadn't come to see the boat, or even to buy slaves. He was there to pick up a grandfather clock. He was building himself a new house outside of Sutton and he'd ordered this clock from Europe and he wanted it to come as fast as possible, and the fastest way for it to come was by slaver. He'd heard how carrying things on a slaver was seven kinds of bad luck, but still, because he was so anxious to get the clock, he let them send it that way. The clock rode in the captain's cabin and was all padded up with cotton, and boxed in, and crated around, and wadded secure. And he'd come to get it, bringing a wagon to carry it out to his house and surprise his wife with it.

Dewitt and everybody was waiting, but first the crew went down and cracked their whips and herded this long line of Negroes out of the hold. The women had breasts hanging most down to their waists, and some carried black babies. The men, their faces was all twisted up sullen as the inside of lemons. Most all the slaves was bone-naked and they stood on deck, blinking; none of them had seen the sun in a long time. The auctioneer and his Negro walked up and down the row, as always, inspecting teeth, feeling muscles, looking over the goods, you might say. Then the auctioneer said, "Well, let's bring up this troublemaker, what say."

"No, sir!" yelled the captain.

"Why not?"

"I told you. I don't want him brung up until the rest of these niggers is off the boat."

"Yes, surely," said the auctioneer, but looked sort of blank. And so did his Negro.

The captain rubbed that shining grease-spot wound. "Don't you understand? He's their chief. If he says the word we'll have more trouble here than God has followers. I had enough already!" And he rubbed that spot again.

The crewmen pushed them Negroes down the gangplank and the folks on the dock stepped out of the way and watched them go by. Them Negroes even SMELLED angry, having been crammed together, each of them with no more room to himself than a baby in a crib. They was dirty, and mad, and ready for a fight. So the captain sent down some crewmen with rifles to keep them company. And the other crewmen, twenty or thirty there was, they just stood on deck fidgeting and shuffling. Folks on the dock knew right off what was the matter: them crewmen was afraid. You could see it in their eyes. All them grown men scared of whatever was down in the hold of that boat chained to the wall.

The captain looked sort of scared himself and fingered his wound and sighed and said to his mate: "I reckon you might as well go down there and get him." And to the twenty or thirty men standing around: "You go down there with him—all of you. Maybe you can manage."

Folks held their breath like youngsters at a circus waiting for a high-wire fellow to make it to his nest, because even if an old deaf-blind lady had-a been standing on that dock, she would-a known there was something down in the hold that was getting ready to make an appearance. Everybody got quiet and over the waves slapping against the hull they could hear all them crewmen tramping downstairs, the whole swarm of them in heavy bro-GANS, taking their time about informing that thing in the hold it was wanted on deck.

Then, out of the bottom of the ship, way off in some dark place, came this roar, louder'n a cornered bear or maybe two bears mating. It was so loud the sides of the boat bulged out. They all knew it was from one throat since there wasn't no blending, just one loud sound. And then, right in front of their eyes, in the side of the boat, way down near the water line, they saw a hole tear open, and splinters fly, splashing like when you toss a handful of pebbles into a pond. There was a lot of muffled fighting, pushing, and hollering going on, and after a while this fellow staggered on deck with blood dripping from his head. "God damn—if he ain't pulled his chain outen the wall of the boat," he says. And everybody stared at that hole again, and didn't take note that the crewman had just passed on from a cracked skull.

Well sir, you can believe that folks got into close knots for protection in case that thing in the bottom of the ship should somehow get loose and start a-raging through the peaceful town of New Marsails. Then it got sort of quiet again, even on the inside of the ship, and folks leaned forward, listening. They heard chains dragging and then saw the African for the first time.

To begin with, they seen his head coming up out of the gangway, and then his shoulders, so broad he had to climb those stairs sideways; then his body began, and long after it should-a stopped it was still coming. Then he was full out, skin-naked except for a rag around his parts, standing at least two heads taller than any man on the deck. He was black and glistened like the captain's grease-spot wound. His head was as large as one of them kettles you see in a cannibal movie and looked as heavy. There were so many chains hung on him he looked like a fully-trimmed Christmas tree. But it was his eyes they kept looking at; sunk deep in his head they was, making it look like a gigantic black skull.

There was something under his arm. At first they thought it was a tumor or growth and didn't pay it no mind, and it wasn't until it moved all by itself and they noticed it had eyes that they saw it was a baby. Yes sir, a baby tucked under his arm like a black lunch box, just peeping out at everybody.

So now they'd seen the African, and they stepped back a little as if the distance between him and them wasn't at all far enough, as if he could reach out over the railing of the ship, and down at them and pop off their heads with a flick of his fingers. But he was quiet now, not blinking in the sun like them others, just basking like it was his very own and he'd ordered it to come out and shine on him.

WILLIAM MELVIN KELLEY *is the author of the novels* A Different Drummer, dem, Dancers on the Shore, *and the African-American literature classic,* A Drop of Patience. *He has taught at The Writers Community, The New School, and the State University in Geneseo, New York.*

DIANE LEFER

La Chata

La Chata's mother curses the chickens in Spanish. The rest of the
time she speaks Zapotec with its Indian shushes and clicks. When
she bathes, she goes behind the bamboo palisade that La Chata built
in the corner of the yard. She takes off her blouse and lets down her
hair. The water comes cold from the hogshead and she pours it over
her body with a plastic cup. Bare breasted in the patio, she looks old.

The old man, her husband, can't see. He sits straight backed on
the hard chair, his cane between his legs. When he pounds the cane
on the ground, she goes to him and helps him to the hammock. In
the hammock, he settles himself and draws up his knees.

The women help the men to move. At the other end of the compound, Toño's cream-colored wife helps him into the cement-block
room, the only room with a bed.

The old man spits. He lifts his head to hear Marilinda's creamy
giggle and Toño's gasp, a burst of air like a swimmer breaking surface.

"My daughter Chata knows how to work," he says. "My son only
knew how to get married."

Inside the room, Marilinda turns on the radio. Chata bought the
stereo console and built the cement-block room around it. Since no
one would come to the village to put in windows, she hitched a ride
down to the port, asked questions, bought glass and frames, and did
it herself. When Toño and Marilinda got married, La Chata gave
them the room. Then the house was more than a collection of bamboo shacks and La Chata built a brick wall around the yard and put
up the iron door.

The old man knows Chata, his baby, can do anything.

Tita Carmen from across the way throws open the door that no
one thinks to bolt. "Have you seen the dead man?" she asks. "They
just fished him out."

There has been another drowning. It's a mystery. People have gone to swim in the river for hundreds of years and no one from the village has ever been lost. But when strangers from the refinery try to swim, they put a toe in the water and are sucked right down.

La Chata's mother mutters to hear the news. She understands more Spanish than anyone guesses. She also knows about Tita Carmen, that she goes to the city now and then and gets arrested and comes home all bloody. It's politics. She's a wild woman now.

The old man rocks in the hammock, grinning to hear Tita Carmen's voice. "Yes, there's a war coming," he says. "We're going to have another war."

The music stops and the radio announcer tells about the bomb that went off in the city, five people dead.

"*Ay, qué feo!*" cries Tita Carmen. "Who could do a thing like that?"

"You're the revolutionary!" says the old man who should know better than to use that word out loud.

"*Ay,* but how awful! Maybe I'm not after all."

The mother thinks Tita Carmen will soon be wilder than ever. She thinks she understands. When she was a girl and her parents were killed, hadn't she been the same? How could people be that way, she'd asked. Violence was wrong. How could people kill? Why did they have to argue? Why couldn't they live in peace? It bothered her so much, it hurt, and it bothered her until she wished she had a gun and could kill them all.

"Revolutionary or not," says the old man, "you're welcome in my humble home."

"It's Chata's home," says Tita Carmen. "She built it."

Toño could have built it. He helped to build the refinery. Gave up on school and let the fields grow wild and took a salary. Once it's built, La Chata warned him, then what will you do? They'll only need people with skills. You'll have no job and we'll have lost our land.

But he took the job and bought bits of black lace for Marilinda and electric curlers to do her hair. He bought a mahogany wardrobe and a Japanese music box.

"I've been promoted to foreman," he said one day, and when he refused to fake the time sheets, they pushed him under a truck.

"Will your job be waiting for you when the cast comes off?" asked La Chata.

"My Chata!" says the old man. "When she was a girl, I didn't want her to go to school. Think of that! Now she's a modern woman, with an education and a government job, and probably she has herself a man there in town." He swings wildly in the hammock until his wife helps him back to the chair. "Well, she's old enough now. A woman of twenty-two. She has the right."

In town, La Chata eats breakfast in the marketplace, a glass of orange juice with two egg yolks floating on top. The women who squat with their baskets and tubs and children cluck to see her hurry. They are fat and imperious as ever and don't know this life won't last.

Chata takes the bus to work, to the new school the government built for the people. She waits for the director to come and unlock the gate.

Two women in the opposite doorway invite her to sit inside with them, out of the sun. Their room is like a cave. The women are embroidering together, working on the same piece of black velvet. The fabric is stretched on a frame at table height and the two women sit at either end, rolls of silk thread set up between them like a chess game. They bend over the velvet with their needles. La Chata's eyes hurt, watching the flowers unfolding in the dark.

I'll end up blind like my father, she thinks, and she wonders again what she ought to do. If she got leave from work, maybe she could drag him off to the city. It might be cataracts and they could operate. But without promising him his sight back, she'll never convince him to go. What if it isn't cataracts? It would be terrible to raise false hopes.

La Chata would like to talk it over with someone. She thinks of the director. He knows something of the world and he would listen carefully. But no, she doesn't like the way he listens, curious to learn the workings of the savage mind.

He arrives at 8:15 and she hurries across the street to join him. When he unlocks the door, La Chata props it open with some bricks from the street.

Inside, the patio is mercilessly sunny. There's a water tap in the corner where the garden is supposed to grow, and by the other wall, two filthy toilets without doors. The classrooms are painted a sickening green. The windows which face the street have no panes, and the north wind blows in dust, and the people passing by toss in garbage.

The director leaves to go to breakfast and Chata gets the broom. She sweeps out paper, dirt, fruit rinds and broken glass as the children start to arrive. The girls wear short cotton dresses that let their panties show. The boys wear dirty little T-shirts and no shoes. Some of the children help with the cleaning. They carry garbage out to the street. Others cup their hands for water from the tap while some just scream and jump around.

When the school day starts, the children go into the classroom and screech out a high-pitched song, incomprehensible and in perfect unison. They jump up and down from their seats and run in and out of the room. The fruit vendor stations himself at the door and La Chata doesn't care. The children run out to buy candy and oranges, they dash to her desk so she can approve their scribbles. The children crack nuts and spit out shells and orange seeds to settle in the dust. They take out pencil stubs and scraps of paper and sprawl on the ground while they write out their vowels. Sometimes two children will consult with each other and point at La Chata before asking her for money.

Two nurses appear in the patio and set up folding chairs. They vaccinated the schoolchildren months ago and now they have been sent to immunize the rest of town. People have been notified. The nurses sit on their folding chairs and wait.

When the children go home, there's a hot wind in the street and La Chata goes walking. There are five dark little stores in town that use loudspeakers to advertise their wares. Maybe the owners will announce that the nurses have come. She visits the stores and talks to fat, bare-chested men. Then she returns to the school.

The women in the opposite doorway call to her. The nurses are sitting and waiting, bored in the sun.

The afternoon class arrives. Children drink from the tap and splash each other and scream. Girls whisper together and take turns on the open toilets while their friends form nervous walls.

La Chata used to think education was the first step, the key. Teach the people to read, she thought. But the only books they sell in town are illustrated romances and comics. Once she wanted to study. She wanted to help children and her parents and her kid brother Toño. And herself. Now La Chata doesn't read, except when someone hands her something political. Then she studies the ideas carefully for clues—how to move forward—and she is careful not to talk about what she reads.

At the end of the day, Chusito's panel truck is waiting outside the school. When he's traveling this route, he always stops to offer the teacher a ride as far as the highway turnoff. They head down the hill and bump along the rutted road, through the high grass outside of town, while Chusito brags about his ignorance.

When they reach the river, he slows the truck as he drives through the shallows. He opens the door, grabs a bucket from somewhere at his feet, and fills it with water.

"Radiator trouble." He rolls the "r's" sonorously, as though announcing the winner of a race.

He leaves La Chata at the turnoff and she gets a lift in a trailer truck. Buses don't run to the village but there's always someone driving out toward the refinery that's still being built. This truck carries concrete tubes. The sun is going down and they follow the river's edge.

It's dark when La Chata leaves the truck. Now it's an hour's walk to home: the familiar path, the fireflies, wind roaring in the wild bamboo. The stars whirl and move above her like animals uncoiling in the sky, and somewhere there's a fiesta. She can hear the music pulsing through the night. It's dark now, but she knows where she's going. Here, at least, she knows the way. She can see the cross on the riverbank, marking the spot where strangers drown.

The old man is talking about modern medicine. It's a new world, full of wonders, at least for some people. His daughter Chata would know.

Toño comes out of the room. "Did you hear the radio? In the capital, everyone's gone on strike."

Everyone is silent.

Then the old man says, "Do you think La Chata is coming home tonight?" You never knew when she might get a ride. He smiles. "She drinks beer now," he says. "Two, three, or four bottles, like a man."

The mother hopes La Chata will get home. Someday she'd like to ask her about the old man's eyes, if there isn't something that can be done. But you can't have private talks in Zapotec. What you say in dialect belongs to the village, the whole village hears you, the old man would hear her talking about him. In dialect, words spread so fast, she believes they enter dreams. He would hear every word, even in his sleep.

Someday she'd like to talk to her daughter, privately, about all this politics and the trouble that's coming, but there are no words in Zapotec for some of the things she'd like to know. The mother doesn't understand about politics. She speaks no Spanish, except for curse words, and so she has no opinions.

Marilinda is looking for split ends, but even she can hear the radio going on—bombs and shootings and strikes.

The mother thinks about her daughter. La Chata never greets anyone with hugs anymore. No hearty *abrazos* for her. The mother has watched her daughter shake hands with people, cool and polite. Was that part of being modern? Or was it part of being a beautiful girl with a job? Of having to take rides in trucks with any strange man going your way?

Is La Chata happy? she wonders. What is her life like?

And she wonders, What is going to become of us?

The old man is the first to hear someone at the door. He struggles to sit up in the hammock and reaches for his cane. He slams it against the pounded earth floor.

"My Chata!" he says.

DIANE LEFER ON COMMUNITY

For years, I felt very much a member of my neighborhood community in New York City but knew no other writers and worked in
complete isolation. Anxious to meet people who shared my writerly
concerns, I went to an open reading, where a man invited me to attend a session of his workshop. I happily followed him back to his
apartment, where of course there was no workshop though I did have
an interesting—if uneasy—time hearing about this stranger's life as
a recently released prisoner on parole.

Then, in 1977, a story of mine was published and led to an invitation to a prestigious writers' conference where older male writers
with modest fame drank too much and sexually exploited, while
physically and verbally abusing, the more attractive of the young
hopeful female writers. They either mocked or ignored everyone else.
I returned home thinking how lucky I'd been that I'd never social-
ized with writers before. Nothing would ever stop me from writing,
but—aside from a couple of new friends I did make in that hostile environment—I no longer wanted anything to do with other people in
my field.

So what made me apply to The Writers Community a few years
later?

My writing was hit or miss. I knew I needed other writers to talk
shop and exchange manuscripts, to learn from. I needed other people
in my life who wouldn't keep telling me how stupid I was to live on
a starvation budget while working temp jobs and writing fiction no
publisher wanted. I had a good feeling about The Writers
Community workshop, which was to be led by Nicholasa Mohr. I felt
safe sending my work to a woman, besides which I'd enjoyed
Nicholasa's fiction about Puerto Rican New York. (Years earlier, I'd
dropped out of college and run away to Mexico. Many of the stories
I was writing took place there and I had a special interest in Latino
writing, which had only grown stronger after one of the drunken
stars of that writers' conference dismissed the work of all Spanish-
tradition writers—including Cervantes, Borges, and García
Márquez—as too parochial to be real literature.)

From the first session of Nicholasa's workshop, I felt I'd found a home. Our group ranged all over the map in terms of age and background and race and culture. What we had in common was a commitment to writing and to mutual respect. We genuinely wanted to see one another do well. I learned a lot about editing others and myself, but I also found what I most needed to see: that creative people—including the most talented and professional—don't have to be narcissistic and competitive and exempt from the dictates of simple human courtesy.

I've since gone on to teach and have tried to replicate that sense of community and support. Writing is a private act; sharing it is intimate. I keep that in mind whether at Vermont College with graduate students or in the Bronx at the workshop I led for senior citizens, where one woman told me, "This is the one place in my life where I talk and someone listens."

The Writers Community nurtured me while helping to hone my skills as writer, teacher, and listener.

DIANE LEFER *is the author of the short story collection* The Circles I Move In. *She teaches in the M.F.A. Writing Program at Vermont College and the Writers' Program at UCLA Extension. A native New Yorker, she recently relocated to Long Beach, California.*

DAVID LOW

Winterblossom Garden

I

I have no photographs of my father. One hot Saturday in June, my camera slung over my shoulder, I take the subway from Greenwich Village to Chinatown. I switch to the M local, which becomes an elevated train after it crosses the Williamsburg Bridge. I am going to Ridgewood, Queens, where I spent my childhood. I sit in a car that is almost empty; I feel the loud rumble of the whole train through the hard seat. Someday, I think, wiping the sweat from my face, they'll tear this el down, as they've torn down the others.

I get off at Fresh Pond Road and walk the five blocks from the station to my parents' restaurant. At the back of the store in the kitchen, I find my father packing an order: white cartons of food fit neatly into a brown paper bag. As the workers chatter in Cantonese, I smell the food cooking: spare ribs, chicken lo mein, sweet and pungent pork, won ton soup. My father, who has just turned seventy-three, wears a wrinkled white short-sleeve shirt and a cheap maroon tie, even in this weather. He dabs his face with a handkerchief.

"Do you need money?" he asks in Chinese, as he takes the order to the front of the store. I notice that he walks slower than usual. Not that his walk is ever very fast; he usually walks with quiet assurance, a man who knows who he is and where he is going. Other people will just have to wait until he gets there.

"Not this time," I answer in English. I laugh. I haven't borrowed money from him in years, but he still asks. My father and I have almost always spoken different languages.

"I want to take your picture, Dad."

"Not now, too busy." He hands the customer the order and rings the cash register.

"It will only take a minute."

He stands reluctantly beneath the green awning in front of the store, next to the gold-painted letters on the window:

WINTERBLOSSOM GARDEN
CHINESE-AMERICAN RESTAURANT
WE SERVE THE FINEST FOOD

I look through the camera viewfinder.

"Smile," I say.

Instead my father holds his left hand with the crooked pinky against his stomach. I have often wondered about that pinky: is it a souvenir of some street fight in his youth? He wears a jade ring on his index finger. His hair, streaked with gray, is greased down as usual; his face looks a little pale. Most of the day, he remains at the restaurant. I snap the shutter.

"Go see your mother," he says slowly in English.

According to my mother, in 1929 my father entered this country illegally by jumping off the boat as it neared Ellis Island and swimming to Hoboken, New Jersey; there he managed to board a train to New York, even though he knew no English and had not one American cent in his pockets. Whether or not the story is true, I like to imagine my father hiding in the washroom on the train, dripping wet with fatigue and feeling triumphant. Now he was in America, where anything could happen. He found a job scooping ice cream at a dance hall in Chinatown. My mother claims that before he married her, he liked to gamble his nights away and drink with scandalous women. After two years in this country, he opened his restaurant with money he had borrowed from friends in Chinatown who already ran their own businesses. My father chose Ridgewood for the store's location because he mistook the community's name for "Richwood." In such a lucky place, he told my mother, his restaurant was sure to succeed.

When I was growing up, my parents spent most of their days in Winterblossom Garden. Before going home after school, I would stop at the restaurant. The walls then were a hideous pale green with red numbers painted in Chinese characters and Roman numerals above the side booths. In days of warm weather huge fans whirred from the ceiling. My mother would sit at a table in the back, where she would make egg rolls. She began by placing generous handfuls of meat-and-cabbage filling on squares of thin white dough. Then she delicately folded up each piece of dough, checking to make sure the filling was totally sealed inside, like a mummy wrapped in bandages. Finally, with a small brush she spread beaten eggs on the outside of each white roll. As I watched her steadily produce a tray of these un-cooked creations, she never asked me about school; she was more concerned that my shirt was sticking out of my pants or that my hair was disheveled.

"Are you hungry?" my mother would ask in English. Although my parents had agreed to speak only Chinese in my presence, she often broke this rule when my father wasn't in the same room. Whether I wanted to eat or not, I was sent into the kitchen, where my father would repeat my mother's question. Then without waiting for an answer, he would prepare for me a bowl of beef with snow peas or a small portion of steamed fish. My parents assumed that as long as I ate well, everything would be fine. If I said "Hello" or "Thank you" in Chinese, I was allowed to choose whatever dish I liked; often I ordered a hot turkey sandwich. I liked the taste of burnt rice soaked in tea.

I would wait an hour or so for my mother to walk home with me. During that time, I would go to the front of the store, put a dime in the jukebox and press buttons for a currently popular song. It might be D3: "Bye, Bye, Love." Then I would lean on the back of the bench where customers waited for takeouts; I would stare out the large window that faced the street. The world outside seemed vast, hostile and often sad.

Across the way, I could see Rosa's Italian Bakery, the Western Union office and Von Ronn's soda fountain. Why didn't we live in Chinatown? I wondered. Or San Francisco? In a neighborhood that was predominantly German, I had no Chinese friends. No matter how many bottles of Coca-Cola I drank, I would still be different from the others. They were fond of calling me "Skinny Chink" when I won games of stoop ball. I wanted to have blond curly hair and blue eyes; I didn't understand why my father didn't have a ranch like the rugged cowboys on television.

Now Winterblossom Garden has wood paneling on the walls, formica tables and aluminum Roman numerals over the mock-leather booths. Several years ago, when the ceiling was lowered, the whirring fans were removed; a huge air-conditioning unit was installed. The jukebox has been replaced by Muzak. My mother no longer makes the egg rolls; my father hires enough help to do that.

Some things remain the same. My father has made few changes in the menu, except for the prices; the steady customers know they can always have the combination plates. In a glass case near the cash register, cardboard boxes overflow with bags of fortune cookies and almond candies that my father gives away free to children. The first dollar bill my parents ever made hangs framed on the wall above the register. Next to that dollar, a picture of my parents taken twenty years ago recalls a time when they were raising four children at once, paying mortgages, and putting in the bank every cent that didn't go toward bills. Although it was a hard time for them, my mother's face is radiant, as if she has just won the top prize at a beauty pageant; she wears a flower-print dress with a large white collar. My father has on a suit with wide lapels that was tailored in Chinatown; he is smiling a rare smile.

My parents have a small brick house set apart from the other buildings on the block. Most of their neighbors have lived in Ridgewood all their lives. As I ring the bell and wait for my mother to answer, I notice that the maple tree in front of the house has died. All that is left is a gray ghost; bare branches lie in the gutter. If I took a picture of this tree, I think, the printed image would resemble a negative.

"The gas man killed it when they tore up the street," my mother says. She watches television as she lies back on the gold sofa like a queen, her head resting against a pillow. A documentary about wildlife in Africa is on the screen; gazelles dance across a dusty plain. My mother likes soap operas but they aren't shown on weekends. In the evenings she will watch almost anything except news specials and police melodramas.

"Why don't you get a new tree planted?"

"We would have to get a permit," she answers. "The sidewalk belongs to the city. Then we would have to pay for the tree."

"It would be worth it," I say. "Doesn't it bother you, seeing a dead tree every day? You should find someone to cut it down."

My mother does not answer. She has fallen asleep. These days she can doze off almost as soon as her head touches the pillow. Six years ago she had a nervous breakdown. When she came home from the hospital she needed to take naps in the afternoon. Soon the naps became a permanent refuge, a way to forget her loneliness for an hour or two. She no longer needed to work in the store. Three of her children were married. I was away at art school and planned to live on my own when I graduated.

"I have never felt at home in America," my mother once told me.

Now as she lies there, I wonder what she is dreaming. I would like her to tell me her darkest dream. Although we speak the same language, there has always been an ocean between us. She does not wish to know what I think alone at night, what I see of the world with my camera.

My mother pours two cups of tea from the porcelain teapot that has always been in its wicker basket on the kitchen table. On the sides of the teapot, a maiden dressed in a jade-green gown visits a bearded emperor at his palace near the sky. The maiden waves a vermillion fan.

"I bet you still don't know how to cook," my mother says. She places a plate of steamed roast pork buns before me.

"Mom, I'm not hungry."

"If you don't eat, you will get sick."

I take a bun from the plate but it is too hot. My mother hands me a napkin so I can put the bun down. Then she peels a banana in front of me.

"I'm not obsessed with food like you," I say.

"What's wrong with eating?"

She looks at me as she takes a big bite of the banana.

"I'm going to have a photography show at the end of the summer."

"Are you still taking pictures of old buildings falling down? How ugly! Why don't you take happier pictures?"

"I thought you would want to come," I answer. "It's not easy to get a gallery."

"If you were married," she says, her voice becoming unusually soft, "you would take better pictures. You would be happy."

"I don't know what you mean. Why do you think getting married will make me happy?"

My mother looks at me as if I have spoken in Serbo-Croatian. She always gives me this look when I say something she does not want to hear. She finishes her banana; then she puts the plate of food away. Soon she stands at the sink, turns on the hot water and washes dishes. My mother learned long ago that silence has a power of its own.

She takes out a blue cookie tin from the dining room cabinet. Inside this tin my mother keeps her favorite photographs. Whenever I am ready to leave, my mother brings it to the living room and opens it on the coffee table. She knows I cannot resist looking at these pictures again; I will sit down next to her on the sofa for at least another hour. Besides the portraits of the family, my mother has images of people I have never met: her father, who owned a poultry store on Pell Street and didn't get a chance to return to China before he died; my father's younger sister, who still runs a pharmacy in Rio de Janeiro (she sends the family an annual supply of cough drops); my mother's cousin Kay, who died at thirty, a year after she came to New York from Hong Kong. Although my mother has a story to tell for each photograph, she refuses to speak about Kay, as if the mere mention of her name will bring back her ghost to haunt us all.

My mother always manages to find pictures I have not seen before; suddenly I discover I have a relative who is a mortician in Vancouver. I pick up a portrait of Uncle Lao-Hu, a silver-haired man with a goatee who owned a curio shop on Mott Street until he retired last year and moved to Hawaii. In a color print, he stands in the doorway of his store, holding a bamboo Moon Man in front of him, as if it were a bowling trophy. The statue, which is actually two feet tall, has a staff in its left hand, while its right palm balances a peach, a sign of long life. The top of the Moon Man's head protrudes in the shape of an eggplant; my mother believes that such a head contains an endless wealth of wisdom.

"Your Uncle Lao-Hu is a wise man, too," my mother says, "except when he's in love. When he still owned the store, he fell in love with his women customers all the time. He was always losing money because he gave away his merchandise to any woman who smiled at him."

I see my uncle's generous arms full of gifts: a silver Buddha, an ivory dragon, a pair of emerald chopsticks.

"These women confused him," she adds. "That's what happens when a Chinese man doesn't get married."

My mother shakes her head and sighs.

"In his last letter, Lao-Hu invited me to visit him in Honolulu. Your father refuses to leave the store."

"Why don't you go anyway?"

"I can't leave your father alone." She stares at the pictures scattered on the coffee table.

"Mom, why don't you do something for yourself? I thought you were going to start taking English lessons."

"Your father thinks it would be a waste of time."

While my mother puts the cookie tin away, I stand up to stretch my legs. I gaze at a photograph that hangs on the wall above the sofa: my parents' wedding picture. My mother was matched to my father; she claims that if her own father had been able to repay the money that Dad spent to bring her to America, she might never have married him at all. In the wedding picture she wears a stunned expression. She is dressed in a luminous gown of ruffles and lace; the train spirals at her feet. As she clutches a bouquet tightly against her stomach, she might be asking, "What am I doing? Who is this man?" My father's face is thinner than it is now. His tuxedo is too small for him; the flower in his lapel droops. He hides his hand with the crooked pinky behind his back.

I have never been sure if my parents really love each other. I have only seen them kiss at their children's weddings. They never touch each other in public. When I was little, I often thought they went to sleep in the clothes they wore to work.

Before I leave, my mother asks me to take her picture. Unlike my father she likes to pose for photographs as much as possible. When her children still lived at home, she would leave snapshots of herself all around the house; we could not forget her, no matter how hard we tried.

She changes her blouse, combs her hair and redoes her eyebrows. Then I follow her out the back door into the garden, where she kneels down next to the rose bush. She touches one of the yellow roses.

"Why don't you sit on the front steps?" I ask as I peer through the viewfinder. "It will be more natural."

"No," she says firmly. "Take the picture now."

She smiles without opening her mouth. I see for the first time that she has put on a pair of dangling gold earrings. Her face has grown round as the moon with the years. She has developed wrinkles under the eyes, but like my father, she hardly shows her age. For the past ten years, she has been fifty-one. Everyone needs a fantasy to help them stay alive: my mother believes she is perpetually beautiful, even if my father has not complimented her in years.

After I snap the shutter, she plucks a rose.

As we enter the kitchen through the back door, I can hear my father's voice from the next room.

"Who's he talking to?" I ask.

"He's talking to the goldfish," she answers. "I have to live with this man."

My father walks in, carrying a tiny can of fish food.

"You want a girlfriend?" he asks, out of nowhere. "My friend has a nice daughter. She knows how to cook Chinese food."

"Dad, she sounds perfect for you."

"She likes to stay home," my mother adds. "She went to college and reads books like you."

"I'll see you next year," I say.

That evening in the darkroom at my apartment, I develop and print my parents' portraits. I hang the pictures side by side to dry on a clothesline in the bathroom. As I feel my parents' eyes staring at me, I turn away. Their faces look unfamiliar in the fluorescent light.

II

At the beginning of July, my mother calls me at work.

"Do you think you can take off next Monday morning?" she asks.

"Why?"

"Your father has to go to the hospital for some tests. He looks awful."

We sit in the back of a taxi on the way to a hospital in Forest Hills. I am sandwiched between my mother and father. The skin of my father's face is pale yellow. During the past few weeks he has lost fifteen pounds; his wrinkled suit is baggy around the waist. My mother sleeps with her head tilted to one side until the taxi hits a bump on the road. She wakes up startled, as if afraid she has missed a stop on the train.

"Don't worry," my father says weakly. He squints as he turns his head toward the window. "The doctors will give me pills. Everything will be fine."

"Don't say anything," my mother says. "Too much talk will bring bad luck."

My father takes two crumpled dollar bills from his jacket and places them in my hand.

"For the movies," he says. I smile, without mentioning it costs more to go to a film these days.

My mother opens her handbag and takes out a compact. She has forgotten to put on her lipstick.

The hospital waiting room has beige walls. My mother and I follow my father as he makes his way slowly to a row of seats near an open window.

"Fresh air is important," he used to remind me on a sunny day when I would read a book in bed. Now after we sit down, he keeps quiet. I hear the sound of plates clattering from the coffee shop in the next room.

"Does anyone want some breakfast?" I ask.

"Your father can't eat anything before the tests," my mother warns.

"What about you?"

"I'm not hungry," she says.

My father reaches over to take my hand in his. He considers my palm.

"Very, very lucky," he says. "You will have lots of money."

I laugh. "You've been saying that ever since I was born."

He puts on his glasses crookedly and touches a curved line near the top of my palm.

"Be patient," he says.

My mother rises suddenly.

"Why are they making us wait so long? Do you think they forgot us?"

While she walks over to speak to a nurse at the reception desk, my father leans toward me.

"Remember to take care of your mother."

The doctors discover that my father has stomach cancer. They decide to operate immediately. According to them, my father has already lost so much blood that it is a miracle he is still alive.

The week of my father's operation, I sleep at my parents' house. My mother has kept my bedroom on the second floor the way it was before I moved out. A square room, it gets the afternoon light. Dust covers the top of my old bookcase. The first night I stay over I find a

pinhole camera on a shelf in the closet: I made it when I was twelve
from a cylindrical Quaker Oats box. When I lie back on the yellow
comforter that covers my bed, I see the crack in the ceiling that I
once called the Yangtze River, the highway for tea merchants and
vagabonds.

At night I help my mother close the restaurant. I do what she
and my father have done together for the past forty-three years. At
ten o'clock I turn off the illuminated white sign above the front entrance. After all the customers leave and the last waiter says good-
bye, I lock the front door and flip over the sign that says "Closed."
Then I shut off the radio and the back lights. While I refill the glass
case with bottles of duck sauce and packs of cigarettes, my mother
empties the cash register. She puts all the money in white cartons
and packs them in brown paper bags. My father thought up that
idea long ago.

In the past when they have walked the three blocks home, they
have given the appearance of carrying bags of food. The one time my
father was attacked by three teenagers, my mother was sick in bed.
My father scared the kids off by pretending he knew kung fu. When
he got home, he showed me his swollen left hand and smiled.

"Don't tell your mother."

On the second night we walk home together, my mother says: "I
could never run the restaurant alone. I would have to sell it. I have
four children and no one wants it."

I say nothing, unwilling to start an argument.

Later my mother and I eat Jell-o in the kitchen. A cool breeze
blows through the window.

"Maybe I will sleep tonight," my mother says. She walks out to
the back porch to sit on one of the two folding chairs. My bedroom is
right above the porch; as a child I used to hear my parents talking
late into the night, their paper fans rustling.

After reading a while in the living room, I go upstairs to take a
shower. When I am finished, I hear my mother calling my name
from downstairs.

I find her dressed in her bathrobe, opening the dining room cabinet.

"Someone has stolen the money," she says. She walks nervously into the living room and looks under the lamp table.

"What are you talking about?" I ask.

"Maybe we should call the police," she suggests. "I can't find the money we brought home tonight."

She starts to pick up the phone.

"Wait. Have you checked everywhere? Where do you usually put it?"

"I thought I locked it in your father's closet but it isn't there."

"I'll look around," I say. "Why don't you go back to sleep?"

She lies back on the sofa.

"How can I sleep?" she asks. "I told your father a long time ago to sell the restaurant but he wouldn't listen."

I search the first floor. I look in the shoe closet, behind the television, underneath the dining-room table, in the clothes hamper. Finally after examining all the kitchen cupboards without any luck, I open the refrigerator to take out something to drink. The three cartons of money are on the second shelf, next to the mayonnaise and the strawberry jam.

When I bring the cartons to the living room, my mother sits up on the sofa, amazed.

"Well," she says, "how did they ever get *there*?"

She opens one of them. The crisp dollar bills inside are cold as ice.

The next day I talk on the telephone to my father's physician. He informs me that the doctors have succeeded in removing the malignancy before it has spread. My father will remain in intensive care for at least a week.

In the kitchen my mother irons a tablecloth.

"The doctors are impressed by Dad's willpower, considering his age," I tell her.

"A fortune-teller on East Broadway told him that he will live to be a hundred," she says.

That night I dream that I am standing at the entrance to

Winterblossom Garden. A taxi stops in front of the store. My father jumps out, dressed in a bathrobe and slippers.

"I'm almost all better," he tells me. "I want to see how the business is doing without me."

In a month my father is ready to come home. My sister Elizabeth, the oldest child, picks him up at the hospital. At the house the whole family waits for him.

When Elizabeth's car arrives my mother and I are already standing on the front steps. My sister walks around the car to open my father's door. He cannot get out by himself. My sister offers him a hand but as he reaches out to grab it, he misses and falls back in his seat.

Finally my sister helps him stand up, his back a little stooped. While my mother remains on the steps, I run to give a hand.

My father does not fight our help. His skin is dry and pale but no longer yellow. As he walks forward, staring at his feet, I feel his whole body shaking against mine. Only now, as he leans his weight on my arm, do I begin to understand how easily my father might have died. He seems as light as a sparrow.

When we reach the front steps, my father raises his head to look at my mother. She stares at him a minute, then turns away to open the door. Soon my sister and I are leading him to the living-room sofa, where we help him lie back. My mother has a pillow and a blanket ready. She sits down on the coffee table in front of him. I watch them hold each other's hands.

III

At the beginning of September my photography exhibit opens at a cooperative gallery on West 13th Street. I have chosen to hang only a dozen pictures, not much to show for ten years of work. About sixty people come to the opening, more than I expected; I watch them from a corner of the room, now and then overhearing a conversation I would like to ignore.

After an hour I decide I have stayed too long. As I walk around the gallery, hunting for a telephone, I see my parents across the room. My father calls out my name in Chinese; he has gained back all his weight and appears to be in better shape than many of the people around him. As I make my way toward my parents, I hear him talking loudly in bad English to a short young woman who stares at one of my portraits.

"That's my wife," he says. "If you like it, you should buy it."

"Maybe I will," the young woman says. She points to another photograph. "Isn't that you?"

My father laughs. "No, that's my brother."

My mother hands me a brown paper bag.

"Leftovers from dinner," she tells me. "You didn't tell me you were going to show my picture. It's the best one in the show."

I take my parents for a personal tour.

"Who is that?" my father asks. He stops at a photograph of a naked woman covered from the waist down by a pile of leaves as she sits in the middle of a forest.

"She's a professional model," I lie.

"She needs to gain some weight," my mother says.

A few weeks after the show has closed, I have lunch with my parents at the restaurant. After we finish our meal, my father walks into the kitchen to scoop ice cream for dessert. My mother opens her handbag. She takes out a worn manila envelope and hands it to me across the table.

"I found this in a box while I was cleaning house," she says. "I want you to have it."

Inside the envelope I find a portrait of my father, taken when he was still a young man. He does not smile, but his eyes shine like wet black marbles. He wears a polka-dot tie; a plaid handkerchief hangs out of the front pocket of his suit jacket. My father has never cared about his clothes matching. Even when he was young, he liked to grease down his hair with brilliantine.

"Your father's cousin was a doctor in Hong Kong," my mother

tells me. "After my eighteenth birthday, he came to my parents' house and showed them this picture. He said your father would make the perfect husband because he was handsome and very smart. Grandma gave me the picture before I got on the boat to America."

"I'll have it framed right away."

My father returns with three dishes of chocolate ice cream balanced on a silver tray.

"You want to work here?" he asks me.

"Your father wants to sell the business next year," my mother says. "He feels too old to run a restaurant."

"I'd just lose money," I say. "Besides, Dad, you're not old."

He does not join us for dessert. Instead, he dips his napkin in a glass of water and starts to wipe the table. I watch his dish of ice cream melt.

When I am ready to leave, my parents walk me to the door.

"Next time, I'll take you uptown to see a movie," I say as we step outside.

"Radio City?" my father asks.

"They don't show movies there now," my mother reminds him.

"I'll cook dinner for you at my apartment."

My father laughs.

"We'll eat out," my mother suggests.

My parents wait in front of Winterblossom Garden until I reach the end of the block. I turn and wave. With her heels on, my mother is the same height as my father. She waves back for both of them. I would like to take their picture, but I forgot to bring my camera.

DAVID LOW *works as a book editor and writer. His short stories have appeared in the* Ploughshares Reader, American Families, *and* Under Western Eyes. *The recipient of a Wallace Stegner Writing Fellowship, a New York State Arts Council Grant, and fellowships from the MacDowell Colony, Yaddo, and the National Endowment for the Arts, he lives in New York City.*

THOMAS LUX

The People of the Other Village

hate the people of this village
and would nail our hats
to our heads for refusing in their presence to remove them
or staple our hands to our foreheads
for refusing to salute them
if we did not hurt them first: mail them packages of rats,
mix their flour at night with broken glass.
We do this, they do that.
They peel the larynx from one of our brothers' throats.
We devein one of their sisters.
The quicksand pits they built were good.
Our amputation teams were better.
We trained some birds to steal their wheat.
They sent to us exploding ambassadors of peace.
They do this, we do that.
We canceled our sheep imports.
They no longer bought our blankets.
We mocked their greatest poet
and when that had no effect
we parodied the way they dance
which did cause pain, so they, in turn, said our God
was leprous, hairless.
We do this, they do that.
Ten thousand (10,000) years, ten thousand
(10,000) brutal, beautiful years.

An Horatian Notion

The thing gets made, gets built, and you're the slave
who rolls the log beneath the block, then another,
then pushes the block, then pulls a log
from the rear back to the front
again and then again it goes beneath the block,
and so on. It's how a thing gets made—not
because you're sensitive, or you get genetic-lucky,
or God says: Here's a nice family,
seven children, let's see: this one in charge
of the village dunghill, these two die of buboes, this one
Kierkegaard, this one a drooling

nincompoop, this one clerk, this one cooper.
You need to love the thing you do—birdhouse building,
painting tulips exclusively, whatever—and then
you do it
so consciously driven
by your unconscious
that the thing becomes a wedge
that splits a stone and between the halves
the wedge that grows, i.e., the thing
is solid but with a soul,
a life of its own. Inspiration, the donnée,

the gift, the bolt of fire
down the arm that makes the art?
Grow up! Give me, please, a break!
You make the thing because you love the thing
and you love the thing because someone else loved it
enough to make you love it.
And with that your heart like a tent peg pounded

toward the earth's core.
And with that your heart on a beam burns
through the ionosphere.
And with that you go to work.

THOMAS LUX*'s most recent books of poetry are* Split Horizon *and*
New and Selected Poems, 1975–1995. *He has taught at The Writers
Community and currently directs and teaches in the M.F.A. program in
poetry at Sarah Lawrence College.*

WILLIAM MATTHEWS

The Dream

A sparse hill. Above it, the early evening sky, a flat,
blue-gray slate color like a planetarium ceiling
before the show's begun. Just over the hill and rising,
like a moon, the stuttering thwack of helicopter rotors

and then from behind the hill the machine itself
came straight up and stood in the air like a tossed
ball stopped at its zenith. It shone a beam of light
on me and a voice that seemed to travel through

the very beam intoned—that's the right word,
intoned—*We know where you are and we can find
you anytime. Don't write that poem. You know the one
we mean.* Then all was gone—the voice, the beam,

the helicopter and the dream. I'd lain down for a nap
that afternoon and slept through dusk. Outside the sky
was flat, blue-gray and slate. I'd no idea what poem
they meant. I lay swaddled in sweat five minutes

or an hour, I don't know. I made coffee and walked,
each muscle sprung like a trap, as far as the bridge
over the falls. I'd have said my mind was empty,
or thronged with dread, but now I understand

that in some way I also don't know how to say
I was composing with each trudge these words.
Until I steal from fear and silence what I'm not
supposed to say, these words will have to do.

WILLIAM MATTHEWS ON COMMUNITY

Writers belong to a special community of other writers and readers, but this special community has no spatial reality, and thus its relationship to the larger community is like that of individual leaves in a forest. An outfit like The Writers Community gives writers a home for their dedication to writing and a platform from which to make themselves heard in the larger community.

WILLIAM MATTHEWS *is the author of ten collections of poetry.* Time and Money, *his latest, received the National Book Critics Circle Award. He has also published two books of translations and a volume of essays. He has taught at The Writers Community and currently teaches at the City College of New York.*

FLORENCE CASSEN MAYERS

Your Poem: Boat to Saltaire

Delete episodes of rain,
details of leaf fall,
erase all reference to sunset,
eliminate geese migration,
cross out grey, keep Great South Bay,
keep waterway, change wetland,
cancel deer, omit gull, swan, light,
lightning's OK, unsure about lighthouse.
Find a better word for evening.
Cargo's good, exploit
contents of King Kullen cartons,
broom handle, sponge mop,
six-pack, eggs, Kellogg's, bread. Keep
cat in carrying case, pushcart.
Expose like radar East Island's
green outline before it appears. Save
Forgive the man who's sleeping, save
Forgive me, save
the ferry *Stranger*
brings me to you in the dark.

FLORENCE CASSEN MAYERS *has published her poetry in the* Atlantic Monthly, Poetry, Paris Review, Western Humanities Review, Epoch, Poetry Northwest, *and other publications. She received the Madeline Sadin Award from the* New York Quarterly. *She also writes and designs a series of award-winning ABC art books for major museums.*

JANE MILLER

The Poet

You would procure the oil of forgiveness from the angel
at the doors, and get a small branch for a tree
that finds no use until it becomes a bridge over a river.
You have a premonition, while crossing,

about the wood's fate, and rather than step farther,
cross on foot. The wood lies dormant for centuries
until it's dug up and three victims die on it,
scattering the Jews. Unable to discern The
cross from those of two thieves, you place them in the pit
of the city and in the early hours hold each above

your head, and with the third are brought to life
zipping between buildings at high speed, shifting
into fifth out a disembodied ramp.
The thrill in the air is sexual, the ballpark darkened
and the holograph of the shut airport glowing,
your headlamps trained on mall light in fog made
more intimate and infinite by the collapse
of time, cement bits swirling your sealed space
to the strains of violins. It's the dawn of an era.

Time does not improve it. You live in a sunny place
and work in a sealed building. 10 mph on Interstate 405
by 2000. The twentieth century, begun in Vienna, has ended
    in California.
. . . gas meters on your left and electric meters on your right.
Ahead, at the end of a passage, out in the light
a flight of concrete stairs. As you climb

you see the big towers of the financial district
fifty stories high a few blocks away . . .

The sense of entering a city nobly, walking the freeway at night
before it's torn down, hearing Portuguese, German, Japanese,
French, Chinese, seeing views of the bay, metallic, choppy,
and of the suspension bridge, and the ships, this is over.
About the demolition, a few warnings, like those about the
    earthquake.

The clack in the streets of Vienna, a carriage door slamming
and a continuous fountain, though far away, seem no farther
than the broken freeway. The bells of the tower, quiet.
The stones smooth and brilliant in moonlight.

You are in a car with music and air-conditioning and a phone.
Softly, the classical station massages you.
You know in the back of your head
the best of your creative life has been siphoned away
by desire and money, desire in general and money in comparison
with others, but between one abstraction and another you yourself
quietly and fiercely participate in a disappearing place,
one you loved and were prepared to enter
with great humility, bathed in tears and barefoot.

Equipped Thus, You Sought an Entrance Here

I sit akimbo on the top of a stoop splayed
like the set of Russian steppes in *Potemkin*
down which the baby carriage careens
I'm sweating out the sunset
containing poorly my determination
to keep you in my life this time
physically that unforced
puckered smile above your funny jaw
your earnest gaze fake when you see me
which nearly crosses when it's late
you're late of course by now
I expect this although we've only met
a few times since your death
I can't believe the couples of queers
who crowd the booth
a lesbian film debuts
a sultry muggy Friday in the city
I knew as a child to which I come
to see your fate sleeping like a kid again
our roles apparently reversed
for my part I look in on you
and you in turn join me around town
carelessly sometime next week
I catch the film much overhyped
of courtship and desire
the players seem like friends to me not lovers
adolescents experiencing their feelings
calculating their chances there's nothing
like the thrill of your arrival hopeless
endless under the flare of the marquee
you're visibly moved you're going to let me kiss you
peremptorily turning a cheek

disappointing me because from this move on
you go into your withheld self
there but elsewhere as we meander
Little Italy's summer fest Chinatown the outdoor life
maybe live another ten years as a satiny sunset
another few days as an upper air pollutant

JANE MILLER ON COMMUNITY

Since working at The Writers Community, I have been aware of my need to interact with writers outside the academic environment in which I make a living. I had the pleasure of organizing a workshop for the elderly in the Tucson area, under the auspices of the Lila Wallace-Reader's Digest Foundation, and for three years participated in its mysterious success. I say "mysterious" because the workshop went through many alterations and teaching strategies and still maintained enormous appeal in the community. With no official degree to hand out, no awards, no public support, the men and women who participated, under crushing physical conditions for many of them, wrote from the heart and taught me more about vitality and commitment than my many years in the institute of the creative writing program. Perhaps the very nature of an institution drains spontaneity and commitment and leaves many of our young writers disillusioned; or perhaps the older writer has the purest of motivations—expression at any cost, whatever the embarrassment, the lack of formal training, the time demand. In any case, I found the outpouring of writing that spoke from the soul to be inspirational.

JANE MILLER *is the author of* Memory at These Speeds: New and Selected Poems, *among other collections. She has also published* Working Time: Essays on Poetry, Culture, and Travel. *Her awards include a Lila Wallace-Reader's Digest Award, a Guggenheim Fellowship, two National Endowment for the Arts Fellowships, and, for* August Zero, *the Western States Book Award. She has taught at The Writers Community and is currently with the creative writing program at the University of Arizona.*

CAROL MUSKE

The Wish Foundation

O holy talk show host,
who daily gives us twenty minutes,
no holds barred, on loneliness,

who has provided, for my particular
amusement, this fat hairy man
in a T-shirt that says he likes sex,

pronouncing himself an "impressionistic
person": describe now for us the child
sent by the Wish Foundation. Hold up

her photograph, say haltingly, that
she died and is buried here,
as per her last request: to fly to

Los Angeles. Then to fly forever beneath
its shocked geologic expression.
To land in Los Angeles, like Persephone

descending the sunset stairs, out of a sky
the color of pomegranate, and through the curved glass
of the ambulance hatch—to be photographed through

the lengthening reflections of exit signs. Persephone
crossing eight lanes, in the rapids of pure oxygen,
descending, recasting the tidy shape of elegy.

Under the overpass, where kids throw
things down on cars, through the gates
and over the machined hills to machined

stones: descending to be where she wished to be.
Where on clear days you can see the city.
Where you can see down the coast

to the cones of the reactor, settling
on the slide, down to the famous rides
of the famous amusement park

where they load the kids into bolted seats
and spin them around a center fixed, but
on a moving foundation. O talk show host,

somebody had to imagine it: how
they would slide hard into what happens.
Fear and desire for more fear. No despair,

would you say? but that sense of black acceleration,
like a blacker wish. I'd say Grief put that new
dress on her. Grief combed her adorable hair.

Then: *which hand* said friendly old Death.
And she stepped away from the foundation
into a sky that all my life, dear

host, I've seen fill and refill
with indifferent valediction: overhead
those stupid planes from the base

flying wing to wing and their shadows
on the earth, somebody's stupid
idea of perfect symmetry.

De-Icing the Wings

They are de-icing the Eastern shuttle.
Men in yellow masks stand on the wings
in the hard sleet and hose gold smoke
over the hold. The book on Cubism
in her hands shakes when they rev the jets.

She is going somewhere to teach somebody something,
to talk to people sitting in solemn rows,
an orchard of note-takers, writing the words
dadaist disassociation over and over.

She can't find the page in her lecture notes
where Bergson says an image is the visual equivalent
of a musical chord . . . so maybe she can just walk
into the classroom, throw away the book and say:

Here's what your teacher did wrong in her life—
and here's what's wrong out there on the runway.

Look how we try to de-ice the surface,
in large-handed, smoky swipes at intimacy,
not getting down to the fragile metal,
the trouble-armor which, under nonstop,
high stress, disintegrates in thin air!

Something like these hands, students,
which have not held another body with love
in weeks. They hold the book to the heart,
defensively. They keep the fine, stylized
stream of interrogation flowing close
to the text, providing a pure reading of intention

similar to the recognition of hunger in another.
Or like a description of passion in language
utterly riveting, where what the author desires
beats so near to the surface.

If you love literature, question its critics—
who are to that beautiful effort as landing
gear and flaps are to the wings—

still extended beneath your teacher, holding up
as always, growing warmer now, by degrees.

CAROL MUSKE *is the author of six books of poetry, most recently* Red
Trousseau *and* An Octave Above Thunder: New and Selected Poems.
She is also the author of Women and Poetry: Truth, Autobiography and
the Shape of the Self. *As Carol Muske Dukes she has published two novels,*
Dear Digby *and* Saving St. Germ. *Her awards include fellowships from
the Guggenheim Foundation and the National Endowment for the Arts.
She has taught at The Writers Community and currently teaches at the
University of Southern California.*

CHARLOTTE NEKOLA

Alibis

Della leaned over the side of her bed and lifted up the arm of her record player. Celeste had showed her how to tape a penny on the arm instead of buying a new needle. Now Della moved it carefully back to the third cut of *The Doors* album, side one, for the twelfth time that afternoon.

Celeste leaned against the opposite wall and flicked her cigarette into the giant abalone shell Della had given her to use as an ashtray.

"What do you think that song means," Celeste said to Della, "when they say 'break on through to the other side'?"

"Well," Della said, "I think it means, you know, the other side." She said the last as if it should be understood.

"Oh yeah, exactly," Celeste said.

"Yeah, exactly," Della said, and they resided for another few minutes in their agreement. Della fanned herself with a peacock feather, bought along with *A Coney Island of the Mind* at Sherman's Used and Rare Books in downtown Providence. Della had spent the night before at Celeste's, and then they rode the bus downtown together to Sherman's.

Mr. Sherman had caught wind of the times and branched out his repertoire. In one section of the store, he sold incense, rolling paper, glass prisms, and yin-yang medallions, along with the serious-looking paperbacks with grainy black-and-white photographs on the cover, poems by Denise Levertov or Sylvia Plath, something strange by Djuna Barnes. Or a small pocket volume of *Howl* or a magazine called *Evergreen*. Any one of them was inscrutable enough to meet their needs. They liked best what they didn't completely understand.

After the song "Crystal Ship," Della leaned over again and set the arm to replay just that one cut again. No question, you could say it was hypnotic.

"I had to hear it again," she told Celeste. "I mean, I had to."

"I know just what you mean," said Celeste, blowing smoke toward the window.

The voice on the album drew out to a hoarse whisper, a confidential aside, a revelation of the true inside place.

The days are bright
and filled with pain

"That is so true," Della said.

"Yeah," said Celeste.

Enclose me in your
gentle rain

"Crystal meth," said Della. "That's what I heard the crystal ship is. The 'rain' part." Della had never tried this, knew boys who had, but it involved needles. That was over the line for her.

"Do you think it was just that?" Celeste asked.

"No, more," Della said.

"Yeah, more," Celeste said, and although they did not say it, in an obscure way each of them hoped that the "more" part could be them. They thought they would have taken in Jim Morrison, the poet, anywhere in any kind of rain, but neither of them knew exactly what form enclosing him would take.

Now it was time for the piano solo in "Crystal Ship," hollow like a recital in a big dark hall. Della thought it went even deeper than the song itself. She and Celeste lived for the piano solo, had even met a guy at a party that could play it by ear, Nick LoPardo.

They had never tried the solo themselves on the piano, but they had met Nick LoPardo, and that seemed like enough. The fact that he wore his blue jeans low and kept a beer bottle in one hand at all times made it even better. Della and Celeste had stood next to the piano.

"This is the best line," Celeste said. Now Morrison's voice had dropped down to the despair level, bordering on final truth.

Oh tell me where
your freedom lies
the streets are filled
with alibis

"Yeah, alibis," Celeste said. "That is so true. So fucking true."

"But it's not 'the streets are full of alibis,'" Della said.

"What do you mean?"

"It's 'the streets are fields that never die.'"

They pulled the needle back again to the beginning of the cut and let it play.

"You're right. Fields that never die," Celeste said.

"That is so, you know, fucking true," Della said.

They entered the zone of the piano solo again. It was a little like opening a fun house door, entering a dark room with no particular floors or wall, maybe where Steppenwolf had been. Della and Celeste were there now. You could get there with Jim Morrison, or some guy who could play the piano solo, or had a motorcycle, or did a good job of leaning against buildings and looking aloof and pissed off at the same time.

For the same reason it was necessary to spend time hanging out outside the luncheonette or by the railroad tracks, watch guys curse and throw glass down on the tracks, light each other's cigarettes, stand in leather jackets that only partially stood up to the wind.

Celeste and Della watched them resist the rest of the cold in a way that said, this is fucked up, this wind is eating me. But it was their job to let it go by, just go by, without acknowledgment.

"It's a bitch," the guys might be saying. "It's fucked up."

"It" had something to do with what they couldn't figure out, about a cycle of dogs biting their own tails, which is how they knew their lives might turn out, only they didn't quite get it yet. They couldn't really see what it was, but they knew in advance it was bad.

"Yeah," another one said, "it's bad, but this is good stuff," and offered the rest of a joint. Then they smoked, and laughed, the corners of their eyes turning up in a sort of wise glee, like a Cheshire cat, that they hoped would last.

"Yeah, not bad," and they all laughed like they had the key to the same obscure universal joke.

So they felt okay, standing in the waste place, the end place, of unused train tracks, gravel, broken glass, old refrigerator parts, the no place. Nick LoPardo went there, and had said at the party, to Della and Celeste, "Why don't you come down to the tracks tomorrow?"

They had gone and been the fringe girls at the railroad tracks, worn their short skirts and suede jackets, deepened their eyeliner and brown shadow, stood parallel to each other, so they could pull it off. Phil Z., said to be a big-time dealer, even heroin, was there. And small-timers, Rat, the two Jerrys, and Nancelli. They would accept you if you made the trip down there, if you could stand around in the same way, cold and standing too straight.

"So Della and Celeste, you made it," Nick said, with a flourish of his arm, as if they had just entered a turn-of-the-century ball. He passed them a joint silently, holding it in the most cool way, the rest of his hand covering the joint so you couldn't see it.

Sooner or later Della and Celeste would have to get aligned with one of the boys or another, in order to stay at the tracks. You had to have a stake there, and if you were a girl, just your presence was not enough. You yourself were not a stake.

Now that Della had been to the tracks, she could say to Nick, the next time she saw him at school, "So who was at the tracks yesterday?"

"Mark Russo, Jim O'Brien, Frank DeWolf, Tony Lopaccio, Eric Flynn," he said, each name in full, as if each were a recognized sovereignty, or an established institution. "And Linda was there with Tony, and Kim was there with Eric."

Girls did not stand stiff in small groups and say "It's a fucking mess" or "It's a bitch" or "The streets are fields that never die." A girl like that would be stealing too much, like she knew, really knew and could say what it was, that was a bitch.

It would make her a bitch to say that, and no girl wanted to be one of those. It was a state of being for pissed-off boys to name, not for girls to actually become.

So girls went with guys to the railroad tracks to hear the words said. They took their communion, they smoked pot and lit up cigarettes, blew out smoke in the manner of long-time smokers who just blew it off, incidentally, to the side and went right on with what they were saying. There was only one thing they needed to say, to keep their place: "Oh really."

If a guy said "Szabo's getting a van and splitting for the coast" or

"Flynn dropped out, he's working at the Gulf station," a girl just said, "Oh really?" Because it had already been said, it was now history, it was the tragic way of the universe. "Oh really" made the recitation of history go on and on. It was a way of being a nice girl in a bad place, of putting out a little without really having to put out then and there.

Sooner or later there was an alignment to be made, a girl came "with" somebody, and since Della and Celeste had come with Nick, it was assumed that one of them was for him. One of them would have to enclose him. Neither one of them were particularly in favor of this, but it was necessary to get to the tracks.

"I mean, like, do you like, *like* him?" Della finally asked Celeste.

"He's okay. What about you?"

"He's okay."

"So let's both just hang out with him. They can think he has both of us."

The arrangement worked out for all three of them. Tony Lopaccio leaned over very close to Nick one day and said, "So, uh, Nick, what's it like, you know, two at a time?"

"It's the kind of thing you have to experience to know," Nick said.

"Can you believe what that jerk asked me?" he told Della and Celeste later.

Celeste and Della made it their policy to stick together, to alternate saying "Oh really" so they didn't lose their place. The tracks were close to the other side, like the piano solo. The tracks, the piano solo, and the other side seemed to all be places that a girl could not reach alone.

Now it was time for Jim Morrison to come back in, to wind up "The Crystal Ship." His voice cracked right at the edge of hope and despair,

> The crystal ship
> is being filled
> a thousand girls
> a thousand thrills

Della and Celeste didn't talk about this part. There was something shameful about it. *A thousand girls,* a ship stuffed full of girls, like girls in a cake, all of them spilling out for Jim Morrison. Della and Celeste would just be one of the thousand girls, the thousand thrill girls. Deep down they knew this and it was no use talking about it.

Yet the music sounded so conclusive, so tragic, so beautiful. Was it really known, anyway, how much you were supposed to pay attention to the words? The next song, "Twentieth Century Fox"—that couldn't really mean them?

Only two summers ago Della and Celeste had catalogued and drawn every species of anemone on Block Island and watched *The Story of Marie Curie* twelve times on the Dialing for Dollars Movie. They waited for the scene where Marie found radium still glowing, at night, when she returned to her lab. They loved this woman, who had found something strong enough to blow up the world, by returning patiently to her laboratory every day and night. No one would have dared call Marie Curie a twentieth-century fox.

But they let the ending of "Crystal Ship" go by: "A million ways to bliss." Girls were part of the "bliss," and Jim Morrison said "I promise this." He promised.

They let it go by, dimming themselves so they could stay on the dark and cozy journey toward the no place where Steppenwolf, Jim Morrison, and Nick LoPardo all wore black T-shirts and recounted tales of history. Where girls said "Oh really."

"But I like 'the streets are filled with alibis' better," said Celeste.

"You're right. It's so much better," Della said.

"Yeah, alibis," Celeste said. "Completely better."

"I'll always think of it that way," Della said.

"I will always, always think of it that way," Celeste said.

But for now, they let the rest go by.

CHARLOTTE NEKOLA ON COMMUNITY

When I was thirty-one, I was working on poems and had been accepted at a well-known MFA program in New York. That fall, sitting in my first poetry workshop, I was very excited. We all waited for a well-known poet, whom I greatly admired, to come in and teach us.

The poet blew in the door an hour and a half late and mumbled something about losing his way back from Cape Cod and Latin America. During the remaining hour he said the best thing for the class to do would be just to remain silent for the rest of the semester.

I was unfortunately already too old for that and still had time to recoup thousands of dollars of tuition money, so I dropped out. That's when I first discovered The Writers Community, which offered workshops with equally well-known writers who took their work as teachers seriously. I worked with Carolyn Forché and James Galvin, and later, when I started writing fiction, Michael Cunningham. At the time, the tuition was a mere twenty-five dollars, and you could even have that waived in return for service, in the spirit of community.

Contrary to the myth, writers don't always love working in isolation. It is a dream to find a group of serious young and old artists sitting together to help each other out, with the generous advice of an experienced professional and the support of a committed artistic director. The modest fee makes this community truly accessible.

My classmates were committed to their writing and to their lives outside of class—you had the sense of them working in the larger community of the world, not just a school. Ten years later I find that many of my classmates have published books, had their work published in journals, teach writing, and work in major publishing houses or as editors of literary magazines. And no, we did not have to remain silent.

CHARLOTTE NEKOLA's *first book,* Dream House: A Memoir, *was selected for the Graywolf Press Rediscovery Series, which reissued it in paperback. Her poems have appeared in* Calyx, New Letters, Massachusetts Review,

Big Wednesday, Cottonwood, *and other publications. She is also the coeditor of* Writing Red: An Anthology of American Women Writers, 1930–1940. *The recipient of a Major Hopwood Award, a fellowship from the New Jersey Council on the Arts, and the Schweitzer Fellowship in the Humanities at State University New York, Albany, she is associate professor of English and creative writing at William Paterson College.*

SANJAY KUMAR NIGAM

Charming

Every morning, Bhola Ram, a snake charmer at Humayun's Tomb in New Delhi, waited for tourists. Even before the buses stopped, he would jump aboard. Up and down the aisle he'd walk, playing eerie music on his wooden clarinet, a wicker basket containing his cobra hanging over his shoulder. As soon as the bus came to a halt, Bhola Ram would hop off, throw the basket on the ground, and charm his lazy cobra out, while tourists climbed down. They'd watch his *tamasha*, clattering in more languages than Bhola Ram could keep track of. Then they'd toss him a few coins or rupees, on their way to the tomb.

Foreign Indians were the stingiest. They'd watch for a while, bring their children close, and leave without giving any money. Or, if their children asked for some money to give, the father would grudgingly hand over a few *paisa*, saying in English, but sometimes in Hindi: "This is nothing—you see it all over India." On occasion, Bhola Ram would get fed up with hearing this and explain that you couldn't see his *tamasha* all over India, not a show such as his. There was only one place in the whole world where you could see his *tamasha*, and that was right here. "So you're very lucky," he'd tell them. When they in turn laughed, Bhola Ram would become angry. "Get back on your air-conditioned tourist bus!" he'd shout. "Traitors to your motherland!"

Bhola Ram was supposed to give the bus drivers a tenth of the take from each *tamasha*, but he always gave them less; if caught, he claimed he couldn't reckon. Through charming (and cheating bus drivers), he had acquired enough wealth to rent a garage in one of the better neighborhoods of New Delhi, and to send his two sons to respectable private schools so they might become something other than snake charmers. Being a charmer, though a tradition in his family, was not a respected profession. He wanted his sons to join the government service, even though they might earn less.

One day, just before the Asian Games, there was a constant flow of buses, packed with foreigners of every color and shape. His cobra danced all morning and afternoon, and Bhola Ram made nearly two weeks' worth of money in a single day.

It was approaching dusk, and along came one last bus, full of journalists covering the Games. As usual, Bhola Ram climbed aboard with his basket, piped his tune, jumped off, and threw his basket on the ground. The top of the basket rolled away as he began to charm his cobra. The journalists snapped pictures of Bhola Ram as they got off. He played and played, but his cobra didn't come out. He was an old cobra, lazy to begin with, and now, after such a long day, very tired. "One last time," Bhola Ram said lovingly to his cobra, and played the cobra's favorite tune.

The cobra's head rose out of the basket. A cheer erupted from the crowd. But the tired cobra couldn't rise any further. He sank back into the basket. Bhola Ram, who believed himself the best charmer in the world, was acutely embarrassed. He began to play variations on the cobra's favorite tune, such beautiful variations that, had they been recorded, they might have won Bhola Ram immortality.

The cobra couldn't resist, and soon the snake was dancing with great verve and grace. Bhola Ram was enraptured—over his music and his cobra's dancing. He'd never seen a cobra dance so magnificently in all his forty-three years! Excited photographers flashed away, shouting encouragement. One, five, even ten rupee notes flew towards him, amid a shower of jingling coins, heightening the effect of the music.

Bhola Ram was so excited he hit a false note. Except for Bhola Ram and his cobra, no one noticed the error—the cheering, the flashes, the monsoon of money, kept coming. But the cobra stopped dancing. It rose on end, eyes blazing. In fifteen years, Bhola Ram had never seen his cobra behave this way. He stopped playing and the crowd fell silent. The charmer circled the angry cobra. The snake shot out at Bhola Ram and bit his calf.

The crowd gasped. Bhola Ram knew the fangs and venom glands

of his cobra had been removed long ago, and the cobra had been tested on a stray dog. Still, his cobra had never tried to bite him. Never!

The cobra lay stretched out on the ground, exhausted, almost dead. Someone was getting a taxi to take Bhola Ram to the hospital. Bhola Ram gazed at his cobra with the rage of a father irremediably wronged by his son. The cobra looked back timidly. But Bhola Ram felt no pity. He grabbed the listless cobra at the head and tail, stretched him to his full length, bit him into two equal wriggling pieces, and let them fall to the ground. The pieces squirmed a while longer, then lay still. Bhola Ram gazed up at the evening sky, his face and clothes dripping with cobra juice, and cried over the death of his eldest son.

The journalists rushed over to Bhola Ram, snapping pictures of him and the two pieces of cobra, asking questions he was in no mood to answer. They insisted he go to the hospital. He told them there was no need, as his cobra had no poison in him. Are you sure? they asked. He was sure. They inquired about his name, his address, and scribbled in their notebooks. Someone gathered his earnings—over two hundred rupees—and handed the money to Bhola Ram. He wouldn't touch it, the money of child slaughter. The journalists whispered among themselves, passed some more money around. A white woman journalist presented him with the stack—now nearly a thousand rupees. After some urging, Bhola Ram pocketed the money, for the education of the cobra's brothers.

Eventually the journalists went away. Bhola Ram returned to the spot of the killing. He picked up the two cobra halves and put them in the basket, joining them as best he could. He placed a hundred rupees inside and covered the basket. "What have I done?" he repeated, again and again, in extreme anguish. He begged forgiveness of the cobra halves and prayed to the Naga god for mercy, asking what penance he should perform.

He sat alone at Humayun's Tomb, past dark, past the time when the homeless crept in to sleep till dawn. It was a moonless night. Numb and woozy, Bhola Ram looked up at the stars. Around midnight, he set the basket on fire. The flames licked up the night and threw long slender shadows against the outer walls of the tomb. It was as though the cremation of the dead snake had given rise to hundreds of snakes, each dancing wildly to a different tune. Bhola Ram watched his beloved cobra turn to smoke. After an hour, only sparks and ashes remained. Bhola Ram left.

He wandered aimlessly, tortured by remorse. But gradually his grief turned into anger. How could his cobra have attacked him? His cobra, whom he had raised, fed meat to—even when his family couldn't afford it; he chose not to recall that the meal was a dead rat or mouse, which his family didn't mind forgoing.

A constable stopped him in the street. "Go home," the constable warned. "We are on the watch tonight, because of the Games. There could be trouble." Bhola Ram had had enough trouble for one day and went home.

"Where have you been?" his wife asked him, when he finally returned home. "Were you drinking?" She sniffed his breath before he could answer. "Or have you gone back to your old ways?" She examined his face. He shook his head. "You are lying," she decided.

He protested, glancing at the children's door. "Listen, just listen!" he said.

"I'll listen. And don't worry, the children are asleep. They have exams tomorrow. But what do you care? Such a father you are! What is the story this time, Bhola? Men can never be trusted, I should have known."

In his self-deprecating mood, he pitied her. He thought: She is right. She is a good mother, living only for her children. And I am an irresponsible father, an even worse husband. So what, if she is wrong today?

He recounted what happened, and she listened, horrified. "You bit our snake in two? Are you mad? How will we live?" She repeated the last question. "How will we live? How will we support the children? I shall have to serve sahibs now, listen to the abuse of their children, clean their dirty dishes and wash their filthy clothes. We will have to return to that shack in the trans-Yamuna slums. Or worse, go back to our village and starve! Do you remember what it was like during the drought? Bhola, you did a terrible thing. It would have been better if you had come home drunk from the brothel."

He pulled the money from his pocket and waved it in her face.

"Oh, my!" she said. She counted the money and smiled. She was silent for a while. Finally she said, "He was an old snake anyway."

By morning, Bhola Ram was famous. There were pictures of him and the cobra halves on every newspaper in India, as well as in many outside the country. One headline, side by side with "Asian Games Begin," read, "Snake Charmer Bites Cobra Back." The first paragraph of the article read:

"Outside the tomb of the Mughal emperor Humayun, father of Akbar the Great, a poisonous cobra bit a snake charmer yesterday evening, while he was performing before a crowd. Undaunted, the snake charmer, one Mr. Bhola Ram, attacked the hissing creature back. A terrible battle ensued, the cobra up on its tail, lunging and lashing at the fearless man, who, like an acrobat, dodged each poisonous thrust. Eventually, Mr. Bhola Ram caught the undulating cobra by its ends, and bit the creature in half. Mr. Bhola Ram said he was not afraid of the snake's venom and, even upon the insistence of the crowd, refused to see a doctor."

Reporters were banging his door, even before his children had left for school. These reporters were Indian, eager to get part of the story after having been scooped by their foreign counterparts in their own territory. They wanted to know about Bhola Ram's sons, his village, what he thought about the current political situation, who his favorite film stars were. He answered thoughtfully. His wife watched from the kitchen, constantly rolling her eyes, much to Bhola Ram's vexation.

He made six hundred rupees that morning. If they had been foreign reporters, he reflected, he could have made six thousand.

Soon after, a man from the circus came and asked if he would charm cobras in the big tent, occasionally biting one in half. They would pay fifty rupees a performance. Bhola Ram said he had already bitten a cobra once, and that was one time too many. Cobras didn't taste very good. He was the best charmer in the world, wasn't that enough? "No," the man from the circus replied.

"You were a fool to refuse," his wife told him. "Fifty rupees a performance, two performances a day, a third on weekends: we could have lived like *sarkari* officers!"

"But what if there was still some venom left in the cobra?" he asked, though he knew this to be unlikely, and even if this were so, he could simply avoid the head, where the venom glands were located.

"I could die!" he roared.

"Nobly," his wife replied.

That night he dreamt of snakes, writhing and dancing, attacking him in strange, forbidden places. He woke up with an erection, distressed. "What is the meaning of this peculiar dream?" he asked himself.

"What is bothering you?" his wife inquired when she brought him morning tea.

"I had a dream."

"Is that all? So did I. I dreamt we lived in a *mahal* on a mountain in Kashmir. You were a prince with a beautiful voice. You sang to me, and I to you, as they do in films. We were so deeply in love. And do you know?"

He shook his head.

"Bhola, we had our own three-wheeler! Our sons were *nawabs*, each with a servant." She smiled coyly and said in a soft sweet voice, "You came back one night from charming with a gold necklace."

Bhola Ram returned that evening with a silver necklace which contained sixty percent nickel. After dinner, his wife put the children to bed early, then coaxed him into the bedroom, where incense burned and sandalwood paste lay next to their cot. She removed her sari and petticoat in dim light as he admired her huge round buttocks, her breasts swinging like juicy mangoes.

She caressed him in many places, but he could not be aroused, imagining her hands to be snakes, so troubled was he by the previous night's dream. After several hours, she was utterly exhausted. He readied for the assault.

"Bhola, you are impotent," she said after a long ponderous silence. Yet she had said it so calmly that he was taken aback. He gazed at her intently. She appeared genuinely pleased. She kissed him and they went to sleep.

In the morning, he rushed off early, to see Doctor Nath, an old sex therapist whose advertisement he'd seen painted on the walls outside Humayun's Tomb.

He told the doctor about his dream.

"You are a homosexual," the doctor pronounced.

This was exactly what Bhola Ram secretly feared. He spit in Doctor Nath's face and left without paying.

For a good part of the afternoon, he strolled aimlessly through Connaught Place, wondering, with increasing anxiety, about his homosexuality. He decided he wasn't one yet, but was intrigued, recalling boyhood experiences long suppressed. He thought of grown men doing those things, and imagined many other things grown men might do. He became excited. He realized he stood at calamity's brink.

He stopped off at Humayun's Tomb, where he was now more famous than the dead emperor. Every vendor wanted him to eat at his stall—free. He had *chaat, aloo tikya,* Campa Cola, tea and spiced cucumber. He ate till he started to belch.

Someone suggested renaming the place "Bhola Ram's Tomb." But others pointed to the facts: Bhola Ram was not yet dead; he was Hindu and must be cremated, not buried; the government would take forever to change the name, and then there might be Hindu-Muslim riots.

Bhola Ram found his friend Jagdeep, the oldest snake charmer around. Jagdeep had retired some years back and was supported by his sons. He said charming was in his blood and spent much of the day keeping Bhola Ram company between buses.

"Ah, a celebrity comes my way."

"It is strange, no?"

"You must be pleased."

"Yes, Jagdeep *bhai,* but . . ."

"But what?"

"Do you think I'm a homosexual?"

"You've been to Doctor Nath too, eh?"

"How do you know?"

"Every snake charmer in Delhi goes to Doctor Nath. Even I went to him, twenty years back. He tells everybody they are homosexuals. I think he is. He must do this to find men to love."

"He is so old."

"And you think old people don't like sex?"

"Not so much."

"I'm sure it must be very lonely being an old homosexual. It is very lonely being old. Here in India, it is not like America and England, where one can be a homosexual in the open and find other homosexuals easily. In America, they even have beach colonies where everyone goes about nude. They are very advanced."

Advanced was not exactly what Bhola Ram would have called it, but he felt he must defend India, especially since he heard they were getting trounced in the Games. "It is very easy to get a prostitute in India," he said with pride.

"That is true," answered Jagdeep. "You have a point."

Bhola Ram told Jagdeep about his dream, omitting certain details. "If you are a snake charmer," said the old man, "it is not unusual to dream about snakes."

Bhola Ram began to take morning walks, swinging his arms the way retired army colonels do, his head tilted slightly upward. People pointed at him, greeted him courteously and deferentially, as if he were a *sahib*.

But soon the Games came to an end, and the city returned to normal. Strikes, power failures and water shortages arose once again. The world forgot Bhola Ram. No more journalists, no more money. People stopped pointing at him in the street. Some even snickered at the snake charmer who walked like a retired army colonel. Disheartened at the fickleness of his fellow men, he meditated long evenings on the evanescence of good fortune and fame. But soon the bittersweet satisfaction of this quiet resignation lost its charm. Solitude turned into boredom. He quarreled with his wife.

"You will buy a new cobra tomorrow," she ordered him one evening, after their usual tussle.

All the next morning, he searched about Delhi, Old and New, for a cobra. He saw many, but none like his old cobra, which he'd begun to miss a great deal. These city cobras were other men's snakes. He took a bus into the hills and got off a few miles from where he grew up. Eventually, he caught a tenacious cobra, defanged it, extracted the venom glands, and brought the snake back to the city.

A day later, Bhola Ram was back at Humayun's Tomb, jumping on tourist buses, playing his wooden clarinet, throwing his basket on the ground, charming his cobra. His libido returned, and he spent himself outside his home.

Seven years passed. Bhola Ram's belly grew and his teeth began to fall out. His children were in the higher secondary, topping, aspiring to government service or professional careers — and embarrassed by their father's livelihood. His wife had become intensely religious of late, an affliction many middle-aged Hindu women of their locality were suddenly prone to. Every morning, she filled his mouth with *prasad* and sacred water when she returned from the temple. He seemed to have a permanent vermillion mark on his forehead, so many times had she done his *teeka*. Only last month, Jagdeep had died. Bhola Ram missed him dearly, and there was no one to idle time away with between buses.

Bhola Ram smoked *beedis* much of the day, allowing a younger charmer most of the business, though he took two or three buses in the afternoon. Although he was proud of his sons, the young charmer seemed more like a son than his own. Charming was not such a bad profession. It had been good enough for at least five generations of his family.

He had stopped frequenting brothels, the impotence being physiological this time — owing to sugar in his blood, the doctor said — but he continued to stay out late, drinking with his friends. His wife began to leave his bedding outside their room when he came home late, and soon he was sleeping in the hall no matter what time he returned.

During a *tamasha* one particularly hot summer afternoon, Bhola Ram's cobra bit him. The crowd gasped. He picked the cobra up by its head and tail, stretched it out, and was about to bisect it with his teeth, when a man shouted, "Are you crazy?"

"I'm going to kill this cobra," announced Bhola Ram, rather dramatically, the outstretched cobra writhing in his hands.

"Why? The poor snake has no venom in it anyway. You are a nut."

And the man walked away, as did the rest of the crowd, laughing at the mad snake charmer.

Humiliated, Bhola Ram set the cobra down. The snake scurried back into its basket. For a long time, Bhola Ram sat under a tree, inhaling the warm exhaust-laden air of the city, thinking with a clarity he had not previously known. Darkness eventually came, and he rose to meet his friends at the liquor shop.

SANJAY KUMAR NIGAM *was born in India and moved to the United States at the age of one. His stories have been published in* Grand Street, Kenyon Review, *and* Quarry West. *A short story collection is forthcoming from Penguin Books-India. He has held residencies at Yaddo and the MacDowell Colony and is currently at work on two novels.*

SONDRA SPATT OLSEN

The Butcher's Girl

On the quiet streets of our Brooklyn neighborhood I saw her on my way to school, one of those girls who look like women from far away. I saw the butcher's girl, frightening in her womanliness, advancing slowly upon me along Avenue S. As she drew nearer, her unmistakable shape with its outthrust bosom grew more threatening. She had a face as blank as a coal-chute door and moist, gleaming black eyes; upon her broad red cheek was a small black mole with a hair in it. At this time she was an eighth grader, and I was nine years old.

On other days she appeared in her father's shop sitting on an upturned milk box amid the sawdust and the blood smells. I saw her sometimes carrying out her father's commands, trudging along the sidewalk after school with a large brown bag against her breast. At times I was invisible to her; her cowlike gaze passed over me, and I breathed more freely. At other times she paused and moved closer to me, close enough to brush me with the crackling brown paper. "Where you going?" she said. If I had no ready destination, I felt forced to accompany her, blocks away.

What did she want of me? Not sparkling conversation, for though I could chatter easily, I was silent in her company. Her weighty combination of sex and stupidity rendered me dumb. Also, my own plumpness, an excess of baby fat merely, drew me closer in repulsion to her tremendous flesh.

On this day she approached me hurrying more than normally, her breasts slowly shuttling sideways. Her lips were parted with that mystical look of high rapture. "You busy after school?"

I had a Brownie meeting on Tuesday, and a piano lesson on Wednesday, but today was Thursday, and I had not yet learned to lie to save myself.

"Uh-uh."

"I got to take my graduation picture," she said. "I need someone to deliver for me. You get the tips. They're good on Thursday. You ain't got much walking, either."

I allowed myself to breathe because I knew that my mother would never let me ring the doorbells of strange houses. This had been proven at Girl Scout Cookie time as well as at Thanksgiving, when I was not allowed to join the roving bands of costumed kids chanting "Anything for Thanksgiving?" door to door.

"My mother won't let me."

"Don't tell her."

This was an argument I had never expected. While I grappled with it, she continued, "Just tell her you was helping out after school."

Stupefied by her shrewd, certain tone, I agreed, at the same time feeling a dead, sinking helplessness.

"Come right to my father's after school. Don't carry no books."

"What do I do with my books?"

"Leave them in school, but don't leave them in the shop. My father don't want no books in his way. He'll throw them in the fat barrel."

I left my books behind the friendly counter at Harry's Candy Store and entered the butcher's shop at three o'clock like a sacrificial lamb. Herman the Butcher stood in a businesslike way behind his woodblock, his dull cleaver beside him. His ruddy cheeks, red lips, and large white teeth reminded me of steak. It would do me no good with him to say that I had all A's on my report card, that Mrs. Bensen, our English teacher, had read my composition aloud with eloquent praise and then tacked it in the corridor for the whole school to see. If I had felled an ox, he perhaps would smile on me.

"Take these to Mrs. Lipsit, Mrs. Brown, and Mrs. Cunningham. I got the addresses written on the bag. Then come back here. Maybe I got more for you." He wiped his fingers on his rosy apron. "You do good, you can make money when Pearl is away."

I staggered out of the shop. The bell rang sharply behind me before Herman could call me back. "I wouldn't use Herman even for soup bones," my mother had once said with some violence. "He can keep his credit." She shopped for meat at Mr. Ganz, the kosher butcher. "His meat is cleaner."

Mr. Ganz's store on the next block seemed bare rather than clean. Perhaps he was going out of business, for his showcase stood empty except for two or three yellow plucked chickens and some long brown chops. Mr. Ganz himself was thin and nervous with a narrow black mustache. He often smiled gloomily when he came out of the icebox, as if he had seen something to his disadvantage inside.

On the street, my reason returned to me. I read the penciled addresses and plotted a course. If I was clever, I would get home free, and my mother would never know. I would donate my tips to charity, to the Girl Scouts.

Mrs. Lipsit's was easy, only one block over, a corner house with a sunporch. Through the window panels I could see who was coming and run if needed. Mrs. Lipsit herself came to the door, unknown to me but wearing a reassuring frilled apron and tortoiseshell combs in her upswept hair, just like my mother. Just like my mother, she was polite, said "Oh, my goodness" when she realized she had no tip handy, and kept me waiting for a long time beside the forest-green sunporch door while she scouted out a dime.

My load and heart were lighter as I slipped along the sidewalk, swinging my fat blond pigtails in play. Mrs. Brown lived three blocks further toward Water Street on the stagnant bay, a fascinating place with huge exposed sewer pipes and a rotten smell—just across the border of my permitted territory.

The Brown house was dark and forbidding, with overgrown hedges that must be breached to reach the side door. The front gate was bound with a padlock—out of the question. The nicked slimy green door held no reassuring window. The bell did or did not ring. I put my ear to the splintery panels to see if I could hear footsteps, and suddenly the surface shifted. I stumbled and looked up, inhaling the sour breath of an old man in a dirty khaki sweater and ragged pants. "Your meat," I said with remarkable aplomb, but the old man only looked at me crooked and banged the door shut.

I reread the paper bag. Herman's scrawl was ugly but unmistakable: 9812 Water Street. I knocked, but no one came. I waited about fifteen minutes, thought about leaving the package leaning up against the moldy green door, looked inside it, saw bulging sausages as well as several other stained parcels, thought better of it, and walked slowly away in despair. There was no point in delivering the third bag; if I had to return to Herman in shame, one undeliverable would be just as bad as two. Rubbing my shin where the hedges had scratched me, I found myself walking in the direction of the bay. I was already done for, I reasoned, so I might as well go down to the water.

I heard wild screams ahead of me. A rowdy gang of boys was playing stickball in an untidy line near the shore on the other side of Water Street. I recognized them without knowing in particular who they were, yet I knew from the silhouettes of their cowlicks and bony shins in rolled-up pant legs and sagging socks that these boys were my traditional enemies, just as they knew me by my pigtails and neat Trimfit anklets in my sturdy school shoes. I heard the violence in their shrieked repeated name-calling. In a few moments if I crossed the street, or even perhaps if I didn't, they would chase after me, calling me names and perhaps throwing rocks. I had been hit on the temple by a snowball in February by a boy who had called out cheerfully, "Look at me!"

I kept on walking along Water Street until I came to a street I had never seen before called Blossom. I saw no flower gardens, only a dank row of brick stoops extending back in the direction in which I had come. Clutching my parcels to my light sprigged dimity chest, I slowly and curiously made my way up Blossom Street. The air seemed to be growing darker and damper. Nightfall was coming, or it was about to rain. I pretended I was in my bed, imagining an exciting journey.

The cries of the boys were soon out of earshot. They had never even glimpsed me, and I was safe. I decided to make another stab at delivering Mrs. Brown's meat, but when I came to the intersection which should have shown me Barker Street, the sign said Blackhorn. I wasn't lost, since I was within a block or two of my destination, but I was mystified. What was Blackhorn?

As I pondered, a man came up the street toward me. I was puzzled about him, for he was obviously not a schoolboy or a delivery boy. At that time of day all the grown men were at work; those left were schoolboys, the elderly, or tradesmen. This fellow seemed about college age and very well dressed in a brown-belted jacket and tweed trousers. He wore a cap at a jaunty angle over his fair curly hair. He was singing a popular tune I very much liked: "Now is the hour/When we must/Say good-bye." Just as he came abreast of me and my packages, he stopped and sang "hello" at the point where he should have sung "good-bye." I thought this very witty.

When he said, "May I help you with those parcels, little girl?" I naturally thought of the wolf in "Little Red Riding Hood." Nonetheless, for reasons which must have had to do with his snapping blue eyes and the regularity of his straight small nose, I handed my packages to him, and he gave me a smile of the most piercing sweetness. He then began to run away from me as fast as he could go, disappearing at the corner of Water Street and speeding towards the bay, the huge sewer pipes, rowdy boys, and rotten smell.

I continued walking along Blossom Street away from the bay, my face all screwed up to prevent tears falling out of my eyes, and gulping very loudly to force the tears down my throat and into my stomach, and scuffing my shoes with their metal tips very loudly on the sidewalk to cover up my gulping, for crying, I knew, was very stupid. No one stopped me or took any notice of me until I came to a wide shopping street which bore the same name as my shopping street. I thought it might be the same, turned in the right direction, and soon found myself at Herman's Butcher Shop.

On a milk crate in front of the shop, her red hands laced together on her broad stomach, sat Pearl, the butcher's girl, in old black sneakers and a new ruffled white organdy and dotted Swiss graduation dress. Bursting into loud wails, I rushed over to Pearl and threw myself on her mercy, or rather into her lap, right at the spot where her crisp peplum was crushed by her bosom. "I was robbed! A boy stole my packages! What will I tell my mom?"

I could feel the gentle pressure of Pearl's breasts as she leaned over me. She didn't understand what I was saying and made me repeat the message. Then she sat for a long time, blinking. "Don't you worry," she said finally.

She rose and went into the butcher's shop, while I remained kneeling, the sidewalk pressing cruelly into my knees. She returned soon, her black eyes gleaming. "I fixed it with my father," she said. "He does what I say."

"Is he going to make me pay for the meat?"

But Pearl only shook her head. "Don't worry. I fixed it." She sat down and squashed me into a hug.

As I lay in her lap, embracing her scratchy stomach, being comforted and admired as a helpless baby is admired, I felt for the first time the warmth of unconditional love. It seemed to me I was not so awful, after all. In a moment, the feeling had gone.

"We'll be friends," Pearl said. "I'll walk you home every day. I'll visit you at your house."

I imagined my mother's haughty rolling glance, her scornful stare. My mother's legs were slim in glossy nylons. Her small polished shoes were dainty, her underpants pink and fresh. Everything she did was excellent.

I saw Pearl's bulky entrance through our narrow garden gate, her cracked black sneakers treading our Chinese rug. I heard my mother whisper, "stupid," and also, "piano legs."

How could I bring home such a creature? What would people say? Wouldn't that make me a butcher's child, too?

"No," I groaned, breaking free with difficulty from Pearl's grasp. "Not now." I stood and began to compose myself, patting my eyes. "But thank you very much for your help. Thank you, anyway."

Pearl's black eyes looked duller, like stones. The hair in her little mole, which I had forgotten, sprang to my attention. "You don't have to pay for the meat," she repeated. "I paid for it myself from my tips."

Although I tried to be thankful and said I was thankful, I felt an ugly grating in my heart. I turned and ran.

Until the end of the term I took a long circuitous route to avoid meeting Pearl on my way to school. If I glimpsed her slow advance, I darted down a side street. Once I crouched behind two enormous metal garbage cans in the alley behind the movie house. Once I reversed direction and scooted home, pleading a sudden headache. I never let her get near me again.

In the fall Pearl went safely off to Eastern District High School, where she earned a general diploma. For years after, I saw her strolling along the sidewalk to Harry's for a candy bar or lingering for a smoke near the dusty butcher shop window. Although she gave me a look with a lapidary gleam to it when I could not avoid her, we never spoke.

SONDRA SPATT OLSEN *is the author of* Traps, *a short story collection for which she received the Iowa Short Fiction Award. She recently completed a comic novel and a second story collection. She is a lifelong New Yorker.*

SONIA PILCER

FROM *Teen Angel*

From where Sonny Palovsky sat, she could hear everything. The whole soundtrack of Humboldt Junior High School 115, and no one bugged her except when she had to go back to Homeroom and face Mrs. King, who had a mug like a rotting eggplant, only it was uglier. But in the stall, with her and Ruben Ortega's initials carved above the toilet paper dispenser, she was royal. Queen Pee of the third-floor girls' room, second stall to the right. Look, if Dobie Gillis could hang his haunches on "The Thinker" (you know, that sculpture where you could swear the guy's sitting on a pot), why couldn't she? All who sought audience with Her Royal Hindness, née Lady Bullshitsky of Washington Heights, visited her here. She granted favors. *I'll let you copy my algebra homework.* But not too many people came except for Paulette Williams. While she mopped and stacked paper towels, she told dirty jokes that were pissers. *What did the blind man say as he passed the fish market? Hi, girls!* She'd be sitting in History and think of one and die laughing all over again. *What's the difference between a young prostitute and an old whore? One uses Vaseline; the other, Poli-grip.* Ha ha ha! And once she started, she couldn't stop laughing, and then the teacher would make her stand out in the hallway until she could control herself. *Why do farts smell? So the deaf can enjoy them too.* But how could someone stop laughing *ever* from a real good joke? Especially when you were stuck in a special class for snots with high reading scores who all thought they were D-g's gift. So she was sitting fifth period out, *Thanks, I don't think I'll dance this one*, when a folded piece of three-hole looseleaf paper was passed to her under the stall. She unfolded it and gasped. "Palovskee, wait till everyone leaves. TEEN ANGEL." She almost *plotzed* into the bowl. Could they want her? *Me?*

Sonny peeked under the stall and recognized D.B.'s fat calves. (Peek and ye shall find.) Her Midnight Coffee stockings had a run

from ankle to thigh like the painted lines between lanes of the New
York State Thruway, which her family chugged every summer, pots
and pans clanging, to some crummy bungalow colony in the Catskills
with a name like Blue Paradise. D.B. wore an ankle bracelet with
pearls and two golden hearts, and black leather ankle boots pointy
enough to castrate a roach. Sonny's heart bounced like someone was
dribbling it.

Jezus. A Teen Angel wanted to talk to her. They fought, fucked
(all she ever did was fart!), even the teachers were scared of them.
Their hair was teased higher, their eyeliner painted thicker, darker,
a solid black line from the bridge of the nose out to both lobes, their
lipstick a ghostlier shade of white. Cross a Teen Angel and say *say-
onara* to your life. They didn't take no shit from nobody. And they
wanted to talk to her? *Me?* Sonny waited until the bathroom was
empty, not daring to breathe.

"Okay, listen carefully 'cause I ain't going ta repeat myself," D.B.
(short for De-Bra which held Humboldt's most colossal bazookies)
whispered. "If you want to see what being a Teen Angel is all about
we'll meet you in the alleyway of 725 Riverside Drive. At four o'clock
sharp. That's on 155th Street. Okay?"

Sonny nodded eagerly, only D.B. couldn't see her.

"Do you hear me?" she demanded.

"Oh, I'm sorry. Yeah, I'll be there. Sure."

"Okay. I'll walk out first. You are forbidden to leave until five
minutes have passed."

Sonny's eyes followed the boots out of the stall, past the sinks.
"And make sure you come alone—unarmed!" The bathroom door
slammed. *JEZUS IN A JALOPY! Me? They must really be hard up.*

She unlatched the door and examined the stall next to hers. All
kinds of stuff was scribbled on the wall, but there was a fresh entry
scrawled in Flame-Glo lipstick: a big heart with TEEN ANGEL
printed in the center, pierced by a knife. What was she getting herself into? She could be murdered. Slaughtered. Even die.

As she walked out of the stall, Sonny prepared her face for the
mirror. Tough-but-sort-of-sexy-yet-sweet-but-not-goody-goody. *Okay,
stick 'em up. Got you covered. You just can't get away with that kind of shit*

anymore. Oh, hello beautiful. Yes, I'd love to go dancing with you. Do you really think I'm terrific looking? Rummaging through her patent leather clutch, she found a plastic comb with a long, pointy tip which she poked into her beehive. On good days, when there was no humidity so her hair didn't frizz, it stood four inches. She teased a few stray hairs and sprayed with a can of extra-hold hairspray. *Okay. Even better than that. I love you. SMOOCH!* At least, she felt decently foxy, sort of, until she had to go to Algebra and face Mr. Gross (he had long hairs growing out of his nostrils and blackheads the size of raisins), who suggested she eat rice "cause it's binding, Miss Palovsky" and all the flatulence in her class cracked up. Lenny Weinstein said out loud so everyone could hear how she ate Shit Krispies for breakfast, and that's why she went to the bathroom all the time. At least, she went when she had to. The chickenshits in her class were so scared they crossed their legs and held it in all day. No soiling their special behinds. After all, you could get germs from *them*, a disease of the privates. *"But Mister, I is a sergeant."* Even pregnant. Sonny's mother taught her to crouch above the seat like she was a raincloud about to shower. But how could anyone drop a decent-sized whopper midair? *Tinkle, tinkle, little turd, how I wonder—oh, my word—BLITZKRIEG!* They'd all die if she became a Teen Angel. No one would dare mess with Palovsky.

At ten minutes to four, Sonny, who sometimes called herself Suzanne, even though it wasn't her real name (no one knew that), stood in the alleyway of 725 Riverside Drive, slouching so that most of her weight fell on one bent knee and she looked two inches shorter. She always did that when she had to stand on line somewhere and towered over everyone like a tree. Adults said she was tall for her age and how she'd appreciate it when she got older. Tall? She was a prehistoric bird with long spindly legs that looked like linguine in stockings and size nine feet. Her figure was nonexistent and the most prominent part of her body was her old yapper. The boys in her class came up to her ribs, the girls fit in her shoe. And all the teachers hated to look up to her and besides "you're not made out of glass and no one can see through you"—did she ever say she was?—so she always got seated way in the back of the classroom like an avocado

plant. As hard as she wished on birthday candles, first stars, dande-
lions, as often as she crossed her fingers and toes (she could, too)
that puberty would wave its magic wand over her sixty-nine-and-a-
quarter gangly inches of length, ninety-five pounds of from hunger
scrawn and arouse her body from the deep sleep of premenstruation—
*Please, God. I'll go to temple. One set of knockers. I'll learn Hebrew. And an
ass that's round and curvy*—nothing happened.

For the third time, she went out to make sure she got the building
number correct. A loud banging sound startled her. A rat scurried
out of the water pipe and took a flying dive into a half-eaten can of
ravioli sticking out of the garbage can. Sonny shifted her weight to
the other leg. Maybe they told her to come as a joke, like the time
Rose Steiner invited her to a party at her house and when she got
there with a present bought with her own money, no one would open
the door.

Why would they want her anyway? Even if she *had* devoted
her life to being like them. Ever since seventh grade, she wore her
makeup just like a Teen Angel. She even tried to talk like them. But
she'd never be one of them. They thought she was a *shmuck,* but she
wasn't. At least, she didn't want to be anymore and maybe if she
tried real hard, but then again . . . She heard footsteps approaching
from behind. "Don't move an inch," a muffled voice commanded.
Sonny's heart galloped. *They came.* That was something. She was
scared shitless.

Ten long fingernails painted the color of teeth held a black scarf
in front of her. It was placed over her eyes and tied in the back of her
head. *Hey, fellas, it's dark in here!* She tried to save her hairdo, but a
hand slapped her fingers. Someone else started to turn her around
several times, then pushed her to another person, and then another
person spun her around. Sonny's Hostess Twinkie from lunch threatened to erupt. *You better be cautious, I'm getting nauseous.*
YECHHHH . . . Only kidding . . . Now she was led down a long ramp
and then it seemed as if she was walked for several miles but the air
never changed. It continued to smell of garbage and she could hear
the distant rumble of washing machines and dryers. A door groaned
open and another voice announced, "Non-initiates cannot enter the

House of Teen Angel with their eyes open." Sonny was led in, pushed roughly and then thrown down on a cold metal surface. The blindfold was removed. Sonny looked around.

It was blacker than Sidney Poitier's asshole, no offense. But with the little bit of light that leaked through from under the door, and as her eyes adjusted to the darkness, Sonny made out an enormous black-bellied boiler with a thick pipe running over her head. Wherever she looked, a pair of Teen Angel eyes peered back at her. *Smile. Oh, Shit! Cheese.*

Judy Gucciano, Teen Angel Warlord, known as the Gooch, stared at Sonny without moving a muscle in her face. She had a Danny Thomas hook that hung so close to her mouth that she could pick her nose with her tongue. When she drank soda from a can, she almost drowned. She was short, curvy, with a reputation for giving out as many free samples as the Fuller Brush man. When you were that ugly, you had to. But she had smarts. The Gooch masterminded all Teen Angel extracurricular activities like breaking into Lynn's on 182nd Street so's everyone could have a new fall wardrobe. What the Gooch said went. Even guys were scared of her.

"Name," Mary Kelly commanded. She was secretary because she had the best penmanship. All her t's were crossed with curlicues and her i's were dotted with daisies. She held a spiral notebook with TEEN ANGEL stenciled in sparkles on the cover which was their Slam Book. It contained all the confidential information about who went with who, and how far they went, pet names, favorite songs with all the words to them, boss expressions like "It is better to have loved and lost than not to have loved at all," and everyone's measurements. She wrote with a pen that had a flashlight on its tip.

"Sonny Palovsky."

"Thpell that," Mary lisped. She couldn't pronounce s's, c's, th's and z's, and whenever she tried, she spit all over herself. Every Tuesday and Thursday morning, she had to go to Speech Clinic on the fourth floor where Mrs. Alexander gabbed about being in the theater and how she once *played* with Sir Laurence Olivier. *See you later, masturbator.* Mary just sat there, staring miserably into a mirror as she tried to make the tip of her tongue touch the roof of her mouth—"The thells thea thells by the thea thore"—without swallowing her gum. She saved bazooka wrappers. That's how she got her transistor radio. Mary was so thin and small-boned she didn't have a shadow. That was because her mother was a fat slob. So she was permanently on the two-finger diet which consisted of sticking her two fingers down her throat after each meal. But she had a ponytail down to her waist like Connie Stevens, except hers looked like a garden hose.

Sonny spelled her name, carefully pronouncing each letter. Mary looked up momentarily from the notebook as if trying to decide whether she was being made fun of.

"Addreth?"

"Six eighty-nine West 161st Street."

"Wow! That's right across the street from where I live!" Dot exclaimed, her blue eyes crossing at the bridge of her nose. Sonny groaned to herself. The one retard in the gang would have to live across the street from her. Dot wore orthopedic shoes and plastered her pimples with flesh-colored paste called Erase. And she had unbelievable BO. The only reason she was a Teen Angel was because she owned every record on the chart for the last three years.

"Age?"

"Fifteen." Sonny hesitated. "Well, almost."

"When are you going to be fifteen?"

"August."

"What class are you in?"

Sonny wanted to lie but she knew they'd find out. "9SP1," she said softly.

"What did you say?"

"9SP1," she repeated a little bit louder.

"How come you're not doing your homo-work?" the Gooch jeered.

"Thpecial progressth!" Mary hooted. "Thpecial people. Why you must be *fairy* smart."

"A study wart," D.B. said.

"NO! I'M NOT!" Sonny cried out. "I don't study at all. I swear!"

"She probably thinks she's real smart," Marilyn added.

"No, I don't. SP stands for stupid people," Sonny protested. "You wouldn't believe some of the bozos in my class. They might get good grades but they're so dumb they think a blow job is something you do to a flat tire."

Some of the girls laughed. Sonny grinned hopefully.

"Thilence!" Mary interrupted.

"No one told you that you could speak," D.B. said sternly. "Now we'll open the floor to questions. Only speak when you are spoken to. And just answer the questions."

"No bullshit, Palovsky," the Gooch said, continuing to stare at her.

"Why do you want to be a Teen Angel?" Crystal Gonzales asked. She was pretty, even if she was a Rican. She wore a St. Francis of Assisi uniform which consisted of a navy blazer and skirt with a white blouse. And she had the meanest ankle boots with needle toes.

"Cause you're the bossest girls around."

"What would you do to be a Teen Angel?" Hansy asked. She was so dumb she got left back in the CRMD, which was a class for retards. She failed in Potholders.

"Anything!" Sonny exclaimed passionately.

"Anything?" the Gooch asked, staring so hard that Sonny felt like she had cigarette holes all over her face.

"Anything."

"Would you thteal a car?"

Sonny paused. "Where's it parked?"

"Hubcaps? Aerials?" Hansy asked.

"Sure, how many do you want?"

"Do you have a JD card?" Marilyn asked, having recently earned one herself when she was caught with five Dion albums in her loose-leaf at Klein's.

"No," Sonny said, "but I'll get one."

"Can you fight?" D.B. asked.

"Sure."

"Do you have brass knuckles?" Crystal asked.

She didn't know what they were but nodded anyway.

"A chain?"

"Of course." Hers had a Jewish star on it but it was buried under her sweater.

"When did you get your period?" D.B. asked.

Sonny gulped. "Oh, when I was eleven and a half."

"Bra size?"

"32A," Sonny said matter-of-factly.

"She's bullshitting us," the Gooch hissed. "You're wearing an undershirt."

"No, I'm not," Sonny cried out. *Yes, she was. Damn it.*

"How far have you gone?" D.B. asked. She wore a black stretch top which showed every curve and swell of her *bosoms*, a tie clip on her collar and a virgin pin on the left side just in case there was any question.

"All the way and back."

"How many times?"

"Enough."

"Yeah?" Dot asked impressed.

"Yeah." *Will someone get this creep off my case.*

"Describe one of your—er—many experiences," D.B. said doubtfully.

"Well, let's see which one would be the best one to tell you guys . . . There are so many . . ." Sonny said, stalling for time and trying desperately to recall something she'd heard. "Oh yeah. Okay. There was this guy I used to know. Named Ruben—"

"Ruben who?" the Gooch interrupted. She used to go around with Ruben Ortega and still had the hots for him.

"Uh," Sonny thought quickly, regretting her slip. No one, of course, knew about her crush. "Ruben Fettucini . . ."

The Gooch continued to look suspicious.

"Anyway, we had a thing. Ruben Fettucini and me. So one day he was fingering me . . ." She paused momentarily for effect. *Here goes.*

"Well, I'm creaming all over the place like I'm a vanilla sundae and having a terrific time. All of a sudden, he pulls his finger out and says, 'Hey baby, I think I dropped my ring in your twat.' So I says to him, 'Well loverboy, go back in and look for it.' I'm enjoying it anyhow. So he sticks his finger all the way in but he still can't reach it.

He puts in another finger and then still another one. 'Hey, what's happening down there?' He says, 'I still can't find my ring in your pussy. My momma gave it to me for graduation and if I come home without it, she gonna kill me.' So I says, 'Don't give up, dollface.' So he sticks his whole hand in and I feel him rummaging inside of me like I'm a Macy's shopping bag. But still no ring." Sonny stopped again and looked around. Everyone seemed to be into her story. She silently thanked St. John, patron saint of the third-floor girls' room, where it had been delivered to her.

"So this goes on for a while, as you might imagine. Meanwhile I've come so many times I'm wet as a slush pond. So he pushes his whole arm in but the ring is still out of reach. Then he sticks in his other arm and you might not believe this, but before I know what's happening, he sticks his head in and *this dude is crawling inside of me!* Well girls, we all like them big and hard but I must say, this is a little bit much. 'I'm still looking,' he calls out to me. I bend down over myself and yell, 'HURRY UP ALREADY! I HAVE TO GO HOME FOR DINNER!' He just strolls around in there until he sees something shiny and bright ahead of him. 'Hey, Sonny! I think I see it!' he yells out to me. 'Come on, already!' I scream back. What does he think I have all day to be diddled?"

"Stop it! I'm going to pee in my pants!" Hansy howled.

"Where was I? Oh yes. So Ruben starts running ahead and would you believe, there's Tony Alfredo, my ex-old man, standing next to his red Camaro shining his brights. 'How'd you get here?' Ruben asks him. Tony looks him up and down. Then he says, 'Never mind that. If you help me find my car keys, we can drive out of this dump.' 'Hey man,' Ruben interrupts him, 'that's my girl's vagina you talking about.'"

"Holy shit!" Marilyn squealed in delight.

"But that doesn't sound possible," Dot said. "Did that really happen to you?"

"She's totally serious," D.B. said, shaking her head.

"That was so bad." Crystal was laughing so hard that her eyeliner dissolved into black pitiful tears.

"I don't think Rube ever found his ring," Sonny said sorrowfully.

"Can't you just see that guy walking around down there. I mean, weird," Mary said.

"This is an emergency," Hansy cried. "I gotta take a leak or I'm going to pee right here."

"You think you're pretty smart, don't you?" The Gooch stood up. "The last time I heard that one, it was a black guy with a Cadillac."

"Then she was jiving us?" Dot asked, her eyeballs darting in all directions, unable to focus.

"No, Dot. It was for real," D.B. said sarcastically.

"Teen Angel conference," the Gooch announced. She walked out shaking her ample ass, followed by D.B., whose skirt hem was dropping out in the back. Mary, Hansy, Crystal, and Marilyn filed out behind them. Dot winked at Sonny, closing the door behind her.

Sonny could hear their voices outside but was unable to make out the words. She knew she blew it. The Gooch hated her on sight. *Why did she have to tell that nerd story?*

The door opened. The Teen Angels marched in, taking their former seats.

The Gooch began. "We have decided on an initiation task for you, Sonny Palovsky. If you perform it well, you're in. If you don't, forget it. And there better be no more bullshit from you."

"You have to get a thcumbag, you know, a rubber—," Mary said.

The Gooch interrupted her. "Am I the Warlord or not around here? Palovsky, a prophylactic, and you have to bring it back full of semen. Do you understand?"

"Yeah," Sonny said, groaning to herself. Where would she ever get a scumbag? *Scumbag?* She had never even seen one of those things. As for semen, they might as well want Jackie Kennedy's stool. But she said, "Sure."

"Tomorrow. Same time, same place," D.B. said.

"Can't I have a few extra days? Danny's out of town. And Ron's gonna be busy tomorrow. Stan's sick . . ."

"Couldn't we give her a couple extra days?" Dot asked meekly.

"Tomorrow," the Gooch concluded.

Oh, feces.

SONIA PILCER ON COMMUNITY
A Writer's Appreciation

This is a fairy tale of a fledgling writer, until recently under the spell of a wicked troll, who begins her first novel. She gets this image, or is it memory, of long legs in off-black stockings and roachkiller boots, dangling from a red Thunderbird parked at 161st Street in Washington Heights. The year is 1963. Five girls with teased-to-the-limit hair, black eyeliner slathered from lobe to lobe, lipstick a ghostly shade of white. They are trying to sound tough as they pass one Salem cigarette between them. With a few strokes, the novice novelist transforms herself and her lumpish girlfriends into a femme street gang called Teen Angels.

She rewrites her first chapter at least fifty times. This is years before computers, and each time she changes a word or phrase, she laboriously retypes the whole page. She tells herself she's working on a novel, but does she believe it? Not at all.

The wicked troll, disguised as a kindly college writing teacher, sealed her fate in a tangle of briars and thorns. "Honestly, who do you think could possibly be interested in reading about a Jewish girl growing up?"

Besides, she's never known anyone *personally* who's actually published a book, or even written one. Yet she keeps on writing.

Somewhere, she notices a flyer for a fiction workshop. Manuscript required. Send up to forty pages. No fee. She mails her uncertain seventeen pages.

Here's where the fairy-tale part begins. Two weeks later she receives a notice that she's been accepted for the workshop—and a note written in a human hand. "I can't wait to work with you on your novel!" Signed by the writer C. D. B. Bryan.

He called it a novel! Me! Mine! He writes for the New Yorker. This sends her into a frenzied week of typing at her Olympia. By the time the workshop begins, she has over forty pages.

The Writers Community, in 1977, is housed in a large ground-floor apartment in a pre-war building on 89th Street between Park and Lexington Avenue. Even during the day, with the lights on, the cavernous rooms with their dark wood floors are dim. The workshop is held in a room with a long banquet table, where class members sit with manuscript pages stacked in front of them. There are several smaller rooms with bookshelves and a backroom for secret flirtations and a quick smoke before class.

In addition to all those initials before his name, C. D. B. Bryan dazzles with his long, lanky frame, choir boy hair, Tom Wolfe suits and foppish hats, his cultivated manner, and by contrast, his outrageous, no-holds-barred remarks. The author of *Friendly Fire*, a powerful nonfiction book about Vietnam, is in the throes of personal chaos, which he shares with the class. The atmosphere in the room is electrically charged. The fiction writers eat it all up.

The young novelist comes weekly, bringing at least one new chapter with her, sometimes more. The positive feedback is addictive. She wants to please her teacher. And he seems to wait eagerly for each installment. At page one hundred, he promises that he will show her novel to his agent—when she has 125 pages. The carrot glitters brightly, not too far away now.

She writes every morning for four hours, takes a shower, and rides her bicycle to the advertising agency that subsidizes her. She brings in twenty-five more pages in two weeks. C. D. B. Bryan agrees to show her 125 pages to his agent.

A good fairy can turn pumpkins into carriages, and rags into magnificent raiments (as a troll can rip out the lining and make pumpkin puddles). After class that evening, C. D. B. Bryan takes her out to Elaine's, where she floats past Woody Allen's table. They are seated with a view of the room. Elaine herself joins them for a few minutes. He introduces her as a wonderful new talent.

Later, Cinderella sips her chardonnay. She is observing actor Roy Scheider, who sits at the next table, talking animatedly with a beautiful woman in a white turban, when C. D. B. B. confides in her about *his* novel-in-progress.

She keeps on writing, but now there is the feeling of a warm and receptive universe out there. *Teen Angel* is no longer just a filament of her imagination. It exists, and therefore she does too.

The agent writes her that he likes what he sees, but he wants to see more. One hundred seventy-five pages. Then he'll meet with her. Another carrot glistens as she continues to work. But the wheels have been set in motion.

She will reach page 175 and be invited to meet the agent. His office is in an old building on 40th and Park Avenue. Upon entering, she notices lots of tiny rooms with locks. "That's where we used to lock up the writers so they'd finish their stories. Afterwards," the agent, who's even taller than C. D. B. B., chuckles, "we'd take them out for drinks."

A year later, there will be 278 pages. *Finis.* No. The ending doesn't work. The budding novelist is sent back to rewrite from the middle of the book to prepare for a new ending. This will take six months. Her ending will be rewritten, and retyped, at least fifty times. But then the truly miraculous occurs: *Teen Angel* is sent out into the world. Pub date: November 1978.

The novel has its own life. *Publishers Weekly* and *Kirkus* like it, the *New York Times* is on strike. There's a paperback and an English sale. It's banned in South Africa, and Universal offers an option. She will write the screenplay with director Garry Marshall, for which she will be remunerated handsomely, but the movie will never be made. End of fairy tale.

I was too young and too raw to grasp my good fortune at the time. It's only now, from a distance of nearly twenty years, fifteen of them teaching young writers not unlike myself then, that I understand my debt.

Writers need nurturing. Their hope is slender, their confidence mercurial. The Writers Community gave me space to work in, a mentor and peers to help me grow. Imagine, an honorary workshop, where you don't have to pay (or just a nominal fee). Such generosity, such support to the hungry artistic soul.

So I say thanks to The Writers Community for my first lucky break. And thank you, C. D. B. B., who gave *Teen Angel* its most memorable quote: "Author Pilcer should be given a major literary award, then have her mouth washed out with soap."

SONIA PILCER *is the author of four novels:* Teen Angel, Maiden Rites, Little Darlings, *and* I-LAND: Manhattan Monologues. *She adapted* I-Land *as a theatrical play, which was produced by the Road Theater in Los Angeles and the Thirteen Street Repertory Theater, where it ran for over six years. She has also written for television and film. She currently teaches writing at Berkshire Community College and is completing her new novel,* Stung by a Serpent.

STERLING D. PLUMPP

Martyr

(for the children of David Theys)

1

I will sing
you the true

blood dripping
cabin legends
in lines forming a
cross where I witness

horrors of open
eyes listening

because among
my people suffering
is a celebrant

language we speak

I chant no
more auction blocks
for me
no more
auction blocks

for me
no more
no more

and I hear your shouts
for freedom
in *gumboot dances*

mining ore
mining ore

mining

choreographing dramas
of assassins in *pata*
pata embraces
with comrades fallen

2

You were my eyes
while I was in Welkon

and the hearts of children
struggling one
more mile one
more mile

were my ears listening
to new suns rising
from debris of bones
and dried blood

children struggling
one more mile
shovels in hands

inventing history

where a world can
see ladders pointing
toward a sky any
person can climb with
out disqualification
because of skin or
dialect or gender or
rituals at prayer time

I chant
in that great getting up morning

I chant
steal away
steal away
steal away
steal away

I chant
Lord don't you move this mountain
just give me the strength to pass
I chant
Jesus speaks
speaks so sweet

I hear
the shuffles of the angel's feet

3

Murder the daily bread
of those with dreams

big enough to swallow
galaxies is

plentiful in your land
in my land

It is never
easy to calculate
numbers for it

for "Silencing Those
Who Create Freedom"
is always the top

rated television program every
where you got thieves
wearing masks

They kill those
whose voices come
like yours from
chromatic districts of
peoples' dreams

singing jobs
singing bread
singing houses
singing education
singing equality
singing no more racism
singing no more terrors

and I chant
at the very time
I thought I was lost
my dungeon shook
and my chains fell

4

I sometimes feel
like a jubilant *toi toi*
calling names of the fallen

and I know
you David
host of my Welkon visit
host of my dreams for freedom

you teacher of Civics
lessons I cherish

I know

you are in
side the memory
where songs bathe
you in honey

and place your name
in the feelings
which yield one
man one vote
one woman one
vote and one
child one

hope

now ain't
that good news
good news
good news

Tell me
ain't that good

news

STERLING D. PLUMPP ON COMMUNITY
Literature and Commitment

I am an African-American and my identity arises out of the brutal separation of Africans from the west coast of Africa and their eventual introduction into the New World. Therefore, since I cannot possibly define myself without addressing political issues such as racial discrimination, gender discrimination, and class domination, I incorporate into my art these forces, which have shaped me—forces I struggle to overcome. Although I am collectively an African-American, I am also a member of the "oppressed majority," whether it be on account of race, gender, or class. The legacy of African-American culture, however, is one committed to art that is at once communal and excellent. I come from the tradition that produced Negro spirituals, folktales, blues, jazz, gospel, and rap; it is a cultural context whereby oppressed and "voiceless" African-Americans forge a language and worldview to affirm their humanity and communicate it to the world.

Yet once an individual begins to put things on paper, he or she must be very careful. This is to say that the bourgeois exploiters of the world do not have any monopoly on excellence. Here I am recognizing the excellence of expressions in the literatures of many cultures—Greek, Roman, Jewish, French, English, Indian, Chinese, Japanese—moreover, I am affirming that oppressed people are bound to the mandates of literature without being bound to narrow expectations of elitist and Eurocentric zealots.

I cherish works by women, African-Americans, and other minorities, and I want these works to tackle the motley issues confronting the oppressed without blinking. But I want these committed writers to do so with the intent of producing outstanding literary works. No,

I do not have any "canonical texts" to suggest as models, but I do observe that the works of certain select individuals—e.g., Pablo Neruda, Nadine Gordimer, Keorapetse Kgositsile, Audre Lorde, John Edgar Wideman, Leon Forrest, Eudora Welty, Lorca, Nicolas Gullien, Sonia Sanchez, and Toni Morrison—privilege the desires, dreams, and disappointments of oppressed communities without sacrificing literary excellence.

Finally, I feel that the doors of experimentation must be kept open for any writer. I do not believe that literary cloning of the imagined texts of white males, who support the status quo with respect to oppressed individuals, is the way forward. I suppose what I am hinting at is that I support literature that exposes and affirms the worlds of disadvantaged groups, and I support their literary creations as valid. Moreover, I support literacy for all people, so that they will have the knowledge and skills to inform themselves about available literary conventions and practices.

David Theys was my host in the Orange Free State while I visited South Africa in 1991. He was a leader in the Civics, the communal structures developed to govern townships after Apartheid structures had been rendered unable to govern. Theys was active in the Bronville Civics (Bronville is a so-called Colored township near Welkon). Thabong is the Black township for the same region. He was a miner whose specialty was environmental control. I received word that he was brutally murdered hours before I wrote the poem, "Martyr," included here.

STERLING D. PLUMPP *is the author of* Johannesburg and Other Poems, Blues: The Story Always Untold, The Mojo Hands Call, I Must Go, Hornman, Portable Soul*, and* Half Black, Half Blacker. *His work has appeared in* TriQuarterly, Negro Digest (Black World), Callaloo, Obsidian, Black Scholar, *and* Black American Literature Forum. *He is a professor of African-American studies and English at the University of Illinois at Chicago and taught at The Writers Community at The Writer's Voice of Chicago in 1995.*

NAHID RACHLIN

Happiness

As I pack, my eyes keep going to the photograph of my mother and myself that I had taken from an old album and now sits on my desk. Finally Lily and I are ready for the trip to Iran to find Mother. We will be leaving in three days and be there in four days, losing one day travelling. Incredible in a way. It took six months to get visas—we had to prove we had our mother and relatives there to visit and to get new passports with photos in which our hair is covered by scarves and we wear raincoats—a dress code required by the new regime, which we too will have to follow when we arrive. Even purchasing tickets was difficult, since not many airlines go to Iran these days. But of course it will be worth all the effort if we finally track Mother down.

In the photograph both Mother and I are dressed up. I must have been around ten or eleven, not long before she left us. I am wearing a blue dress with a pleated skirt, a blue ribbon in my hair, white shoes and socks. Mother is wearing a liver-colored dress, high heels, and a hat with her black hair flowing out from underneath it. She is slender, her eyes dark and dreamy, her lips almost heart-shaped. Could it have been taken that day when I looked up at her, as we stood on the steps of the church, and saw tears rolling down her face? A little later that day I found her sitting in a chair by the window in her room, smoking a cigarette, looking sad and withdrawn. "What's wrong Mom?" I asked. "I miss my sisters, my family," she said in her heavily accented English. Adding more vaguely, "This isn't the way I was raised." Only later I understood what she meant—she had converted to Catholicism only to please my father and his family. It was fourteen years ago that she vanished from our lives—I was only thirteen and Lily eleven—but the pain of it is still so fresh.

How could she just vanish like that? At first she sent us presents, with the briefest notes—for my lovely daughter Miriam, or for my beloved Lily—but she never gave us a return address. I still have some of the presents—a pink-and-blue hand-knit sweater (which of course no longer fits me), a flower-shaped barrette (which I still wear occasionally, though it is all worn), and a doll with braided black hair that I keep on my dresser. I used to take it to bed with me. A warm and comforting wave would rush over me as I thought, this is from my mother. I would see my mother's face close to mine, feel her arm around me, hear her whispering to me, telling me stories, as she used to do before she left. After a while her notes and gifts stopped. I wrote her many letters, sending them to Aunt Mahin to forward to her, begging her to come back, asking her forgiveness for the mischiefs Lily and I had done, which I was sure were part of the reason she had gone away. I promised to be a good girl, to obey her. I spoke of lonely nights, how empty the house was without her. Then I wrote Aunt Mahin, asking her why Mom was not answering my letters, but she never gave me any clues. I had begun to have horrible visions of Mother locked up in a remote mental hospital or worse, dead.

But then there was the letter six months ago that started the idea for the trip to Iran. Coming home from the office, where I do temp work, intending to continue until school starts in the fall, I noticed an air letter among the envelopes I pulled out of the mailbox. It was from Iran. My mother? My heart almost leapt out of my chest at the mere thought. I dashed inside, dropped my bag on the living-room floor, and sitting down on the chair, opened the letter. I know more Farsi now than when Mother lived with us—learning it has been a part of my obsession with her. The letter was from Aunt Mahin. "I passed on your letter and the photograph to your mother. She said she's glad you have your father to go back to. And Darien is such a lovely child. She cried seeing his picture. All I can tell you about your mother is not to worry. She is fine and she thinks about you, Lily, your father, all the time. She has never stopped having you in her heart. But keeping a distance from you is the only way she can live her new life, one that she can fit into better . . ." I breathed deeply, painfully.

Perhaps the decisive force behind her finally responding after all these years, even though it was no more than a brief message sent through her sister, was the letter I wrote to her. "I'm back living with Dad. Divorced. Darien is four years old. I wish I had you to talk to throughout all this. Lily too just broke up with someone she was going out with. A lot of broken hearts here. How are you, are you happy? . . ." I had enclosed a new picture of Darien in it.

Did Mom see my moving in with my father as a desperate act, evoking guilt in her that she is not here for me; did it simply make her yearn for what she has left behind?

Is it strange to have moved in with my father at the age of twenty-seven, with a four-year-old son? A weakness? There are of course many benefits. I can save on rent and go back to school with the money I got from selling the house my ex-husband and I had lived in. Darien has more space to run around in—his room here, once belonging to Lily, is practically as large as the whole apartment we moved to after the divorce. Anyway I love this house with its views of the beach from practically every room and its huge palm-filled yard.

I close the suitcase and go into the kitchen to get dinner ready. As I beat the eggs for a cake, I think of Lily and me coloring eggs for Easter when we were children. Mother would add some designs to them herself, stripes, dots, little chickens. We would pile up the eggs in a basket and put it on the dining room table. I remember clearly the last time I saw Mom. She was wearing a blue linen dress, navy low-heeled shoes, before she went out the door and never returned. I don't recall, though, whether she was carrying any luggage or whether, before leaving through that door forever, she displayed any extra affection toward me and Lily.

My father tried to be both parents to us. He came home from work on time to shop and cook. He was the one who read or told us stories at night. Most of the time he put on a cheerful front, but once I caught him crying—he was leaning on the patio railing, in the twilight, holding his head between his hands, and tears were streaming down his face. I asked him what was wrong and he held me to himself and said, "Nothing, nothing, life just gets sad sometimes." "Daddy, you won't go way from us like Mommy did, will you?" "No, no, of course not," he said, wiping his tears and pulling me up into his arms. "I'll be here with you forever." But insecurity lingered with me. I asked him over and over, "Do you love me?" He was always reassuring: "You and Lily are my whole life, I love you more than you can imagine."

I can't complain, he gave us what any father could, but all his attention didn't compensate for the loss, the trauma of Mother's sudden departure.

Dad comes in and helps me set the table. The dining room is filled with light because of its south-facing windows. The thick oak table is still the same from years ago, and underneath it there are carvings Lily and I made—a round smiling face, a tree. I used to do my homework at this table while I watched Mom work in the kitchen. My interest in school and studying dwindled after she left. It was all so irrelevant. In the classroom I would daydream about my mother instead of listening to the teachers, imagine us in a room with no people or sounds to disrupt our complete focus on each other. That indifference to school followed me all the way to college. When I dropped out after one semester, one of my teachers said, "You aren't living up to your potential."

Dad and I sit down to eat, with Darien on a chair between us. Dad attends to Darien, cutting up a piece of veal for him, wiping the sauce getting on his face. Dad is much more subdued than I remember him from when Mom was still around. He used to be flamboyant, loud, assertive. He liked to joke all the time; he would suddenly turn on the music and start dancing with Mom or with Lily or me.

Darien gets up and goes to the TV. He turns the channels until cartoons come on. He takes his plate and begins to eat there by the set.

I ask Dad, "How was your day at work?"

"Not so good. One of the young women went hysterical, she threatened suicide."

"Oh, no! Anyone I met when I came there?"

"Janis, the redheaded, freckled girl."

"I remember her."

Dad says suddenly, "The happiest days for your Mom were after each birth, first you and then Lily. . . . She's going to come back. She'll want to claim her family one day." He adds more forcefully, as if he sees a clear analogy, "I work with runaways, I know they finally want to return home." Maybe in the back of his mind he thinks of my mother as young, when he just met her, her image then. "You and Lily could try to bring her back."

He and Mom never got divorced officially. Once when I asked him why, he said, "You know how hard it is for a Catholic to get a divorce" (though he is no longer a practicing Catholic). And then, "Anyway she's going to come back." They had met in Iran, where he had gone to represent his pharmaceutical company, his job then (later he quit that job and began studying to become a social worker, what he does now). He had seen her at a friend's house. Within a few months they were engaged, though they hardly knew each other. She had pleaded with her parents to let her marry him (they were opposed to his being an American), and finally they gave in. She had been only eighteen and my father twenty-five. In the United States she had gone to college but then stayed home when she had Lily and me. She had developed an interest in flower painting (a few of her paintings, of a bunch of tulips, a large iris, two roses, hung on the walls of the living room). These are the bare facts. The rest, the yearning, the pain, the blame and self-blame following her going away, is more elusive. Lily, Dad, and I have gone over the events so many times that they have become like rounded, washed-over stones you find at the bottom of a stream.

After finishing dinner Dad helps me clean up, then he goes to his room and I take Darien into the bathroom to give him his nightly bath.

It is seven o'clock. Andy is half-an-hour late. I almost wish I had not started going out with him again when he came back to L.A. from New York. He stays up all night watching old movies and works a few hours a day as a paralegal to make a bare minimum living and keeps writing scripts, hoping one day he'll have a breakthrough. His hair is always disheveled and almost as long as mine. He is almost too much the opposite of Chuck, my ex-husband. Life had run smoothly for a while with Chuck, mostly due to his sense of commitment and dedication to everything in his life. As a manager of a supermarket, he had an elaborate file system for the bills, every bit of money that came and went, receipts to be used for tax returns. He was good at fixing things around the house. It was his resourcefulness and attention to detail that had helped him move from the position of clerk to manager.

What went wrong exactly between us? I remember a vague depression settling on me and growing. Even simple things befuddled me. I asked myself, in continuous self-doubt, am I doing the right thing rushing to Darien every time he starts to cry, do I give in to his demands for milk or give him the pacifier too quickly? Is it wrong that I put him in our bed when he wanders into our room at dawn? "You've become impossible," Chuck said, when he came home and found me sitting idly on the sofa, the house in a jumble. Sometimes he zoomed out and didn't come back until the middle of the night. And then one evening he said, "I can't take this anymore," and left me for good.

The phone is ringing. I pick it up.

"Hi, I'm going to be an hour late." It is Andy. "I'm just at an important point in the script."

"You're already half an hour late."

"I know. You understand, don't you?"

"I guess so."

I should start with someone new, instead of hanging on to a problematic relationship. I have to grow stronger . . .

I end up meeting him at the eight o'clock show of a movie, *Sleepless in Seattle*, we hadn't planned to see. As we watch he keeps whispering in my ear how he would do certain words and scenes in the movie differently. After it is finished we go to Rioja, a Mexican restaurant, just opened. We sit in a dim corner in the back, have sangria and mixed plates, and keep talking about the movie, more than I can bear.

We go to his apartment in a run-down section of Venice, then directly to his bedroom. I wonder if the main thing that keeps us together is sex. We are good together in that sense. He likes making love in different spots of his apartment, but mostly right here, where two large mirrors on the walls reflect our bodies as they intertwine, lock inside of each other.

When we lie back, sweaty and spent, all I feel is an emptiness.

"What are you thinking about?" he asks.

"Nothing."

"You can't be thinking about nothing."

"Don't you wonder where we're heading?"

"No."

We get out of the bed and go into his small living room with a tiny kitchen extending from it.

"I'll get you your herb tea," he says and goes into the kitchen while I sit on the sofa with some of the foam showing through torn spots in the fabric. He comes back with peppermint tea for me in the red polka-dot cup he knows I like and a beer for himself and sits next to me.

"So you feel good about going to Iran?" he asks.

"Happy and nervous. You know, I still miss my mother."

"Yeah. I can understand, sweetie. I missed my father for years, still do, after he and my mom split and he went to live in Mexico."

The TV he never turns off drones in the background. He intermittently drifts away from our conversation and focuses on the images on the screen. His own screenplays echo what he watches, sitcoms, mysteries, soap operas. His connection with what goes on around him is somewhat flimsy and tenuous; maybe so is mine.

I leave before midnight. At home, I tiptoe into Darien's room and check on him. He's asleep, so I go to my own room and get ready for bed. I have a hard time sleeping; I toss and turn. In a way it's good that living here keeps me from spending too much time with Andy. I would never stay in his apartment an entire night or let him spend a night here, where Darien and Dad would overhear conversations, the creaking of the bed. Dad himself is reticent about the women in his life. In fact he has never mentioned anyone specific to me or introduced me. He has acknowledged only having "women friends." Every year I expect him to announce to us that a romance has developed in his life, someone just widowed or divorced or a woman he met at work, but it hasn't happened yet.

I finally fall asleep and I wake from a dream about Mom. The two of us were standing together at the rail of a cruise ship. We were wearing identical red dresses, black patent leather shoes, and gold necklaces. Mom began to laugh. "They're going to get us mixed up," she said.

Oh, it feels so much like it really happened, not just a dream. I do resemble Mom; Lily has always looked more like Dad, has his light brown hair and blue-gray eyes. I used to think I was closer to Mom than Lily was, that being the firstborn gave me a special place with her, and Lily was closer to Dad. Now Lily rarely visits Dad; she keeps herself busy, maybe too busy, with her work in the cosmetics department of Bullock's and with a string of boyfriends. She appears to be more easygoing than me about life, but I wonder.

In two days we'll be in Isfahan . . . we'll be with Mother. Images of the one time she took Lily and me, children then, for a visit to Iran come to me in bright flashes. We stayed in a big house in a village just outside of Isfahan, an oasis at the edge of a desert. The desert was beautiful. So were the mountains in the distance—they changed color from brown in the sun to salmon at dusk and then deep blue with the darkening sky. Wolves and jackals lived in the mountains. Next to the house was an orchard with a spring in the middle of it. Lily and I and other children roamed through the orchard and picked fruit from the trees and ate them; we swam in the spring. At night we slept under mosquito nets in the courtyard, where the stars and the moon were brighter than I had ever seen. I remember the sounds from that visit—the whistles of nightingales at dawn, the howl of the owls in the evening, the shriek of the jackals in the middle of the night, which made me crawl into Mother's bed for protection. And the voice of the muezzin three times a day calling people to prayers. Many, many relatives came to the big house and fussed over Lily and me, gave us presents—jewelry, clay animals, rag dolls. I remember Mother whispering things to her relatives about religion, a certain concern on their faces at what she said, a certain nervousness on her part. These images and sounds have come to me on and off through the years, like a dream, they are so disconnected with L.A.

Except for that visit Mother stayed remote from her own culture—she followed another religion, observed different holidays, spoke English rather than her own language. We, her children, were all American, and she did little to make us understand or be a part of her culture. But in general she wasn't a part of American culture. She kept to herself, had few friends. She was shy with other mothers. She never went to open school day or PTA meetings. At our birthday parties it was our father who took charge, decorating the house with balloons and colorful streamers and arranging games and the party bags to give to the children to take home. She smiled pleasantly at the other mothers but rarely engaged them in conversation. When she left us, Father lied to us about her. "She's sick, she went to recuperate at her own family's house." But as time went by and there was no sign of her, he said, "She's liking it there too much but don't worry, one day you'll come home and see her waiting for you."

We have been here in Isfahan for five days now and have only five more days left of the trip. Lily and I must get back to work and I to Darien—I can't bear the separation from him. I keep wondering what he is doing, at this moment, for instance, though I know between Dad and his babysitter, he's fine, is in good hands.

The long flight from the L.A. airport, via Turkey to Teheran, and then the bus ride from Teheran to here went quickly—Lily and I were so intensely engaged in our speculation about Mother. The hotel, in the center of the city, near the main square, is modern and seems to be filled with businessmen—a group of Japanese men are often sitting in the lobby and two German men have been eating breakfast in the dining room.

When we arrived in the hotel, immediately after washing up and a quick snack in the dining room, we began our search. But when we went to Mahin's address we were told by a young girl who answered the door that she had moved away. Strange since Aunt Mahin's address has always been the same. "Are you sure?" I asked.

The girl stared at me, looking insulted. She didn't know her new address, she said.

Now I continue my search alone, without Lily's help—after the first frenzied attempt, Lily has been taking tours arranged through the hotel—trying on my own to trace Mother through shopkeepers, the bank, the post office. I have done little else than search for her— I only allowed myself to visit a few sights in this ancient city, the Shaking Minarets, a building that sways when you lean against it, and the Masjid-e-Imam, a mosque with great Islamic architecture.

I notice a photography shop among a row of shops, displaying handmade vases, painted pen cases, silver jewelry. I look at the photographs behind the window—one of a family together, one of a bride and groom. I go inside and ask the woman standing behind the counter, "Do you have any photographs of the Anjomani family, I'm a relative from America."

"Yes, some we took at a wedding. There have been several weddings in the family."

Though I was hoping for it, I didn't expect her answer.

"Can I look at the photographs."

She opens an album and quickly looks through it. Then she pauses on one page. A woman standing next to a man in a courtyard strongly resembles my mother—older of course, but with the same features, particularly the eyes.

"Is this Pari Anjomani?"

The woman nods. "And that's her husband."

Husband? My mother is still married to my father. He could be a relative the woman is mistaking for a husband. The man in the photograph is burly-looking with rather coarse features and a big mustache twisted upward, very masculine and yet conveying kindness.

"Do you have her address?"

She fumbles through a stack of papers, mostly bills and receipts on the desk. "Here is Pari's address. They live in Ashtarjan."

"How far is that?"

"About an hour on the bus." She writes down the address and gives it to me. She tells me how to find it among a maze of lanes.

"Do you want me to take photographs of you, as you see we do very good work?" she asks.

"Definitely, I'll come back with my sister." I thank her and leave, eager to tell Lily what I have found out.

Lily comes out of the bathroom with the towel wrapped around her, water glistening on her skin, dripping down her hair. I notice the large bruise on her arm, which she has said is from Jarred playfully biting her. Her relationship with men worries me sometimes, though I am not proud of my own broken marriage, all the meaningless affairs I have had since.

When I tell her about the address I have found she says, "I hope it isn't a false lead."

Outside the window I see mist has gathered in the air, obscuring the view. Only the dome and minarets of a mosque are clearly visible. A brown finch comes and sits on the windowsill, its wings wet, probably from bathing in the hotel's courtyard fountain.

She is finished drying herself and begins to dress. "I met a really cute French boy on the tour. He's gorgeous." She studies my face for my reaction. "I gave him the phone number here."

"Oh, Lily," I say in a tone I try to keep light.

After Lily is dressed we go to eat in a restaurant near the hotel—serving the usual *chelo kebab* and *koreshes*.

A waiter comes over to take our order. Lily smiles at him. He smiles back flirtatiously, lingers a bit, trying to talk to her in English. She looks striking even though her hair is all covered up.

After the waiter walks away, she says, "I wonder what happened to Maurice."

"Who's Maurice?"

"You know, the man I met on the tour. He didn't call."

"You know you're playing with fire. This is an Islamic country. We're covered up because we aren't supposed to be temptations to men. You can get arrested and go to jail if you're seen with a man who isn't your husband or brother or father."

"Don't worry, I'll be careful . . . if I ever see him again."

After we are finished eating, we walk for a while through the main square, which is bright with gas lamps. Many people, the women wearing *chadors* or *rupushes* and scarves, are walking around, going in and out of shops or sitting in restaurants and cafes.

When we return to the hotel, in the lobby the clerk hands a message to Lily.

"He did call," she says to me, showing me the pink slip.

I glance at the message. "Maurice requested that you call him back." Underneath that a phone number is listed.

"Are you going to call him?"

"Maybe."

I know my trying to talk her out of it would have little effect.

Later as we lie in bed I feel like we are children again, close and yet separated by our different dreams. But what are my dreams exactly? Sometimes it is as if I am someone I am reading about in a bad novel.

I wake in the morning with the rays of sun shining on my face. Lily is not in her bed. I look at my watch. It's ten o'clock; I have overslept. I get up and start for the bathroom. I see my name written in large letters on a yellow sheet of paper lying on the side table and I pick it up. A note from Lily.

"Miriam, I hope you don't mind but I'm going to spend the day with Maurice. I found him waiting for me in the lobby this morning. You go on your search alone, see you tonight."

I cringe inwardly. How could she spend this, of all days, with a man she will never see again once we leave Iran? Is she more pessimistic than I am, or more indifferent to Mother? I think of her as a teenager telling her friends that Mother had died. Right after Mother left us, though, we talked about it all the time and sometimes I would wake in the middle of the night and hear Lily crying to herself in her room.

I get off the bus in Ashtarjan and walk along the river that runs through it, passing a mosque, houses built of mud or stone huddled together on the other side, green pastures, a few orchards. I have covered up even more carefully, wearing my darkest scarf and a plain gray *rupush*, which I bought to replace my raincoat. The sunlight, so lucid and golden, adds a luster to everything, and the most squalid sights take on a richness. The snow-covered mountains surrounding the village seem to shelter against harsh desert winds and it is cool as I walk.

I come to a little square, its shops carrying the essentials—sugar, rice, matches—and with a flowerbed at its center. A mill, a low clay building with a tower, stands on one side of the square and a dilapidated rooming house on the other. Then I come to a cluster of narrow lanes snaking off a main wide avenue and begin to look for the address. At an intersection stands a mosque, with a group of women wearing black *chadors* sitting on its steps, waiting for something, it seems. Next to the mosque is a huge poplar tree with a hollow made in its center, and an old man is lying on a mat spread in the hollow. Children have collected around him, taunting him, throwing coins to him. I keep thinking what a different world this is from L.A. and wonder how my mother, who had lived in L.A. for so many years, could live here.

I see "Gol Abad" written on the wall of an alley. There it is, I think excitedly and turn into it. One side of the alley is lined by gardens and orchards with flowers and fruit showing above the crude walls surrounding them; houses stand on the other side. Some of the houses' doors are open, and I have glimpses of hallways, courtyards. In one hallway two children are kneeling and playing with marbles. Then I am in front of number twenty-eight. I stand back and look at it. It is an old, seedy-looking house, sagging a little. Weathered blue tiles surround the dark, heavy door. The appearance of the house is softened somewhat by the row of small fruit trees planted in front of it and that ever-present golden sunlight. The mere thought that my mother might be inside there fills me with awe. I hear my heart thumping as I ring the rusted bell. It has been fourteen years since I saw her last—how will she react to my turning up at her house, how will she explain what she did to us? I feel a palpitation in my heart almost as if I am about to reunite with a lover. I put my head on the door and listen for sounds inside. I hear children's voices and then a woman's barely audible voice. I begin to cough. I remember when Mother left us I developed a cough that would not go away. Father took me to a doctor and got a prescription. Later, when I was older, he told me the medicine was a placebo, that the doctor had said my cough was from nervousness.

"Mother, someone is knocking," I hear a boy saying, and then footsteps. Could I have the wrong address, the wrong person?

The door is opened and a small boy stands before me, staring at me with his dark eyes.

"I'm looking for Pari Anjomani. Does she live here?"

The boy begins to run back inside. "Mother, Mother."

I stand frozen in my spot. In a moment I see a woman approaching in the dim hallway. My eyes are riveted on her, and as she comes closer I can see that she is the same person as in the photograph, with a strong resemblance to Mother. "Are you Pari?" I ask through a constricted throat.

She nods, staring at me without recognition.

This may be a different Pari altogether. But her eyes . . . "Do you know who I am?" I ask. She keeps staring. "Miriam."

She flutters her hand in the air as if about to shut the door on me. Then she says, "Oh, Miriam, Miriam, you came, why did you . . . I'm so happy to see you . . . you shouldn't have come," she says, confusingly, in a whisper.

"Mom, I've been searching for you, Lily and I." I walk into the hallway and we embrace.

"Please don't tell my other children who you are. I'll explain everything, my Miriam, my dear daughter."

My mother's four children, two boys and two girls ranging in age from around four to ten or so, play in the courtyard while she and I sit in the living room talking. Chickens and goats are roaming around the courtyard. I recall how frequently I would come home, in L.A., and find Mother leaning over a flowerbed, weeding, planting, watering. And then those flower paintings. I don't see any paintings like that on her walls here, but the courtyard before us is flush with flowers.

The walls are whitewashed, the floors covered with tiles, chipped here and there, the furniture is simple and hard. On the worn mosaic-covered mantle above the stone fireplace stand a few blown-up and framed photographs and clay animals.

"Let me get you something to eat," she says.

"I'm not hungry."

"Why didn't Lily come with you?"

I hesitate, grope for an answer. "She had to rest. She got a stomachache."

"Why don't I get you a cool drink. *Doogh, sharbat?*"

"*Doogh* is fine." I detect a strange formality in my tone.

She gets up and so do I and we go into the kitchen. The kitchen is large with whitewashed walls also and smells pleasantly of spices. Baskets heaped with fruit or with garlic, onions, and other vegetables, lie on a tiled counter; copper pots and pans hang from hooks. She takes out a jug of *doogh* from a stumpy-looking icebox, pours some in two glasses, and we go back into the living room.

I am hoping she will say our letters never got to her, that she will explain her hiding from us, that she will say she never knew we were trying so hard to get her back, but another voice in a deep gray spot of my mind asks, how can any of that be possible?

She says suddenly, "I'm sorry I haven't been in touch."

"Haven't been in touch" is too light a phrase to capture the magnitude of the loss I have been living with, but everything about this woman, my mother, is startling, verging on the absurd, unbelievable. I am not the same person I was when she left. I have been through a divorce; I have a child; I have moved out and back into my father's house. Some of my dreams have been shattered, others substituted. Why do I expect Mother to be the same as years ago?

She begins to knit, with blue and green yarn. "A sweater for my youngest son," she says.

Memories, half-faded, spill over me. She, sitting under a tree, knitting a sweater then too, for Lily or me. She and Lily standing in the living room of our house, arguing about something, Lily saying to her with the bluntness and cruelty of a child, "Mom, you don't understand, you're from another world." Myself ashamed of Mother's accent, blushing when she speaks to my friends. Mother crying and saying, "I don't know what's the matter with me."

"Mom, why have you been hiding from us? Tell me, what made you leave?"

My mother hangs her head down and does not say anything. When she lifts her head I see her eyes are glistening with tears. We both take sips of our *dooghs* and I have a momentary illusion of closeness to her, the way I did as a child, sitting with her, feeling protected. So many times I have woken in the middle of the night from dreams about Mother, so often I have lain in the dark, thinking of questions I would ask her. During those wakeful moments I felt that some piece of my own existence would always be missing unless I saw her, talked to her.

Two hours later we're still sitting there, with me urging her to talk to me, tell me what happened. Finally she says, "One day I was alone in the house. You and Lily were at school and your father was out working. I was feeling depressed. There was a knock on the door. I went to open it, thinking maybe it was a neighbor, though I had not really become friendly with any of them. When I opened the door I saw a man standing there. He said abruptly, in a familiar tone as if he knew me, 'I finally found you, do you know how long I've been looking.' I couldn't believe it, but it was Parviz, a boy I had known in our neighborhood. He had asked my parents to let him marry me, and I would have if your father hadn't come along. I was so shaken to see him . . ."

It's just a friendly visit, he had said. But then they had gone for a walk in Marina Del Rey. They talked about the old times. After a while she was thrown into a state of something like delirium. She was not sure where she was, what country, beside what body of water. Was not sure about her age or who this man was, holding her arm. His presence, his touch, both had calmed and excited her. Strange. But what calmed her was his sheer presence and what excited her was what he had opened up, puncturing a capsule in which powerful memories had been hidden away. His visit pulled at her like a magnet during the days that followed. Suddenly everything around her— the beaches, the pastel, precarious-looking houses, the canyons still holding rubble from fires, charred hillsides where houses had once stood—all seemed without any meaning or clues, desolate.

She stops. I am too dazed to say anything. I remember how she used to withdraw into some inner compartment, and now I see it as a retreat when she could no longer bear what went on around her. Still her dreamy look, her sitting in a corner and staring into the darkness, had not seemed to signal anything so drastic. Finally I ask, "Is he the person you live with now?"

She nods. Then she startles me by saying, "We got married when I came here."

"But you're married to my father."

"No one here knows that, except for Parviz of course. It would have terrible consequences for me if they knew."

My eyes focus on the pictures on the mantle. Then I spot the man looking like the one in the other photograph I saw in the shop.

"Did you ever love Dad?" I ask.

"I was very young when we met. I was swept away by the idea of living in America. But it took every atom of my existence to try to adjust to it. I did my best but then something broke with Parviz, would have sooner or later anyway. There was a lack I couldn't fill."

I think of the lack I have been feeling for so long, which seems to have stunted my growth. I assume the same is true about Lily. We have been blown this way and that way like unanchored ships struck by a wind.

"True, he's possessive, jealous, but in some ways I feel more free with him than I ever did with your dad," my mother says. "We can laugh together."

One of her daughters comes over to us. My mother says to her, "She's a friend visiting from America." Then turning to me she says, "She's my oldest daughter, Manijeh."

I smile at Manijeh. She stares at me with her large, dark eyes, leans over and whispers something to Mother and Mother whispers something back. Then Manijeh dashes out.

"She wanted to know if you're staying here. My children love having visitors. She wanted to bake something for you. She's a wonderful child, perfect."

She is a substitute for me, I think painfully.

Mother is looking animated now; her eyes are glistening. And I am aware now also that the house, in spite of its decaying condition, has a happiness to it.

"What does he . . ." I have a hard time saying "your husband," and an equally hard time saying his name.

"He's a carpenter, builds cabinets, closets." There is a touch of pride in her tone. "He's a good man." She reaches forward and holds my hand. I feel a tremor in her hand. "But Miriam, if you love me, if you truly care about my well-being, you have to promise to forget about me, at least a while longer. I have no choice."

I nod. I think of my father still hoping for her return, his saying to me, so many times, his face thoughtful, furrows between his brows, "I work with runaways . . ."

"I'd better go back," I say, looking at my watch. "There's only one bus going to Isfahan this afternoon. It leaves in half an hour."

"Wait," she says. She walks into the adjacent room and comes back out, holding something in her hand. "Here, I want you to have it, a memento."

It is a gold necklace—a heart with a tiny latch on it, hanging on a chain.

"Open it," she says.

I open the heart, expecting a photograph of herself, instead it's of her four children, a row of tiny heads.

"Remember me through them," she says.

I put the necklace in my purse and get up. We walk to the outside door together. There, we pause and embrace. As I pull away, I see her face from memory, warm, dreamy, discontent. When I come back to the present, to her face now, I see it is content.

Outside, before I turn around, I hear Manijeh's voice from the yard. "Did the American leave already?"

"Yes," my mother says, without elaborating.

I walk rapidly to the bus station. Being in motion is calming me down somewhat. What is Lily going to think, what is her reaction going to be, other than, "I always knew she had forgotten us"? Maybe I am better off keeping the meeting with Mother a secret, leaving Lily out of it. But then I know I will have to tell her. Just before I reach the bus depot, I take the heart Mother gave to me from my purse and throw it into the river. I stand by for a moment and see it sinking to the bottom. At the moment I have a clear feeling that I am finally freed from some constraint. I can begin to focus on my own happiness. After all, that's what Mother has done.

NAHID RACHLIN ON COMMUNITY

Working alone is an aspect of writing that I don't value. In fact I find it to be a disadvantage. As long as I have been writing I have sought out groups with which to share my work and obtain feedback on the work itself. Writing groups are a way of providing such feedback.

Years ago, when I heard about The Writers Community, I was immediately drawn to it and applied to be a student. Several years later I became a teacher there. Both as student and teacher I found the experience to be exciting. I was surrounded by people who asked questions, had concerns, not just about the process of writing and publishing but about the lifestyle and outlook of a writer. For one thing being a writer entails a great deal of uncertainty—would anything you write get into print, can you make a living this way? Writing is so different from other fields in which feedback and paychecks are steady and can be counted on.

At The Writers Community I discovered that not even a group of writers was enough. The machinery of writing won't work unless the group meshes with the community at large. The public lectures and classes and day-to-day contact with a variety of people I found at The Writers Community have given me and my work the context, the breath of life.

NAHID RACHLIN, *born in Iran, has been writing and publishing novels and short stories in English for many years. She is the author of three novels,* Foreigner, Married to a Stranger, *and* The Heart's Desire, *as well as* Veils, *a collection of stories. She has held a Doubleday-Columbia Fellowship and a Wallace Stegner Fellowship and has received the Bennet Cerf Award, the PEN Syndicated Fiction Project Award, and a National Endowment for the Arts grant. She has both studied and taught at The Writers Community and currently teaches at Barnard College and in the M.F.A. writing program at Warren Wilson College.*

ROBERT RICE

Moving to Town

At the trial Lucy Booser told the judge that if her husband hadn't
insisted on going to the casino, she never would have blown up
his tractor. It was the Indians' fault, really. They were the ones
who started all the trouble, building that gambling joint just four
miles from Lucy and Odus's farm. Jackpot Junction, they called
it, and everyone in southern Minnesota could talk about nothing
else.

In the beginning it wasn't too bad, just a bingo parlor that didn't
amount to nothing in a shed on the reservation. Lucy herself had no
use for gambling of any kind, but some of the neighbors, it's true,
did play bingo, and she supposed she could understand how it might
not be too sinful to sit in a church basement on Friday night and
spend a dollar or two, as long as it went for a good cause like the
church day school. Not to the Indians, of course. She was sure most
people felt like she did and the bingo joint would go broke.

But then they went and put up the big building, three stories
high, white stucco, and put slot machines in it and card games.
People from all over the state started coming to see what was happening, and lots of them gambled. "Well, if they're stupid enough to
do that," she told Odus, "I hope they lose everything they got."

When their nearest neighbors, the Gustafsons, started going, she
let them know how foolish they were. "Those Indians are just trying
to take your money," she said.

But Edith Gustafson told her it was fun. Besides, they had a real
nice restaurant there now, the food was good and cheap. Over coffee
she described how the casino looked inside, and even though Lucy
didn't want to she listened in grim wonder.

"In the middle," Edith said, "there's blackjack tables, and it's
open all the way up to the roof. There's real wood paneling on the

walls, walnut I think, and that green carpet's so thick it feels like you're walking on your lawn."

"Well, our church is nice, too," Lucy said.

"The best part is the slot machines, though. There must be thousands of them, all shiny and lit up with lights that flash. They ding and hum all the time, like some kind of space music."

Odus put down his coffee cup with a faraway look in his eyes. His whiskers rasped as he rubbed the back of his hand across his mouth. Right then and there Lucy knew she was in trouble.

"You'll never catch us in there," she said to Edith, loud enough so she knew Odus heard. He wouldn't admit he was hard of hearing and it drove her crazy, the way he turned the TV up so loud.

"Them Indians," she said. "They're just in it 'cause they're too lazy to work. They live on the reservation so they can live off us."

"Maybe," Edith said.

But Lucy could see she didn't really agree with her because she changed the subject.

While she and Edith had a second cup, Odus went outside. To tinker with his tractor, Lucy knew. Since he retired and rented out the land all he did was play with the old thing and putter around in his garden. Over the years the garden had grown bigger and bigger until he needed the tractor to plow it.

"Stop raising all that stuff," she told him. "We can't eat it all."

But every spring Odus plowed up a little more ground behind the hog barn and planted a new kind of muskmelon or more sweet corn. Even when it rained he spent every summer morning there, and when he wasn't in the garden, he was messing with that tractor.

"You're almost eighty years old," Lucy told him. "You should be taking it easy. You've got no business working that hard at your age. And look at me. This house is too much for me to keep up. Let's sell this place and move to town."

But when she said that, Odus would get up and go outside, or if it was a winter night and he couldn't, he'd turn the TV up and ignore her.

Lucy would have to go into her bedroom to get away from the noise, and she couldn't help but feel a little sorry for herself. Fifty years of hard work she had given him. All it had gotten her was a bad back and high blood pressure. A cozy little house in town, having the neighbors over for coffee, taking life easy for a change—it didn't seem much to ask.

Even after Odus hired a maid for her, a young Indian woman she didn't approve of, it didn't really change anything and she let Odus know it. "This place is falling apart," she said one morning when he came in for coffee. "Last week it was the roof on the hog barn. This week the well's flooding. God knows what it'll be next week. You can't keep things fixed up like they should be. Did you drain that well yet?"

"I ain't looked this morning."

"I'll bet it's full of water again."

Odus just looked out the window and chewed his sweet roll, then took a sip of coffee and set his cup down on the clear plastic she kept over the tablecloth. She sighed in exasperation, reached over and moved the cup onto his saucer.

"I think I'll drive over to Jackpot Junction," he said.

Lucy couldn't have been more horrified if he'd told her he was turning Catholic. "What?"

He pushed back his chair and stood. "I'm gonna see what's there. I'll be back."

"Are you crazy? You know what Pastor Onstad says about gambling. What'll the neighbors think?"

"I ain't gonna gamble. I'm just gonna look. And the neighbors have all been there."

"Not in the middle of the day."

Odus ignored her and walked into his bedroom.

For a moment she sat at the table, listening to him open and close drawers looking for clean socks and underwear. Then she stood and wrapped Saran Wrap around the Styrofoam tray of sweet rolls and spread a dish towel over the salt and pepper shakers. She picked up her cup and saucer and carried them out and put them in the sink, then pulled open a drawer and searched through the can openers and jar lids until she found what she was looking for, an old skeleton key.

Odus was reaching into his closet for the white shirt he wore to church, standing with his back to her, when she pulled the bedroom door quietly shut and turned the key in the lock.

She tucked the key into her apron pocket and went to the front room window and gazed out. A bird feeder made out of an old bicycle wheel stood on a post in the lawn. She had bought it on the spur of the moment at a craft sale in Montevideo, much to Odus's scorn. As she watched, a breeze caught the spokes and turned the wheel slowly. The feed cups attached to the sides swung so they always stayed upright. "The birds like that," she'd told him the other day. "When the wind blows it around they get a ride."

"You ever seen a bird on that thing, Ma?" he said.

That made her mad. "I haven't been looking."

Now she heard the bedroom doorknob turn, then Odus's voice. "What the . . . ?" It rattled as he pulled on it. "Ma," he shouted, his voice muffled. "Come here once. Push on this door. It's stuck."

She smiled and watched the bird feeder turn. If the birds would just give it a chance, she knew they'd like it.

"Ma? You out there?"

"I'm here," she said.

"Come here and push on this door."

After a moment she said, "It's not stuck. I locked it."

"Hah?"

"I locked it," she shouted.

Silence. Then a puzzled, "The hell." More silence. Finally, he said, "What the devil for?"

"You're not going to that Indian gambling joint."

He muttered something she didn't catch. Then she heard the bed squeak as he sat down on it.

Lucy smiled to herself and went down in the basement to wash clothes. The avocado Kenmore automatic washer Odus had bought her sat against the wall, unplugged. Her old wringer machine got the clothes cleaner. Humming, she attached the hose to the hot water faucet and ran water into the washing machine tub.

At eleven-thirty she stopped and went upstairs to fix lunch. She put the morning's coffee back on the electric range and put white bread on a plate, then bologna and Velveeta on another and carried them to the table. When the coffee was hot, she turned off the burner and went to the bedroom door.

"Odus, lunch is ready," she shouted. "If you promise not to go to the casino, I'll let you out."

There was no answer.

She put her ear to the door and listened but heard nothing. He must have gone to sleep and she decided to let him have his nap, pleased with her generosity. She took the key from her apron and put it in the lock and turned, and pushed the door open a crack.

Odus wasn't on the bed. She pushed the door a little wider, stuck her head in the room and looked around. It was empty. The curtain caught between the closed window and the sill told her how he had escaped.

Furious with herself for forgetting the window, she swung the door open so hard it hit the wall. But as she turned to leave she decided not to let him know she had discovered his escape. She drew the door closed and locked it again, then sat down at the table and ate two bologna and Velveeta sandwiches.

She had finished the laundry and was just lying down in her room for a nap when she heard a car drive into the yard. She knew from the sound it was Odus and resisted the temptation to get up and look. A few minutes later the kitchen door opened and he came in whistling.

Lucy lay still and closed her eyes, pretending to be asleep in case he checked on her. But he didn't. He walked past her room, probably with his muddy shoes still on, and down the hall to his bedroom.

A crash raised her bolt upright. It sounded like an airplane had fallen on the house. She hurried to her door, pulled it open and peered out.

Odus had smashed the lock on his door. She stared in shock as he propped a sledgehammer against the wall and walked into his room, still whistling.

Lucy closed her door and locked it with the skeleton key and sat on her bed, hand over her mouth. Worse than she had feared. Only a few hours in that gambling den and they had turned him into a maniac. As she sat wondering what to do—Should she commit him to the asylum over in Willmar? He was obviously crazy, a gambling fiend gone violent. But how did you go about committing some-body? Just call the asylum? At least then she could move into town— as she thought about what to do she heard Odus come out of his room and walk down the hall, not whistling now. She held her breath. He hesitated a moment outside her door, but he walked on and she heard the kitchen door open and close, the screen slam.

A few minutes later she unlocked the door and opened it. The sledgehammer was gone. She went to the kitchen window and moved the curtain enough to peek out.

Odus was bent over in the farthest corner of his garden, pulling weeds from the carrots. After thinking a moment she decided she wouldn't commit him yet. But she knew he would try to sneak away to the casino again. Once in the grip of gambling fever, a man was helpless.

An idea came to her. She hurried out the front door, tiptoed to the car, and pulled the keys out of the ignition. Then she hid them, along with her own set, in the basement behind the Kenmore.

Lucy waited, fixing Odus's meals in silence, watching him out of the corner of her eye, not even mentioning the smashed door. Sure enough, two days later he came in from the garden, went to his room and changed clothes and came out whistling, jingling change in his go-to-town pants. From the window she watched him get into the Ford and hunt for the keys. In a few minutes he got out again and went to his tractor.

He unhooked the wires of the battery charger he kept connected to it and climbed up on the seat. The engine cranked and started with a pop. Then he chugged away in the direction of Jackpot Junction.

Within an hour he was back and Lucy wondered why a man would bother gambling at all if he wasn't going to stay any longer than that. He parked the tractor, hooked up the battery charger, and headed for the house. She stayed in the basement while he changed clothes, but when he left the house again she came up and looked out the kitchen window. He had gone to his garden and she knew he'd stay there until supper.

The tractor sat in front of the machine shed, and she glared at it.

It was a huge thing, faded orange with rear wheels as tall as she was and tiny front wheels angled in at the bottom. The frame had broken once and was held together by four huge bolts and old welds that looked like puckered scars. The engine leaked oil in a steady, slow drip and the battery kept running down from a short circuit Odus was never able to find. When he'd bought it back in 1948, it had been new, like their marriage, and she was as proud of it as he was, how it was the envy of the neighborhood. "You look so handsome up on that seat," she told him, and he grinned.

But now she resented it, a broken-down thing like that. What did he need a tractor for anyway? And it was embarrassing, him driving it to the casino. Next thing she knew he'd be driving it to church. She hated it, hated it like she'd never hated anything.

She put on her oldest overalls, the ones she wore to weed flower beds, and her work gloves and went over to the machine shed. It was gloomy inside, the dirt floor shiny and hard from oil and spattered with pigeon droppings. She didn't like it and never came in here if she could help it.

Lucy pulled the light string and looked around, knowing what she was after but not sure what it looked like. One winter years ago the railroad abandoned the right-of-way and put it up for sale. Odus had thought about buying the ten-mile strip between Redwood Falls and Morton, she remembered, but in the end he decided not to.

"Longest farm I ever seen," he told her, "but it's only sixty feet wide. Couldn't hardly turn the tractor around."

He had worked for the railroad that winter tearing up track. Somewhere he found an old case of dynamite and brought it home. He never told her where he stored it, but she didn't doubt it would be in here someplace.

In the back corner behind a stepladder, after she snagged her overalls on the lawn mower, she found it, an unmarked wooden box with a hinged lid covered with grease and dust. She moved the ladder aside and pulled up the lid. The box was full of gray tubes with printing on them that said *Forcite 40%*.

She picked one up and looked at it. It reminded her of a Roman candle she'd held in her hand one Fourth of July, the year Ruth got sick. She stared at the tube, turning it in her fingers, stung by the memory that ambushed her now like a snake in the flower bed, remembering the suddenness of the fever, their helplessness, the decision to take their daughter to the hospital. And the Studebaker not starting, and the horrible slowness of the tractor as Odus drove it to the neighbors' to borrow their car, then the frantic race to town, her child going stiff in her arms, and then still. Dead before they could reach town.

With a shake of her head Lucy pulled her mind back. She set the tube on the ground and searched through the case for fuses, and she found what she thought must be one, a paper box with a hole in the center that said *Thermalite Igniter Cord, Type B, 33⅓ feet.* She held the box at arm's length, squinting at the directions on the back. "Pull off length desired and cut." That seemed simple enough. She wouldn't need much.

She opened the box and pulled out a coil of waxy green cord, set it down, and went back to the house and got her pruning shears, then snipped off a length of cord about three feet long. She looked at it, wondering how to attach it to the dynamite. Any way would do, she supposed. She tied one end around the middle of the tube and made a nice bow.

Lucy got to her feet, knees stiff, and carried the dynamite to the doorway. Blinking in the bright afternoon light, she shielded her eyes and looked toward the garden. Odus was facing the other way and couldn't see her.

She tapped the tube thoughtfully on her leg, inspecting the tractor. Where to put it? He had left the seat tilted forward with the battery case open. Wires ran from the battery to the charger, on the ground near one of the rear tires.

She stepped up on the foot rest, careful not to get grease on her overalls, and laid the dynamite on top of the battery. "Just you wait till I get some matches," she said.

She was opening a drawer in the kitchen when she glanced out the window. To her horror Odus was walking toward the tractor. She froze, her hand on the matchbox. What would he do to her if he found the dynamite? He was violent, that she already knew, and if he thought she was trying to hurt his tractor, Lord knew what he was capable of. She held her breath, praying for him to go back to the garden.

But Odus folded back the hood and started playing with some wires inside. She stood paralyzed, trying to think of something to distract him, wishing the phone would ring so she could call him in.

As she was trying to decide what to do, he closed the hood with a clang and shuffled to the back. He bent over and did something with the battery charger and the tractor exploded. One moment it was standing there, faded orange in the bright sun and Odus bent over behind the huge rear wheel. The next moment there was a bright orange ball of flame and greasy black smoke and the wheel flying through the air, Odus clinging to it like a life raft.

She ran from the house shrieking, "Not you! I didn't mean you, just the tractor! Why didn't you stay in the garden?"

Jake Gustafson, driving by in his grain truck, saw the explosion and skidded to a stop as Odus and the tire landed on the lawn, taking out the bird feeder. Jake stared at the flaming tractor, then at Lucy, then loaded Odus in his truck and carried him to the hospital. She followed as soon as she could find the car keys.

The doctors told her it was pure good luck the wheel shielded Odus from the blast, and that he landed on top of it instead of the other way around. He had a broken ankle and collarbone, and his ears would ring for awhile, but he'd be all right. Jake Gustafson called the sheriff.

Odus told the judge it was an accident and he was sure Lucy never meant to blow him up. He hadn't even taken the tractor to the casino. He went to town to get a spare part, which was why he'd gotten back so soon.

The judge, Leona Peterson's boy, lectured Lucy about playing with dangerous materials like she was some kind of child and told her this was serious business, as if she didn't know that already. He gave her a night in jail. The sheriff came and took away the dynamite.

In jail Lucy worried a little about what the neighbors would think and how she would explain this to Pastor Onstad, but she decided when he knew the truth he would be on her side, and the neighbors were all gamblers anyway so their opinions didn't count. She sat on her bunk listening to two women in the next cell—Indians, she was sure, although she couldn't see them—complain about how the casino was being run and talk about voting out management at the next meeting.

She had to admit she was enjoying jail a little, although she was glad she had a private room. It had been years since she'd gotten so much attention or stayed up so late. More than ever it made her want to live in town. And now that Odus was laid up and might be limping for months, she thought she had a good chance of talking him into moving.

ROBERT RICE's *stories and poetry have appeared in literary journals such as the* North American Review, Hayden's Ferry Review, West Wind Review, Nebraska Review, *and others, and in magazines such as* Field and Stream. *His first novel,* The Last Pendragon, *published by Walker, was called by* Kirkus Reviews *"a persuasive reinvention of the Arthurian myth." Mr. Rice lives in Bozeman, Montana.*

GJERTRUD SCHNACKENBERG

Darwin in 1881

Sleepless as Prospero back in his bedroom
In Milan, with all his miracles
Reduced to sailors' tales,
He sits up in the dark. The islands loom.
His seasickness upwells,
Silence creeps by in memory as it crept
By him on water, while the sailors slept,
From broken eggs and vacant tortoise shells.
His voyage around the cape of middle age
Comes, with a feat of insight, to a close,
The same way Prospero's
Ended before he left the stage
To be led home across the blue-white sea,
When he had spoken of the clouds and globe,
Breaking his wand, and taking off his robe:
Knowledge increases unreality.

He quickly dresses.
Form wavers like his shadow on the stair
As he descends, in need of air
To cure his dizziness,
Down past the ship-sunk emptiness
Of grownup children's rooms and hallways where
The family portraits stare,
All haunted by each other's likenesses.

Outside, the orchard and a piece of moon
Are islands, he an island as he walks,

Brushing against weed stalks.
By hook and plume
The seeds gathering on his trouser legs
Are archipelagoes, like nests he sees
Shadowed in branching, ramifying trees,
Each with unique expressions in its eggs.
Different islands conjure
Different beings; different beings call
From different isles. And after all
His scrutiny of Nature
All he can see
Is how it will grow small, fade, disappear,
A coastline fading from a traveler
Aboard a survey ship. Slowly,
As coasts depart,
Nature had left behind a naturalist
Bound for a place where species don't exist,
Where no emergence has a counterpart.

He's heard from friends
About the other night, the banquet hall
Ringing with bravos—like a curtain call,
He thinks, when the performance ends,
Failing to summon from the wings
An actor who had lost his taste for verse,
Having beheld, in larger theaters,
Much greater banquet vanishings
Without the quaint device and thunderclap
Required in Act 3.
He wrote, Let your indulgence set me free,
To the Academy, and took a nap
Beneath a *London Daily* tent,
Then puttered on his hothouse walk
Watching his orchids beautifully stalk
Their unreturning paths, where each descendant
Is the last—

Their inner staircases
Haunted by vanished insect faces
So tiny, so intolerably vast.
And, while they gave his proxy the award,
He dined in Downe and stayed up rather late
For backgammon with his beloved mate,
Who reads his books and is, quite frankly, bored.

Now, done with beetle jaws and beaks of gulls
And bivalve hinges, now, utterly done,
One miracle remains, and only one.
An ocean swell of sickness rushes, pulls,
He leans against the fence
And lights a cigarette and deeply draws,
Done with fixed laws,
Done with experiments
Within his greenhouse heaven where
His offspring, Frank, for half the afternoon
Played, like an awkward angel, his bassoon
Into the humid air
So he could tell
If sound would make a Venus's-flytrap close.
And, done for good with scientific prose,
That raging hell
Of tortured grammars writhing on their stakes,

He'd turned to his memoirs, chuckling to write
About his boyhood in an upright
Home: a boy preferring garter snakes
To schoolwork, a lazy, strutting liar
Who quite provoked her aggravated look,
Shushed in the drawing room behind her book,
His bossy sister itching with desire
To tattletale—yes, that was good.
But even then, much like the conjurer
Grown cranky with impatience to abjure

All his gigantic works and livelihood
In order to immerse
Himself in tales where he could be the man
In Once upon a time there was a man,

He'd quite by chance beheld the universe:
A disregarded game of chess
Between two love-dazed heirs
Who fiddle with the tiny pairs
Of statues in their hands, while numberless
Abstract unseen
Combinings on the silent board remain
Unplayed forever when they leave the game
To turn, themselves, into a king and queen.
Now, like the coming day,
Inhaled smoke illuminates his nerves.
He turns, taking the sandwalk as it curves
Back to the yard, the house, the entrance way
Where, not to waken her,

He softly shuts the door,
And leans against it for a spell before
He climbs the stairs, holding the banister,
Up to their room: there
Emma sleeps, moored
In illusion, blown past the storm he conjured
With his book, into a harbor
Where it all comes clear,
Where island beings leap from shape to shape
As to escape
Their terrifying turns to disappear.
He lies down on the quilt,
He lies down like a fabulous-headed
Fossil in a varnished riverbed,
In ocean drifts, in canyon floors, in silt,

In lime, in deepening blue ice,
In cliffs obscured as clouds gather and float;
He lies down in his boot and overcoat,
And shuts his eyes.

GJERTRUD SCHNACKENBERG *is the author of three books of poetry:*
A Gilded Lapse of Time, The Lamplit Answer, *and* Portraits and
Elegies. *She has taught at The Writers Community and has received many*
awards for her writing, including the Rome Prize from the American
Academy and Institute of Arts and Letters and fellowships from the National
Endowment for the Arts and the Guggenheim Foundation.

NTOZAKE SHANGE

serial monogamy

i think/ we should reexamine/ serial monogamy
is it/ one at a time or
one for a long time?

           how
does the concept of infinity relate to a skilled
serial monogamist/ & can
that person consider a diversionary escapade
a serial
one night stand?

         can a consistent
serial monogamist
have one/ several/ or myriad relationships
that broach every pore of one's body
so long as there is no penetration?
do we/ consider adventurous relentless tongues
capable of penetration & if we do
can said tongues whip thru us indiscriminately
with words/ like

              "hello"
"oh, you lookin good"
"you jigglin, baby"
cd these be reckless immature violations of
serial monogamy?

  i mean/
if my eyes light up cuz
   some stranger just lets go/ caint stop hisself
from sayin

"yr name must be paradise"
if i was to grin or tingle/ even get a lil happy/
hearin me & paradise/ now synonyms
does that make me a scarlet woman?
if i wear a red dress that makes someone else hot
does that put me out the fryin pan & into the
fire?

say/
my jade bracelet got hot
                (which aint possible cuz jade aint
jade
            if it aint cold)
but say
my jade got lit up & burst offa my wrist
& i say/
        "i gotta find my precious stones
cuz they my luck"
                & he say
"luck don't leave it goes where
you need it"
            & i say
"i gotta find my bracelet"
            & he say
"you know for actual truth
            you was wearin this bracelet?"
& i say
    "a course, it's my luck"
            & he say
"how you know?"
& i say
        "cuz
    i heard my jade
    flyin thru the air
    over yr head
    behind my knees

&
up under the Japanese lampshade!"
        & he say
"you heard yr jade flyin thru the air?"
        "yes"
            i say
"& where were they flyin from"
        he say
        "from my arm" i say
            "they got hot & jumped offa my arm"
"but/
where was yr arm?"
            he say
& i caint say mucha nothin
cuz
where my arm was a part a some tremendous
current/
cd be 'lectricity or niggahs on fire/
so where my arm was is where/ jade gets hot
& does that imply the failure of serial monogamy?

do flamin flyin jade stones
on a arm/ that is a kiss/ & a man who knows where/
luck is
take the serial/ outta monogamy/ & leave
love?

chastening with honey

by all rites i shd be writin
right to left/ upside down
or backwards/
speech/ shd run garbled & dyslexic thru my
brain/ til i hear yr voice
clearly/ again/

in some other/ life were you a mandala?
are you "OM"?
is shakti-pat/ yr regular metabolic status/
under ordinary circumstances?
oh/there I go again
admirin myself/ unwittingly/
invitin some terribly/ lush *mot palabra son syllable/*
to flail
abt my bangs & lashes
so moist/ you smile/ i remember/ this is arrogance
& it's over

this/ chastening with honey
is nothin/ like the Passion of Christ/
which brought us Lent & we give up meat/
quit our lust/ for blood & bonbons/
Mohammed's trials brought Ramadan/ & we may only
quench our thirst for life from dawn to dusk/
& Buddha/ neath the bo tree/ spread joy abt our
ankles
so long as we rid ourselves of resentment &
impatience/ now Krishna/ is another kind of story/
but goatherds & goatherdesses/ shepherds &

shepherdesses/
all come with chastening.

you may/ sheer this wool/ wet it
braid it til you can wrap it round/ two or three
parallel/ cosmic strings/
just don't/ disrupt the ritual
the leap from maya to nirvana/ overwhelms
unwitting/ arrogance
& *je ne sais que ton insouciance*/ we
can't handle passion/ with the deftness
we associate with civil servants/ in Ibadan or
Bogota/
i am so lucky
this is the essence of life/ you
present yrself/ with the warmth of the Goddess/
the ferocity of Yahweh/ the glee of Shiva/ the
cunning of Coyote/ the de-groovi-licious breath of
Obatala/ like
there was some difference tween yr voice/ this
honey/ fallin off
my body/ & wild hummingbirds from the rain forest
appear
by the A train/ imaginin you some/ tropical flower
pollen
hoverin over Manhattan/ like the Muslim brother's
incense/
maybe/ if i burn you up/ i'd calm down/
the endorphin crazed
birds/ cd go back to the Amazon/   think abt it/
fire/ is a great rite of passage/   the pollen &
the honey & the
flyin birds by my cheek/ oh oh/ i understand/
this is the fall from the Garden.

NTOZAKE SHANGE *is a playwright, poet, novelist, and performance artist. Her many works include the play* for colored girls who have considered suicide/when the rainbow is enuf *and the poetry volumes* nappy edges, A Daughter's Geography, Ridin' the Moon in Texas, From Okra to Greens, *and* The Love Space Demands: A Continuing Saga. *She is also the author of the novels* Sassafrass, Cypress & Indigo *and* Liliane. *She has taught at The Writers Community.*

Miracle Glass Co.

Heavy mirror carried
Across the street,
I bow to you
And to everything that appears in you,
Momentarily
And never again in the same way:

This street with its pink sky,
Row of gray tenements,
A lone dog,
Children on rollerskates,
Woman buying flowers,
Someone looking lost.

In you, mirror framed in gold
And carried across the street
By someone I can't even see,
To whom, too, I bow.

Divine Collaborator

He's the silent partner of everything we write; the
father of all language out of silence.
   Cuss or pray all you want! He owns every one of
our words and is only lending them to us, even when
we write to the one we love madly, saying:
   "My dearest, you must understand my back hurts,
I could not get out of bed. I lay there all day listening
to the rain and dreaming of you aroused by my caresses,
offering your naked thighs to me . . ."
   "Disgusting pig, you must be thinking as you read
this! Remember, love,

                    this is God writing!"

Charles Simic

Charles Simic is a sentence.
A sentence has a beginning and an end.

Is he a simple or compound sentence?
It depends on the weather.
It depends on the stars above.

What is the subject of the sentence?
The subject is your beloved Charles Simic.

How many verbs are there in the sentence?
Eating, sleeping and fucking are some of its verbs.

What is the object of the sentence?
The object, my little ones,
Is not yet in sight.

And who is writing this awkward sentence?
A blackmailer, a girl in love,
And an applicant for a job.

Will they end with a period or a question mark?
They'll end with an exclamation point and an ink spot.

CHARLES SIMIC *is a poet, essayist, and translator. The author of fifteen collections of poetry, he has also translated contemporary Yugoslav poetry and published numerous essays. His books include* Dismantling the Silence, Charon's Cosmology, Selected Poems 1963–1983, The Book of Gods and Devils, Hotel Insomnia *and* A Wedding in Hell. *His many awards include a Guggenheim Fellowship, a PEN Translation Prize, a MacArthur Fellowship, and a Pulitzer Prize in Poetry. He has taught at The Writers Community and currently teaches American literature and creative writing at the University of New Hampshire.*

STEVE STERN

Sissman Loses His Way

The angel Sissman, despite a taste for tailored suits and his pair of magnificent alabaster wings, was in no way an illustrious angel. Neither was he dissatisfied with his position, but was content to remain the kind of functionary angel typically assigned to births of no special note. The current on his agenda was the birth of one Ira Bluestein, destined for a predictably drab and undistinguished life. In order to reach the site of Ira's nativity, Sissman had to follow the map of his life from its terminus in heaven, the angel's starting point, backward through a prosaic history to the moment of his birth. Made of fine buff paper hand-milled from the pulp of glory trees by the celestial cartographers themselves, the map was soft as kid and somewhat elastic. It was indestructible in the timeless element of its manufacture, where it would endure in a heavenly archive for all eternity, but was subject to the usual ravages below.

Following the map was a perfectly straightforward operation, the route clearly delineated by an orderly procession of descending years. Its major crossroads were located at standard intervals, the rare points of interest graphically illustrated, labeled, and dated, highlighted in varying shades of gray and brown. The terrain was monotonously even, with no real obstacles to speak of and few unanticipated turns of events. Everything about this assignment was regular; Sissman had presided over a multitude of similar births in his time. His task was the usual one: to pinch the infant's nostrils, thereby depriving it of the wisdom it would otherwise have been born with. The wisdom in question was the ability to see without obstruction from the beginning of one's life to the end. It was a wisdom that also included the memory of paradise, a memory that would naturally make living on earth unbearable.

Having traced Ira Bluestein's chronology to its source, Sissman alit on the sill of a frost-etched window above Bluestein's General Merchandise. This was on North Main Street in the winter of 1927. He peered into a room where the coal-burning stove, the enamel washstand, the wardrobe, the tintypes, the busy pair about the iron bed, all glimmered from an intensity of hope and travail. Flouting physical law, a little luxury in which the angel liked to indulge, Sissman passed through the window and invisibly approached the bed. As always, his timing was impeccable, a point on which he took particular pride. He'd arrived just as the doctor, puffing in his shirtsleeves and assisted by a hawk-nosed midwife (in this case the child's own grandmother, Rebekah), was dragging Ira headfirst from his mother's belly.

Then it should have been simple enough to slip imperceptibly among them and tweak the infant's nostrils—this before the doctor, wielding scissors like a predatory beak, cut the cord connecting the baby to its mother. But when Sissman reached for the puckered blue-and-red bundle that was Ira, framed by the wings of his mama's splayed-open legs, he encountered a problem. The bubbeh Rebekah had grabbed hold of the angel's arm.

Sissman had seen her type before: the raw cheekbones and steely eyes, rush-brown wig carelessly askew, her shirtwaist stained with blood. She was from the Old Country, where it wasn't uncommon to find people with second sight, though few had retained it after coming to America. This one, it seemed, had kept intact her faculty for perceiving supernatural creatures. Sissman could have kicked himself for not taking proper precautions; a hasty prayer would have sufficed. Evidently the woman had mistaken him for *Malech Hamovet,* the angel of death, come to snatch the child before its time. It was a confusion that Sissman was not above being flattered by, since the angel of death was one of your more resplendent seraphim. But never ambitious himself, he merely wished the tiresome woman would let go her talonlike grasp of his arm.

Resourceful under pressure, however, the angel remembered his other hand, free but for the map, which he dropped forthwith. Then, ambidextrous, he completed the pinching procedure, if not quite as effectively as he might have under normal circumstances:

he left perhaps a vestigial grain of wisdom that could ripen over time, though Sissman seriously doubted it. Nevertheless, chagrined by the clumsiness of what should have been a routine affair, the angel yanked his sleeve out of the woman's grip. With as much dignity as he could muster in that swimming room (while the doctor *patsched* the squalling infant whom he held by the feet, saying, "*Mazel tov*, Mrs. Bluestein, you got here a fine baby boy"), Sissman spread his outsize wings. But answerable now to certain laws, thanks to the error of his detection, he had to fold them up again to exit the window.

He'd flown some considerable distance from North Main Street, his silhouette briefly visible against a platinum moon, when he realized he'd left the map behind. Had Ira's been a more remarkable life, Sissman might have recalled enough of its details to follow them back to their destination (and his) in heaven. But without the map he hadn't a clue. Besides, it wouldn't do to leave celestial artifacts lying around on earth, where mortals might have proof of what they ought to take purely on faith. There was nothing for it but to turn around.

Almost immediately he was faced with another problem. In his haste to get away, the angel had soared clear out of recorded history, into a spectral dimension where time is measured in eons instead of days. As a consequence, by the time he'd changed course and penetrated the thick yellow cloud cover over North Main Street, many years had passed. Bluestein's General Merchandise was long gone, along with most other remnants of the original community: the kosher butchers and fishmongers, the cobbler and used clothiers, the movie house and the storefront synagogue, the trolley lines. Everything that wasn't boarded up was tumbled down into weed-chocked vacant lots. God only knew where the map was, but Sissman could expect no advice from that quarter until he'd returned to kingdom come, the direction to which was anyone's guess from here.

Fortunately for Sissman he had the knack, as did the least of angels, of discerning the echoes and incidents of dreams. He could track down Ira Bluestein by the ghosts of events and fantasies he'd left behind him in growing up, and where he found Ira he was sure to find the map. Despite its urgency, the enterprise didn't instantly appeal to the angel. It wasn't that Ira's experiences were so awfully disagreeable; on the contrary, his youthful exploits—swimming the river, hide-and-seeking among racks of irregular pants, deceiving the rabbi, running errands for bootleggers, gambling with roustabouts, spying on the Widow Teitelbaum in her bath, the times he watched the burning Phoenix Athletic Club from the roof of his building and delivered papers by rowboat in the flood—were as sweet as any boy's. And his dreams—wherein he was often some bold composite of Natty Bumppo, Baron Munchausen, and the sorcerer Itzak Luria— made a colorful gloss on his adventures. It was just that the adventures hadn't lasted beyond his youth—they never did, a truth about humans Sissman always found disturbing. They dead-ended on North Main Street, Ira's adventures, sometime during his thirteenth year, when a war was waging in Europe and his family had moved from the neighborhood. Neither did Ira's dreams survive the exodus.

Sissman dimly recollected having passed over the war years, which had appeared as an asterisk-studded trough on the map, on his way to the nativity. But now, moving forward in time as did the mortals, low to the ground without the benefit of navigational reference, he could feel how war had ruptured the very atmosphere. It had stunned the population, left them marooned from their pasts in a world unsafe for dreaming.

Mr. Bluestein had opened a hardware store in a shopping center near the treeless subdivision where the family lived. When he finished high school, Ira, who'd shown some promise at first then became an indifferent student, went into his father's business. (The war was over and it was said there were great possibilities in business, though Ira, never ambitious, had merely taken the path of least resistance.) Here the trail became more difficult to follow, due to a tedious repetition of events that left only vague impressions in the air. Sissman couldn't help comparing them unfavorably to the indelible phantoms of Ira's boyhood, where even a walk to Catfish Bayou was a journey into uncharted fastnesses to battle rival magicians and so forth. Years that, on a map, should have required only brisk negotiation here slowed the angel down; they threatened to mire him in the wearisomeness that now seemed a betrayal of a once lively past. The

angel's disappointment was so palpable it seemed to add weight
to his wings, making the simple act of flight a hobbled chore.

Still, attuned as he'd become to the rhythm of human experience,
Sissman relentlessly pursued the dull hum that was certain to lead
him straight to his prey. He found Ira Bluestein—a frowning, multi-
chinned man in an appalling plaid sport jacket and a pastel knit shirt,
a few thin hairs combed over his freckled scalp—on a crisp Sunday
afternoon in October of 1981.

He was seated at the bedside of his grandmother Rebekah, in a
room redolent of disinfectant and stale gardenias at the Daughters of
Zion Nursing Home. She'd outlived practically everyone, Rebekah,
hanging on to her life with a tenacity that fascinated her grandson,
who couldn't see why she bothered, given the chronic pain she was
in. He visited her dutifully over the years, every Sunday in fact since
his last parent had died, attending her with the scrupulousness he
demonstrated in all his affairs. But if pressed he might have conceded
an unspoken bond between them, whose nature he'd never been able
to define.

Now her health was rapidly failing, her sere flesh sprouting
whiskers in appropriate places, as if she were already partly a tussock
of earth. But even in sleep her wrinkled face assumed a certain ferocity, her fitful snoring half a snarl. Restless though not wanting to
wake her, having exhausted his Sunday paper, Ira thought this might
be as good a time as any to sort through her effects. Maybe there
was something worth passing on, though he wondered to whom. He
hesitated—this was possibly premature—then decided as well now as
later, her end being only a matter of time. Besides, wasn't he at bottom a little curious? From the drawer of her metal nightstand, he removed a scuffed cigar box, then donned bifocals to inspect the stored
personal treasures inside.

What he discovered was an umber wedding portrait of herself and
her long departed husband, of whom Ira remembered only a dry
cough and an unshaven jaw—the *zaydeh* Abe. There was also a
scrolled marriage contract with Hebrew characters like black fire and
a ticket stub for the steerage section of the steamship *Bratislava*.
There was an embroidered napkin containing almond cookies close

to petrifaction, a silver amulet against the evil eye, a prayerbook out of whose pages fell indigo petals, and an atomizer with a bulb like a swollen thumb. There was a buff-colored parchment folded lengthwise like a map. Examining it, Ira noticed its curious texture, brittle about the creases but otherwise soft as kid. He opened it to find that it was indeed a weathered map, though its loci were not so much places as incidents. The incidents were depicted in deep mahogany tones where they originated, in the lower left-hand corner, fading to ashen grays in their diagonal advance across the years.

Following events in the order they seemed to insist on, Ira traced a boy's dream-appointed adventures to the place where they dead-ended, the gulf—which was a war—separating North Main Street from what the illustrations characterized as a desert of subsequent years. A waste of time. Beyond the gulf the pictures appeared more washed out, with less attention paid to detail, their dates more difficult to discern. You could just make out the young man's ascendancy to manager of Bluestein & Sons Hardware, allowing for his father's early retirement, and his marriage to Myra, a pliant but sickly high school sweetheart with whom he'd been thrown together on account of the similarity of their given names. There was a decade or two of mutual recriminations, each accusing the other of responsibility for the barren marriage, after which Myra passed quietly away. Meanwhile, through no particular fault of Ira's (who by this point in his map-reading had no recourse but to acknowledge the life as his own), the business had prospered, branches opening in several corners of the city. Well-to-do, he was on the board of directors of the new synagogue, a member of the Lion's Club, active in the Temple Brotherhood and the B'nai B'rith bowling league. He was often in attendance at weddings, bar mitzvahs, and funerals but persistently begged off attempts to "fix him up" on the grounds that he was a confirmed widower.

He was lonely, according to the map, and frightened in his bones of growing old, though he hadn't known it till now. Watching at the open window, the angel Sissman knew it, which was what had made it more than his job was worth to push on in his search for Ira Bluestein. Having lost his own bearings in the process, the angel understood what it meant that Ira had been deprived of his at his birth. And for this Sissman couldn't help but feel sorry, unbecoming as it was in seraphim to sympathize with the fates of mortals in their charge.

Retracing his steps via the same route that Sissman had traveled toward him, Ira also felt sorry for himself and his boring life. But his sorrow changed swiftly to anger; the life was after all only humdrum on the map, which had scarcely bothered indicating instances that Ira clearly recalled as fraught with exquisite frustration and pain. Never mind occasional joy. Who had drawn up the *farkokte* thing in the first place, that they should represent his mature experience as a sleep-walking lockstep toward death? All right, so he was only human, shivering in his skivvies like everyone else, but for this he was entirely to blame? No, Ira decided, the fault was not in himself but in his mapmaker! At that moment Sissman, with his typical flair for timing, threw up the sash and entered the room to snatch the map away.

What happened next should never have. What should have happened was that Ira, relieved of the map by an invisible force, would also have been bereft of the memory of having seen it. But that's not how things turned out. What happened was that Ira saw the angel. This was maybe because Sissman's uncharacteristic intimacy with the earth had left him more dustily material. Or was it Ira's shock at perusing his own arid history that had done it—jarred loose the long-dormant grain of vestigial wisdom that the angel had failed to expunge? The grain had fallen into some fertile furrow of Ira's brain, where it was brought to instant fruition. In any case, it suddenly seemed to Ira that the promise at the beginning of one's life ought to be realized later on. It seemed that the future might yet hold some surprises. Of course there was always alarm at seeing your life for what it was, but the fact remained that it was your life, and no stuffed shirt of an angel in his tailored worsted—now somewhat the worse for wear—had the right to snatch it from you so rudely.

Launching himself from his chair, Ira made a desperate lunge for the map, which prompted a tug-of-war.

"In the name of all that's holy-oly-ly," demanded Sissman, employing his mightiest reverberation, "let go already!"

But Ira patently refused to do so, hanging on for dear life. This was no easy exercise for a pudgy-fingered man in his middle years, who suffered from sciatica and shortness of breath. His bifocals slipped from his nose, and he was certain he felt his hives coming on. Nevertheless he gripped the map as doggedly as his grandmother had clung to the angel's arm so many years before.

"I don't like to have to pull rank-ank-nk," barked Sissman, surprised to find that he meant it profoundly, "but you asked for it." Then he extended the awful width of his alabaster wings. Their shadow filled the narrow room in a manner that seemed ominous to the angel himself, as if an umbrella had been opened indoors.

Wondering that his heart hadn't stopped, Ira managed to hold firm. "You don't scare me," he blurted in unsteady defiance, giving the map a yank that pulled the angel momentarily off balance. Summoning outrage, Sissman retaliated by beating his wings. Their cool wind whipped the curtains, scattered molting feathers, caused a wheelchair to spin in circles, and lifted both the angel and his antagonist from the linoleum floor. Airborne, Ira still struggled to hang on.

"*Nishtikeit-tikeit-keit,*" shouted the hovering Sissman, all patience spent, "you want I should carry you back before your time?"

Although they'd already ascended to the ceiling, Ira assured him through slipping dentures, "You're not taking me"—click—"anywhere!"

That's when the buff paper, aged considerably among Rebekah's keepsakes and moreover stretched to twice its ordinary length, tore apart. Ira fell to the floor with an earth-shaking *thud* and sat clutching his portion of the map to his heaving chest. Having retained the smaller portion—whose route led from the present moment (where a demarcation of recent vintage indicated a struggle) across the featureless expanse of Ira's last years—Sissman attempted to fly through the ceiling. But, still corporeal, he bumped his silver head against the cork and was forced to fold his wings for a less exalted exit through the window.

No sooner had he set about following the map, however, than the angel became disoriented once more. What perplexed him was the way the lay of the land seemed to change before his eyes, the colors turning like a leaf aging backward from gray and brown to a rich russet red. The previously flat thoroughfare of Ira Bluestein's hours, where they began the gentle grade toward their conclusion, was becoming as circuitous as a seam in a crazy quilt. Incidents appeared where none had existed, bumps and declivities where before had been unbroken plain. There was mischief afoot, embarrassing behavior during business hours, liquidation sales, settled scores, withdrawn accounts, travel by night through a geography whose drama supplanted routine.

There was the bubbeh Rebekah who, having slept soundly through the commotion, sat up friskily in bed and called for her Jewish fish. Her grandson had kissed her parchment brow to bid her a tender so long, then returned the map for safekeeping to her treasure box before stepping off its ragged edge. He was headed who knows where, beyond the known world at any rate, into mysterious parts rumored to be sites of lost neighborhoods, places dense with peril and romance. Here and there—as Sissman tried to make out his itinerary—the wilderness through which Ira journeyed was dotted with gardens, suggesting that the wayward shmo had recovered his memory of paradise. Nothing could be taken for granted anymore; thanks to the angel's bungling, a mediocrity was playing hell with the meticulous craft of the cartographers of kingdom come. A nobody was distorting his own destiny after a fashion that constituted an unauthorized miracle.

This wouldn't do. It was highly irregular and Sissman ought to put a stop to it at once, though he was currently at a loss as to how to proceed. All he knew was that he had to act quick. If he didn't turn around and stick close to Ira Bluestein for the wild remainder of the mortal's days—a proposition that promised to be, God forbid, interesting—he might never find his way back to heaven again.

STEVE STERN ON COMMUNITY

To emerge from your writing is like surfacing from an underground shelter after a bomb. The world outside the well-lit, symmetrical confines of your story is rubble. Lonely, you walk around blinking in the toxic sunlight looking for other survivors. So imagine your exhilaration when among the walking wounded—among the mad and disfigured and broken in spirit (who are also incidentally your audience, no matter that they're too defeated to hear what you say)—you meet someone who looks no better off than the rest, who nevertheless inquires with concern, "How's the book going? Myself, I'm having some problems with point of view . . ." Such is a writer's relation to community.

STEVE STERN *is the author of two collections of short stories,* Isaac and the Undertaker's Daughter *and* Lazar Malkin Enters Heaven; *two novels,* The Moon and Ruben Shein *and* Harry Kaplan's Adventures Underground; *and a book of novellas,* A Plague of Dreamers. *He has also published two children's books. He is the recipient of a number of awards, including the Edward Lewis Wallant Award, a Pushcart Writer's Choice Award, and an O. Henry Prize. He has taught at The Writers Community and is an associate professor of English at Skidmore College.*

TERESE SVOBODA

Polio

If you play hide-and-seek in the dark, you won't get polio, said Mrs.
Then she went in. We slapped at bugs that liked the porchlight until I turned it off and said, Let's watch TV instead.

You're it, said one and then the other in the porch corners. For talking.

I didn't count or close my eyes but they went away anyway. Except the littlest with her wet diapers. I carried her to base, then put her down. Then I did this jig we had to know for the school musical and someone cleared his throat like he was waiting.

Game over, I shouted and climbed base, not a very big tree.

I hated baby-sitters worse than baby sisters, the one on the ground crying, wanting up. From where I was I could see Mrs. with her legs crossed in front of the TV with a doctor show on and our bowl of popcorn half snacked up. In six short years I could be Mrs. too. I had breasts, my shorts were that short, I knew about babies.

She's wet, I said, loud into the dark. You scared her, I have to take her in. I knew they wouldn't stay out without me, even if the boys said, It, It to each other.

The sitter switched channels to news as soon as we settled. Bedtime, she said.

No. We had consensus, I said. I used the word from the news.

We were moving toward the suitcases, the ones stacked in the corner with the winter clothes supposed to be turned soon into summer. She laughed at consensus and left with the baby.

Never, I said after her.

We unstacked the suitcases, threw out the clothes before Mrs. even found a diaper. The boys were especially fast. The smallest was already sitting in a trunk when she came back, the whole kit and kaboodle pretty much empty. Mrs. shut it on him.

In the dark you won't get polio, she said, and picked up the trunk and carried it to the door. It's fun, said the boy after some silence, so anybody who could fit climbed into the others. Then there were six cases by the door and me with the baby who said, Click, click.

Okay, said Mrs. and went into the kitchen for some more of this bottle she kept refilling with water after she poured some into a Coke.

I let everybody out since they wanted to switch, everybody but the last girl since the lock on that one stuck pretty much always. But after a while, after we tried a bobby pin and then a nail and then a paper clip—or rather me, since the others had started watching TV—it finally came loose with Dad's hammer.

Mrs. came in with the new noise and said, Give me that baby, who of course wanted her own bottle and was crying. But no, Mrs. couldn't find the nipple and the baby hated the cup which was still filled with what Mrs. had been having so she said, If you play chute you don't get polio either.

Chute? Or Shoot? We didn't know until she'd wrapped the baby in some of the thick winter things lying around and tossed her down it.

At the bottom, in the basement, lay always a huge mound of laundry, a lot of diapers mostly, so the baby—who was quiet for a while, Mrs.'s intention—broke nothing. Of course, then we all wanted a turn and I think one of the boys sprained his wrist but he knew better than to tell in front of Mrs. and went to bed right away, like the rest of us.

A consensus? asked Mrs. Then, in the dark, she told us a story about a house very much like ours that had someone walking around it and around it, putting his face in the windows, and then coming in, and he had polio.

What's this polio thing? It's boring, I said.

Nothing, said Mrs. Go to sleep, she said and snapped her gum that she wouldn't share with us but that Dad had left us. Nothing, but my brother has it, said Mrs. Then she breathed in all our faces and said, Don't let the bug bite.

Mom, I said in the morning. Besides, she wouldn't give us the gum.

Mom laughed. You know how many sitters would sit with all of you, or at what price? Anyway, I've heard she's going to have one of her own. What could be better?

TERESE SVOBODA ON COMMUNITY

I've always been heartened by the hunched forms of writers at their machines, silently straining to find out what they mean. We're the last cloistered community, eschewing the ball game or a night at the movies for a chance to get closer to the point. People may make fun of us, but that's because, as my mother used to say, they're afraid of us. There's power in this community, power produced—if for no other reason—by the extreme concentration it requires in a world full of distraction.

TERESE SVOBODA's *books include the novel* Cannibal, *which won the Bobst and Great Lakes prizes and was featured in* Vogue. *She is also the author of three collections of poetry. Her most recent book is* Mere Mortals, *a volume of translations. She lives in New York City.*

SHARON THOMSON

Community Life

(1)

Each has her own
berth, one bureau. No smoking,
no mirrors. No. One mirror
like a sliver, at the foot of the second floor
hall where I bow each morning
before it, that cracked thing. Suck in
belly   pat bottom   adjust collar   stretch
as in dance—an exercise—me
in pieces, face locked
into its face pose: no pretense,
no give.

(2)

The day begins and I am filled
with good intentions.   Light strikes
the bare wood floors, the haze is rising.
Stairs creak under the weight of us
going down to

breakfast. I am sure
to not go out of turn, to keep our line
even   hold the fork back, not taking
more than a fair share. Being new
here I imitate the rest of them, settle
into their ways. Small talk. An August breeze

seeps in. One by one
they finish and are gone, screen door
slamming. A beat
at each exit. My heart pounds.
I scrape their plates, scavenge
for scraps left behind.

(3)

The property is green and lush, in hills
just west of the Hudson: fields
cabins   slopes   and wild fruit   a bench
from which the whole of our land
is visible. I have not yet
tired of the view nor intricacies
of those who live within it though my heart
goes back to the city and I am eager
for mail   poised
at the head of the driveway   I am
as they say, among strangers here, forgetting
the dark part of what's past, the underbelly
of the familiar.

(4)

Our hermit, the potter, has a shed
in the back woods. Primitive
and lean. She hauls water,
won't talk; her voice
is written   *bring clay*
thursday morning and monday afternoon.

I do it. The wheel is turning,
her hands ride the mound. I am fixed

for a while   in this dust
something holds: the bareness she goes on.
Going unnoticed at the outside wall
I smell must in the wood.

(5)

. . . almost collapsed. Sun
like a devil across my back
bent into digging, potatoes emerging
three or four to a hole. *Oh*

come now, you can do
better. I had to straighten up,
had to lean against the pitchfork. Sunstruck:
ground tipping out from under   I saw
down by the corn in neat rows   so many
of us fading into stalks
as if the body were lost   then present
in the next person. There was a ringing
all around. I had to stop.

(6)

At night, the house dog roams
after woodchucks, breaks necks
with a fast bite, delivers them
at the door. He howls
to be let in. It's always the same:
dog pantings   good night   too many
crickets   the faucet
I'm clean   my shadow is doubling

beyond the oil lamp   moths beat
blindly at the screen. Groan. Someone's

bad dream getting tossed off. Off.
A wheeze. Their breathing
is a comfort.

(7)

Already, it's like the fall. Cool. We pick
and preserve what's done,
what can rot. It's easy
reaping and one has come who makes
me laugh. She's young yet, lifts
rocks   vats   throws back
her scarf   axes wood.
Firewood. There's a lightness
and it extends. Love:
here in the fields, Canada
geese honking down. The sky
is thick at the rim.

(8)

Crimson—the foliage
thins. We're pulling corn stalks
out by the roots and stacking
them. I'm making friends, recognize
kindnesses but something more
is required of me. I can see it
in the distance, my uneasiness
at their approach   welcome   their casual stance
before the fat, crisp
stacks; afraid
even now, as a torch is put
to our gatherings and my arms
fold and each long leaf hurries
toward its stalk in the burning.

(9)

We close in.
It's a simple service: her body
wrapped in a white shroud is prayed over.
Hymns. Hands clasp. Four stand-up candles
mark the corners
of her coffin. I was the one
who found her dead, it was
as I've told them: no sign
of pain, no clutching
at the sheets. She was gray;
the look, the expression was odd
and not her own.

(10)

Bare. Bare. It's all sticks
and on the ground: what's fallen. Sick
with fever, I'm propped
on pillows and removed, this season
like a film before me: rain, pods—
hundreds—splitting from the limbs
of the locust. Nothing is left

I am skin   empty
hot, they say, so hot when they visit
and whisper of me in the doorway. There's a cool hand
and a figure above. I lie still
for her   I drink
what she brings, smoke lifting
in spirals from the cup.

(11)

I woke early. Dressed. Quietly
left and went in darkness
to the ridge   east   yes,
I was commanded
like a child

like a child
when the bell sounded
Attention! and I used to straighten
hands fixed on the edge
of my desk. Patient. There was a sense
of things staying. I was taken
year by year

now through dry leaves
up this slope. Black.
Light. The sky has a line,
is divided. *Come to me.*
Be mine. Finally, said.

(12)

Each step locks me in snow
deep, past the knees. My breathing is short
and fast from trying. Our house stands
white, in the dusk, far away. It excites me:
the idea of danger, as if I were
broken   lost in the heart
of a wild place, a piece of moon
limping high above the hill, no tracks
but mine.

(13)

She has my hand   *I want*
to show you   points to the field,
plans for spring. A hard wind
hits, whips at her hair. March.
Mud slopping under our boots   collars up   I touch
the holy medal in my pocket, with a thumb
follow the lines of a figure
there: serene, her long robe,
the baby she holds. The sun
is about to break through,
something's in the air: my name
is hung in the air, a call
from the others, waving
at the edge of the field . . . Sharon . . .
There's a crack of orange light.
Now. A blackbird
lifting off dips its wing
and squawks. The past is done.

SHARON THOMSON ON COMMUNITY

The poem "Community Life," published in this anthology, was
inspired by my initial contact with The Grail—an international
women's movement committed to spiritual search and social action.
As described in the poem, my first experience of living in a Grail
community in 1977 was so utterly transforming that I later chose to
become a permanent member of the movement, dedicating my skills
as a poet, performer, and teacher in service to The Grail. Living out
this commitment to function as an artist on behalf of my community
has been both a challenge and a privilege.

It has asked certain things of me. It has asked that I create works
in response to the needs of the community, that I enlarge my voice
to include more than my own personal need for self-expression, that

I allow the community to not only inspire but to be actively involved in the process, often having direct input into the final product, and that I develop a way for them to have this input with creative, imaginative results. In this way the community is enriched, while the creativity of its members expands and becomes more.

But I also am enriched, and my work expands and develops in ways that would probably never happen without the context of my community. Throughout the years I have been asked to apply my skills to forms and media that I might never have otherwise considered: speeches, sermons, articles, publicity, grant writing, alternative education, small group facilitation, workshops on poetry writing as a spiritual path. Most importantly, I have been given encouragement and support to develop Poetry Ritual Theatre—a concept of participatory, multi-media theatre directly inspired by my experience of celebrating, praying, and ritualizing within The Grail—as a way of working with communities outside The Grail. Thus I am able to participate in The Grail vision of personal and social transformation while remaining true to my own talents and interests.

And there is always an audience. There is always an outlet. There is always the community waiting, often eagerly, to receive what I have to bring to the life of the whole. So I am lucky. I am blessed. I don't have to struggle to have my work heard, or published, or performed. I don't have to compete with others in order to be received. My contributions are welcomed, as I welcome the diverse contributions of each of the others with whom I share this community.

I have often thought to myself: this is the way it once was, long ago, back in time, when the center of life was the campfire, and poetry was a chant, a particular sequence of sound and rhythm with magical properties sung as the voice, and will, and spirit of a people. I have thought: this is the way it was when words and music and movement and graven images and thoughts and matter and spirit were one, back in time, when all the members of the tribe had access to the dimension we now call art, and the artist was not on the fringe but rather, like the fire, at the heart of it all.

Of course, I think these thoughts only in certain special moments. For community life is, in the end, just another kind of life, with all the problems inherent in everyday living. Yet, in the midst of it all, I always know that I am not alone, that my work does not exist in a vacuum of private experience and isolation. I always know that I and my work are rooted and brought to fruit in something larger than myself. I always know that I have something to give and a place that needs me to give it, a place where I belong. Through my willingness to not just be an artist in relation to a community, but to become a part of that community with all that I am, I have found a way to be and to create that is ultimately uniquely satisfying.

SHARON THOMSON, *a performance poet, has taught for New York State Poets in Public Service and The Writers Community, where she had previously studied. She is presently National Program Consultant and Poet-in-Residence for The Grail, an international movement of women committed to spiritual search and social action. She is also founder and artistic director of the Poetry Ritual Theatre, a multi-media participatory theatre experience. She received the Poet of the Year Award from Xavier University's* Athenaeum *magazine, as well as a grant from the Kentucky Foundation for Women to assist the completion of her next theatre piece,* Rage and Healing: A Ritual by Surviving Warriors, *which concerns breast cancer as an environmental disease.*

MEG WOLITZER

FROM *This Is Your Life*

It was her sister who taught her how to hyperventilate. They sat facing each other on the bed, and they panted together like a husband and wife in a Lamaze workshop. When they could just about take no more, they felt that identifying swoon, the oxygen leaving their brains for good, the cells dying en masse. One day Erica put an end to it. She couldn't be bothered anymore, she said; she had other things to think about. Suddenly her walls were lined with posters; huge, disembodied heads of folk singers loomed down from above the bed and the dresser. Voices started coming from the stereo speakers: trembly underwater sopranos singing about medieval woodnymphs and slain labor leaders. But the 1960s had already ended, and the records were strictly from the remainder bin. Buffy Sainte-Marie had a big orange 99-cent sticker slapped over her face.

Erica's room grew lush with things to touch, and fiddle with, and smell. Something was always burning in a dish. Once she bought a wand of incense from a man in a white robe on the subway and was later appalled by the literature he had sweetly handed her with her purchase:

Thank-you for Buying "Lovely" Patchouli Incense.
You're contributions will Go to help FIGHT the Rise
of worldwide Judaism.

Still the incense burned, and now Opal stood and breathed in the bad air of her sister's room and thought longingly of how they used to hyperventilate together, and how all of that was finished.

In the past, sitting cross-legged on Erica's bed, the two sisters would allow their breathing to quicken. It was those first moments that Opal liked best. Erica had made a rule that they must keep their eyes closed, but sometimes Opal would crack open an eye and watch her sister heaving for breath, her shoulders moving up and down. It was embarrassing to see this, but somehow necessary. Erica was like a big sea creature that had washed up onto a rock, and Opal was the sea creature's diminutive sister. If someone had burst into the room then, it would have seemed crazy: two girls gasping for oxygen when there was certainly enough of it to go around. But no one *would* burst into the room; even the baby-sitters knew enough to keep their distance. Sometimes Opal would hear one of them practicing a routine in the den. She grew used to hearing the distant swoop and mutter of a voice, the rise and fall of words out of context. She rarely paid much attention, preferring the company of her sister. In Erica's bedroom it was just the two of them, breathing and falling.

One evening when they were hyperventilating, Opal actually thought she had died. She thought she had slipped into some narrow, dark province where she would be held forever. It was like all the hiding places she had ever found in the apartment: like the alley behind the refrigerator, where you wedged your body in and stood flush against the humming coils and wires until you were discovered. And you were always discovered; that was a given. But now Opal felt as though she might never get out, might never come to. She could not move, she could not open her eyes.

Good-bye, she thought, good-bye. She remembered Charlotte's babies at the end of *Charlotte's Web*, and the way they had parachuted off into new, separate spider-lives, calling good-bye to Wilbur even as a current carried them along. She had wept then, as she had wept pages earlier during Charlotte's death. It made sense to cry at someone else's departure, someone else's death. But this now, this was worse; Opal was mourning only herself. She would be found in her culottes and headband and knee socks. She saw herself being lifted gently, held in some anonymous adult arms and carried from the room.

That was when Erica reached out and shook her.

"Earth to Opal," Erica said, and Opal's eyes flew open like a doll's. "You should have seen yourself," Erica said, but her voice was kind.

No more was said about it. Together the two sisters caught their breath and went into the kitchen to hunt for supper. There was always a baby-sitter around to serve as a vague supervisor. Their mother had hired a string of young comedians to take care of Opal and Erica when she herself was away—men and women whom she had discovered at various comedy clubs around the city. She paid them decently and gave them a place to stay and a telephone to use and a pantry stocked with interesting food. The apartment was never empty; there was always the sound of one of the baby-sitters in the background, obsessively practicing a routine. The baby-sitters were extremely lenient, youthful parents who let you do what you want and eat what you want.

Tonight Danny Bloom, who was doing a three-day baby-sitting stint, came out of the den and asked if they needed anything. He was a thin man in his late twenties, with a body like a piece of bent wire. His humor, said their mother, was very physical. He moved around a lot onstage at the Laff House, where she had discovered him.

"You two doing okay out there?" Danny asked them.

"Yes," Opal and Erica chorused. "We're fine."

"Well then, I think I'll keep practicing," he said. "I'll come out again in time for the show. She said she's doing all new material tonight."

When he had disappeared down the hall, Erica and Opal boiled water for wagon-wheel pasta and slathered Fluff on crackers. They ate in silence, and when they were through they flipped through their homework for a while, dreamily shuffling pages. Illustrations of colonial life drifted by; women in long dresses sat at butter churns, backs straight, hands busy. Erica and Opal looked up from their homework every few minutes, checking the clock. At eleven-twenty Erica carried in the television set, and Opal pulled the swivel chairs up close to the screen. Together in the kitchen with the heat from the stove and the soft, granular light of the television, they waited for their mother to appear.

Opal watched the long loop of commercials as though it were an opening act. It was strange; you barely had to focus on the commercials, and yet you still knew what they wanted you to buy. Opal loved television and watched as much as she could. You had to watch the shows closely, but during the commercials you could just let your thoughts fall around you while the music jumped and the coffee spilled and the bottle of detergent came to life and danced.

Opal swiveled her chair in time to the music and thought of all the things that crowded around her. She thought of the people she worshipped in the world: her mother, and her sister, and the new art teacher, Miss Hong. A few years before, she had worshipped Mickey Dolenz of the Monkees. She thought she had been shrewd about loving Mickey; everyone else loved Davy Jones, and the chances of ever getting *him* were slim, at best. More realistic to go for Mickey, with his elastic face and squinting eyes. No one else took Mickey seriously; they all went for the easy charms of Davy: the soft British accent, the tender skin. Opal remained patient, did not make a big issue out of her theory. She thought of Mickey constantly, wondered what time of day it was in California and whether he grew discouraged by all the letters Davy received. But as the months passed, and the flurry died down, Opal thought of him less, and somehow her love for him was unmoored. It had been her decision; she had not had to be forcibly restrained, like some older girls at school who tried to sneak into hotel rooms or backstage at the Westbury Music Fair. She had restrained *herself,* and suddenly she was way past the whole thing.

Everything kept changing as quickly as a film strip, frame after choppy frame. You loved someone and then you didn't, and then you loved someone else. You wept over a spider's death when you were eight, and a few years later you read that same death scene again with a cool, critical eye. You thought of ways in which E. B. White might have made the scene more true to life; you thought of writing to tell him.

There were very few things in the world that stayed hinged to you for too long. Each year there was a new teacher at the front of the room, a new arrangement of chairs and desks, a new pale color slapped over the walls around you. Every class had a classroom pet: a guinea pig that drowsed in its window cage while you traced the outlines of the seven continents. You spent a whole year of your life caring for this animal, stroking its nervous fur and sliding in trays of pellets, and when the end of the year came, the animal was left back in the second grade while you kept moving up. You all knew that there would be another animal awaiting you in the third grade: a parallel rodent needing stroking and holding and water and food.

Now the commercials ended, and the theme music began, and suddenly Danny Bloom raced into the kitchen and perched on the countertop behind Opal. First there was the monologue, and a little joking around, and then Opal's mother was brought onstage. Sitting between Johnny and Ed, with the skyline tableau stretched out behind her, she gestured broadly and flooded the entire screen. In that moment the two men disappeared, were swallowed up, and even the skyline was eclipsed. All that remained was an ocean of dotted fabric—her mother's fashion trademark—and the helpless laughter of the studio audience. They kept laughing and didn't show signs of ever stopping. This is what is meant by "convulsive laughter," Opal thought.

"I'm glad she's on first tonight," Erica said. "Not like last time when that woman from Sea World was on with her animals, and Mom got four minutes."

Things had changed since then, they acknowledged. Their mother was now allowed to come on first and ease into the still-cold chair by the desk. She was frantic tonight; she was huge and luminous. *My mother the moon,* Opal thought. *My mother the explosion.* Opal could not take her eyes off her mother. She was madly in love with her, as was half the country. Everyone wanted to meet her, talk to her, somehow nudge up against her.

"It's worse in California," Opal's mother had said. "Out there, everyone's lying in wait with their autograph books. They *expect* to see celebrities. They come right up and touch you; it's like a petting zoo." But Opal knew her mother wasn't significantly upset by this; it was clear that in some ways she took pleasure from the touch of strangers. Opal imagined her mother gliding down a street in Los Angeles under an archway of palm trees, while all around her, hands reached out to brush her cheek, her hair, the edge of a dotted sleeve.

Opal had not yet been to California. "I want you girls to stay in New York for now," her mother said, "and have as normal a life as possible. I don't want you to start missing a lot of school and falling behind. I know the situation isn't ideal, but the baby-sitters take good care of you, and I'm only a phone call away."

Opal begged to be allowed to go with her, but the answer was always the same. "Soon," she was told. "I promise you, soon."

But when, exactly, was "soon?" The word was used to represent any given period of time; it was fluid and could change shape freely. "I will be back from L.A. soon," her mother would say as she stood before her closet, selecting dresses from the rack with the help of her assistant, Cynthia, who always leaned toward the loudest, most spangle-dipped items. Then a week or two might go by, during which Opal had her hair braided systematically each morning and her lunch packed by a live-in baby-sitter. *Soon, soon,* came the voice, this time over the telephone, but even long-distance it was as soothing and persuasive as a hypnotist's.

Finally, her mother would return. It might be winter in New York City, with snow gathered in ragged drifts, but the limousine would pull up at the curb and the doorman would fly out to greet her, and she would emerge a dusty, mottled, coastal pink, her nose peeling, her suitcase swollen with citrus fruit. California seemed a remote tropical island, having little to do with anything that went on here, in New York City, where the snow fell for days, and the world seemed locked permanently into winter. In California, Opal imagined, you were served crescents of papaya on a terrace overlooking the water, and speed-shutter cameras were always hissing at you like locusts. Opal would go there soon, she knew. But "soon" kept unraveling with no end in sight.

There were times, during that first year of fame, when her mother was home for weeks on end, either resting or playing a series of club dates in the city. "I really prefer it here," she would say as she got ready to go out for an evening in New York. "The audiences are much more savvy. They laugh with discrimination. Out in L.A., you get the feeling that there's a laugh track going. Everyone's so desperate to have a good time; you could get up there and read a manual about oral hygiene and they would laugh. No, this is where I want you girls to live, not out there in Disneyland."

Sometimes she would sit down for a moment on the bed between her daughters. "I hope I'm doing the right thing," she would say. "Who knows? Maybe if God had really wanted me to be a comedienne, He would have named me Shecky."

Opal and Erica looked at each other and laughed politely. They had reached a point at which they usually understood when there mother was making a joke and were able to respond fairly quickly. But sometimes Opal wasn't even sure whether her mother was funny or not; she'd heard her jokes too many times. At home her mother practiced in the bedroom.

"You girls be my audience," she said. Opal and Erica sat solemnly on the edge of the bed and listened as she ran through her act. She usually opened with some rueful comments about her size. "I do have a weight problem," she said, looking down at herself and shaking her head. Then she looked up suddenly. "I just can't *wait* for dinner!"

Opal thought about this, and understood that her mother was making a little pun. She chuckled politely.

"Women's lib isn't so easy on large women," her mother went on. "I mean, I tried to burn my bra, and the neighbors called the fire department. It took hours to put it out. One of the firemen said to me, 'I don't know what kind of campfire you were making, lady, but those are the biggest marshmallows I've ever seen!'"

Opal and Erica laughed again, hesitantly. Their laughter had a familiar rolling burble to it, like a water cooler. Opal was aware that there were probably some nuances she was missing, certain inflections that seemed to point to the approximate region of humor, although the particular meaning was lost on her. She recognized her own ignorance, her limits in the presence of this huge, wonderful mother. Opal was a knobby girl, especially small for her age. "My little ectomorph," her mother sometimes called her, touching the hair on the back of Opal's neck, making her arch and settle like a cat.

She preferred it when her mother did parodies of songs from musicals, which she had expressly rewritten for her act. Onstage she was accompanied by a piano, bass, and drums, but here in the bedroom, her voice had to survive on its own. She didn't have a brassy voice, as one might have imagined, but instead she sang in a girlish soprano, aiming tremulously for the top notes the way someone might reach for a delicate object on a high shelf.

"Okay, girls," she would say. "Now I'm going to do something from *West Side Story*. This one is to the tune of a song called 'Maria.' You have to know the song, I guess, but just bear with me." She paused, pulled at the throat of her turtleneck sweater, and began to sing:

"The most beautiful sound I ever heard/Pastrami/Pastrami, pastrami, pastrami/Say it loud and there's a carving knife carving/Say it soft, because I'm suddenly starving/Pastrami/I've just eaten a *pound* of pastrami . . ." She stopped singing and clutched at her stomach, rolling her eyes around. Opal was the first to laugh, and Erica followed.

"Oh good, you like that one," said her mother. "I'm glad. Here's another." She cleared her throat and sang. "There's *no* blintzes like *roe* blintzes, like *no* blintzes I know . . ."

After the songs she began to do characters, starting first with her most popular one, Mrs. Pummelman, then doing Baby Fifi, and finally Isadora Dumpster. She poked fun at her own weight problem, in the hopes, she often said, of having it cease to be a delicate subject. It was not this way with most overweight people. Opal thought of Debby Nadler at school, whose mother was a large, gentle ceramicist. Mrs. Nadler was constantly at work in her studio, standing over the wavy heat of a kiln, looking flushed and serious in a red smock. Her heaviness was just another part of her, along with her talent and her kindness and her breathy voice. It was a big package that you couldn't split up; it was all or nothing. And then there was Miss Coombs, the school nurse, whose wide, easy presence was welcome when you were throwing up or had strep throat and had to be sent home. Miss Coombs lay you down on a narrow cot and hovered above you, blocking out the stark glare of the room, and she placed a washcloth over your forehead, smoothing its edges with her heavy hands. Both Mrs. Nadler and Miss Coombs carried their weight around without referring to it all the time, and everyone understood that it would have been wrong to make fun of it, or even mention it. You couldn't make fun of someone's fat mother—the mother had to make fun of herself, like Opal's did—but on the other hand you *could* go up to another girl at school and calmly say, "You're ugly, no offense." The remark would blaze inside that girl forever.

Nobody ever said this kind of thing to Opal. She was popular already, good in gym, and quick at spelling. There was a small amount of cruelty in her, which surfaced at odd times and always surprised everyone, especially her. It sprang from nowhere, painlessly, like a nighttime nosebleed. She found herself occasionally joining in with a few others in the coat room at the end of the day and forming a tight ring around some unfortunate girl. Once they even stooped so low as to gang up on the new exchange student from Seoul, Korea, who couldn't even begin to imagine what they were saying to her in such mean voices.

Opal stood at the periphery, muttering a few vague insults that no one could hear. She barely had to do anything, and still she was liked. It had really all started the day that she brought her class to watch the taping of a television show her mother was on. It was a morning news show, and all the children sat bleary-eyed on the floor at sunrise among a tangle of wires and cables. They were so well-behaved that a cameraman came over and told them they were welcome back anytime. For the rest of the day, Opal was treated with real awe. She found herself at the very heart of the lunch table, being offered sandwich halves and tangerines and an invitation to try Alison Prager's oboe, if she wanted.

After that, Opal had her mother make strategic guest appearances at school. On Carnival Day her mother dressed as a gypsy and sat in a booth, and everyone crowded around. All the other mothers felt snubbed. Mothers in clown suits milled around unhappily, smoking furtive cigarettes in corners. Peter Green's mother sat bone-dry on the plank of a homemade dunking machine, waiting for someone to plunge her into the water, but no one did.

It wasn't that the children particularly wanted Opal's mother to read their fortunes, as she had been prepared to do. Instead, they tore off tickets from a loop, and came up to her booth, shrilling, "Do Mrs. Pummelman!" or "Do Baby Fifi!" and Opal's mother would patiently oblige.

When they got back home at the end of Carnival Day, Opal stood in the doorway and watched her mother take off her gypsy costume. She watched her pull off her pantyhose, holding it bunched up on her hands for a second, as though about to make a cat's cradle of the nylon. Then she dropped it and reached around to unzip her gypsy dress. After that she unwound the turban from her head, and fished out the bobby pins from their hiding places in her hair. All she wore now was a pale yellow slip and two silver-dollar circles of rouge. She looked like a teenage girl sitting alone after a date that has gone poorly. That happened to girls sometimes, Opal knew; she had just begun reading books from the Young Adult section of the library. The books had titles like *Ready When You Are* or *New Girl at Adams High* or *Seventeen Means Trouble*. Sometimes in the book the boy stands the girl up at first, or else he says something terrible to her, like, "Oh, here come my friends. Let's pretend we're not together, okay?" Now Opal's mother looked so sad and exhausted that Opal had to look away. This was the only time she ever remembered wanting to look away from her.

Most of the time, like now, Opal could not get enough. As she sat in the kitchen watching the show, she laughed easily at all the familiar lines. Her mother torpedoed joke after joke, and everyone was satisfied. Opal could hear the beefsteak laugh of Ed McMahon, louder than anyone's.

When the audience finally quieted down, the camera closed in tight and her mother said, "I'd like to take this moment to send a special message to my daughters back in New York." No one moved. "If you're watching this, Opal and Erica," she said, "then you're in big trouble. You're supposed to be asleep now! It's a school night!"

It was like talking to her mother on a television phone, the kind that *My Weekly Reader* had insisted would be installed in every home by 1970. Opal had lived in fear. What if you were on the toilet and the phone rang? What then? But the threats had proven idle. *My Weekly Reader* also swore that America would go metric within the next few years. Opal had been terrified, knowing her own stupidity with ounces and inches, let alone kilos and meters. But this, too, was just a scare, designed to alarm, then be forgotten. Everything settled down, went on as usual. Her mother showed up on television, sent satellite love messages to the East Coast, and later that night, after the credits rolled and her mother stood as if at a cocktail party with Johnny and Ed and Rita Moreno, Opal drew back the blanket on her bed and slipped inside.

Lying alone in the dark, she could hear the baby-sitter practicing down the hall, and then the sound of Erica preparing for sleep in the next room. There was the usual banging around, drawers sliding open and shut, and once in a while Erica would open her door and a line of music would drift out: ". . . And when will all the killing stop?/We cry into the rain . . ." Then the door would close again and Opal couldn't hear anything more. Erica's music was so depressing lately, and yet this was the way she liked to fall asleep at night; this was her lullaby of choice.

Opal flipped over onto her side and lay close to the wall. She summoned up an image of her mother onscreen, a pulse of color and motion. She was excited for a while, thinking about the show, but then the excitement shifted into something else. Now in her mind she saw her mother joined by her father, her sister, and finally herself. The whole family was up there, all spread out like the little winking lights of the *Tonight Show* skyline. They blinked at each other from across a great distance.

No, she thought, amending it slightly. She, Erica, and her father were all little lights, but her mother was something else entirely. She was a zeppelin traveling across the sky, traveling from light to light, and everyone was pointing at her. Cars stopped on the road. "Look!" children cried. "Look! It's Dottie Engels!"

In the next room, her sister was already asleep, but now Opal was wide awake.

MEG WOLITZER *has just completed her fifth novel,* Surrender, Dorothy. *Her previous novels include* Sleepwalking *and* This Is Your Life, *among others. The recipient of a grant from the National Endowment for the Arts, she has taught at The Writers Community, the Iowa Writers' Workshop, and Skidmore College. She lives in New York City with her husband and sons.*

Copyright Acknowledgments

About the Editor

Laurel Blossom is the author of three volumes of poetry, *Any Minute, What's Wrong*, and *The Papers Said*, and she is the editor of the anthology *Splash! Great Writing about Swimming.* She has received grants from the National Endowment for the Arts, the New York Foundation for the Arts, and the Ohio Arts Council. She is cofounder of The Writers Community, the master-level workshop and residency program of the YMCA National Writer's Voice.

About the Series Editor

Jennifer O'Grady is Program Director of the YMCA National Writer's Voice. She holds an M.F.A. from Columbia University and her poems have appeared in *Poetry, Harper's,* the *Yale Review,* the *Kenyon Review,* the *Georgia Review*, and elsewhere. Her awards include the Billee Murray Denny Poetry Award.

Interior design by Will Powers
Typeset in American Garamond
by Stanton Publication Services
Printed on acid-free Glatfelter paper
by Edwards Brothers, Inc.

MORE ANTHOLOGIES FROM MILKWEED EDITIONS:

Changing the Bully Who Rules the World:
Reading and Thinking about Ethics
Edited by Carol Bly

Clay and Star:
Contemporary Bulgarian Poets
Edited by Lisa Sapinkopf and George Belev

Drive, They Said:
Poems about Americans and Their Cars
Edited by Kurt Brown

The Most Wonderful Books:
Writers on Discovering the Pleasures of Reading
Edited by Michael Dorris and Emilie Buchwald

Looking for Home:
Women Writing about Exile
Edited by Deborah Keenan and Roseann Lloyd

Minnesota Writes: Poetry
Edited by Jim Moore and Cary Waterman

Mixed Voices:
Contemporary Poems about Music
Edited by Emilie Buchwald and Ruth Roston

Mouth to Mouth:
Poems by Twelve Contemporary Mexican Women
Edited by Forrest Gander

Night Out:
Poems about Hotels, Motels, Restaurants, and Bars
Edited by Kurt Brown and Laure-Anne Bosselaar

Passages North Anthology
Edited by Elinor Benedict

The Poet Dreaming in the Artist's House:
Contemporary Poems about the Visual Arts
Edited by Emilie Buchwald and Ruth Roston

Sacred Ground:
Writings about Home
Edited by Barbara Bonner

Testimony:
Writers of the West Speak On Behalf of Utah Wilderness
Compiled by Stephen Trimble and Terry Tempest Williams

This Sporting Life:
Contemporary Poems about Sports and Games
Edited by Emilie Buchwald and Ruth Roston

Transforming a Rape Culture
Edited by Emilie Buchwald, Pamela Fletcher, and Martha Roth

White Flash/Black Rain:
Women of Japan Relive the Bomb
Edited and translated by Lequita Vance-Watkins and Aratani Mariko